Finding Margaret Fuller

Finding
Margaret Fuller

A Novel

ALLISON PATAKI

Ballantine Books
New York

Published in the United States by Ballantine Books,
an imprint of Random House,
a division of Penguin Random House LLC, New York.

BALLANTINE is a registered trademark and the colophon is a
trademark of Penguin Random House LLC.

LIBRARY OF CONGRESS CATALOGING-IN-PUBLICATION DATA

Names: Pataki, Allison, author.
Title: Finding Margaret Fuller : a novel / Allison Pataki.
Description: New York : Ballantine Books, [2024]
Identifiers: LCCN 2023009186 (print) | LCCN 2023009187 (ebook) |
ISBN 9780593600238 (hardcover) | ISBN 9780593600245 (ebook)
Subjects: LCSH: Fuller, Margaret, 1810-1850—Fiction. |
Women journalists—United States—Fiction. | Feminists—United States—
Fiction. | LCGFT: Biographical fiction. | Novels.
Classification: LCC PS3616.A8664 F56 2024 (print) |
LCC PS3616.A8664 (ebook) | DDC 813/.6—dc23/20230629
LC record available at https://lccn.loc.gov/2023009186
LC ebook record available at https://lccn.loc.gov/2023009187

Printed in the United States of America on acid-free paper

randomhousebooks.com

2 4 6 8 9 7 5 3 1

First Edition

Book design by Virginia Norey
Frontispiece art by Nora/stock.adobe.com
Butterfly art by BillionPhotos/stock.adobe.com

For my oldest friend, also named Margaret.
Also a bold and beautiful woman.

Humanity is divided into men, women, and Margaret Fuller.
—EDGAR ALLAN POE

How can you describe a Force?
How can you write a life of Margaret?
—EXCERPT OF A LETTER FROM
SAM WARD TO RALPH WALDO EMERSON

Finding Margaret Fuller

Prologue

Concord, Massachusetts
July 1850

M R. EMERSON LOOKS THROUGH HIS STUDY WINDOW to see Sophia and Nathaniel Hawthorne marching toward him. Up the Cambridge Turnpike they come, side by side, no doubt carrying some delicious morsel of gossip, as they are just now returning from a visit out at Melville's.

Melville, the poor soul, Mr. Emerson thinks. The tortured man struggling to throw off the final strangling clutches of his great toil, his seafaring saga of the one-legged captain and the white whale he hunts. Melville needed Hawthorne's companionship in order to finish; he said it outright. And so Hawthorne went, dutiful wife at his side. Hawthorne, who is still floating from his recent triumph with Hester Prynne and her scarlet letter.

Has Margaret seen it yet? Mr. Emerson wonders. *Has she pieced it together?* A woman who takes a lover and unashamedly bears his child. A lone woman brave enough to live in defiance of the Puritanical judgment and brimstone that try, in vain, to engulf her. A meeting of the lovers in the forest—surely Margaret will see herself when she encounters that scene. They all know about those magical afternoons of dappled light and pine-tinged breezes; of Margaret sitting in the sun, her chestnut hair loose and untamed.

Even Sophia knows. Long-suffering, saintly Sophia Hawthorne, who has seen so many women—and now men, given the tangle with Melville—fall in love with her husband. Attachments that, if she's taking an honest accounting, are not sufficiently discouraged. But she'll never leave her Nathaniel.

Here come the pair of them now, turning off the lane and up the front walk to Mr. Emerson's home, Sophia clutching Hawthorne's arm like she might tip over without his support. Therein lies much of the reason why Nathaniel picked her over all the rest: because she would fall without his steadying support. Hawthorne may woo women like Margaret Fuller, might crave their bright-eyed attention, yearn to kneel in thrall before their power. But for a wife and companion? He's made a different choice.

Mr. Emerson's eyes narrow. Sophia looks pale—paler than usual. And their pace—there's something not quite right about that pace. Too hasty. No one rushes about like that on the gentle lanes of Concord. The Hawthornes are approaching with more than mere gossip from Melville.

Mr. Emerson turns from the window and crosses his study, making his way through the entry hall toward his front door. When he opens it, Hawthorne nearly barrels into him.

"Emerson," the man pants. "Thank God you're at home." But Emerson is so often at home, it should not come as any real surprise. Sophia grips her husband's arm.

Mr. Emerson eyes each of the Hawthornes in turn, his voice low as he replies, "Yes, hello. What is it?"

Sophia's wisp of a voice is barely audible. "It's Margaret." She need not clarify; there is only one Margaret for him, for all of them.

"Yes? What of her?"

Hawthorne looks to his wife, a wordless communication, then back to his friend. "She's . . . she's gone."

A tightness encircles Mr. Emerson's throat, and he swallows against it. "Gone?" What can they mean, *gone*? "Her ship's expected to dock in New York Harbor by the end of this month," Mr. Emerson manages, but his tone is a bit strained.

Hawthorne offers only a quick shake of his head. That strangling sensation grips Mr. Emerson once more, and he raises a hand to the doorframe, bracing as he leans toward the Hawthornes. "What can you mean by this?"

"We've only just heard." Sophia's voice quivers. "Her ship . . . a storm. Off the coast of New York."

Mr. Emerson's mind, his incomparable mind that has earned him the title the Sage of Concord—the mind that has gathered them all together, here in Concord, to give America its glorious decade of original thoughts and letters—that very mind trips and falters now. He can barely keep the threads together as Hawthorne weaves a most terrible tapestry: An ill-fated Atlantic crossing. A captain lost at sea to smallpox, then a fierce summer storm. The final stretch of the journey from Italy to America. The shoreline of New York in sight, and yet, a fractured ship stuck on an unyielding sandbar. Close enough for the souls on board to hear the shouts of the on-lookers lining the beach, and yet too far to survive the stormy swim. Margaret, swept away, along with her baby and the man she's made her husband. Their bodies pulled under by cruel and roiling waves. So that's what Hawthorne means by *gone*.

Mr. Emerson feels as though his legs might give out. "Thoreau," he says to the Hawthornes now, and he reads in their expressions that they do not understand. "Thoreau!" he roars, knowing he will rouse the entire street. But that's his intention. Thoreau is just next door; surely he'll hear. But *is* he next door? Or did he spend the night out on Walden Pond? Mr. Emerson can't recall. "Thoreau!" he bellows once more.

A door opens, but it's not Thoreau's. It's at the Alcotts' home. Mr. Emerson groans. Bronson Alcott is just the wrong person for a moment such as this. But fortunately it's not Bronson who appears at the threshold. It's Louisa May. That's fine, Louy can hear this. Louy ought to hear this.

Mercifully, Thoreau does emerge a moment later, trotting toward them. And now it's a flurry of motion outside the Emerson home. Whereas a few breaths ago it was the Hawthornes delivering this terrible news, now Mr. Emerson brings his friend into this dreadful confidence. "Go now," he tells Thoreau. "To New York. The beach called Fire Island. You must get to Margaret before anyone else. You must find her manuscript. Call on Greeley, you can stay with him. If Greeley is not in town, then Poe will help. Or Whitman, even Longfellow. Just get there. Get there as quickly as you can. You must get to the wreck. Find her. Find her book."

If he's too late to save her, if Mr. Emerson cannot claim the body of Margaret Fuller from its watery grave, then perhaps he can save her words. It's the least he can do after all this time. Given the many debts he has yet to repay her—and now never will—he can make amends in this one way. He can tell her story. Because the fact that the world does not yet know it? Why, that is a tragedy nearly as grave as any shipwreck.

PART 1

Chapter One

Concord, Massachusetts
Summer 1836

I KNOW THAT MR. EMERSON IS EXPECTING ME. IT WAS he, after all, who invited me here. And yet, as I approach the front door of his grand white home, I feel a twinge of nerves. I pause, staring up at the house, an imposing structure set back from the Cambridge Turnpike, hemmed by a fence, the columned porticoes and rolling green lawns lending the place a simple, stately elegance. "Bush" is what Mr. Emerson called the estate in his letters, when he wrote to invite me from Cambridge out to the country for a week's visit.

He'd read my newspaper tribute, Mr. Emerson explained, to his beloved brother Charles, so recently deceased of tuberculosis. He'd found that my words had touched his heart, providing some small balm to the pain of the untimely loss. I was a young writer of great promise, Mr. Emerson declared, his fine cursive filling the front and back of the page. As one of New England's most established lecturers and perhaps its most prolific writer, he, Mr. Ralph Waldo Emerson, took great pride in being able to support individuals like me. Even women, his words implied, though he had not stated that outright. But really, he hastened to add, the primary purpose of the visit was to provide companionship for his wife, Mrs. Lidian Emerson, now in the final months of her confinement before the expected arrival of their first child, and barely able to leave her bed.

"He's collecting friends and thinkers to his side," Eliza Peabody had told me, when she welcomed me into her Boston parlor for tea on the eve of my planned departure. Eliza, my friend of several years, and I had gravitated toward each other as two of the only young ladies in the Boston and Cambridge writing circles who shared the twin stains on our reputations of being unwed *and* wishing to work as published writers. We had an audacity to us that frightened many, an independence of spirit and circumstance that made us not a little bit threatening to some of the men who wrote about freedom and lectured about liberty. An independence that allowed me to accept an invitation such as this one from Mr. Emerson, to stay as his houseguest in the country.

Eliza was in a position to tell me what I might expect from a visit at Emerson's estate, as she herself had made the very same three-hour journey by stagecoach from Boston to Concord on more than one occasion to accept a similar invitation—or was it a summons?—to the Emerson home.

"He knows of you, Margaret. Knows your reputation, evidently even knows some of your writing," Eliza said, stirring a pinch of sugar into her tea as she held me with her intense, inquisitive gaze. I did my best to bite back the flattered smile that pulled on my lips. To think, my work had been read—and enjoyed—by a man such as Ralph Waldo Emerson. Certainly there were many who found my work and my passions unladylike, even unnatural. But not Mr. Emerson, it seemed.

Eliza went on: "Sophia and I were with the Emersons out at Bush in the spring." While Eliza was a celebrated wit and lady of letters, her sister Sophia was known to excel at painting. "It promises to be interesting, my dear, to say the least. A chance to glimpse the great Sage of Concord at home."

And now here I stand, clutching my cloth bag and gazing at the front door of Mr. Ralph Waldo Emerson's home. I glance down at my dress, a simple poplin of dove gray, a cream-colored kerchief tied modestly around my neck. I pat the skirt and then raise my gloved hands to make certain that my chestnut bun is tidy, the curls bobbing down the nape of my neck, giving myself one final prink before I knock.

I'm expecting a servant of some sort, perhaps a housekeeper or cook, but the man who greets me at the door is none other than Mr. Ralph Waldo Emerson himself—I know his famous face. "Oh, yes, Mr. Emerson?" I shift my bag from one hand to the other, forcing a bright tone even as I feel my cheeks grow warm. "Hello."

Mr. Emerson looks at me, one corner of his mouth tilting upward, the hint of a half smile, and then he extends a hand in greeting. "And this must be the famous Margaret Fuller of Cambridge at my doorstep?"

I take his outstretched hand and let out a puff of breath that sounds like a warble. I'm struck by the deep timbre of his voice, and by his informal manner—I hadn't expected either. Already he's caught me back on my heels, so I square my shoulders and summon a casual smile as I reply: "I don't know about *famous*, but I *am* Margaret Fuller indeed."

His smile grows from partial to full as his blue-gray eyes catch a lively glimmer. And then he sweeps his arm up, performing a slightly theatrical bow. "Welcome to Concord. Please, Miss Fuller, won't you come inside?"

I accept his welcome and step past him, out of the warm summer afternoon and into the cool and airy quiet of the Emerson home. The foyer is bright and high ceilinged, with a gracious stairway and wooden banister before us and spacious rooms off to each side. I stand still as my host asks after my journey and I tell him it went smoothly. There is neither sight nor sound of any other person in the home, which lends the handsome place an almost temple-like tranquillity. I clutch my valise as Mr. Emerson ushers me across the front hall and into a room lined with books. His study, I suppose. A large mahogany desk occupies pride of place, topped with a tidy stack of papers and a pen tipped into a dish shaped like a bird. Beside it sits a half-filled inkwell. The room smells of books and firewood.

Mr. Emerson stands beside his desk. "What refreshment can I offer you, Miss Fuller, after your hours-long journey? Some tea? Coffee? Water? Ah, or we do have some nice cider, which our dear handyman has pressed for us."

"Water would be fine," I answer. As he pours us two cups from a pitcher on a nearby side table, I take the opportunity to subtly study his appearance. Ralph Waldo Emerson is tall and slender, dressed in a tidy suit with a cravat that hugs high and tight around his neck. I know from his reputation as a great speaker and writer that Mr. Emerson is a few years older than me, thirty-three to my twenty-six. Nevertheless, he has an undeniably youthful vitality about him; perhaps someone so filled with deep thoughts and ideas cannot help but overspill with an uncoiled sort of energy.

"Thank you." I accept the water from his hand and take a sip. Our eyes lock for a moment and I allow my stare to linger in his cool gaze, before I remind myself to look away. I take another sip, my throat feeling dry, and I tell myself it's because of the three hours on the turnpike.

"Sit, please." Emerson gestures to a sofa of red velvet across from his desk, then he crosses the room to shut the door. I take note of the fact that I have not sat alone in a room with a man since my father's death. I blink, glancing down toward my hands in my lap. But Mr. Emerson does not seem to find this closeted state of affairs unusual in the least, as he takes his own seat in a rocking chair behind his desk.

"Well, Miss Fuller, thank you for coming all this way." He reaches for the nearby poker and jostles the logs in the hearth, just a small blaze given the warmth of the summer afternoon.

I nod. "Thank you for your gracious invitation."

"It has been a matter of great interest to me for some time . . . meeting you."

I can barely mask my surprise; I had supposed the chief purpose of my visit was to offer company to Mrs. Emerson. I reply only, "Oh?"

"The Most Well-Read Woman in America," he says with a flourish of his long-fingered hands, then he sets his gaze back on me. "That's what they call you, if I'm not mistaken?"

"Person," I reply, my voice quiet but certainly audible.

Emerson tilts his head, eyeing me with a bemused expression. "Pardon?"

"Person," I state again, this time just slightly louder. "What I've been called is 'the Most Well-Read *Person* in America.'" Almost as soon as I've said it I regret doing so—the importance of first impressions and modesty being what they are. Particularly in a lady, and a junior one at that. Mother is always reminding me of this, chiding me when my pride or boldness seems too much. And Father did the same. *Margaret, my girl, you are the Much that always wants More.* The thought of Father—his words, his memories—it all causes my vision to swim for a moment, until I remind myself not to get lost in the pull of these daydreams.

Mr. Emerson is looking at me most intently. I sit up taller in my seat. My host offers me half a smirk, and then he speaks again: "Won't you please tell me how it is that you are so well educated?" He tents his long fingers, looking at me over their tips. "Where was your formal schooling?"

"I was sent to be finished at Miss Prescott's Young Ladies' Seminary."

"Ah, yes. Groton?"

I tilt my head. "But I would not say it was at Miss Prescott's that I acquired my education."

Mr. Emerson lifts an eyebrow.

"I left the boarding school after only one year," I reply.

"Why is that?"

"Because I had more Greek and Latin than any of the teachers. It was not a worthwhile investment of my time, nor of my father's money."

Mr. Emerson chuckles, the skin around his pale eyes crinkling. "Well, then, if not at Groton, where *would* you say you received your prolific education, Miss Fuller?"

"From my father," I answer.

Mr. Emerson tips back in his rocking chair and muses aloud, "He must be a most singular man, seeing fit to allow his daughter such a robust education."

"Was," I correct him, clearing my throat. "He *was* a most singular man. We lost my father, Timothy Fuller . . . last year."

Mr. Emerson nods once, slowly, and I see that he's absorbing this—the fact that just as I first entered his awareness by publishing an elegiac tribute to his brother at the time of his death, I was also nursing the wound of my own beloved father's passing. That we share the twin griefs of these recent and fresh heartaches.

"I am sorry for that, Miss Fuller," he says, and I can hear that he means it. "I would very much like to hear more about him, and his success in raising such an exceptional daughter. That is, if you might be willing to share?"

"Yes, of course," I reply, taking a quick sip of water. Because I *am* willing to speak about my father. About how he had hoped for a son, but when I was born, the eldest of his eight children, he'd been determined to raise me—and teach me—like his boy instead. I share how he had me reading and reciting Latin and Greek by the age of six, drilling me from morning until well past dark, long after other children my age had been tucked into their warm beds with gentle songs and kisses.

"Yours sounds like an unusual youth," Mr. Emerson remarks, holding me in his gaze.

"Most unusual," I agree. "Unnatural, even." I look down and pat the folds of my skirt, my mind mulling over so many hours now filed into the past, and yet always in my memory and thoughts. "My father loved me a great deal, you see, but I believe—or, at least, I very much felt—that his love was always conditional, determined by my performance. He expected excellence at all times and in all things. To my six-year-old self he declared: 'Mediocrity is obscurity.' "

When Mr. Emerson speaks next, it's a question that I am not expecting. "Did you ever rebel?"

"I remember one time, yes." Now it's my turn to flash a wry smile. "Sundays were our day of rest. I was granted a break from my lessons with Father. On Sunday I was permitted to put aside my Virgil and my Homer. And so one Sunday—I believe I was seven— I wandered into our family library and I selected a book for my own pleasure. It was the plays of William Shakespeare. I remember I began with *The Tempest* and was immediately engrossed. Miranda was a young lady entirely at the mercy of her devoted but exacting father. They occupied an island unto themselves. It felt so fantastical and yet somehow so familiar. I could not stop reading. But Father, when he found me, was not amused. In fact, he was furious. Or perhaps even worse . . . deeply disappointed."

"Why was that?"

Now I feel positively lively with storytelling. I answer: "Father told me that Shakespeare was tawdry and unfit for my impressionable young mind."

Emerson chuckles, and so do I. "So he ordered me to put the book away at once. But then he went off to do something else, and I went back into our library, where I once more took up the forbidden book, and I secreted it away with me. Up to my bedroom I brought Master Shakespeare, where I read him for many more happy hours. When Father came to summon me to supper and saw that I'd buried myself in the forbidden text, in spite of his disapproval, he was livid. But I did not much care."

Mr. Emerson lets out a hearty laugh, a warm, smooth sound, and I find myself basking in his approbation. But when he speaks next, the change in tack catches me by surprise. "You do know," he says, "that my wife, Mrs. Emerson, is looking ahead to a most joyful and anticipated event?"

I nod, feeling a sudden stab of embarrassment. Embarrassment at Mr. Emerson's alluding to something as delicate as childbirth. But even more so over the fact that I have been invited here to serve as Mrs. Emerson's companion in her confinement and yet I've neither met nor asked after her. Instead, her husband and I sit here behind a closed door as I speak about my life and books and so much else. "Yes," I answer after an instant, my tone tenuous.

Mr. Emerson appears entirely unfazed as he says, "Well, all I can say is that I very much hope, should our child ever see fit to rebel against the authority of his own beloved parents, that his transgression might be something as noble as the clandestine reading of William Shakespeare."

We both laugh at this, and that softens some of my feelings of unease from a moment earlier. "All that to say," he goes on, "for however you and your father may have disagreed over the merits of Mr. Shakespeare, I find myself convinced that your father did an indisputably meritorious job in educating you, Miss Fuller. And, aside from that one moment of discord you may have shared, I have no doubt that he was most proud of you."

My cheeks flush with warmth, and I look toward the nearby hearth. Emerson continues: "I've had the pleasure of reading your recently published translation of Goethe, and I was most impressed."

"Thank you," I say. Now the warmth within me swirls with a heady tinge of satisfaction, a rippling of pleasure at hearing that my work has been noticed—and appreciated—by a writer as renowned as Ralph Waldo Emerson. The same Mr. Emerson who now stares at me with a quizzical expression. "But you cannot be more than twenty-five, Miss Fuller."

"Twenty-six," I reply.

"So young." He quirks an eyebrow, his gaze still fixed on me. "And yet you've published quite a bit in *The American Monthly Magazine*. I've enjoyed your thoughts on everything from Goethe to Shelley to Byron. Dare I even hope for something soon on Mr. Shakespeare?"

I smile at this, but my tone is serious when I say: "As I was raised like an eldest son, and as I remain the leader of my siblings, it does fall to me, now that Father is gone, to provide for them and my mother." What I don't say aloud—but what I'm certain that Mr. Emerson understands—is that my hand has been put to paper as much by necessity as by my inner desire for creative expression. That I am one of that new and vulgar breed who seeks to earn wages and even make a living as a writer. And an unwed woman writer, at that.

"Yes, of course," Mr. Emerson replies, his brow softening in a thoughtful expression. "Your mother . . . I would be most curious to hear about her, as well. That is, if you are willing to share?"

"I am always happy to speak of Mother," I say, and I mean it.

"How did they meet?" he asks.

"While crossing a bridge over the Charles River. He was coming from Boston, she from Cambridge, and they nearly collided in the middle." I smile at this story I've heard so often, and then add a remark of my own, stating, "And I believe that was the only time in his life that Timothy Fuller ever met anyone halfway."

Mr. Emerson laughs at this. "So then, was it a pairing of opposites?"

"In almost every way. Mother was little more than a child herself when she met Father, not yet twenty. He was so much older, and so serious. She was beautiful and soft-spoken. And somehow Mother was the only person, other than me, who could ever manage to make Father smile."

Emerson takes all of this in, his eyes kindled with attentive interest. "And is Mrs. Fuller a reader like you and your late father?"

"Not at all," I answer, then I hasten to add: "That's not to say Mother is not intelligent. But her interests always turned more toward domestic matters. She was happiest in our garden. And I will admit that the gladdest hours of my childhood were spent with her in that little plot. She'd tell me tales of fairies, or show me how to clip the clematis and honeysuckle. I would have spent every hour of the day with Mother there, had I been permitted." I barely suppress the sigh that seeps out of me. "But there was always another baby. Always another little boy or girl, one after the other, who pulled Mother away. And always Father, pulling me back to the books."

There's a momentary pause, a silence that stretches but does not seem to make either of us uneasy. Eventually, he speaks: "But now you are taking care of her. I'm certain she appreciates that."

"Yes." I nod. "I must. It was the promise I made to Father right before I shut his eyes."

Mr. Emerson tips his chair back. "You speak metaphorically, I presume?"

"No." I shake my head. "I was the one beside his deathbed in the final days. It fell to me to shut his lids after the fever finally claimed him."

Mr. Emerson almost frowns as his body tilts toward me, saying: "Your father did indeed place severe expectations on you, Miss Fuller."

I swallow. "In life . . . and in death." When I speak again, my voice is low, and the words are in Latin: " '*Possunt quia posse videntur.*' "

Mr. Emerson has no trouble translating: " 'They can conquer who believe they can.' "

I nod.

"Virgil, I believe?"

"Virgil's *Aeneid*. And my life's credo. When Father died, I knew that I had to push all youthful thoughts from my mind. Father's investments were not nearly enough to live on. We had the big farm to maintain, and my siblings needed food and schooling. Mother seemed to wilt before me, until soon she was little more than a shadow. They all depended on me to eat—and to live. If ever I regretted being born a woman, it was then."

Emerson braids his fingers together, resting his chin atop his hands. A moment of thoughtful silence, and then he says, "If you were a man, there would have been no question of your entering the breadwinning crowd. And quickly distinguishing yourself in order to earn wages."

"I believe you are correct," I reply, my tone flat.

"So then . . ." Emerson exhales. "It was quite a burden placed on those narrow shoulders of yours."

I sit up straight, pulling back the narrow shoulders he has just referenced. When I speak next, there's an undergirding of defiance to my tone. "I was too strong to be crushed."

His eyes narrow. I go on: "I've not let any obstacle in life thwart me, and I have no intention of doing so now. And this is how you find me, on the cusp of my move to Boston, where I shall enter the wide world as a woman, and earn my keep in order to provide for my family."

A slight dip of his chin, then he says: "With your writing."

"My writing, yes. And teaching."

He nods at this, still eyeing me with that direct, appraising gaze that makes me feel a bit exposed. I resist the urge to fidget in my seat, but instead meet his stare head-on. Eventually, it is Mr. Emerson who speaks. "Well, Miss Fuller, you've been most generous in meeting me in such a place of confidence. I apologize if I ask too much, but you see, I very much wished to know how it could be that a person such as you came into being." Mr. Emerson looks at me as though I'm some jigsaw puzzle that he has yet to piece entirely together.

Now I take a sip of water. As I'm doing so, Mr. Emerson seems to arrive at the same thought that I had a few moments earlier, which is that we have yet to speak much of Mrs. Emerson. "Might I be so bold as to presume, Miss Fuller, that were I inclined to share a bit of my own and Mrs. Emerson's story, you might be willing and inclined to listen?"

"Of course," I reply, sitting forward on the velvet couch.

"Mrs. Emerson and I married a year ago." I nod; this much I already know. Mr. Emerson is an eminent enough scholar and public figure that I know, too, that he was widowed just a few years before that. His first wife was a celebrated beauty and heiress, young, his great love before she succumbed to tuberculosis. Ellen is the name I remember reading, Ellen Emerson. Ellen died suddenly, leaving Mr. Emerson with a broken heart and her vast inheritance. His new wife is reported to be Ellen's foil in many ways. Not younger than Mr. Emerson, but older. Serious, pious, lacking in any sort of great beauty or charm. But perhaps she's a steadying, world-wise ballast in the wake of such a shattering heartache.

"Why have you never married?" Mr. Emerson asks now, his head tipping to the side.

"That did not last long," I remark.

His brow creases; he's unsure of my meaning. My fingers tap the plush velvet of my seat as I throw him a wry smirk. "I shared, and then you offered to share. But now the light has turned back on me."

Mr. Emerson smiles at this; his eyes are two pools catching shards of sunlight. "It's just another quandary . . . one of the many things about you that mystifies me, Miss Fuller. Why, you are intelligent, pleasant to speak with, you are—well, your . . ." And now the great and learned Mr. Emerson appears to fumble in search of words. His hands sweep toward me, upward and downward, in a gesture I can only surmise has something to do with my appearance. "Only to say, your physical bearing . . ."

I take mercy on him. "Perhaps you mean that my outward appearance is not so offensive as to render me entirely unmarriageable."

Mr. Emerson's cheeks flush. "Quite the opposite, and you are clever enough to know that."

I look down at my skirt, feeling that my own cheeks have now darkened. Yes, I know that. I know that my thick, dark hair, auburn in my youth but now a rich chestnut, does attract the admiration of many. My eyes are a shade of dark blue that I once heard my parents describe as *lovely* when they did not know I was listening. I've never had suitors, have never been formally "out" in society, what with my father's determination that I would be educated like a Harvard lad rather than presented like a Boston debutante, but I know enough to guess that some gentlemen find me attractive. That is, until I speak. Once I get onto a topic such as Dante or Goethe, young gentlemen typically nod politely and turn away. My physical appearance may be attractive enough to elicit an initial interest, but the fully formed mind is most off-putting.

Except to Mr. Emerson, it seems. He is the first gentleman I've ever encountered—other than Father—who appears eager to plumb my thoughts and mind in such an earnest and inquiring way. And I have to admit that I find it exciting. More than exciting. Exhilarating, in fact. And for this reason I am willing to answer his question with candor. "You ask why I have never married? My reason is that I have no interest in captivity."

Mr. Emerson laughs at this, an unself-conscious sound, even a bit youthful in its jollity. Sitting back in his rocking chair, he lifts his eyebrows as he repeats my word: "*Captivity?*"

I nod, meeting his earnest expression with frankness. "To be candid, I've not yet met the man who wants me for a wife. And I do wonder if I ever will, given my disinclination toward voluntary subjugation. But yes, even if I were to find the man who was willing to take me on, would I want to enter into a state where suddenly all of my property, all of my earned money, all of my opinions, and, I daresay, even my body were suddenly the property of a man? No." I shake my head, aware that what I'm saying is most scandalous, even for a man as forward-thinking as Ralph Waldo Emerson. But I must be brave; I made my decision long ago that I would not be dishonest, nor would I be ashamed of these truths I carry in my breast. And I have more to say. "Until our great and free society should see fit to declare that freedom ought to apply not only to men but also to women, I cannot see that marriage would be a state I could abide."

I fall silent, my heart pounding against my chest, and I wonder if

Mr. Emerson can hear its thrashing in the quiet of the room. A log pops in the hearth, sending up a small spray of ash. Eventually, my host breaks the silence. "Please, Miss Fuller, when you meet my Lidian, would you be so kind as to refrain from telling her that I am her captor?" He says it with a rueful smile, and I can see, with relief, that I have not offended him. In fact, he seems to accept my sentiments, even if he may not entirely agree.

"I don't see you being the sort of man who would treat his wife as such, Mr. Emerson."

"That is high praise, coming from you."

"Shall I meet her now?" I ask, glancing toward the closed study door. What must she be thinking? Surely she heard me enter the home. How long ago was that?

Mr. Emerson taps the arms of his chair. "Mrs. Emerson is abed. She'll ring when she is ready to receive visitors. In the meantime, would you like me to show you where you'll be staying for the week?"

"That would be nice, thank you," I answer, and we rise to leave the study. Out in the foyer, I am expecting Mr. Emerson to lead me up the stairs, nearer to his wife's bedroom, perhaps. Instead, to my surprise, my host walks me across the front hall and right to the door closest to his study. "After you," he says, stepping aside. I enter an elegantly furnished room, with a large bed carved of black walnut and covered in a cream-colored bedspread. A row of windows offers a lovely view over his well-kept gardens and stately old chestnut trees. A bedside table stands furnished with a washbowl and pitcher of green and white porcelain, and the desk is equipped with a full inkstand and fresh paper.

"I know you will wish to write while you are here," he says. "I promise to keep you swimming in ink."

I nod appreciatively. The best part of the room, I decide, is the plush wingback armchair tucked between two of the windows, covered in red upholstery that matches the red rug on the wooden floor. It'll be perfectly situated to catch the sunlight from the morning until the evening, and I imagine it will suit quite well for both reading and writing.

"Firewood will be brought in each morning. In addition to our woman in the kitchen, Nancy, we also have a handyman, Henry David. He has a room upstairs. He's a writer, too. You'll meet him. Brilliant man, that Thoreau, and quite capable around the house. So we trade room and board for his help at Bush. He'll keep you supplied. We call this the Red Room. Will it be all right?"

I've never had a room this comfortable before, nor even a room entirely to myself. "It's lovely," I answer. "Thank you."

"Good, good." Emerson slips his hands into his trouser pockets. "Well, then, shall I leave you to freshen up?"

I nod, happy to settle in and unpack before Mrs. Emerson invites me to visit with her. But before he leaves me, Mr. Emerson pauses, hovering at the threshold of my bedchamber. "Miss Fuller?"

I turn toward him. "Yes?"

"I was planning to take a walk. I like to do so every afternoon before supper. You'll find that Concord has that effect on you—in the summer, the day can't help but draw you out of doors. Of course, the same can be said in the spring, and in the autumn, and in the winter. Would you . . . care to join me?"

I shift on my feet, looking to my bag, then back to my host. "As long as Mrs. Emerson will not need me?"

"As long as Mrs. Emerson does not need you, of course," he quickly agrees.

"Then, yes. I would very much like that. It would be nice to stretch my legs after the journey."

"Wonderful. Shall we meet out front in half an hour?"

"That would be lovely, Mr. Emerson."

He turns to go, then pauses one more time in the doorway, looking toward me. I am not expecting what comes next, when he asks: "Would you do me the great honor of calling me Waldo?"

I stare at him, taken aback. He goes on, "It's what my friends call me, you see. And I'd very much like to name as a friend 'the Most Well-Read *Person* in America.'"

Chapter Two

I EMERGE TO MEET MR. EMERSON—NO, *WALDO*—AT OUR appointed time, but he's not alone. Standing beside him on the broad front lawn is a wild-looking man whose dark curls wind like an unkempt wreath around his unshaven face. In appearance, he's the opposite of Waldo in nearly every way; Waldo is tall and tidy, well-groomed in a crisp three-piece suit, while this other man does not appear as if he would ever consider owning a comb or a cravat. He is short, with light, bright eyes that give him the fiery look of some sort of prophet, or perhaps some feral Pan who has just walked up, barefooted, from out of the wild wood. He leans on a dirty shovel.

Waldo, perhaps noting my bemused look, gestures to the bare-footed man beside him. "Ah, Margaret, here you are. Please meet my good friend and even better handyman, Henry David, or Mr. Thoreau if you prefer formality, though Thoreau certainly does not."

"Thoreau will do just fine," the man says, extending a dirt-caked hand for a shake.

"Hello, I'm Margaret. Nice to meet you."

Thoreau's grip is strong, the top of his hand covered in a thicket of hair, and I decide that indeed he must be part faun. "And you, Margaret," he answers. Thoreau is only a bit taller than me, but sturdily built, his face and arms golden from the sun.

"Thoreau here helps Mrs. Emerson with the household chores, and he gives my fruit trees and vegetable beds their best chance."

Waldo gestures across the yard, where a lively array of trees stand in full leaf, many of their limbs heavy with ripening fruit—apples, pears, even an arbor covered in clusters of grapes. Toward a large barn tucked back from the road there are vegetable beds scored in tidy rows of dark soil. "He was just giving me an update on my tomatoes. Ready to pick any day."

"Then I've come at just the right moment," I say, looking from Waldo to Thoreau.

"Of course you have." Waldo smiles, then turns to his handyman. "And we were just planning to take a walk to the river. Margaret has promised us a week of her time, so I thought I'd show her around our little village."

Thoreau leans on his shovel, nodding. "Delightful day for the river." He sees us off with a wave and turns back toward the vegetables.

Waldo and I make our way up the front walk, a path lined in smooth marble stepping stones, and through the front gate. We turn out onto the Cambridge Turnpike, the very same road by which I arrived on the stagecoach, only now we head in the opposite direction of Cambridge, merging onto the Lexington Road. "Just a mile this way to the river," Waldo says, pointing ahead. We fall in step, side by side, as the Concord countryside unfurls before us.

We pass brick and wooden farmhouses as we go, none so grand or stately as Bush, but all of them tucked back amid lush and verdant gardens. Some of the homes are surrounded by orchard trees pearled with fruit, others with pastures growing thick and green ahead of the haying season. Picturesque stone walls delineate the thriving, fertile farmlands, and cows and horses that appear content and well-fed graze in the gentle afternoon sunshine.

Carriages and carts roll past at regular intervals, and Waldo nods politely as he walks beside me. "I find an evening walk helps my appetite at supper. And I thought that perhaps you might be willing to . . . well, that is . . . I would very much like to thank you."

"For?" I ask, glancing sideways at him.

"For earlier . . ." Waldo takes my arm to navigate past a young lad wrangling a boisterous dog, tugging on the tether to keep him out of the dirt road. "For how much you shared with me."

I nod. The truth is that I found it a relief to open up as I had. To speak so candidly with another person. To share about Father and Mother, and my childhood, and books. To have someone ask me questions and then earnestly listen to the responses. With Waldo I get the sense that he does not want me to bridle myself, to hide the intensity of my thoughts or the depth of my feelings. And that makes him a first. "Mr. Emerson . . . er, Waldo. I am happy to be a friend to you."

He looks at me for a long moment, eventually offering the flicker of a smile, and then he says: "I live quite alone, you see."

Surely my expression shows my confusion.

"Oh, not alone in the house," he adds. "Lidian is there. And Thoreau. But, rather . . . in the solitude of my mind . . . and my books." He glances at me, his brow knitting in a thoughtful look. "Does that sound terribly strange?"

I shake my head. "Not strange at all." I know precisely what he means.

The buildings are closer together now, and the traffic grows thicker. We pass the massive white structure of the old Unitarian church, its white belfry soaring higher than any other structure on the horizon. After that I see a rusty red-brown building with a lively din seeping out of its opened windows and a sign overhead identifying it as Wright's Tavern. A massive old oak grows just before the town green, and Waldo explains that it was under this tree that the first English settlers declared their intention to found the village of Concord, two hundred years earlier.

"And there is J. W. Walcott's," he says, pointing toward a tidy façade across the busy square. "Dry goods," he adds, "sugar, flour, tea. And over there is our bank, and that's a boardinghouse, managed by Thoreau's aunts, in fact. There's the apothecary. But let's continue past all this, for I am interested in showing you a quieter place."

We navigate the horse and foot traffic of the village center and its crowded commons. It strikes me that even though this is the busy and bustling heart of the town, it is nothing compared to the clogged streets of Cambridge or Boston. From the snippets of passing conversation that I do make out, it seems as though people out here walk slower, with more time to stop and chat, to banter about prices or weather or the woes of their fruit trees.

Waldo occasionally nods or touches the brim of his hat. He greets the people passing by or looking out from a storefront, but we carry on with our own private exchange, easily bandying all manner of topics back and forth. Uncomfortable silence is not a problem we encounter; Waldo seems to wish to play Socrates for me. And I don't mind, not at all.

In fact, I thrill at the chance to go deeply into conversation with him. "What do you fear, Margaret?" he asks me as the foot traffic thins and we walk up a gentle incline, striding away from the crowded center of the village. It's quieter now.

I barely have to think about his question, but quickly answer: "Stagnation."

"Then it's no wonder you have disavowed marriage," he quips.

I grin, throwing him a sideways glance. "Mr. Emerson!"

He shrugs. "I jest. My Queen Lidian is a saint. But it's just . . . oh, marriage *is* a confounding institution—I'll grant you that much."

I look out over the meadows that now surround us, gentle green dotted with the occasional burst of color—purples and golds and rusted yellows. I breathe in the sweet tang of the thick summer grass, then I let out a long exhale and say: "For me, marriage just always seemed an unnatural state of being."

"And why do you say 'unnatural'?" he asks.

"Of course I have no experience in the matter . . ."

"I desire to hear your thoughts, nevertheless. You have experience being a member of humanity."

"Well, then . . . love is a bonding of the souls," I muse aloud. "But marriage as a legal institution is a bonding of the physical bodies. Once one's soul no longer feels itself bound to the other, why, then, doesn't marriage become a sort of entrapment of the body and the being? For that reason I chose the word *unnatural*."

Waldo pulls his eyes from mine and looks straight ahead, out over a world that is green and golden and fertile. He does not answer my question, but instead says only: "Miss Margaret Fuller, who shall never wed."

"I won't say *never*."

"I asked you what you fear. I expected you might say spiders, perhaps. Or maybe wolves in these woods. And you tell me instead: *stagnation*. And then proceed to offer me the most thoughtful argument against marriage that I've ever heard."

"Fine, then," I say, laughing to myself. "You want something less philosophical and more material? Then I will give you my modified answer: water."

"Water?"

"Yes, I fear water."

"You do realize that I'm walking you toward the water? You could have told me you'd rather not—"

"No, not a river. That's all fine." I wave my hands. "I mean the sea."

"Why do you fear the sea? Can't you swim?"

"I can. But when I was a girl I had the most vivid nightmares."

"And what happened in these nightmares?" Waldo asks.

I fold my arms together before me, my gaze fixed straight ahead. "I dreamed I was surrounded in a great flood . . ." I say, my voice hard, entirely at odds with the gentle warmth of the countryside all around us. "I could not swim my way out."

Waldo exhales a whistle of breath. "I can see why that would give you a lasting fear."

I turn toward Waldo now, meeting his gaze as I add: "I believe it was Father's doing."

I see that this catches him by surprise. "Why is that?"

"How he worked my little mind. I never could find my ease in the evenings. I'd be so overwrought, and I could never sleep. And then, when I *did* sleep, I'd wake with the most chilling nightmares."

Waldo's face creases. "My poor Margaret." He leans toward me and puts his hand on mine. I look down, realizing, for the first time, that I'm not wearing gloves. I feel a jolt at his warm touch—it's immediate, and it causes me to step back slightly.

He notices, and quickly removes his hand from mine. The trembling cord between us snaps. And then he looks away and raises his hand, his tone bright as he gestures in front of us. "But speaking of water, we've arrived at the Concord River. I hope it does not strike you as dreadful."

I had not even noticed that we had approached the river, so intent was I on our conversation. I come back to the present moment and stare out over the pastoral scene of greens and blues—there is nothing frightening at all in the placid beauty that unfurls before us. The Concord River flows wide and lazy between its banks, two shores bathed in the golden light of the late-afternoon sun and fluffed with wild cabbage and thick ferns. Just before us a stand of paper-white river birches rise up from out of the water. More wildflowers color the scene in patches of purple, white, scarlet, and yellow.

I gaze in silent appreciation before saying: "It's quite different from the Charles River I'm used to."

"Yes," Waldo agrees, running his fingers down the curled, peeling bark of the nearest river birch. We fall into step beside each other, ambling slowly along the grassy bank of the river. "Did you walk along the Charles often?" Waldo asks.

"Any chance I could get," I reply.

"It's a fair bit busier than our stretch of the Concord," Waldo says.

"Busier, and noisier. And then, of course, there were the Harvard fellows hollering as they would row their boats along the river."

Overhead a chickadee studies us from a branch of a silver maple, warbling out a warning to its friends. We both pause and watch the bird for a moment, and then Waldo says: "You do know that I am a Harvard man."

I recommence my walking. "Yes, I know." Does he hear the bitterness in my voice? I manage a milder tone as I venture: "The great Harvard University. To men it's a temple of learning. Nothing forbidding about its stones, bricks, and books. To me, it was only ever a fortress, one which I would never be permitted to breach."

Waldo absorbs this, looking out on the blue-green river in thoughtful silence. I go on: "I told you how my parents fetched me from Miss Prescott's Seminary and brought me home at fourteen."

"Yes," he answers.

"Well." I lean down, pick up a small rock, and send it with a plunk into the river. I watch the growing rings that its weight pushes outward. "After that, I would walk down to the Common and try to speak with the Harvard boys."

"What about?"

"Anything. Whatever they were willing to speak about with me," I answer with a shrug. "Rousseau, Dante, Cervantes."

"I'm sure you bested each one of them in turn."

My eyes slide toward Waldo's, and I hear Mother's admonishing in my head; I hope I'm not being too brazen. "Until my parents forbade me from going. Mother was afraid that word would get out that the Fuller girl was debating Harvard boys in public. They knew it would ruin whatever slim chances I might have had in . . . well, at getting a beau. Anytime after that, whenever I had the excuse to walk past those red-brick buildings . . . I remember just standing outside that library, yearning to go in. Wondering what I might find, if only I could be permitted to enter."

We've stopped walking. I lean down and pick a nearby wild-flower, a pale pink profusion of petals bursting out of a cheerful yellow center. Waldo leans down and picks another just like it. "Swamp rose," he says. "Far too modest a name, I've always thought, for such a thing of beauty." I gaze at the small blush-colored petals appreciatively. And then Waldo does something I had not been expecting: he leans forward and tucks his prize into my dark hair. I stare up at him, unmoving, our eyes meeting as he settles the flower into place behind my ear. His fingertips just barely graze the skin of my cheek as he withdraws his hand, and I smell the fragrant summertime perfume, a sweetness that makes me slightly dizzy. I blink once, and then again.

When I've opened my eyes, Waldo has stepped back, and his gaze sweeps out over the shimmering ribbon of the Concord River once more. His voice is calm as he says: "I think it was a sort of mercy that you weren't permitted inside Harvard."

I lift an eyebrow, questioning his meaning.

He picks another wildflower, twirling this one in his fingers. "Your mind has a sharp audacity to it. A wildness, even. It hasn't been dulled by rote memorization or recitation. Yes, the Fuller girl has done just fine for herself. In spite of the library books that she was denied."

I nod once, slowly, but don't offer anything in reply. We begin walking again, side by side, our shoulders nearly touching. I pinch my pink flower between my thumb and forefinger as I say, "Self-learning was the only option for me."

Waldo looks in my direction, eventually answering: "And self-reliance is the natural and beautiful result."

The afternoon is a warm one, and we've walked quite a way; I'm thankful that my poplin is lightweight, but I'm certain my cheeks are flushed.

"Yes, that's good. I quite like that. Self-reliance." Waldo snaps his fingers, declaring: "Oh, Margaret, speaking with you, it does something good for my soul." We've stopped walking again and now our bodies turn, angling toward each other as we pause just beside the fence that leads up to his house. Waldo is smiling like a lad many years younger as he says: "Thank you for meeting me here. For coming along with me."

Does he mean the walk? The conversation? The weeklong visit? I wonder. And then he does it again: he reaches for my ungloved hands and takes them both in his. Lifting our hands, he gives me a quick, unself-conscious squeeze, and I can't help but smile at his earnest goodwill, his exuberance and enthusiasm.

"Waldo, I must thank you, as well. It's been . . . well, this year has been a challenge." I swallow. I could go on, explaining that this *life* has been a challenge. Father's illness, and then his passing. Mother bringing me into her confidence, revealing the truth of just how bleak the future would be were we to try to survive on the remnants of Father's dwindling estate. I know more hard work awaits me when I move, alone, to Boston. Work to support myself and my family. But this, today, it's the first time I've had any peace for myself to simply, well, be. To think. And to speak freely with Ralph Waldo Emerson like an old friend—it's both delightful and entirely surprising. I add: "It's generous of you to have me here for this brief stay. I . . . I quite like Concord."

He crinkles his features into an odd, appraising smile as he holds my gaze. And when he speaks, it catches me by surprise that he says: "You have the busiest blue eyes, Margaret Fuller. As if they are dancing. I love to see it all, fresh, as you see it."

I can't help but laugh at this, a full, throaty laugh. I can't quite fathom the fact that the Sage of Concord has become such an immediate and natural friend, one now commenting on my busy, dancing eyes. It's difficult to grasp all that has transpired in just a few hours. Hours that, truly, passed like mere minutes. Waldo releases my hands and I raise my wildflower to my nose to inhale its intoxicating perfume, and also to mask how broad my smile is.

It's not until we turn toward the house that I notice, with a start, that the front door is wide open, and there's a figure standing out front. She's not smiling, but her eyes are alert, and they are occupied in that moment with darting from me to Waldo and back again.

I hear Waldo's quick intake of breath before, an instant later, he remembers himself. He manages a calm tone as he starts to walk up the path and says to me, his eyes only momentarily glancing toward the wild rose that he's tucked into my hair: "Come, Margaret, I'll introduce you to Mrs. Emerson."

Chapter Three

M RS. EMERSON STANDS AT THE THRESHOLD OF HER home, a tall figure draped in afternoon shadows and simple muslin, with a high collar and a bulge at the midsection where her child grows within. As I approach, I make a quick sweep of her figure, noting the plain crucifix that rests against her neck. Her dark hair, parted in the middle and pulled into a tightly braided bun, frames a wide face of round features. A smile might have done much to soften their impact or lend some small measure of beauty, but Mrs. Emerson's mouth is fixed in a straight line.

"Ah, my dear Lidian!" In contrast, her husband approaches in a bright, lively mood. "It does my spirit good to see you risen from bed." Emerson pauses several feet short of his wife, and I notice that he does not extend a hand to touch her, nor does he place a quick, comfortable kiss on her cheek. Instead, he gestures toward me. "Lidian, please meet our guest, Miss Margaret Fuller, formerly of Cambridge, and soon to be of Boston. But for a week, of Concord."

"Mrs. Emerson, it is so nice to meet you," I say, taking a step closer.

"And you, Miss Fuller." She folds her hands before her broad middle. "It's good of you to come to keep . . . me . . . company."

"I hope my arrival did not disturb your rest. Waldo—er, Mr. Emerson has been kind enough to show me the river and some of your village."

My hostess nods, her granite-colored eyes resting on the pale pink rose tucked behind my ear. Then she turns to her husband. "Thoreau has been my helper."

"Has he? Good man."

"He brought me my tray of bread and milk."

Waldo clasps his hands together. "And will you join us at the table for supper?"

Lidian shakes her head, looking to me, then back to her husband. "No. But Nancy has set the meal for you. I will ask Thoreau to help me back to bed. I've been standing here for some time now, and I feel quite tired." Thoreau appears just then from elsewhere in the yard, as if answering her summons. He sets his shovel against a broad chestnut tree and lopes toward our hostess. Lidian accepts his outstretched arm for support, then looks to me once more. "Welcome again, Miss Fuller. I hope you will make yourself at home." Her water-gray eyes slide from me toward her husband, and then she turns to Thoreau with a quick bob of her chin. The handyman takes up the arm of the lady of the house, and he leads her back inside, where I see them make their way toward the stairs.

Waldo and I remain outside, a few steps shy of reentering the quiet home. He watches his wife's slowly retreating figure as she labors up the stairs. Then he says: "Thoreau is a great comfort to my wife. For that I am glad. Lidian has suffered during this . . . ordeal. Fatigue and aches. Only a few more months and these troubles shall be behind her. But where are my manners?" Waldo turns his gaze back toward me. "Are you hungry?"

"Very," I answer honestly, noting that I haven't had a bite since before my stagecoach journey.

"Thoreau will join us once he has Lidian settled. Let's have some supper."

We enter the house and Waldo leads me into the dining room, where a simple but appealing spread fills the rounded mahogany table—I see plates of bread and cheese, a large bowl filled with salad greens, and a tureen steaming with what appears to be a fish stew. Now I'm even more aware of my hunger, and I happily take the offered seat at the table set for three. Waldo serves out three bowls of the warm stew, passing the first one to me in the seat to his right. Thoreau reappears and joins us a few moments later, taking the seat to Waldo's left, across from me. A silent look passes between Emerson and Thoreau, concluded when Thoreau gives a slight nod and Emerson looks down toward his supper. I gather it is Emerson thanking him for tending to his wife.

Waldo says a quick blessing as we bow our heads, and then I notice with a jolt of surprise that Thoreau begins his meal by sticking his fingers into his stew bowl and plucking out a morsel of fish, which he proceeds to pop directly into his mouth. From the look of his darkened fingers, he has not washed up since his work in the garden! Emerson takes no note of this. I stifle the urge to laugh into my bowl.

Hunger truly does make for the best seasoning, and the stew is delicious, warm and flavorful. My first mouthful tastes of garlic and lemon, with a hint of pepper and parsley. I'm taking quick, appreciative spoonfuls when Emerson breaks the silence, asking: "Is the meal to your liking?"

I dab the corners of my mouth with my linen napkin before answering: "Very much. Thank you."

"And I know that you're enjoying yourself," Waldo says, turning to Thoreau, who is slurping his broth most appreciatively, his bowl raised to his lips like a cup. Waldo smiles, then turns back to me. "Thoreau here is a most helpful man around the house. In addition to the gardening and the care he provides for Mrs. Emerson, he makes Nancy, our cook, feel quite flattered at mealtimes. And sometimes he even helps her cook."

"You sound like the perfect housemate," I say.

"And then you must add in that he's a prize to have in the woods. He can whistle any birdcall you might throw at him."

I look across the table at Thoreau, whose light eyes are smiling. "Is that so?" I ask.

"Do the phoebe," Waldo says. Thoreau sits back in his seat, swallowing his bite of stew before he closes his eyes and lets out a whistle. It fills the dining room: a two-note call, from high to low, that sounds much like saying the name itself. *Phoe-beee.*

"Very nice," I say.

Waldo raps the table. "Now do the bobolink, I quite like that one." Thoreau's next whistle is an erratic series of undulating notes.

His body dances as he does it and I cannot help but laugh. "I feel as though I'm in the forest," I remark.

"How about this one—can you name it?" Thoreau looks to me and then toward Waldo, his expression bright. He whistles a high note and then a series of quick, hard-hitting staccatos.

"I know that one." Emerson raises his hand. "You've gone easy on us. Chicka-dee-dee-dee."

"There you have it, Waldo." Thoreau nods approvingly. "You're a woodsman yourself."

"I try." Emerson turns to me and says, "Mr. Thoreau has a gift with birds, turtles, squirrels, and the pen."

"You're a writer as well?" I ask, helping myself to a serving from the cheese board.

Thoreau offers a modest shrug of his thick shoulders. "I write, that is the truth. Though I'm not certain that anyone other than Mr. Emerson here has yet to call me a writer."

"You can be bashful, but I'll be honest. Mr. Thoreau is brilliant with a pen," Waldo declares. "That is, when it comes to words. You ask him to put that pen to figures or balance ledgers? It's a fright."

Thoreau turns his gaze to his friend, a look of playful indignation on his features as he raises his hands. "Why should I trouble myself with figures and balance ledgers? Why, any sum that I must do, I should be able to do on these five fingers. Ten, at most."

"Oh, money. Thoreau has sworn off the stuff entirely." Waldo flashes me a rueful smirk. "That's all very well and good, though one does need a roof over one's head."

"What does money have to do with building oneself a roof?" Thoreau asks. "Again I say: I have these two hands. And is there not wood enough in the forest?"

"But the stuff did pay for your time at Harvard, after all."

I look at each of them for a long moment, absorbing their bandying, this talk of money and life and writing, and then I muse inwardly: Waldo has his roof over his head, and a very fine one at that, because of his dead wife's fortune. The plentiful food on his table, as well. Thoreau, too, has a roof over his head because of Emerson's dead wife's fortune. And yet Emerson is clearly generous with that money, opening this house to Thoreau. Inviting guests like me, Eliza Peabody, and others to enjoy the richness of his company and thoughts. I can't very well begrudge him the fact that he has come into enough money to live purely, to feel no weight on his shoulders or timepiece binding his hours as a writer and a thinker. Enough money, even, to support another writer in his own household, as well.

And yet, the fact remains that for me, it will never be so simple. I turn back to my supper, grateful in a new way for this nourishing spread before me, knowing that in just one week's time, I will have to work for every meal I take, and for every meal that I can provide for my family back home on the farm.

Outside the windows, the summer sun has slipped down. A soft lilac glow has settled over the gardens and the fields, and the lanes of Concord beyond. Mr. Emerson's dining room fills with shadows and Thoreau hops up to light the candles. As we finish our dinner, he stokes the small fire at the hearth, and now the room feels bright and cozy.

Though we finish the meal, none of us appears ready to retire quite yet. Instead we remain at the table, talking about books and writing and the beauty of the Concord River. Thoreau reaffirms Waldo's earlier statement, telling me that my exile from Harvard was in fact a blessing, as Thoreau, even more than Emerson, seems to support a rugged sort of solitary study. He has us laughing like children as he demonstrates more birdcalls, including the brazen shrieks of the blue jay and the jaunty warble of the cardinal. I am satiated from the meal and pleasantly tired from the long walk. *I cannot remember the last time I felt this at ease,* I think, looking from Emerson to Thoreau, feeling indescribably grateful for their enlivening company.

Eventually, after how long I do not even know, it is Thoreau who yawns. "I plan to rise early tomorrow to catch the fish before the sun," he declares.

"Indeed," Waldo agrees, setting down his napkin. Thoreau puts out the fire at the hearth as Emerson and I snuff out the candles. When the room is dark, Thoreau bids us good night and trots up the stairs without a candle, disappearing into the small room right at the top. He is, I imagine, a man so in tune with his nature that

sleep must enfold him as soon as he puts his head to the pillow. I
envy that.

Emerson and I stand in the dim front hall now, just the pair of
us. He's kept two candles lit, and he hands me one, keeping the
other for himself.

Our faces flicker in the candlelight. "Thank you for supper," I say.
My voice sounds loud in the quiet space.

"Thank you for making it so much more than simply supper,
Margaret."

Waldo sees me to my bedchamber in candlelit silence. We pause
at the threshold of my room. Waldo raises his candle and I open the
door, stepping past him, pausing to meet his eyes. "And thus con-
cludes your first day in Concord," he says, his voice low, almost a
whisper.

I nod. What a day it has been.

"I suppose I shall retire to my study to read for a while," Emerson
says, glancing at the doorway that's only a couple strides from
mine, before turning his gaze back toward my bedchamber. His
eyes linger for a moment on my bed. And then he stares back into
my eyes. Suddenly I don't feel tired at all, but instead notice the
clamoring of my heartbeat. I manage a calm tone as I say: "Enjoy
your reading, Waldo."

His gaze holds mine, his pale eyes glinting with candlelight, or
perhaps something else. "Thank you, Margaret. Enjoy your rest. No
nightmares allowed here, all right?"

I smile. "If you say so." And with that I enter my chamber and
softly shut the door, remaining fixed in place as I take in a long
breath. And because he stands on just the other side of the thin
door, I can hear perfectly well that he, too, remains fixed in place.
There are no soft footsteps, no receding shadows. Instead I know,
without seeing, that Waldo is lingering outside my bedchamber. It's
several long minutes before I hear him turn, hear the creaking of
the wooden floorboards as he steps away, leaving me alone with the
quiet candlelight and a mind filled with noisy, whirling thoughts.

Chapter Four

I WAKE TO AN UPROARIOUS DIN THE NEXT MORNING. The sounds that rouse me come across the bright morning with a clamor of carriage wheels and horse hooves. I rise, padding across the room in bare feet and my nightgown to peer out the window, past the gardens and toward the turnpike. In the street beyond the fence, a man bellows.

I dress quickly, moving through my toilette and selecting a simple summer tarlatan of pale purple with a white collar. When I open my bedroom door I nearly collide with Waldo, who stands in the front hall looking out the window. He turns to me with a grin. "Ah, Miss Fuller, good morning."

"Good morning," I say, feeling a bit bashful at the sudden memories of the previous evening. How late we stayed up. Just how much we talked—and shared. That, and the fact that other than my father and brothers, I've never had a man walk me to my bedroom, nor have I seen a man early in the morning like this, even before taking my coffee.

Waldo's expression is unreadable, but then his eyes sweep my appearance, and he asks: "How did you sleep? Were you comfortable?"

"Very well, and yes. Thank you. But . . . I thought I heard a terrible racket on the street just now."

"You did," he says with a knowing grin, looking back to the window. "That is the sound of the Alcotts returning home."

"Who are the Alcotts?" I join Waldo at the window, peering out to the street, where a carriage and horse are tied to a hitching post at a nearby house, a mountain of luggage tied to the carriage roof. I don't see any people.

"Bronson and Abba, and their three little girls," Waldo says. "A lovely family, if a bit . . . colorful. Come, let's take a quick breakfast and then we ought to call on them."

Emerson's sunlit dining room is already set for the morning meal, the air rich with the pleasant aromas of coffee and toasted bread. I accept a cup of coffee and a heap of berry preserves on top of my toast, and I happily tuck in as Waldo tells me more about the Alcotts. How the patriarch, Bronson Alcott, began as a traveling peddler, moving from town to town offering all manner of goods, as well as his wild and entertaining stories.

Along the way, Bronson Alcott wooed and wed the affluent and well-educated Abigail May, daughter of one of America's oldest families—whom he has renamed with the pet name Abba. The couple now have three lively girls, Anna, Louisa May, and Beth. "It was around the time of his marriage to Abba that Bronson decided the salesman's life was not for him, and now he fancies himself something of a pioneer in the world of education," Emerson explains, taking a slow sip of coffee.

"Is he a Harvard man like you and Thoreau?" I ask.

"Oh, no," Emerson says, sounding like he might laugh. "I don't believe Bronson Alcott had any formal schooling past the age of eight." He replaces his coffee cup in its saucer. "And yet, his ideas on children and education do have a unique brilliance. He has quite a following. He gives successful lectures—his talks are always well attended. And with the earnings from those talks Bronson was able to open the Temple School in Boston, a coeducational school for young children."

I sit back in my chair. "Coeducational," I say, musing aloud. "I like very much that Mr. Alcott offers his school to boys *and* girls."

Emerson nods. "Oh, you'll find much common ground with Bronson Alcott on his philosophies for educating girls."

"I'd like to meet this man," I declare.

"And I'd like to introduce you to him."

. . .

WE STEP OUT into a bright, warm morning and walk up the lane until we pause before a brown home, spacious enough, if not stately, with the carriage tied out front. The home is set back from the road on a slight hill, with flowers and fruit trees coloring the space, and a sprawling elm casting a pleasant canopy of shade over much of the front lawn. I spot a lanky man climbing on the parked coach. He whistles a tune as he reaches up to untie the profusion of luggage that is piled atop the roof.

The man, entirely consumed with his attempts to unfasten the cords holding the luggage, does not notice us.

"Bronson Alcott, welcome home." Waldo speaks up to the traveler. "Orchard House was far too quiet without you and the family."

Now the man turns, the floppy beige hat atop his head going lopsided, his pale features broadening into a wide smile. "Mr. Emerson!" He hops down in one jaunty leap, his long legs and arms calling to mind the image of a grasshopper.

Bronson Alcott is dressed entirely in black, his clothes simple and, from the looks of it, in need of a good laundering. He has honey-colored hair and clear blue eyes, and he looks to be a bit older than me, though he still bears an undeniably youthful energy and attractiveness. He holds in his hands, for some reason I could not provide, a tambourine. He looks from Emerson to me and then replies: "Greetings, neighbor! And who is this?"

"Bronson, please meet Margaret Fuller, newly arrived from Cambridge, and kind enough to visit Lidian and me for a week at Bush."

"*The* Margaret Fuller! Here in our humble Concordia? You are most welcome! Most welcome indeed."

I smile at this, taken slightly aback by Bronson Alcott—by his effulgence, his rumpled appearance, his neighborly words. "Thank you, Mr. Alcott."

"Please, it's Bronson among friends. We are most informal here in Concord, isn't that so, Waldo?"

"So I've told her."

Bronson taps his tambourine against his leg, eyeing me from under the brim of his floppy hat. "And how is your visit so far?"

"I've only been here a day. But I'm very much enjoying myself."

"And we've only just arrived back from Boston. Here for the

summer before the workaday calls us back to the big city. But looking forward to several months of the woods and wild blackberries."

"And we are glad to have you back," Waldo says, looking up toward the home on the hill. Right then I hear a tinkling of laughter from indoors, the sound of children on the other side of the opened windows.

Bronson pulls my attention back to the street. "Margaret, Waldo has shown me some of your writings. I am your humble admirer. It is a special treat to return to Concordia and see that you are to be my neighbor—why, it makes our arrival even happier."

The fact that Ralph Waldo Emerson has taken the time to share my writings with Bronson Alcott fills me with the warm embers of flattered satisfaction, and I can't help but smile at this. Just then, the door to the house swings open and I hear a woman's voice calling out. "Bronson? Have you any sight of the kitchen wares yet?" A tall, slender woman appears, followed by what can only be described as a disgorgement of rambunctious little bodies that spill out all around her, with much squealing and laughter as the three small figures bolt down the hill toward us. We three adults, standing here talking, are mere obstacles in what looks to be their game of chase as they run right past us.

"Abba!" Bronson Alcott calls to his wife, and she steps from the doorway. "I have not! Because I have much more pressing matters to attend to at the present moment, such as meeting the illustrious Margaret Fuller and receiving the eminent presence of our dear friend Ralph Waldo Emerson." Abba looks at each of us in turn. Her face is shadowed in a brimmed bonnet, and her dress is a simple blue worsted, but she, like her husband, is an attractive person. She greets me with a polite smile, then turns to my host. "Waldo, how lovely to see you. How is Lidian?"

Emerson tucks his hands into his pockets, rocking on his heels as he answers: "She is . . . valiant."

Abba tilts her head sideways with a knowing expression. "Still suffering from the headaches?"

"Among other things."

Abba Alcott offers a nod, gazing out over the lawn, where her own three offspring are now leaping about with joyful squeals. Two of the girls are fair like their father. The eldest wears a single golden braid down her back, and the youngest, whose flaxen ringlets bounce as she toddles around trying to keep up, appears to be no more than two years of age. The two bigger girls—I guess them to be around five and four—are playing what looks to be a game of horse and rider. The middle girl has darker coloring, her mahogany hair pulled back in two tails with bows coming untied. She is playing the part of the horse, while the eldest sister follows behind issuing orders like a prim lady.

"Her troubles shall pass soon enough," Abba says, sending a weary smile in the direction of her daughters. "The burdens of her condition will soon be but a passing memory as her joy—"

"Abba, my dearest one, where are our manners?" Bronson interrupts. "We must offer our guests tea."

Abba turns to her husband in mute but apparent disbelief. Her expression makes plain her incredulity at the fact that, after a three-hour journey on the turnpike, with three small, boisterous children and an entire household strapped most precariously to the roof of a coach—the bags and trunks which her husband has yet to bring down—she's expected to wait on us with hot tea.

"Oh, please do not trouble yourselves," Emerson hurries to interject. "We are only here to say hello."

But Bronson insists: "No, no, we *must* have tea. We have much to catch up on."

After a pause, during which time her husband does not meet her eyes, Abba sighs. Then she marches dutifully off toward the house without a word of protest, merely asking us to give her a few minutes to draw the water from the well, and to get a fire going and the kettle to boil.

Waldo and I exchange a glance. Abba closes the front door, perhaps a bit more vigorously than necessary, as Bronson's satisfied nod seems to tell us that it's all in hand. I turn to look out over the yard. "Your girls are happy to be here," I remark.

"Oh, indeed. They love Concord. But then, they seem happy wherever we go."

"What are their names?" I ask.

"Anna is our eldest. She's a veritable angel. She's holding Beth, our youngest. And that one, the least lovely, is our Louisa May. We call her Louy."

At that precise moment, Louy runs by at a full canter, issuing a snorting exhale that sounds impressively similar to that of a horse. This sets the actual horse, tied to the hitching post, into a flurry of excitement, and the animal's loud neigh sends the girls into peals of hysterics, with Louy throwing herself onto the grass in a fit of giggles. I can't help but smile as I watch her guileless mirth. She may be the least lovely in her father's eyes, but Louy also appears the least likely to care for any designation of loveliness. The bows in her pigtails are now fully untied, and her dress, which looks like at one time it might have been white, is dirt-streaked and torn at the hemline. She is my immediate favorite.

Bronson interrupts my thoughts. "They are a lively trinity, to be sure. You know I'm an educator?"

"Waldo was just telling me, yes."

"I'm an expert." Bronson says it with total frankness, still clutching the tambourine in his hand. "I believe that we humans, we could be as good and pure as the divine walking the earth. And it is the children who will teach us the way. But that one . . ." Bronson points toward his middle daughter with an expression that looks like admiration mixed with a large dose of befuddlement. "She would challenge the patience of a saint. The others are fair, you see, with my light eyes. But Louisa May . . . you can see there is more darkness in her. More that still wants for purification."

I glance at Bronson with a small laugh, certain that now he is jesting. But then I note his earnest, unsmiling expression, and it occurs to me that in fact he is being entirely serious. I shift on my feet, momentarily at a loss for any response, wondering: *Does he not notice that my own hair is dark?*

Mercifully, I am spared from this awkward exchange when Louisa May lets loose a fresh shout. "Mr. Thoreau!" I see Thoreau bounding up the Alcotts' lawn, moving like a puppy that's just been let off his tether. He runs to the girls, arms outstretched, and they barrel into him, tackling him until all four of them are a pile of limbs and laughter spilling across the grass.

"Ah, Mr. Thoreau is a great favorite of my children," Bronson says with delight. "He teaches them their lessons sometimes, taking them along the river. He shows them how to find the places where the fox kits play. Where to locate the best wildflowers and summer blueberries."

Thoreau joins seamlessly in their game, appearing to play the part of a horse right beside Louisa May, and suddenly their joy is even more giddy than it was a moment earlier. It's a side of Thoreau, a playfulness, he must reserve only for children. He looks completely at ease.

Eventually the game is paused and Thoreau joins us, panting, greeting Bronson with a hearty handshake. Louisa comes right up and sits on his feet, so that he won't be able to walk anywhere without carrying her along like a barnacle. "Mr. Thoreau! Did you miss us terribly?" she asks, tugging on the hem of his stained trousers as she looks up at his sun-browned face.

"I've cried myself to sleep every night since you left." Thoreau hangs his shaggy head in a theatrical mope. Louisa likes this; she laughs, her giggles like a wood chime.

"But!" Thoreau raises a finger. "You've returned just in time."

"Why is that?" Louisa's dark eyes sparkle.

"Have you remembered what I told you to look forward to?" Thoreau dips his face down toward her. "A most special event that would happen this summer?"

Louisa hops to a stand, bouncing as she answers: "The Queen of the Night! Is that it?"

Thoreau claps his hands together. "Indeed."

"Is she ready?" the girl asks.

Thoreau leans forward so that his eyes are level with Louisa's, and he speaks in a conspiratorial whisper: "Her buds have appeared. Every day they grow larger and larger, and her stem has just started to lean. I believe Her Majesty shall be ready any day now."

Louisa smiles wide, then, without a word, she grabs the tambourine from her father's hand and dashes off to share this news with her sisters. Thoreau watches her go with a look of kindly affection before he turns back to us adults. He must see my confusion, because he says, "I have a *Cereus* cactus, in a pot in the back of Emerson's garden. She's a most lovely, most rare specimen. All the way from Mexico. They call her Queen of the Night. She blooms for one night only; it's called the Dance of the Night Blooming. And you have come just in time."

Louisa runs back to our huddle and I'm amazed at how quickly her little legs can carry her about. Now she wraps her arms around her father's waist. "Oh, Father, can we see it? Please? *Please!* Can we stay up past our bedtime, late into the night, to watch the queen open her petals?"

Bronson's wide hat flops as he nods. "I don't see why not."

Just then Abba reappears at the doorstep, her face crinkled in apologies. She can't find the kettle, she declares. Her May family china is put away and she is overwhelmed by all that must be sorted and unpacked; might we please come back for the offered tea the next day?

"Think nothing of it, Mrs. Alcott. We've trespassed too long as it is," Emerson replies good-naturedly. "Mr. Thoreau and I shall assist your husband in bringing down these trunks from the coach and then we will leave you in peace." Just then little Beth begins to squeal, clinging to her mother's skirt, as if to answer Waldo that there shall be no peace at the lively, chaotic Alcott home. Nevertheless, we will leave the road-weary family to get settled.

But not before Thoreau promises Louisa May three different times that we will be certain to fetch her as soon as the Queen of the Night begins to unfurl her petals.

THOREAU'S POTTED QUEEN offers no excitement that evening, as hoped for. Nor the next. Each evening we gather after dark, hoping for signs of the much-anticipated night blooming, but, like all queens, this one keeps her own time.

"I won't deny my disappointment," Emerson declares the next morning at breakfast, after yet another uneventful night in his garden. Both Lidian and I sit with him, though Thoreau is already out, at work in the vegetable beds. Emerson's tone is dismayed as he looks to me. "She's taking so long, and now you might miss the blooming."

Already I've been in Concord for five days—the next day is the last full one of my weeklong visit. I take a sip of my coffee, touched by his care. And also deeply disappointed that I might miss something that the whole town seems so eager to witness.

Emerson stares at his plate as he ventures, "That is . . . unless you might extend your stay?" He poses it tenuously, like a question. I pause, mid-sip, coffee cup pinched between my fingers. Lidian sits silently across from me, but I see how her eyes dart toward her husband.

The truth is, I would love to extend my stay in Concord. I'm not needed in Boston, not urgently, until late August, when my pupils will begin their scheduled studies. Would I relish more time here? Yes, I would. I've loved my week in Concord—the company, the conversations, the walks through the summer greenery.

Before I've formed my response, Emerson presses on: "Lidian, don't you think Margaret should stay? She's such wonderful company to us both. I don't like to think of the Red Room empty again so soon."

My eyes slide back toward Lidian. I watch her features arrange themselves into a taut, self-possessed smile. She places a hand on the swollen globe of her belly and then, her voice like a reed, she answers: "If that suits Margaret, then yes. Of course she should stay." Lidian looks from her husband to me. "You are most welcome."

"Thank you both," I say in reply, but I'm looking only at my hostess. "I'd like very much to stay. Only . . . I do not wish to impose. Wouldn't you like your home back?"

"It's no imposition at all," Emerson declares. "Isn't that so, Lidian?"

"Yes," Lidian answers with a curt nod. And I'm not certain whether she's answering her husband's question, or mine.

THAT NIGHT, THOREAU comes bounding into the dining room at suppertime, his hair even more wild than usual around his flushed face. The petals of the *Cereus* are swollen to plumpness, he declares. "It's tonight. It can't possibly wait another night."

"Hear, hear!" Emerson cheers, looking to me with a broad grin, and I can see the handsome young lad of Harvard in his animated features. Lidian has already retired upstairs, complaining of a headache after breakfast and skipping midday dinner, tea, and supper altogether. Emerson, Thoreau, and I are all excitement and anticipation as we hurry through our meal and Thoreau dashes off to alert the Alcotts of his long-awaited news.

At eight o'clock Emerson climbs the stairs to listen outside his wife's door. He knocks softly but receives no response from within, then he descends without a word.

Together he and I make our way out into the garden, where night has fallen and a sizable crowd has gathered in the back, with Thoreau standing at its center. Louy and Anna stand at his side, each one holding a candle. My eyes adjust to the shadows and I see that the creamy white petals of the Queen of the Night have started to unfold, like a fine lady's fan opening one crease at a time.

The night is a warm one. Some in the crowd whisper, some giggle, but most stand in a sort of reverent and silent vigil. It is all so intoxicating: the scent of the flower, the twinkling light of the candles being held aloft around the garden, the giddy titters of the Alcott girls. The whole assembly has the feel of a fairy's summer scene.

Emerson stands at my side, close enough that I can hear the rise and fall of his breaths. As we watch the flower making her slow, inching progress, the scene takes on an air of spiritual solemnity. Even Louisa seems to grow calmer, almost peaceful, as if partly entranced. Thoreau tells us all how the flower hopes to gather pollinators on her one night of activity—bats, moths, and beetles. These visitors will come after midnight, to land on her massive petals that will stretch as long as a child's arm.

As we stand there for an hour, and then two, my own bare arms begin to grow chilly. I wish I had thought to bring a shawl. At first, I suppose that the brush against my side is some casual mistake of Emerson shifting on his feet. But when it happens again a moment later, I look down and see his palm resting on top of my hand. My eyes fly upward to meet his.

I can't seem to look away. He leans forward, and for a confused, breathless moment, I wonder if he intends to kiss me. And then I wonder: How might I react? But his lips don't find my own; instead, they pause beside my ear. His breath tickles my skin, sending a ripple of goose bumps over me as he whispers: "I know how that flower feels."

I peer at him with a questioning gaze, my heart hammering against my rib cage. I'm grateful for the veil of darkness that covers this entire garden, hiding what I am certain is the scarlet flush of my face. When Waldo goes on, his voice is still a low whisper, his words intended only for me. "When I am with you, I expand."

I force myself to breathe out, slowly, as I nod. He pulls his hand away from mine, but he keeps his body close. And he continues to keep his body close for several more hours as we watch the Queen of the Night in her seductive, exotic dance. I can feel the hum that pulses between us, a heat, invisible and yet thick enough to touch. The heady perfume of the flower makes me a bit woozy and I close my eyes. I think of Shakespeare and Grimm and so many others, and I marvel at the fact that none of their fairy gatherings can compare to this summer night in Emerson's garden.

We stay until just after midnight. The Night Queen opens and stretches until she has reached her full and resplendent shape. She is ready for her many lovers. And when the viewing is over, when the crowds disperse and the Alcotts return to their home and Thoreau slips off and Emerson walks me, silently, back into his house, right up to the door of my bedchamber, we take our leave of each other with nothing more than a chaste good night.

And even though I *did* have the chance to see the blooming, neither Emerson nor I raise the topic of my departure the next morning. Without further discussion, it seems it's been decided that I'll stay with the Emersons in Concord for another week.

Chapter Five

WALDO IS EXPANSIVE THE NEXT MORNING. HE TAKES his seat at the dining room table, looking fresh and well-groomed, eager to tell stories. Lidian, too, has dressed and come down to breakfast, and Waldo begins regaling her with the details of last night. "Oh, Lidian dear, you would have loved it. The perfume was unlike anything we have from these northern flowers. You would have fancied yourself in the tropics. I am sorry you missed it."

Lidian takes a small bite of plain toast, her expression dim opposite her husband's bright enthusiasm. When she speaks, her lips look pinched. "I am sorry to have missed it, as well. Perhaps you can write a poem about it."

Emerson cocks his head, answering only: "That's an idea."

I take a sip of coffee, looking down at my trembling hands, hoping that neither Waldo nor Lidian can tell just how fraught my own thoughts are. The truth is that my mind is restless; I did not sleep well, brooding as I recalled the hours spent in the garden with Waldo, watching the night blooming. We'd been in the garden surrounded by many others, rather, but it had *felt* like just the two of us. What was this, I wondered, that was happening between us? What was this spark that flew back and forth whenever we were near?

It is a feeling that is entirely foreign to me, and while I find it pleasant, to be sure, I also find it terribly unsettling. With his attention and his interest, is Waldo perhaps quenching some thirst I've long felt, but have not yet articulated to myself? Perhaps the void left by my exacting, withholding father? Or is it the presence and affirmation I've always craved from my distracted, fragile mother? Or perhaps he is the professor I've always yearned to learn from? Or—and this may be the most terrifying consideration of all—are Waldo's attentions stoking some fire within me that no interested suitor or beau has ever yet kindled?

I do not know what to make of it all. Nor can I understand how *he* feels—he, who seems so entirely untroubled, even ebullient, as he speaks to his wife mere hours after touching my hand in the darkness of his garden. My mind cannot make sense of it, my mind that can study and work for hours without pause; these quandaries of the Emerson household I am finding impossible to reason out.

"Rain all day," Waldo remarks, interrupting my brooding. I follow his gaze across the room toward the windows, where drops of water pearl the glass panes.

"Yes," I say, looking at both of the Emersons in turn. "I think I'll use these damp hours to write." Writing to my mother might clear my head, I tell myself.

"A fine idea." Waldo settles his napkin on the table. "And perhaps if the skies clear, we can walk later?"

I hear Lidian inhale a quick, sharp breath. I swallow my sip of coffee without tasting it. Before I can answer, Lidian interjects: "So, then, it's settled?" Her hand strokes the mound of her midsection, the belly that fills the space between her chair and the table. "Margaret will stay with us for another week?"

"She has graciously accepted our offer, Mrs. Emerson," Waldo says, smiling brightly.

"Good," Lidian says, though her wooden tone seems to say quite the opposite.

"I thank you for your hospitality," I venture, looking to my hostess. "I hope I won't be an imposition."

"Not at all, Margaret," she says, meeting my eyes straight on, her hand fanning out over her swollen middle. "After all, what is one more week? Mr. E. enjoys running our home like a hotel."

I nod, attempting a feeble smile, then I excuse myself from the table, guessing that perhaps Mrs. Emerson might appreciate having a few minutes alone with her husband. And the full day of unrelenting rain means that Waldo and I do not walk together that afternoon, which I find to be both a relief and a terrible disappointment.

AFTER THAT, WE settle into a sort of routine in the Emerson household. Breakfast in the bright dining room, though Lidian often prefers to take her tray of bread and milk in bed, and Thoreau has often left by the time I emerge from my guest room. After coffee, Waldo and I break to our separate rooms, where we write in solitude. He tells me that he's working on a collection of essays that he hopes to publish in the autumn. I fill my hours with writing to Mother as well as the half-dozen families who have hired me to tutor their daughters in the autumn with private lessons. It is how I will earn my wages to support my rented room in Boston and to send money back home to Mother and my siblings. When I have time remaining, I work on a Goethe text that I am translating from its original German into English.

We break for midday dinner. Lidian sometimes joins us, and a few times Abba Alcott comes with the girls, as well. Thoreau prefers to take his midday meal out on the river or while working in the gardens. After we've eaten, if Lidian feels up to it, I offer to read to her in her bedroom. One day I take dictation for her as she sits on her chaise longue beside the window and answers a letter from her cousin in Plymouth. Otherwise, Waldo and I like to take a long daily walk, ambling through the woods and the meadows that surround Concord with their lively summer splendor. In the late afternoons, we sit beside the Mill Brook or return to Bush and read to each other beneath the gracious shade of the tulip tree.

Unlike his wife, who prefers the dry and moralistic prose of Belsham, or verses from the Bible, Waldo reads to me from his own drafts, sharing passages of his new essays. He pauses often to think through an idea, and I punctuate his reading with questions or comments of my own. Sometimes he takes my suggestions, other times he doesn't. I find his language so engrossing that often I'm surprised when he puts down his pages to tell me it's time for supper.

AND THUS PASSES the better part of another week, with a peaceful enough rapport, even if that peace feels, at times, fragile. Even if I do feel frequent pangs of guilt that I'm enjoying Waldo's company so much, just as he's clearly enjoying mine. But nothing untoward happens—ours is a kinship of the mind. On several afternoons, a late-summer storm rolls in, bringing with it thick, marbled clouds and a sudden downpour of rain. But inside the home, we manage to avoid any unpleasant storms.

Toward the end of my second week, Waldo and I set out on a walk that brings us past Orchard House, where we spy Louisa May and Anna at work in the yard. Bronson Alcott expects his girls to put in long hours in the summer garden; these plots comprise the primary source of the family's foodstuffs, and now the beds lie full with squash and tomatoes, peppers, peas, and pumpkins.

But it's not among the vegetables where we find Louisa that day. The girl is standing in the middle of a patch of sunflowers taller than she, speaking to each brown-and-yellow face like she might greet a gathering of friends. Waldo and I share a silent, appreciative smile, not wishing to interrupt or embarrass her.

After a moment, Waldo clears his throat and the girl turns. "Oh! Mr. Emerson! Miss Fuller!" Louisa's dark eyes go round. "I didn't see you there."

"Good day, Miss Alcott."

"I was just speaking with my sunflowers," Louisa says unselfconsciously.

Waldo walks up to her side. "Is that right?"

"Plants fare better when we humans speak loving words to them," she explains.

I like this very much. "You are a true student of Mr. Thoreau," I remark.

Louy smiles at this, but then her face turns serious. "Well, Anna tells me she's too proper to fritter away her time speaking to plants that don't have ears to hear." She crosses her arms before her chest, issuing a woebegone sigh. "So it falls to me to speak to the whole garden."

"A most important job," I say. "And do you give them all names?"

"Names?" Louy looks at me askance. "Goodness, no. They are *plants*, not puppies."

"Oh, yes, of course. Pardon me; it was a silly question."

"It's all right." Louisa reaches forward and plucks a few seeds from the nearest sunflower. "I take these to feed the chickens."

"Lucky chickens," Waldo says. "May I tell you a secret?"

"Yes!" the girl answers, her dark-eyed gaze brightening.

Waldo leans forward and speaks in a conspiratorial whisper: "You keep some of those seeds for yourself, and if you roast them over the fire and sprinkle them with a generous pinch of salt, they make for a most delectable treat."

Louisa nods solemnly at this, taking his instructions to heart. Then, after a thoughtful pause, she whispers back: "Don't tell my sisters, all right?"

"Why is that?" Waldo asks.

"Because then they will want some. And I know this is a wicked thing to say, but I don't wish to share. Not my sunflower seeds. Not after I've been the one speaking with them all summer."

"I won't utter a word," Waldo assures her, putting his finger to his lips in a most solemn vow of secrecy. Louisa looks to me, and I offer her an allegiant nod to promise the same. When Waldo tips forward and gives the young girl an affectionate tap on the top of her dark head, I see, with a pinching sensation in my heart that I don't quite understand, what a wonderful father he will be.

Then Waldo's pale eyes slide toward me, and he looks almost mischievous. "Oh, Louy, I do have one question for you."

"What's that?" the girl asks, turning back to her task of plucking out sunflower seeds.

Waldo is still eyeing me as he asks the girl: "Do you think our Miss Margaret here is nice?"

"Nice?" Louisa pauses her seed collecting. "Why, yes. She's splendid!"

I smile appreciatively at this. Waldo puts his finger to his chin and goes on. "Well, the reason I ask is because Miss Margaret had promised us a fortnight of her time. But the fortnight has come and nearly gone, and now she's preparing to leave, and I suspect that her departure shall make us all quite despondent. Don't you think that, if Miss Margaret were *truly*—what was it you called her?—splendid, then she would have mercy on us all and consent to give us just one more week of her time?"

Louisa takes the bait with gusto. "Oh, yes! Please, Miss Margaret! Don't leave us. Won't you please stay?"

"Waldo!" I grin, surprised by this. Surprised, and yet undeniably delighted. Entirely tempted by the prospect of just one more week in Concord. But I offer him a wry smile as I say: "I find it unfair of you to pull in Louisa May to do your work."

Waldo makes a face, an adorably innocent face, answering: "I had a feeling you might have a harder time saying no to our Louy here."

"You were correct in that," I admit. "But still . . . it's something I must think on. . . ."

He waves his arms around. "What's not to stay for?"

"Well . . ." I want to stay—of course I want to stay. "But have you . . . does Mrs. Emerson know you've invited me to stay on for another week?"

"I will speak with her directly. Surely she won't mind. Lidian knows how happy you make all of us."

But perhaps that is a problem, I think.

"There are so many things we have yet to discuss," Waldo goes on. "And so many things I still wish to show you."

I fold my hands before my waist, trying my best to appear indifferent. But now I'm more intrigued. "Like . . . like what?"

"Stay," he says with a tilt of his smiling face, "and I'll show you."

BRIGHT SUNSHINE GREETS me the next morning, streaming through my bedroom windows as I rise and dress. At breakfast, it is just the pair of us, and Waldo declares it is time for me to go out on the river. "I've been to the river," I say, taking a sip of coffee. We walk there almost daily.

He taps the shell of a soft-boiled egg, peeling it off in small shards. "But you've not yet been *on* it." His pale eyes flash in my direction. "It's time you float down it."

So late morning finds me and Waldo aboard Thoreau's small rowboat, the *Musketaquid*, drifting out from town, winding slowly around the Concord River's gentle bends. Emerson has decided I need to see the crumbling ruins of the beloved Old North Bridge, so Thoreau sets our course.

As we float, I see that Waldo was correct: being on the river means seeing it in an entirely new way. I tilt my cheeks up to catch the sun's warm golden light. Waldo crosses his legs out in front of him, his hat leaning on his head in a rakish, lopsided tilt, and he tells me about Paul Revere's heroic nighttime ride through this very countryside. He speaks of the resulting military skirmishes that played out right here between the Concord farmers and the hired British regulars, in these very pastures and meadows, beginning our nation's Revolution. "I like to call it 'the shot heard 'round the world,'" Emerson says. "It was all right here. Picture, if you would, rows of our Colonial Minutemen and English Redcoats in lines, where now instead you see these rows of apple trees."

Thoreau, who steers our course with the wooden oars he's hewn for himself, sits in the back of the boat. He's quiet, pensive. I'm not entirely certain whether he's listening to Waldo's stories; perhaps he's listening to whatever it is that the river and the trees see fit to tell him. After a while I turn to him and ask, "And what of the name of your vessel, Captain Thoreau?"

Thoreau's face perks up. "*Musketaquid*? It's the Native name of this river," he explains, his features relaxed in the afternoon sunshine. "It means 'grass.' Look down." I do as he says, eyeing the thick river grasses that sway beneath the surface that his oar now ripples. They dance in the current like long green fingers. I nod appreciatively. He's painted his boat blue and green, and it skims seamlessly through the natural beauty all around us. Though I've told Waldo in the past of my fear of water—my recurring nightmares of oceans and drowning—I feel no fear now, not on this gentle river, not with this gentle oarsman at the helm.

Eventually we come to a bend in the river and I spot a gray-brown home perched back atop a hill, hemmed by an orchard of fruit trees and rolling green pastures. It appears to be some sort of residence, or perhaps a church outbuilding.

"Ah! Here we are." Emerson sits up, observing how I'm studying the wooden structure. "The Old Manse."

"You know the building?" I ask, turning to him.

"I know it, yes. My family built it."

Surely he sees my surprised expression.

"A former parsonage," he says. "It's been in the Emerson family since my grandfather. William Emerson was the pastor in these parts during the American Revolution. Land ahoy, Thoreau, let's put down right here. This is where we shall enjoy our picnic."

Thoreau paddles us to the shore, the hull of the *Musketaquid* running aground with a soft scrape against the muddy bank. Emerson takes my hand and we hop off into a riot of cabbage and ferns. My heeled boots sink slightly into the soggy river mud. Waldo puts a large hamper down on the grassy bank, the Old Manse looming behind us. I look around, appreciating the picturesque scene as the river birches climb up from out of the water, their papery curls of bark flapping in the breeze.

Thoreau remains standing in his boat, wielding his oars to keep the wobbling hull steady. I wonder what he's waiting for, why he doesn't hop down. "Terribly sorry to pass up the picnic, but I can't stay," he says, swaying with ease as the boat bobs beneath him.

"Why not?" I ask.

"Frogs," he declares, looking back out over the water.

"Pardon?" I ask.

Thoreau turns his gaze back in our direction. "I promised Louy and Anna I'd bring them some frogs. I'll keep going, just a bit more up the way, and once I've found a mister and a missus, I'll come back for you."

Before Thoreau pushes off, Waldo has unfurled a blanket, on which he now sets the hamper. He tips open the top, revealing a bountiful spread—apples, a square of cheese wrapped in wax paper, several turnover cakes, and a half-dozen hard-boiled eggs. A cork-stoppered pitcher contains lemonade.

I watch Thoreau drift away, offering us one final wave over his shoulder. I return the gesture, aware, suddenly, how alone we are. "Well, then," Waldo says, standing beside me, as he gestures at the spread. "Shall we?"

"Oh, yes," I say, grabbing fistfuls of my skirt and settling onto the blanket. We sit side by side on the grassy bank, with now only an outcropping of sun-warmed boulders and the lively birds for our company. At Waldo's urging I help myself to some cheese and a turnover cake. He pours us each a glass of lemonade and then peels himself an egg. A silence stretches between us as we eat, though it's not in fact a true silence, as the air all around us is enlivened by birdsong and breezes, the gentle lapping of the water on the shore. When Waldo takes a bite of an apple, the crunch catches me by surprise with how loud it sounds. I turn and smile, feeling as though I've eaten enough.

Nearby I spy a stand of creeping clematis and I decide to rise and pick a fistful of the purple plant. When I sit back down on the blanket, I set to work weaving a wreath, just like my mother taught me to do as a girl. It feels good to have my hands busy, my focus occupied.

My feelings of awkwardness begin to seep away, and I notice how my body softens as I work with the tendrils of clematis. I make a large wreath first, and when I've finished, I place it on Waldo's head. Then I make one for myself and tuck it into my wavy chestnut hair. Waldo smiles approvingly, leaning back on his elbows with his feet kicked out in front.

We sit there, looking out over the water, each of us crowned with wildflowers. "Are we king and queen?" Waldo asks, turning to look at me. I nod.

"Of what?" he asks. I feel his gaze on my arms, my shoulders, my neck, but I keep my own eyes on the water. I consider his question, managing a casual tone as I answer: "This day. We are king and queen of this day."

"That sounds right," Waldo says. Just then a bird warbles, and I look up to its bough, saying: "We need Thoreau to tell us who that is."

I feel that Waldo's eyes are still on me. I turn my attention to the plants growing thick and wild around us. Just as lovely as the creeping clematis are the purple asters and the goldenrod that bloom together in their summer splendor. The scene is lovely, but suddenly the silence hangs thick around us. Waldo's gaze burns intensely—and I feel the urgent need to fill the quiet. "When I was a girl," I say, "I would say prayers to flowers like these."

"What sort of prayers?"

"I'd ask them . . . pray to them, begging that I might one day be as beautiful as they were. As pure."

Waldo's fingers graze the grassy earth, his touch ever so light. "And did they answer your prayers?" he asks.

"I don't know that the flowers did, necessarily. I'm certainly not as beautiful as these asters." Though I *am* pure, in my unwed spinster state. I blink, going on: "But I do believe that this is where I feel the divine. I never felt as though I might meet God in a hard church pew. It's outside . . . here—on the river, in the fields, in the woods— where God reaches my soul."

"I agree with you," Waldo says, his deep voice rich with feeling. "I've always sensed the same—that it's not in the formal traditions or rote ceremonies that we meet our Creator, but here, in God's creation."

"It's only natural, if you think about it." Now that our conversation has moved to the lofty, I feel as though I'm on firm footing once more. The frisson of whatever was passing between us, it feels more appropriate, even pure, when it links us on a mental plane, even a spiritual one. I go on: "As God created us with souls and minds, it is most natural that we should enjoy His natural world. Or else, why else would He, in His divine wisdom, have seen fit to create all of this beauty, if not to speak to us?"

"I think that's exactly right," Waldo says, his eyes bright. "He's a generous God. A loving God." He gestures around us. "And it's here, where our souls may be fully awake—we meet God here." He waves his hands between us and our eyes lock. What he has just said—it is precisely how I feel, as well. Waldo understands. And what we share between us, it also feels as though it awakens my soul.

I'm the first to break our gaze. I don't know how long we've been sitting like this, but I look out at the river for signs of the returning *Musketaquid*. Waldo seems to guess my thoughts, because he says: "Every time I send Thoreau off into the wild, I wonder if he will come back. One of these days, he'll take off for the woods and decide to stay."

I smile at this, for Waldo is not entirely wrong to consider the possibility. "Speaking of the divine," I say, clearing my throat, "that is one of the reasons why I love the Greeks as passionately as I do." I can find firm footing with the Greeks.

"Why is that?" Waldo asks.

"Because in the pantheon of Greek gods, not only is there the emphasis on beauty, and on the natural—but you know what else I especially love about the Greeks?"

"Please tell me."

"The Muses," I declare. "Those powerful forces that inspire creativity and genius. The Greeks knew them to be female." I pause. When I speak next, my voice is full of feeling. "With the Greeks, you see, the goddesses weren't chastised for their boldness or their brilliance. Nor were they told to bridle their power. But rather, their power was intrinsic to their very beings. And to the well-being of the entire world."

Emerson nods at this, staring at me a long while before he eventually says, "I can see full well why the Hellenic goddesses would speak to you. You would have been right at home among them."

I flash him a smile. Waldo's eyes hold mine, then travel up to the clematis around my head. We are so close, our bodies separated by mere inches. My heart begins to hammer, a rapid pace that mercifully cannot be heard, though I can feel it. Without a word, Emerson reaches up to touch my crown, tucking a loose tendril back into place. His fingers linger, and then they appear like they might trace a line right down my temple to my cheek. I feel light-headed, and I can no longer blame it on the perfumed scent of the wildflowers. But just then a deep voice calls out, pulling my focus to the river. "Ahoy!" Thoreau is floating toward us, oars in hand, a bowl perched in the boat before him.

Emerson sits up tall, pulling his hand back. "Ah! Here he is. From the goddess to the frogs." The tension of a moment earlier has snapped, but when Waldo slides his eyes back toward mine and our gazes lock for one final instant, I feel that my heart is still galloping. And he does nothing to slow it when he says, his voice barely a whisper: "Though, I have to admit, I would have preferred to remain on the mount with the goddess."

Chapter Six

WALDO TELLS ME THE NEXT MORNING THAT HE WILL not be at luncheon, nor will he be available for our afternoon walk. I feel a stab of disappointment, but I believe I succeed in hiding it. That is, until he tells me that he, Thoreau, and Bronson Alcott have made plans to ride in the Emersons' carriage to nearby Lexington to see about a rooster and several hens. "Bronson needs to replenish his coop," Waldo tells me, wiping his mouth after breakfast. "Someone at the Alcotts' left a door to the henhouse open." I suspect that Bronson cannot afford the animals and Waldo has offered the funds.

I resolve to carry on with my day at Bush, not revealing how much it piques me that I'm not invited on this ride with the gentlemen. I have plenty of reading and writing to keep my hours occupied, including some translation work on Goethe. Later, Lidian feels well enough to come to the table, so she and I sit down to a midday meal of cold chicken and roasted squash together.

I tell myself that I am only imagining this feeling of prickly unease that stretches, with our silence, across the table. Taking a sip of water, I decide to attempt some conversation. "How has your morning been?"

Lidian gently lowers her fork, taking a slow sip of her tea. When she does speak, it is not to answer my question, but instead, she says: "Margaret, my husband tells me that you will stay with us for a third week."

I swallow. "He invited me, but I wished to ask you if—"

"Yes, he told me last night."

"I must get to Boston soon," I say. "I would be able to stay one more week, but only if it isn't . . . well, only if . . ."

"You seem to really enjoy . . . Concord." Her tone is flat, without a hint of feeling.

Suddenly I have no appetite for the rest of my food. Lidian turns her gaze back to her own plate. There is now a noticeable tension in the room, a string pulled too tight. *What should I do?* But after a moment, Lidian clears her throat, looking back to me, and I force myself to meet her eyes. "I was wondering, Margaret, if you would walk with me after luncheon today?"

I'm startled by the proposition. For the nearly two weeks that I've been here, she's been so uncomfortable—tired, complaining of headaches or other pains. And I would imagine that I'd be the last person whose company she'd seek for a walk. But I answer, "Yes, of course. I'd be happy to."

AFTER THE MEAL, we fetch our bonnets and gloves and make our way outside, turning onto the Lexington Road. The lane is busy with the steady stream of midday horse and foot traffic into the village, but we walk in silence.

We move slowly, Lidian taking lumbering steps at my side. The meadows sprawl around us, the aster and goldenrod dappling the green with their lively golds and purples, but Lidian keeps her eyes straight ahead. I can't help but note the difference: how her husband had responded to the very same wildflowers yesterday with a sort of rapturous reverence and appreciation, while today, his wife does not appear to see anything poetic or inspiring in them at all.

It is also hard not to notice, with our frames side by side, how differently we move. Lidian treads slowly, her pace tenuous, her belly like a heavy parcel she labors to carry. Not only am I eight years younger than her, but my body is strong and unburdened, energized by these past two weeks filled with brisk walks and fresh air, enlivening conversations and even more invigorating companionship.

Unable to bear the silence a moment longer, I remark on the beauty of the afternoon. Lidian nods, barely looking up. "It is good that we are getting out," I say. "The fresh air must be good for you and the baby."

"Perhaps," she answers. "I have a lot of time in my bed."

Her voice sounds a bit short of breath when she asks: "Do you know how I like to fill my time?"

"Prayer?" I offer. I know she is a devout woman.

"Sometimes," she replies. "And do you know how else?"

"Reading?" I venture.

"I think about names," she declares.

I look to her belly. "Names for the child?"

"For the child, yes. Though Waldo has made his preferences clear. Another little Waldo, if it's a boy. Ellen, if it's a girl."

The name of his dead first wife. The young beauty, Emerson's great love. My skin ripples at the thought, but Lidian's voice is toneless, expressing neither approval or disapproval, and her face is inscrutable as she goes on: "But then, other names, too."

"What other names?" I ask, noting how my throat feels dry.

"Well, let's see." She places a hand on her swollen middle. "Lots of other names. Do you know that Bronson Alcott is not his real name?"

I look to her, startled. "I did not know that," I admit.

Lidian smiles, a smile that does not reach her eyes. "No, his name is not Bronson Alcott. His true name is Amos Alcox."

I arc an eyebrow.

"And his wife is named Abigail, though he calls her Abba."

"That's interesting," I say.

Lidian pauses her steps. "My name is not Lidian."

Now I pause, too. "It's not?"

She shakes her head.

"Then what is it?"

"I was Lydia Jackson. But when Waldo proposed marriage, he also proposed a change of name. He felt that Lidian sounded more, oh, I don't know, poetic? So Lydia Jackson of Plymouth was remade into Lidian Emerson of Concord."

I laugh at this, before I even realize I've done so. Her eyes narrow, pinning me with their pale, watery gaze. "What's funny?" she asks.

"Only that, well . . . I'm not actually named Margaret."

Now it's Lidian's turn to be surprised. She tilts her head, holding me in her stare. "What do you mean?"

"My name is Sarah," I say. "Or rather, my parents named me Sarah. Sarah Margaret Fuller. At the age of nine I declared to them that henceforth I would no longer be Sarah. That they were to call me Margaret."

Lidian squints, as if studying me for a long moment, then she turns, breaking our gaze to continue her slow march forward toward the village. She doesn't look back at me as she says: "So you're just like them. All of you . . . *great thinkers* . . . with your desire to remake the world according to your great visions. You all exist on another plane, I suppose, and I'm down here, a mortal, walking with my heavy feet on this earth."

I grasp to find some suitable reply to this, but she goes on before I manage to do so. "Careful, Sarah Margaret, or Mr. E. might wish to remake you, too. Who was that sculptor in the classical readings that all of you great thinkers enjoy so much? Was it Pygmalion? Yes? Well, Mr. E. might wish for you to be his ivory girl."

What is it that I feel in this moment? Guilt? Embarrassment? Relief? Relief, yes, that Lidian has done what I have not yet had the courage to do: to pull these fraught and tense thoughts from the realm of silent strain and set them down at the table, plain, for both of us to acknowledge and address. Now I feel the urgent need to meet her frankness with honesty of my own. "Lidian, please know that that is not at all my interest."

Lidian pauses, and now she's staring at me. I see in the hungry expression of her eyes that she yearns to understand more, to know, then, what my interests *are*. So I press on. "You see, all my life . . ." I sigh, trying to wrangle my disordered thoughts. "All my life I've been lonely." There, I've admitted that. To her, and to myself. I go on: "My father wanted nothing more from me than to see me memorize and recite. Perfection was the only option. My mother, whom I adored . . . well, all I wanted was to play in the garden with my mother, but all I was permitted to do was study in the library with Father. I loved animals, but my parents did not ever allow them in our house. I was never permitted to play with other children my age. Nor would I have found companionship with them, had it been allowed—given, well, how unnatural my upbringing was. So the only refuge I could find for myself was in the world of books. But this escape from my loneliness only served to make me lonelier. Because who in our world has any use for a well-read girl? A girl who can best the boys in intellect, but cannot relate to the other little girls with their ribbons and dolls?"

When I finish speaking, Lidian says nothing. Perhaps she's stunned by how much I've divulged. The truth is that I'm a bit stunned myself. But there's still more.

"All my life, I've had to draw a veil over my real self. No one has ever wanted to know the real me." To my shock, I notice the thin screen of tears that has begun to blur my eyes. "I've been so, well, so very *excited* these weeks to finally meet someone who . . . someone who can be my friend." I swallow, trying to pull the tears back, steeling myself to go on. "And the result is that . . . I now see how I've overstepped your generosity."

With this the tears come unbidden, and my efforts at composure prove futile. How mortifying, I scold myself, to be crying like this on the lane in front of Lidian Emerson. But then, to my great surprise, Lidian does something entirely unexpected.

Lidian leans forward and, with her great belly between us, she wraps her thin arms around me in a hug. I stand there like a child, mute and not a little bit mortified, as she speaks, her tone matter-of-fact: "There, there, Margaret. No need to cry. I understand that."

After a moment she draws herself back, her hands landing to rest on her middle. "Well, perhaps I don't entirely understand it," she says with a shrug. "But I see what you are saying." Her tired eyes scan the scene around us, then return to me. "Forgive me for my coldness. I've been so covetous. You see, Mr. E. does not usually offer people much more than half a smile. Oh, with children I suppose it's different. But adults? And yet . . . you make him laugh . . . all the way up to his eyes."

I swat at my own eyes, feeling unspeakably foolish for crying like this. But also unspeakably grateful for her candor. "He sees me as a pupil," I say. "Perhaps a protégée of sorts."

"That may be." Lidian angles her face, staring off for a thoughtful moment. "You aren't the first, well, young lady *pupil* that my husband has invited here."

I bristle at this—it's involuntary and instinctive. At all that's implied by this, whether intentionally done or not.

"And like all pupils," Lidian continues, "your time in this school will end." Now she stares back at me. Her voice carries no malice, only a resolute bluntness as she says: "You will graduate and move on to your next endeavor. While I shall remain here." Lidian looks down to her swollen belly, giving it a soft tap with both hands. Yes, she'll remain here. She is his wife; she will very soon be the mother to his child. And when she gazes back at me, her gray-eyed smile is relaxed, almost beatific. "This is fine, Margaret. It is an experiment to see if the three of us, all strong and decided in our own right, can harmonize together. You, me, and Mr. E."

I feel chastened by her speech. By the forbearance and world-weary patience she sees fit to display before me. Or perhaps, if I'm being honest, what irks me more is her frank but accurate reminder of our proper places. Of the fact that, even though I am the one her husband has indisputably sought out this past fortnight, the plain truth is that I am nothing more than their visitor, while she remains the wife. She is the resident, with Waldo, at Bush.

I may be the one who deeply and truly understands him, the one who can share in the poetry of his soul, just as he understands and shares in mine. I may be more his equal, the one who has a connection to his inner world and can meet him in the higher spaces of his genius. And Lidian Emerson likely sees that that is so. But now she wishes to make certain that I understand something else: *she* is the one who has won the prize, for she is the one who shall live her life with Waldo.

Chapter Seven

Perhaps Lidian Emerson does not truly under-stand Ralph Waldo Emerson. But, in truth, do I really under-stand Waldo any better? Does *anyone* really understand Ralph Waldo Emerson? That question gnaws at me as the days pass and Waldo proves largely absent from Bush, missing at mealtime, no longer inviting me on walks or for afternoons of reading together beneath the shade of the old tulip tree. I can't help but begin to wonder: *Is there some specific reason why Waldo no longer wishes to be in my presence?*

The days pass and I keep busy, writing to Mother at home and to my Boston students, preparing for lessons and enjoying my own walks through the woods and fields. I visit with Louisa May, and Thoreau takes me and the Alcott girls on an adventure through the old-growth forest, to a nearby pond that the girls name Fairyland.

And then, somehow, it's Friday. And I'm sick of swallowing down my true feelings. As much as I've passed the week in determined purposefulness and good cheer, it does pain me, Waldo's steady and inexplicable aloofness. It's my last day—I'll depart by stagecoach the following morning, and I've barely seen him all week, save for passing greetings in the hall at Bush.

I finish folding my clothes and packing my final trunk that after-noon, with an hour to spare before supper. Outside my bedroom windows, the late-summer light falls like a sprinkling of gold. When a dove lets out a doleful coo from a nearby tree, I decide to step out into the garden for a quick walk. I will miss Bush, I'll miss these moments and these chances to amble in the summer beauty, and so I determine not to waste my opportunity now.

I make my way out into the garden. There, I pause to stand under the grape arbor that Thoreau has built for Waldo and Lidian. I look up into the soaring boughs of Waldo's beloved tulip tree, its branches thick and busy with leaves and wildlife. The birds are a clamorous symphony on this evening. Soon, I realize with a pang, the songs of these birds will change, as many in their number will move along. The autumn chill will paint these limbs in shades of ochre and russet. It will be glorious, and I won't see it when it happens. Nor will I see it when these grapes are picked, these heavy clusters that curl and hang all over this arbor around me. I'll be gone, in Boston, when the grapes are pressed and squeezed into juice and preserves. When the Emersons enjoy these treats at their dining room table with Thoreau. When life at Bush, and all over Concord, carries on.

I'm deep in these solitary thoughts when a voice catches me unaware. "Will you miss Thoreau's birdcalls?" I turn, startled. It's Waldo. He walks up, pausing at the opposite end of the arbor, looking at me as if expecting something.

I fold my hands together before my waist. "I had no idea you were out here," I say, managing a casual tone.

"But I knew you were out here."

This sends a tremor through me. I stare at him in confused silence. Waldo glances away, picking at a leaf hanging from a thick cluster of grapes. "Am I interrupting? You seemed deep in thought," he says.

"Oh." I nod, then I shake my head. "No, you're not interrupting me. But, yes, I was deep in thought."

Now his pale eyes slide back toward me, locking on mine. When he speaks next his voice is low, almost gravelly. "You're always deep in thought, aren't you, Margaret Fuller?"

I exhale a puff of breath, then offer a shrug as I reply: "Whether I wish to be or not."

"And would you consider sharing your thoughts with me?"

I swallow, wondering what—and how much—to share. I look up at the leafy limbs that hang all around. "I was thinking about the trees, and the birds," I say.

"And what about the birds?"

"I suppose . . . how I envy them."

"Why is that?"

"Look at the way they nest. The birds, no matter how far they fly, always seem to know their place on this earth. But me?" I cross my arms before me, shrugging. "I feel as though I'm to be a wandering pilgrim all my life."

Waldo's gaze floats downward, landing back on me. "Come now, you know your next destination. Boston. You've got your lodgings and your employment lined up."

"Yes. Tutoring. Is that to be my life's occupation? A single rented room alone in a big city?" The sigh slips out of me; I don't need to say more. Waldo is clever enough to hear and know what is hidden underneath my words. "You've been a ghost this week," I continue. "I've barely seen you." *And now I'm leaving.*

Waldo's face clouds over, a serious expression, and then he says, "I think it is good that you are moving on."

I am hurt by this, and I allow my face to show it. He steps forward and crosses the length of the arbor in three of his long-legged strides. Now there is no space between us. But I'm not expecting it when he takes my hands in his. We stand, staring at each other. In other circumstances—our postures and position, this twilight setting under the arbor in his lovely garden—the tableau might appear as if we are a pair of lovers divulging the contents of our hearts. Or even exchanging sacred vows. But what are we doing, Emerson and I?

Waldo speaks, and his voice is strained, thick with feeling. "Do you not see, my dear girl? You, whose eyes see everything?"

I shake my head, unsure of how to respond. "See what?"

He squeezes my hands in his, and I can feel his heartbeat pulsing in his fingers. "You have me completely at your mercy, Margaret." Or maybe it's my own heartbeat I'm feeling in our braided grip; it's impossible to tell where mine ends and his begins. "You have roused in my soul such a passion and longing—" He breaks off without finishing the thought, but my cheeks flush with warmth.

Emerson shakes his head, adding: "No, not a longing of any . . . not of any base nature. Rather, pure and unblemished, such is my admiration for you. For your mind. For your very soul. And now, well, now I can allow it to remain that way. I must not spoil this"—he lifts our hands, gestures at the space between us—"with any physical weakness. To do so would be to use it up." He exhales, and I notice that I have been holding my own breath.

When Waldo goes on, it feels as though he's plowing through his thoughts as much for his own understanding as for mine. "If we were to act . . . to besmirch this—well, this union between us . . . then what? What would remain? Ours can now stay a pure love, a bonding of two spirits, unprofaned by any baser or fleeting wants."

I feel the threat of tears stinging my eyes. It's almost dark now, and I'm grateful for that. There is too much building within me to keep my face composed. I know that what he is saying is true. There is some powerful and undeniable union between our souls. He's the first man—the first *person*—I've ever met who matches me. In what? In life force.

And yet, I remind myself, it's a fool's errand to think on it too much. To hope for anything more. We can never allow it to be more than, well, this friendship. He's married. His wife is expecting their child.

"Won't you please say something fine and beautiful, Margaret?" His voice sounds parched as it pierces my thoughts. "Something to consecrate this, so that I'm not alone here?"

I swallow, managing only: "Waldo."

"Yes?" He is eager for me to say more, but my words feel choked.

I inhale a slow breath. "You are not alone . . . in feeling this way." I shake my head. "And yet . . ." I try to pull my scattered thoughts into something lucid. "Do you recall how I said I shall always be a pilgrim?"

He looks at me for a long moment, his eyes holding mine through the shadows, and then he nods.

I go on: "I've always known that my life is to be one of movement. Seeking. But this time with you . . . you have helped me to see that it can be more than that. You have helped me to see a clearer picture of who I wish to become. You've shown me that I don't always need to feel alone. But in fact, I might even hope to encounter kindred souls on my journey."

Waldo dips his chin, his face and body angling closer to mine as he gives my hands another squeeze. But there is something final in the gesture. If, a moment ago, we were exchanging vows—even, as he said, consecrating something—then now we are concluding the ceremony. And we will return from the high altar back down into reality.

When Waldo finally speaks, his voice sounds more settled, as if brought back from its feverish edge. "I daresay, Margaret, that you are the butterfly. And perhaps Concord here, or even Bush, has been a most fortunate flower, one that you have seen fit to land on for a time."

"Yes." I want to cry now—I feel tears needling my eyes, but I won't allow it. Tears cannot change anything. The fact remains that I am a woman. And not only a woman, but a penniless, unwed woman. I can't even speak with the directness he can. I know what I have to say, so I say it: "And now I must move along."

He, too, knows it's true. He nods, and then I pull my hands from his, bringing them back to my sides. They are warm from his touch.

From the house I hear a window closing. A golden glow begins to seep out as the candles are lit within. The garden has grown dark, the air has grown cool, it is time for us to go inside.

Waldo draws back his shoulders, standing straight, his body no longer tilted down toward mine. But even though his posture has gone hard, his voice is soft, barely a whisper, as he says: "Then I won't clip your wings. Even as I'll grieve to watch you go."

Chapter Eight

BOSTON IS RIOTOUS NOISE AND BUSTLING COMMO-
tion after my summer idyll in Concord. Horse hooves and the
cries of black-capped coachmen have replaced the gentle song of
the goldfinch and jay, the laughter of the Alcott girls as Thoreau
whistles to the trees. Peddlers and pedestrians call out on the streets,
interrupted by the shrieking staccato of the gulls that circle the
city's wharves and docks. The ducks and the geese peck the crumbs
of bread that little children toss across the trampled grass of the
Common. Unlike the ducks of the Concord River, these birds are
brazen, pushy, all too familiar with roiling humanity—things are
wild in the city, but in an entirely different way.

I miss the meadows and the quiet lanes of the country. Concord's sun-warm goldenrod, the sway of a wispy willow on the
river. Thoughts and memories of my time there start to blur, hazy
like the fringes of a dream, as the days of September shorten and a
crisp new edge in the wind announces the arrival of Boston's autumn. I have no choice but to plunge headlong into the melee of
my new hometown.

I've rented a small room with modest furnishings. My few trunks
are quickly unpacked and I settle in to begin giving lessons to my
young lady pupils. I'll teach them the classics—Dante and Virgil,
Goethe and Schiller—hoping that these works will enrich their
minds, even if next year's autumn will likely see most of them debuted and fêted as society brides and hostesses.

And yet, even as I throw myself into my busy days of teaching and city life, I still find myself, in many moments, thinking long-ingly of Concord. I wonder: *Have the trees turned yet? Have the grapes been pressed? Will I be invited back? Will I have the chance to return?*

My daily walks along the Charles fill me with the desire to see the Concord River again. When I hear the seagulls caw and wail over Boston Harbor, I recall with a pang the gentle birdcalls of Tho-reau. Conversations with Waldo have now moved from beside the hearth in his study to the letters we regularly write to each other—and while I do savor each page of our correspondence, nevertheless, our note writing feels like only a poor and dim substitute com-pared to the actual conversations we once shared.

In late September, Waldo surprises me by sending me an early pre-publication copy of his upcoming essay, which he's titled "Na-ture" and which he expects to publish later that fall. While I des-perately miss speaking with him, at least having his manuscript gives me insight into his mind and thoughts, and I clutch the pre-cious pages, relishing them late into each night, as I would Waldo's company.

And then a bit of Concord does arrive, unexpectedly, at my front door, when I receive a surprising visit one afternoon. The day has been a mild one, with gentle golden light, even as I note how the sunsets are coming earlier with each passing week. My windows are open and the breeze smells clean, rippling my curtains as it enters my small room.

I've just finished my final session for the day, German lessons for a bright young lady who lives with her well-to-do family on Beacon Hill. She's collected her bonnet and gloves and I've seen her out when I hear a rap on my door. Expecting it to be my pupil, perhaps returning to claim some personal item she's inadvertently left be-hind, I smile in greeting as I open my door. But I find a most unex-pected face staring back at me. "Ah, Miss Margaret Fuller!"

Bronson Alcott stands at my threshold. "Mr. Alcott . . . what a surprise! A pleasant surprise."

He hovers at my door, a relaxed, expectant smile on his fair fea-tures.

"Please, won't you come in?"

"Gladly," he declares, removing a rumpled brown cap and stepping inside. I offer him tea and he takes his seat across from me, the only other chair I have in my modest room. The upholstery is pilled and worn, but I don't imagine that Bronson Alcott cares, or even notices. I feel no shame in showing him my humble lodgings—as I suspect I might feel if it were Waldo in my home—because Bronson Alcott's pale eyes don't even seem to look around to take them in. He crosses his long legs before him, his trousers far too short and hitching up above his ankles to show quite an alarming amount of his shins. Then he takes an appreciative sip of tea as I sit opposite, staring at him with expectant attention.

"Miss Fuller," he says at last, looking from his teacup to me. "I come to you as a most humble and needy supplicant. I find myself in dire straits."

"Why is that?" I ask.

"You know that I run a school here in Boston? The Temple School."

"Yes," I answer. Located in the city's Masonic temple, from what I've heard. Bronson has use of the higher floors of the building, and I also happen to know that he's able to afford the rent on the grand place because of a generous gift from Waldo. Bronson Alcott's unique teaching philosophies are well-known across New England, but so, too, is the matter of Ralph Waldo Emerson's assistance in supporting Alcott's educational ventures.

Bronson takes another gulp of his tea before going on: "I am most happy when teaching my bright young pupils, but I cannot do it all. Abba, she tries, but . . . well, the girls consume her."

"Of course." I nod. And I've heard the news, from Waldo, that a fourth child is now expected. Yes, Abba's slate is most full.

"I did have a lovely teaching assistant. Ah, but you know her, I believe." He cocks a blond eyebrow. "Sophia Peabody?"

"Yes, I'm familiar with the Peabody sisters. Sophia and her sister Eliza as well. Eliza has been a dear friend of mine for years."

"Yes, yes, of course." Bronson pauses, his expression clouding over momentarily, and I'm not sure what to make of his look.

"It's my understanding that they are traveling now?" I venture. "In fact, they left Boston so quickly, I didn't even have the chance to say goodbye to Eliza. Where have they gone—with their parents somewhere? I believe I heard Cuba?"

Bronson shakes his head, ignoring my question with a wave of his hand as he goes on: "Fine girls, the pair of them. In fact, prior to Sophia, it was Eliza who worked as my teaching assistant. In any event—" Another wave of his hand. "As you know, Eliza Peabody has gotten far too busy, what with her travels and her plans to open a bookstore of her own. And Sophia, I'm afraid the poor dear just isn't well."

"What do you mean?" I ask.

Bronson leans toward me with a conspiratorial tilt of his head. "The girl is practically a bed case now. You know her father, Dr. Peabody, treats her for headaches. He's tried everything for the poor girl, calomel and opium, but I'm afraid it's only worsened her condition."

"Oh, goodness," I say, sitting back in my chair. Mercury poisoning, that's how I've heard it referred to, when a lady is overdosed with calomel. This is news to me; I haven't heard from Eliza since before her departure for her trip. I press my lips in a tight, straight line, not even trying to suppress my frown, nor my frustration with the fact that far too many women are treated for headaches and nerves with so-called *treatments* that seem to put them into an even more dreadful state. I heave a loud exhale, looking back to Bronson as I say: "Well, then, I hope that their travels to warmer climes will do them all some good, particularly poor Sophia. Sunshine and ocean air, it cannot hurt."

"Indeed," Bronson says, eyeing me intently with his light gaze. And then he blinks, gives a quick toss of his flaxen head, and goes on: "Whatever the case may be, the Peabody sisters have left me quite bereft. My school . . . well, I feel most abandoned. And yet, I'm not entirely without hope." He lifts an index finger, pointing it skyward. "That is because I've found someone whom I now know would be even better than either of the Peabody sisters."

"Oh?" I sit forward in my chair, feeling my heartbeat quicken. "Who might that be?"

"You," Bronson declares with an upward lift of his light eyebrow. "You are to be my heroine. My deliverer. How fortunate shall my pupils be to study with Boston's very own Athena, goddess of wisdom, the genius Margaret Fuller."

I shift in my seat, pressing down a seam of my skirt. "I thank you, Bronson, for the faith you place in me. Your words are too generous. A Greek goddess, my goodness, I cannot claim parity with Athena." I am flattered, to be sure, while also quite surprised. I lift my teacup, then lower it without taking a sip. "And while I admire your philosophies as a teacher, I'm afraid I cannot accept."

"But . . ." He was not expecting that. "Whyever not?"

"I already have a full schedule of my own private students."

"Can't you see them in the evenings? Or on the weekends?"

I tilt my head to the side, considering all of this for a moment. "I don't see how—"

"No, no, Margaret. Hush. I won't accept this. At least, not today. Not before you've had a chance to give my offer a proper and due consideration." He rises to stand, his trousers still hitching up on his too-long legs. "I shall take my leave and provide you with this address for the Temple School. Think on it. Write to Waldo. He'll tell you what a grand place we have." Bronson slips me a card with his narrow, spidery handwriting. "And, how desperately we need your help."

IN THE END, the practicalities of my life force my hand, steering me down a path I had neither expected nor particularly wanted. The financial practicalities, to be precise. Because the truth is: even though I *am* busy, even though my schedule is full with private lessons and tutoring, I'm barely earning enough each week to cover the costs of my food and my modest one-room lodging. And that's not even taking into consideration the greater need I will very soon have for firewood; a Boston autumn can be chilly, but a Boston winter promises many bitter months.

And there's more. There's an added burden that weighs on me from the moment I rise from my bed each morning: it falls on me to send money to Mother. Only with my support can Mother properly feed my siblings and keep the farmhouse. Father's annuity does not cover the cost of a family as large as ours, and my tightfisted uncle has made it plain to me in more than one written response that he will spare no additional funds beyond what my father's estate has allocated for my mother's monthly allowance. My father did not die a wealthy man, nor did he leave enough to adequately support his widow and large brood.

If I'm being fully honest with myself, there is one more factor. While I never imagined a future for myself as a teacher in a children's school, it *has* stoked my pride to be invited by someone as eminent as Bronson Alcott. The Peabody sisters have fine reputations as some of Boston's most learned women, and to take a job as their successor will enhance my reputation among the intellectual circles—it might even help me to get my future works published.

Waldo helps to tip the scales on that account; when I write to him, inquiring after his opinion, he urges me to take Bronson's offer. Alcott's school is held in high regard as one of Boston's pre-eminent programs for children, he explains. And the fact that he accepts girl pupils as well as African Americans—I see only positive outcomes from being a part of such a forward-thinking institution. So I dash off a dozen letters; I move my sessions with my young lady pupils to evenings and weekends, and then I write to Bronson Alcott with the news that I will accept the position at his Temple School.

I STAND BEFORE the door of Boston's Masonic temple, a classical-looking building of grand Corinthian columns and an imposing pedimented rooftop. Behind me, the intersection of Temple Place and Tremont Street is a noisy, crowded juncture, roiling with carriages and foot traffic. To my delight, it's Louisa May who appears at the door. She rocks from her heels to her toes, the two tails of her dark hair coming loose, one ribbon missing entirely. Her face grows rosy when she sees me.

"Louy, my dear girl. How wonderful to see you." I bend forward so that my eyes line up with hers. "But how is it that you've grown so tall in only a few months?"

When Louisa smiles, I see that she's lost a bottom tooth. She pushes the door open wider. "Come in, Miss Fuller."

"Please, my dear. It's Miss Margaret to you. We are pals, aren't we?"

I step inside, where the air is cool and the large space hums with quiet. Our heels echo off the floor and walls as Louisa May skips ahead, leading me toward a wide, carpeted stairway and up to the landing of the second floor. "Come, I'll bring you to Father!"

I follow her lead, if not her coltish pace. My eyes sweep the airy, high-ceilinged space as I climb the steps. I've deliberately come on a Saturday so that the school will be empty of students and I may speak freely with Bronson. He is fortunate in his location; as we reach the second floor, I look around a massive hall, a row of broad windows letting in the autumn light. The place really does feel like a temple, a sanctuary for learning, with its soaring ceilings and or-nate furniture upholstered in plush velvet of wintry green.

Louy skips on, leading me into another large hall, this one with arched doorways and floor-to-ceiling windows. "I'll go fetch Father. He's been waiting for you." With that, Louisa skitters off like a little woodland mouse, and I'm left alone in what I presume must be one of their main lesson halls. Simple wooden chairs are arranged in a broad circle at the center of the great space, a ring of learning. Four antique-looking busts hold forth in each of the four corners of the hall.

I walk to the nearest one and recognize Socrates. I'm studying the rutted, bearded profile, wondering about the identities of the other three statues, when a voice reverberates across the large room, creating an echo and startling me from my quiet daydream-ing. "Shakespeare, Socrates, Plato, and Sir Walter Scott." I turn and see Bronson Alcott in the far doorway. He sweeps his hands up in greeting, striding toward me as he says, "We need a woman to join the ranks."

I like this. "Someday, hopefully not too far in the future," I say with a nod.

"Or else a child," Bronson declares. "After all, children are closer to the divine than we adults are."

I see his point, and I offer a smile as Bronson approaches.

"Thank you for coming here to our humble temple." We shake hands and I look around appreciatively at the grand space.

"Hardly humble. Your school is lovely," I say. "Most impressive."

"Children deserve the best," he says, raising his hands to gesture around the room. And then Bronson points toward the ring of chairs in the center. "It is for that reason, the divine nature of our dear little pupils, that I break from my peers on the question of corporal punishment. I will never strike a child."

I like this, too. Educating girls, calling for the end of slavery, championing equality between the races, disavowing bodily punishment of students—Bronson Alcott's pedagogical philosophies are quite new, some might even say radical, but I agree with him. I thrill at his ideas of teaching girls and the descendants of freed and former slaves. And I'm grateful that I won't be ordered to strike my pupils. I offer him a decisive nod.

Bronson moves his gaze over the chairs, the windows, the soaring ceiling overhead. "This is our holy space. There is nothing more sacred than the pure and good mind of a child. You will join me in this sacred mission, Margaret. I teach philosophy and religious instruction, but I need someone to oversee their recitations and penmanship, geography, arithmetic."

"Yes," I say, taking all this in. I can certainly manage the basic subjects of a child's education.

Bronson's eyes are gazing up as he goes on: "I told Waldo, when he was so gracious as to support my mission and help me to acquire this space: this is an institution that is fittingly in a temple. For we are building a holy place of learning."

I see the passion Bronson has for his calling. I can't help but admire it. He goes on, pressing a hand over his heart as he declares: "Each student of mine is a disciple, and I am the high priest." At this, I am taken slightly aback. I flash him a smile, but I note that his expression is entirely earnest.

I resist the urge to chuckle, knowing how Bronson has a tendency toward the lofty. But I tell him that I'm happy to accept the job. Delighted, he offers me a full tour of his space: the grand hall where he teaches philosophy and holds what he calls his "conversations," lessons that I gather are structured in a sort of Socratic format. Next he shows me the smaller classroom where I am to teach.

After that Bronson takes me up another flight of stairs and leads me into the small apartment on the top floor where he and Abba and the girls stay. I'm genuinely delighted to see the Alcott women there, briefly visiting with them in their cramped little "parlor," giving Abba a hug around her swollen middle and offering her my congratulations. But I decline her offer to stay for supper. "Seeing all of you more often will be one of the great joys of my new position. But today I cannot linger. I have much work to do," I reply. And in truth, when I see the dark half-moons under Abba's eyes, I dread the thought of adding to her workload at a mealtime.

Louy is giddy with excitement at my visit, and declares that she'd like me to move into their small apartment with them. After I've declined *that* offer, as well, she settles for showing me a knit doll she's been working on since she left Concord.

"It's most impressive," I say, squeezing the little doll's lumpy leg.

"Have you seen Mr. Thoreau?" she asks, her brown eyes peering up at me, rounded and expectant.

"I have not, my dear. Not since I left Concord."

"Do you think he'll like this doll I'm making?" She looks down at her efforts. "Will he be proud of how hard I've worked?"

"Of that I have no doubt," I declare.

"He writes me all the time," Louy says, leaning toward me with a conspiratorial whisper. "I keep his notes in a pile under my pillow. He writes to me more than he writes to Anna. But don't tell her that I told you."

"I won't breathe a word of it," I promise, offering her a wink to consecrate my vow.

Bronson hands me a list of my pupils' names and sends me home with a satchel full of books and papers so that I may familiarize myself with where the children are in their studies. It's all very exciting and promising, and my mind feels enlivened as I take my leave of the Alcotts, the looming structure of the Temple School casting a long shadow as I step back out into the graying chill of

Boston's late afternoon. It was not a job I had expected or sought out, but it will be interesting work, and the steady salary will go a long way toward easing my own worries and Mother's, as well.

It's not until the interview is over and I'm walking back home that I realize: Mr. Alcott mentioned nothing to me about payment.

Chapter Nine

I REPORT TO THE TEMPLE SCHOOL ON MONDAY MORN-
ing, as directed. No sooner has Abba ushered me inside and
helped me to get settled in my small classroom, with tidy rows of
desks arranged before me, than the door opens and a crush of pupils comes streaming in, the girls in autumn cloaks and day dresses,
the boys in pressed trousers and smart blazers. They come like a
mighty gushing river, and I'm swept up in the tide of their spirited
energy as I greet them all and guide them to their seats.

They are bright-eyed and red-cheeked, the small children who
settle into their desks and remove their slates and papers. They are
attentive and eager. They are the children of some of Boston's most
affluent, blue-blooded clans, but also the most forward-thinking
and open-minded families, to have enrolled in Bronson Alcott's
place of learning. They are not at all fazed at the sight of a woman
standing before them in a position of authority, just as they are not
daunted by the fact that they sit in mixed company, an equal number of girls and boys.

I take my place before them, delighted by their openness, heartened by the fact that they are growing up to see the world as a
place where little girls may read and write and think, just like their
male peers do. That even the darker skinned among them have
every right to enter this place of precious learning. The continued
molding of their minds and their characters will be in my hands,
and it is an honor that I do not take lightly.

The morning is busy and that makes the hours fly. By the afternoon, I've managed to memorize most of the names of my young students. I see Bronson only in passing, but I note how his face is alight, his passion for the pupils and their education clearly kindling some fire within him.

That afternoon, once the lessons are complete and the students have been sent home, I accept an offer to join Bronson and the family in their small upstairs apartment for tea. He wishes to hear about my first day, and I wish to bring up the matter of my salary, though not in front of the girls. Abba serves us our tea with buttered toast as Bronson flops down on the carpet in front of the hearth. The air outside grows chilly; the sun begins to dip. The scene inside this small apartment is messy and noisy, with the girls flitting in and out of the room, but the fire is warm and the room is cozy.

We sit there, the girls and Abba offering updates on their own day—their errands down at the harbor, at the bakery, at the print shop. The girls are not yet of an age to be enrolled in the Temple School, so Abba sees to Anna's and Louisa's home lessons. Bronson listens with a vague, distracted smile as Louy tells us about her adventures chasing the seagulls across the docks that morning.

Then Bronson turns his blue eyes toward me. "And how about you, Miss Fuller? How was your first day as our Temple's very own Athena, goddess of wisdom?" Bronson has a kind heart, even if his flights of fancy sometimes veer off toward the ridiculous.

Like when, after I've given him my brief report on my first day, he declares: "My dear Marguerite, your words are music to my ears. I knew you were the right person for this position. Why, you shall add enduring glory to female learning." But he does not stop at that. He's speaking now with a lilting cadence that sounds almost like that of a preacher in the pulpit as he goes on: "The integrity of your being and your genius will inspire all your young pupils."

I tip my head sideways, appreciative of his approval, to be sure, but a bit hesitant to fully accept his praise. Had the words been coming from Waldo, I might have taken them more willingly. But then, I very much doubt Waldo would ever speak like this.

"What is on your syllabus tomorrow?" he asks.

"Ovid," I answer. "We will take up the *Metamorphoses*."

"Splendid," he says. And then Abba pronounces that supper is ready and the girls begin to hop about like hares, and so I take my leave, eager to return home before darkness has fully fallen over the city. I have not yet had the private interview with Bronson that I was hoping for, but I can see that it won't happen tonight. My question pertaining to my salary will have to wait.

I DO MANAGE to pull him aside the next day, in a brief moment between lessons. I find him in the noisy corridor and I take my chance to ask him when I can expect payment. The question prompts a fluttering of his blond lashes, his voice wobbling as he says: "Patience, my dear apostle." He throws a look over my shoulder toward a line of students that approach. Then, leaning in, close enough that I can smell his warm, sour breath, he adds: "You've only been here a day."

"Oh, I know that. Of course," I hasten to reply, shifting on my feet. "I was merely wondering, is it by the week? Every other week?"

"Yes, yes, of course," he replies, nodding. The queue of students has reached us, and he raises his hands to them in greeting.

"Which is it?" I seek to clarify. "Weekly? Every other week?"

"Every other week," he says, and he's already in motion, leading the column of students down the corridor toward his lecture hall, his ridiculous long cloak that he wears for teaching fluttering behind him like he's some Roman senator marching into the Forum.

Then that's that. *Every other week*, I repeat to myself, standing alone in the hallway. Noticing, as Bronson walks away, that our exchange has left me with an unsettled feeling in my gut and the unwelcome smell of his breath in my memory.

AS THE AUTUMN days pass, we settle into a busy but steady rhythm. Bronson leads the large lectures on philosophy, religious instruction, and ethics in the grand hall, while I work with smaller sections of the students on penmanship, recitation, arithmetic, geography, and literature. When our paths do cross, I often have to bridle the urge to chuckle—or scowl. I note that not only does he call me "apostle," but he refers to the students as his "disciples," and he is "High Priest Alcott." I bite my lower lip and hope that I manage to conceal how outlandish I find it.

A few weeks later, I am at home on a drizzly Saturday morning, resting and getting caught up on my own personal affairs. I left school the previous evening in quite a lather, as it has now been several weeks, but Bronson has yet to pay me. After the students left for the week I'd sought him out, in his classroom, even stopping by the Alcotts' upstairs apartment, but he was out. Abba had no idea where he was, nor when he might return. "Care to stay for supper?" she offered, her stained apron pulled wide over her growing belly. "Squash soup."

"No, but thank you. I'll see you all Monday." And I'd left without my pay, doing my best to hide my glower from her.

This morning I'm determined not to let my annoyance spill into my weekend. I have two days to myself, with a pair of evening private lessons. I have so much to do, but first, I settle down in my slippers and robe before the fire to tuck into my small pile of unopened mail. I begin, of course, with the letter from Waldo.

It is exciting news from Concord. Waldo writes of his twin joys: his work "Nature" has been published to great acclaim, and Lidian has delivered a healthy baby boy, Waldo Emerson. I read the long letter several times in its entirety, eager for every piece of news from Bush. I am happy for them—happy for Lidian, especially, that it's a boy and thus she does not have to live with a second coming of Ellen Emerson in her home.

I imagine all of them there, together. The family of three, plus Thoreau as a constant fixture and practically a member of their family as well. I *am* happy for them, I tell myself. But then a stab of . . . something . . . aches within. Is it envy?

I blink, forcing that troubling thought from my mind, steeling myself to resist the tempting tug toward melancholy. I fold Waldo's letter and tuck it neatly back into its envelope. Then I press a plain piece of paper onto my desk before me. I'll write to Waldo and tell him I'm overjoyed for him. And I am. He deserves every bit of this happiness. I jab my pen into my inkstand, a soldier loading bullets for battle.

I *am* happy for my friend. And I will never voice aloud, to anyone, the thought that I fight now to quiet: that the bright and
beaming light of Waldo's joy, both professional and domestic, shines
an unpleasant and too-bright glare onto the inescapable fact that
my own professional and domestic situations are less rich than I
would like them to be. Far less so. Because the truth that I do not
wish to face, but which I cannot now deny as I sit alone in my
room, is that I am so very troubled. I am so very weary of the
strains of a life in which I am always working, but never bringing in
enough to feel secure at home. And a life that, at home, is so very
lonely.

Chapter Ten

WHEN I GREET BRONSON ON MONDAY, NEARLY bumping into him in the crowded corridor outside his classroom, I have managed to wrestle myself out of my melancholy. I am even capable of a smile as I share the exciting news I've heard from Concord. Bronson is happy to hear of the birth of the baby boy, but he's even more interested to learn of Waldo's publication. Bronson is eager to publish a work of his own, he tells me.

"And what is your topic?" I ask.

"Why, my disciples, of course."

I stare at him, waiting for more information.

"It's already written, my dear Marguerite. I've been working on it since long before you began here in our Temple. It shall be called *Conversations with Children on the Gospels*."

"I see," I say, speaking over the din of the busy hall. I have not yet read any of Alcott's work, and this manuscript was written during Sophia's and Eliza's time in the position I now hold. "Did Eliza and Sophia help to write it?"

"No, Abba served as my transcribing secretary," he says. "And *you* have given me a great gift in bringing my dream to the light."

My face must show my confusion, because he goes on: "You see, your sharing this news with me this morning, Apostle, was the impetus I needed. It was a providential sign, I believe. I am ready to send my work out into the world."

. . .

THE ALCOTTS INVITE me to join them for supper the following weekend in their apartment above the quiet, empty school. Eager to finally wrangle a private conversation with Bronson, I accept.

I arrive with a parcel of wildflowers for the girls and a jug of apple cider for Bronson and Abba. Now that it is late autumn, the night arrives early, and the space is illuminated by candlelight when I arrive, the fire in the hearth warming the small, low-ceilinged space. The quarters are cramped but cozy, with the three girls sprawled across the rug, playing with their dolls as Abba finishes the meal.

I regret that I may spoil some of this domestic pleasantness, but I simply must speak with Bronson. I've been working at his Temple School for over a month now and I have yet to receive any payment. I'm still tutoring in my scant free time, but it is not enough. I accepted this position because of an urgent want of funds. Funds that I desperately need, as winter is setting in and Mother writes that she is without enough firewood and food to comfortably manage these next few months.

Once the meal is over and Abba has risen from the table and withdrawn from the room to put little Beth to sleep, I see my opening. I glance toward the hearth, where Louy and Anna are consumed in conversation between their dolls, their childish ears innocent and disinterested in the exchange of the nearby adults.

"Bronson . . . Mr. Alcott," I venture. I pull in a breath, willing myself to go on, unpleasant as the topic may be. "I am wondering when I can expect payment for my first month?" I hate that it comes out so tenuous, like a question. But at least it is out.

Bronson sits back in his winged chair, drawing a slow circle with his spoon in his tea, his gaze fixed downward. When he says nothing, I go on: "I hear from my family in Groton . . . and I have my own lodgings here to pay for, and with winter—"

Bronson raises a long-fingered hand, and I fall silent. His spoon held aloft like some teaching tool, he looks at me, and when he speaks, his tone is soft, a voice of willed patience. "Marguerite, please. I would expect more from you. But . . . to concern yourself with the base want of money. Why, it's not beneficial for your soul."

I stare at him in disbelief, my mouth falling open. I throw a glance toward the girls to ensure that they are not listening, but before I can answer, he goes on. "We are called to exist on a higher plane. You, of all people, ought to know this: the material is fleeting and transient."

Now I am incredibly irritated. I sit up a bit taller in my chair, managing a measured tone as I answer: "I see your point. But I can't very well meditate on transcendence when I am too hungry to think straight."

Bronson lowers his spoon back to his teacup, which, I notice, bears the monogram of his wife's family. When he speaks, his voice is barely a whisper. "I beg to differ."

I raise an eyebrow. "You do?"

He nods, a defiant bob of his chin. "Our Savior the Christ had his most powerful and rapturous experiences in the desert when he had not eaten, even going as long as forty days. If he could do it, so can we."

Now I am stunned to silence, while my heart clamors against my ribs at an angry gallop. Does Bronson Alcott truly expect me to go without a salary in this teaching position because Jesus Christ fasted in the desert? The realization that yes, he just might, hardens in my gut.

Bronson sighs, his tone turning soft, plaintive, without a hint of its former defiance. "Several of my disciples are derelict on tuition payments, if you must know."

I narrow my eyes, studying him, and I see, for the first time, the hints of worry on his pale features. But then I look at the spread we've just eaten, and I tell myself this: Bronson Alcott is not expecting his family to go hungry. But mine may be forced to? I'm bracing to say as much, but he speaks first: "My dear Marguerite. I understand your concern."

This has a slightly disarming effect. I lean back in my chair. "You do?"

He blinks, looking into his tea. "And once they have paid, I shall put this all to rights, and you shall be duly compensated. And besides, my work will be published this spring. It will be a monumental work in the educational field. Our precious school shall never want for funds again. And you shall wear a cloak of glory for your work here. Trust me, my dear apostle."

BUT I DO not trust him. In fact, with each day that passes, I trust him less. These are some of Boston's finest families he has enrolled here—surely there must be enough money coming in to pay me, as I carry the lion's share of the teaching responsibilities so that he, High Priest Alcott, can relish his lofty lectures on philosophy and the Gospels. And besides, Waldo has helped him considerably with his expenses. Where is all of the money going?

I decide to write to Waldo with my concerns, imploring him to keep my words between us, as I know the two of them are also friends. But I need his advice on how to manage this situation: I do not want to leave my pupils without a teacher, without my steadying presence opposite Bronson's erratic whimsy, but how can I stay in this post when it appears I am fulfilling the obligations as a volunteer?

"I wish I could define my distrust of Mr. Alcott," I write to Waldo. *"He sees only what he wants. He has very little of any common sense, I fear. There is something in him that unnerves me."*

And yet, my livelihood is in the hands of this man. Not for the first time I lament, with gritted teeth, the fact that I, as a woman, find my fate and well-being in the care of a man so much less capable.

Waldo's letters grow irregular and brief that winter. I presume he's preoccupied with the new baby and flooded with correspondence and invitations after the success of "Nature." Perhaps he's even hard at work on his next project, seeking to maintain the momentum of his triumph. But it's frustrating. I wish I could write to Eliza and Sophia Peabody, as they might have advice on how to approach their former employer, but they are traveling, I know not where. They left so suddenly that it seems few people knew their destination.

But why did they leave so suddenly? Did they experience these same frustrations? Did they know something about Bronson's wayward management? Was it more than simply a resignation—a need to cut ties with the place altogether?

It's a bitter evening, pitch-dark as only the deep winter can be, and I sit in my rented room, slowly turning the toasting fork over my small fire. It'll be another plain dinner, toast and tea, as I cannot afford more. I've just come home from a day of teaching and I've put my slippers by the hearth to warm. I've set the old copper warming pan on my bed to warm the icy sheets. My fingers ache from the constant cold and my skin is chapped from my wind-swept walk to and from the school.

Another fortnight has passed and yet Bronson remains derelict on my payments. Just as disheartening as the lack of payment is the seeping apathy I'm beginning to feel, the withering realization that I'm starting to accept: the fact that I might not ever see the money he's promised. I'm exhausted in both body and spirit.

And yet I cannot bring myself to tender my resignation. I'm staying for two reasons: I care for my students, and I care deeply for the Alcott girls. I want the school to succeed for them, for all of them.

Chapter Eleven

OUR CRISIS COMES TO A BOIL A FEW WEEKS LATER, just as the first hints of spring are beginning to thaw the deep freeze of Boston's winter. True to his word, Alcott has printed his *Conversations with Children*. But rather than the warm and enthusiastic response that he has told us all to expect, the reaction comes as quite the opposite.

I see the work for the first time on the night it publishes, after Bronson has triumphantly placed a copy in my hands on my way out of the school building. Once back home in my rented room, with slippers on and a warm mug of tea in my hands, I tuck into the pages. Only one page in and I begin to feel a swirl of dread.

By the second page, my dread has thickened, and now I feel sick. And yet, I cannot put the pages down. The words are as ludicrous and fitful as Bronson himself, his sentences overwrought and meandering, but it is the subject matter that fills me with the most roiling disquiet.

Virginity.

Conception.

Childbirth.

The sin of lust.

How has Mr. Alcott seen fit to discuss such topics with his young students? And then published these conversations in a text he supposes will be a boon to educators? How can he possibly feel that this is suitable? Even believing, as he's told me on several occasions, that this publication would bring him fame, wealth, and eternal glory?

I am disgusted. I'm barely able to meet his eyes in school the next day, when we pass in the crowded corridor. I still greet Abba, and Louisa May and her sisters, but even that is a challenge at times. I can no longer visit their apartment. I return to my classroom, day after day, only so that my students are not left alone with Bronson.

It's not just me who feels this way—the shock is widespread and fierce. Almost immediately the number of our students begins to shrink, and by the end of the week, many of our pupils stop coming altogether. Scores of parents send angry letters informing Bronson and me that they've pulled their children. Some do not even send a letter at all.

The critics and reviewers must have read with as much shock and incredulity as I did, because their outrage comes like a deluge. All that week, the printing presses churn with reactions to Alcott's book, and the coverage is not favorable. The kindest reviewers call Alcott absurd, his teachings blasphemous. Most are far more scathing: he's either an indecent pervert or a dimwit and ignoramus, many declare. He has no place at the head of a classroom. He has no right to mold the mind of an innocent child.

AS THE WEATHER warms and the book makes its way throughout Boston, a city founded by Puritans, I start to worry that the reckoning might soon be bigger than just diminished class sizes. And then I begin to hear the rumors. Rumors that a very pregnant Abba whispers to me, her weary features pulled tight with the strain of these weeks. The public is outraged. In a city where the outraged public has a long and illustrious history of tarring, feathering, even hanging, what if they come for Bronson? What if they come for all of us?

Once again I feel paralyzed by a sense of obligation, a feeling that I have to stay, not *for* Bronson, but in spite of Bronson. If I leave, who will be here for the students? For the Alcott women?

I feel a bitter sense of satisfaction in one respect: at least he's finally admitted that we can't subsist on his airy thoughts and erratic
whims alone. As more students are withdrawn from the school, the
need for money becomes a crisis. He's certainly not squandering
money on paying salaries. Now he sells his plush green-velvet furniture, his marble busts of the great thinkers. The ridiculous décor
of which he was once so proud. And his profile will never be a bust
keeping company with Socrates and Shakespeare; he sees that at
least.

IT'S A FRIDAY afternoon in late spring. I'm preparing to close up
my classroom for the weekend when I hear a disturbance in the
hallway, the staccato of running feet, and then Louy bursts into my
room. "Miss Margaret? Miss Margaret! We must hide!"

I stand up, bracing myself on my desk. "What is it, Louy?"

"The mob," she pants, her hair a dark mess of curls around her
flushed face. "They're coming!"

My hands round into two clenched fists. I could scream, I'm so
frustrated—furious that Louisa May Alcott must live through this.
Furious, too, that I feel so powerless to spare her from this nightmare. There's only one thing I can do. "Come to my apartment with
me, Louisa," I say, stepping out from behind my desk and marching
toward the door. "We will be far from here and anyone who might
wish to start trouble."

"No." Louisa stands in my doorway, her eyes blazing, her voice a
gasp of disbelief. "You can't leave us, Miss Margaret. And we can't
leave Mother! And Father! My sisters." Her young features twist in
fear. "Please, Miss Margaret. You must stay with us. Won't you?"

I sigh, feeling my entire frame sag. Once again I am unable to
peel myself away from this young, guileless girl, even as I'd happily
leave her father. But I don't really believe that a mob will come.
And I cannot possibly welcome all five of the Alcotts into my one
cramped room—my landlady would never let them through the
front door. Nor can I afford the expense of a hotel. We have nowhere to go. "You're right, Louisa May. We can't leave the others.

We shall stay. I'll stay with you for the night, if it gives you comfort. And I promise that no harm shall come."

We lock up the school, bolting both the inner and outer doors, and then we retreat, a tired and silent troop, up to the Alcotts' apartment. Neither Abba nor Bronson lights a fire in the hearth, and I wonder if it's because they can no longer afford fuel. At least the night is a mild one, with spring warming the air.

No one seems all that eager to sleep, as we huddle together in the parlor, and Abba makes no mention of putting the girls in their beds. Anna is irritable and Beth fusses, picking up on the distress in the room even though she's too young to fully understand. Louisa May tries to comfort both her sisters while Abba paces the dark, empty halls of the top floor, a fretful ghost with a cumbersome mound in her middle. Bronson locks himself away in his study; none of us see him for hours. It's just as well, I note. I'm sure I'd no longer be able to bite my tongue, even in front of his daughters.

Once the girls have finally dozed off on the sofa, Louisa the last one to settle, I cover them with Abba's shawl, since I cannot find a blanket. Then I take a candle and I pad out of the room, marching through the shadows until I reach Bronson's study. I knock on the door.

"Yes?" he asks, his voice muffled, but irritatingly serene.

"It's Margaret. May I come in?"

"Yes, of course. Enter."

I rattle the knob. "Bronson, the door is locked."

"Ah, yes." I hear him rise, then his soft, unhurried footfalls as he comes to unbolt the door. I must tell him, at last, all that I feel. I will resign immediately, and that will leave the students without a teacher. I have come to feel that it's what's best for them; they are mostly children from families with means, they can afford enroll-ment at another school. The dream of a thriving school for girls, for the children of freed slaves, it can no longer happen in this place.

But just as I'm preparing to say all this, just as I'm bracing to push back against whatever prevarications and excuses Bronson might offer, he surprises me yet again. Bronson greets me at his study door with a statement of his own: "We are leaving."

I stand at the threshold in stunned silence for a moment. Then I look beyond him, over his shoulder and into his room, and I see that he's been packing. So that's what he's been up to during these fretful hours, while his wife and daughters have been huddled upstairs, afraid.

"We'll go abroad." He turns, leaving me at the doorway, as he picks up a copy of his book, holding it aloft as if contemplating some sacred text. "Boston is not ready for us. These Brahmins are still stuck in their *Mayflower* charter, thinking they are here on their moral high ground. City on a Hill and hunting for witches and all that. Oh, well. The world is seldom ready for its prophets."

I let out a long exhale, trying to pull my scattered thoughts into some reply. Eventually, all I manage to ask is: "Who is *we*?"

"Pardon?"

"You just said: 'We are leaving, we'll go abroad.' Who is 'we'?" He had better not expect me to play any part in his future plans.

"Why, Abba and the girls, of course. With me."

I nod. Good. Then I'm finally free.

I turn without another word, leaving him with his boxes and his book, and I make my way back upstairs to the apartment. I shut the door quietly. I peek into the bedroom and see that Abba has at last settled on top of her bed while her three girls sleep together on the sofa, entwined in a tangle of limbs, their faces innocent and peaceful in rest. I sit on the winged chair, watching them, keeping vigil, knowing that after tomorrow it will be quite some time before I see them again.

Eventually I doze, waking with a start, unaware of how many hours have passed. I sit up and look to the windows. Outside, the sky begins to thin from inky black to pale purple, the first wispy hints of the coming daybreak. It is quiet. We've made it through the night. I feel my body unclench ever so slightly. The girls are still tucked in and asleep on their family's sofa. I will take my leave without disturbing them, knowing it is safe now for me to do so. I blow a kiss toward Beth, then to Anna, ending with a long gaze down at Louisa May, her face wreathed in her dark waves.

I lean forward and take a lone brown curl of hers between my fingers, savoring its softness for just a moment longer. Then I press a paper note into her hand, a written farewell, and I tiptoe down the stairs, not stopping by Bronson's study on my way.

But I don't go home—at least, not immediately. Instead I go first to my classroom to pack up one box, just what I can carry on my own. Then I walk to the post office, where I dash off another quick letter on some paper I've grabbed from my teaching supplies. I know it's the only paper I'll ever be paid in by Bronson Alcott. But at least that's behind me now. I mail my letter. I hope my message will travel with haste, and be received with a favorable response on the other end.

IT DOES ARRIVE. I know that because, three days later, the familiar carriage comes to a halt outside my door. And there he sits, Ralph Waldo Emerson. He's perched on the driver's seat, the space beside him empty. He's alone, and he's got a grin on his face that reaches me like gentle sunshine after a devastating storm. "Margaret Fuller, I heard you needed a knight and steed?"

"A horse and driver will do just fine," I say, looking up into the soft morning light to meet his gaze. "The fighting I can do for myself, if only a willing carriage will take me from here."

Waldo's features crease into his familiar, fine smile. "I should have known. Margaret Fuller needs no knight to fight for her." He shifts in his seat as if to show me there is room at his side. "Then a willing carriage I am delighted to offer you."

"And I am delighted to accept."

His light eyes hold mine as he hops down and takes my hand, helping me up. "To where shall I bear you?"

I settle into my seat, feeling the warmth of him as he joins me and settles in at my side. I throw him a look. "I was hoping for Concord."

He gives an easy joggle to the reins, setting the horses to trotting, and I can hear the smile in his voice as he declares: "I was hoping you'd say that. Concord it is."

PART 2

Chapter Twelve

Concord
Spring 1837

CONCORD GREETS ME WITH A GENTLE BREEZE, ON IT the rich perfume of new grass and lilacs, as the horses trot happily up the turnpike toward Bush. They know they are nearing home, and I can understand their delight. After a long winter, spring has returned, crowning these woods and meadows in flowers and greenery, and my eyes relish the sights that we pass: the thawed earth carpeted in wildflowers, small clusters of soft white candy-tufts, periwinkle and pale purple phlox.

We've traveled only a few hours out of the city, but it feels as though I've entered a different world, a place where everything is in bloom. Emerson glances at me beside him, surely noticing my gape. "First springtime in Concord, Miss Fuller."

"Yes," I reply, breathing in the warm, floral-scented air as we pass a dogwood tree, its limbs wreathed in riotous pink. "Why, Mr. Emerson, the whole place appears to be decked in petals."

Waldo smiles, his blue eyes as bright as the cloudless sky as he says, "The earth laughs in flowers."

I glance at him, nodding, before turning back for one more appreciative view of the glorious dogwood. "Then Concord is in a veritable state of hysterics."

I glimpse Bush up the lane, stately and white against this bucolic backdrop, and Waldo brings us around to the front. I see Thoreau standing beneath a flowering apple tree, looking very much like the forest faun of my fond memories. At his side is a fat, peach-colored pig with a patchwork of large brown beauty marks splashed across its back. Thoreau cracks a smile as our carriage comes to a halt. "Margaret Fuller, returned to us?"

"Thoreau." I hop down from the coach, overcome with happiness to see my friend again. He reaches forward to take my hands in his and we embrace. Then I step back to look him over. He is already brown from the sunshine and long hours of outdoor chores. His waves of dark hair are even longer than I remember, unruly as ever, giving him the rustic appearance of a sheep in need of a good shearing. I feel pale and diminished from my Boston winter, from my long hours of desk work and my repeated frustrations and anxieties, but Thoreau looks ruddy and full of vim. I hope my stay in Concord might do me some good. "And who is this?" I ask, glancing down at the fat pig nudging the soil at our feet with its snout.

"This is Professor Bacchus Bacon," Thoreau answers. "Bacchus for his obvious enjoyment of feasting. And Bacon, well, for the food he shall never become . . . the fate from which I have spared our porcine friend by making him our own special pet. I was just about to take Professor Bacchus Bacon for a walk."

"Who needs a pet dog when Thoreau walks that thing up and down the lanes of Concord?" Waldo offers a jovial shake of his head. "Oh, but the village children love it. As if Thoreau needed anything more to make him our local Pied Piper."

Thoreau and the pig begin their slow amble down the lane, side by side, and Waldo unloads my luggage. I'm traveling light—one trunk and two bags—and we make our way up the front walk. Bush looks grand, lovely as ever, a crisp white against the newly unfurled green of the springtime bower all around. Waldo escorts me inside.

As I enter the front hall I take a deep breath in, overcome with a medley of smells that hit me as familiar—scents that I had not realized I had been missing: to breathe in the air of Bush is to breathe in the smell of old books and new paper, coffee and fresh-cut flowers. I feel as though I've returned home.

And then I spot her: Lidian. Mrs. Emerson, the lady of the house. I clutch my satchel, freezing midstep. She does not rise to greet me, but rather sits in the parlor, holding the sleeping baby in her arms. She turns, looking to me. And then, to my relief, she smiles. Her face is thinner than the last time I saw her, her features more relaxed, even a bit lovely. Her arms hold the baby as if he's always been there, a part of her, his warm weight on her heart making her complete. The spring sunlight streams into the room from the opened windows, gilding the scene with a soft golden glow. She is Madonna enthroned.

"Lidian," I say, my voice low so as not to wake the baby as I approach. Waldo hangs back, attending to my luggage and hauling my trunk toward the Red Room—my bedroom once more. I go with quiet steps to my hostess. "Motherhood becomes you."

"Margaret, welcome." There is a light in her eyes that was not there last summer, and her long figure is slender once more.

"This must be the dear little Waldo."

"Indeed," she whispers.

"Will I disturb him?"

"Oh, not to worry on that account. Little Waldo is like his father, he sleeps the deep slumber of an untroubled mind." Lidian smiles, glancing down at the rosy face with evident infatuation. She, too, seems less troubled. More at peace. She looks back to me and whispers that the child is a dear. I see that motherhood is medicine for her soul, that she now has someone to receive and return her love in a way that Waldo, her husband, did not seem to do last summer.

"He is precious," I say. "He makes Raphael's cherubs appear plain."

Lidian likes this, I can tell from her easy smile. "Thank you, Margaret. And welcome." She takes in my appearance with an upward sweep of her eyes. I know what she sees: my dusty traveling suit and straw hat, my bedraggled hair flying loose of its pins. I'm sure I look exhausted and ragged, not only from the journey, but from the winter months leading up to it. "You are welcome back at Bush." And as she says it, I see in her eyes that she means it. For that, I am glad.

IT FEELS ALTOGETHER more peaceful in the Emerson house that spring, as the days warm and lengthen. And peace is precisely what I need. We settle into a harmonious routine, the four of us and little Waldo. Thoreau's days are busy with springtime chores—planting his seeds as the New England sunshine turns from tentative to reliable, weeding the vegetable beds, pruning the fruit trees. On most days he knocks at my bedroom door with a harvest of fresh-cut flowers in his hands. "For you, Miss Fuller," he says, extending the fragrant sprays of pear blossoms, quince, and flowering almond.

Lidian is consumed with the baby; her days revolve around his rhythms, his napping and his feedings, and now that he's crawling around, she barely takes her eyes off little Waldo, for fear he'll end up at the hearth or atop the stairs. I notice one difference around the house, which I credit to Lidian's recent entry into motherhood: there are now copious signs of devotion to Mother Mary and the baby Jesus—small statues and icons on the tables and mantels. And a new framed artwork over my bed in the guest room, a lithograph of the Virgin holding her babe. Lidian, who was always pious before, now seems to worship at the twin shrines of Jesus and motherhood.

Waldo and I pass our mornings in happy and productive industry, writing and reading. I've taken on an independent project, translation of a massive Goethe text from German into English, that I hope I might be able to publish. It is good to be back in my beloved sunny guest room, right across the hall from Waldo. Knowing that he's there, working, helps to keep me focused.

Lidian puts the baby down in the mornings for a long nap, and she often rests with him. We all break for luncheon and usually eat as a lively party of five. Thoreau has fashioned a tall wooden chair, and Lidian feeds the baby boiled fruit and mashed bites of potato, allowing Thoreau to take whatever unfinished scraps he can scrounge for Professor Bacchus Bacon.

In the afternoons, when Lidian brings little Waldo up for his rest, Waldo and I read together, usually outside in the garden, breaking to take walks to the river or through the woods out to Walden Pond. The birds, too, have returned to Concord, as have the green leaves of the old oaks and elms. The days grow gradually warmer and I find my entire body softening amid the fresh air and the easy, pleasant companionship.

I have agreed to stay for several weeks, but no one has set a finite date for my departure, and I do not press the issue, happy as I am to be back in Concord. From here, I'm to spend the remainder of the summer on Mother's farm in Groton before I'll need to return to work, this time in a teaching position I've accepted in Providence, Rhode Island.

Waldo has helped me to secure the position, and he assures me that the headmaster of the school will be nothing like Bronson Alcott. "It'll be an entirely different experience, Margaret. Of that I can assure you. The man's name is Fuller. Hiram Fuller. You don't suppose he's any distant relation?"

I shake my head; I know of no relative by the name of Hiram Fuller in Rhode Island. But hearing that he is a man altogether unlike Bronson Alcott *is* a resounding endorsement. "I still do not understand why you gave your blessing and recommendation that I go to work for Bronson," I say that afternoon, as we are walking through an ancient grove of massive hemlocks on the meandering trail out toward Walden Pond.

Waldo sighs audibly beside me, eventually saying: "I did not realize how maladroit Bronson was as a headmaster." He falls silent a moment, looking upward, and then eventually he goes on. "For that, I am sorry. To think that I put you in such a . . . *challenging* situation, I do heartily regret that. Sophia and Eliza Peabody did not tell anyone why they left. They did not make their grievances with Bronson widely known. I was only trying to be a good friend, to find you employment when I knew you needed it. Bronson has a mind that can see purity and goodness. Like in children. He can imagine things not as they are, but as they should be. And yet, perhaps a mind that soars always toward those lofty ideals—well, it can't help but prove totally ill-equipped, unable to function, even, in the face of the world's harsher realities."

"Ill-equipped and unable to function." I repeat his words, my tone wry. "You speak correctly there."

Waldo winces. "I will try to make it up to you, Margaret. Truly I will. And I think that going to work for Mr. Fuller in his school is the right next step."

I take all this in, walking beside Waldo in thoughtful silence, relishing the deep breaths of pine-scented breeze as we approach the pond. The fact of the matter is that I have little choice; either I accept this employment with Mr. Fuller in Providence or I remain with Mother and my younger siblings on the farm—a fate I do not find appealing as a twenty-seven-year-old woman.

IT'S A MORNING in early June, the air clear and bright beneath a sky of robin's-egg blue. Waldo finds me on a blanket in the grass with Lidian and little Waldo in the back. We are laughing at the chickens, the poor creatures toddling about in new leather shoes that Thoreau has fashioned for them, as Lidian has complained that their claws were tearing up the garden. Little Waldo is pointing at one particularly clumsy hen when we notice Waldo appear.

"Good morning," Waldo says as the chickens take the opportunity of his appearance to scatter. Then Waldo announces to us that he has an appointment in Salem to see about a bed for little Waldo. Thoreau has offered to craft one himself from an oak he has felled, but Waldo has his eye on an antique piece.

"Will you ride over with me, Margaret?" Waldo asks. I'm taken aback by the request—it's several dozen miles from Concord to Salem; even in a carriage it will take hours each way, making it an almost full-day excursion. Lidian is now looking at me as intently as her husband. Waldo interjects: "I'd like a second opinion. Lidian, I presume you would not wish to be away for the day?"

Lidian turns her gaze back to the baby, who is plucking out blades of grass. "I would not," she answers, her voice toneless.

"And Thoreau is busy," Waldo says, stuffing his hands into his trouser pockets, looking to me expectantly. Just then I hear Thoreau's hammer, the sounds of his puttering out by the barn. I shift in my seat, rearranging the draped fabric of my skirt, looking from Lidian to Waldo. After a long moment I answer: "I'll ride over with you. If you'd like a second opinion."

"Good," Waldo says, nodding once. "Then that's settled." And yet, the air between the three of us feels, suddenly, quite unsettled.

WE SIT SIDE by side in the carriage, just the pair of us. But we're out in the open air, I tell myself. The bright June sunshine pours down on us, and Waldo waves as we pass familiar faces—there is nothing illicit about this. It's only fresh air and soft breezes, broad sunlight and a casual domestic errand.

We roll into Salem in the early afternoon. It's a bustling town that smells of sea brine and milled timber. Pearl-colored seagulls flit across the cobblestone streets, pecking for scraps. The buildings in Salem appear older than in Concord, weathered by their closeness to the ocean, rows of tired bodies huddled together against the unrelenting winds and squalls coming in off the coast.

Waldo halts the carriage before a store with a broad glass front, its sign boasting antique furniture and elegant household wares. "Here we are," Waldo declares, hopping down from the carriage and then offering me his hand. It feels good to stretch my legs after the long journey. "I've brought us a hamper with luncheon," Waldo says, and I realize just how hungry I am, as well. "Shall we inspect our quarry and then find a nice spot for a picnic?"

I agree to his plan and we enter the store. Half an hour later we are exiting the building followed by a pair of young lads, who set to work strapping little Waldo's new bed to the back of the carriage. I blink, my eyes adjusting once more to the bright afternoon sunshine, and that's when I see the figure before me.

Standing a few paces off, as if awaiting us, is a lone man with long waves of dark hair and a high top hat. He's tall and slender, his face slightly shadowed by the broad brim of his cap, but I can see that he's young, younger than Emerson, perhaps about my own age. I notice, with a slight start, that his eyes are a bright, piercing green— and they are fixed on me.

Emerson sees that I've halted, that I'm staring at this unspeaking stranger on the street before us, and his gaze follows mine. A moment later his features spread into a casual smile. "Ah! Is it Nathaniel Hawthorne?" Emerson strides toward the man, taking his hand in a hearty, familiar greeting. "Good to see you. Should have known you'd be haunting the streets of Salem."

"Mr. Emerson, nice to see you here," the man says, his voice smooth and rich, like dark coffee unsoftened by cream. Then his green eyes glide back toward me, locking with my own. Closer up I can see how handsomely his features are arranged—and yet, it's in a crisp, even cold, sort of way. The cruel beauty of a hawk.

This Mr. Hawthorne quirks an eyebrow. "And this must be the famous Margaret Fuller?"

I feel my body tense, surprised by his remark. "This *is* the famous Margaret Fuller indeed," Emerson says, taking a step closer to me. I feel his hand come lightly to my arm. "Margaret, please meet Nathaniel Hawthorne. Local rogue and Salem's most eligible bachelor."

Hawthorne's eyes remain on me as he extends a gloved hand. I offer him mine as well. "Nice to meet you, Mr. Hawthorne."

"And you, Miss Fuller." His lips curl upward, just the hint of a grin. "Emerson wrote to me that you'd be returning to Concord. Staying with him at Bush."

I feel my cheeks grow warm; I just hope they've not turned red. I raise my hands to my face as though I'm shielding my eyes from the too-bright sunshine. But really it's the too-bright stare of this man.

Hawthorne, perhaps seeing that he's caught me in some disquiet, goes on: "Emerson here apotheosizes when he speaks of you, Miss Fuller."

"Oh?" I rock back on my heels, turning from Hawthorne to Emerson, my puzzlement surely evident. "Can this be true?"

"Indeed he does," Hawthorne interjects, a good-natured and teasing expression sparkling his hawkish features. "As if you were some goddess he's encountered. What was it he called you? Ah, yes. 'The greatest woman of ancient or modern times, and the one figure in the world worth considering.'"

Stunned to speechlessness, my mouth falls open as I look to my friend. Emerson blinks, clapping his gloved hands together, offering a fleeting smile. "There you go, spilling my secrets, Hawthorne. But yes, yes, I'll freely admit it. I am a member of the Margaret Fuller Admiration Society. An enthusiastic member."

My mind is in a spin. I've never been a lady who had a full dance card or a line of admirers. I've never had even one devoted suitor. Father had neither the time nor the inclination to see me debuted into the marriageable set, and then neither did I. And yet Emerson has written to this gentleman—this Hawthorne—calling me a *goddess*?

"I've been most eager to make your acquaintance," Hawthorne goes on, angling his face toward me with a grin, as if these bold revelations of his, and my flustered reaction to them, are all most entertaining. Then his green eyes rove down my figure in a way that makes my cheeks burn with heat.

Emerson steps closer to my side, speaking with a tone of calm, casual joviality: "Your timing is fortuitous, Hawthorne. We've finished our errand and were just about to set up a picnic. Care to have luncheon with us?"

"I wish I could," Hawthorne says, his eyes flitting from me toward Emerson before landing back on me. "But my errands are not finished." He pulls a timepiece from his pocket and gives it a bored look. "In fact, I'm meeting a solicitor on some pressing business for my sisters. Then, sadly, it's back to Castle Dismal."

I have no idea of what he's speaking, but Emerson seems to follow, as he offers a knowing nod, saying: "Ah, yes. And how goes the writing? Can I expect more pages anytime soon?"

Hawthorne puffs out his smooth cheeks, offering an exaggerated sigh. "I toil away, sunup to sundown. When I have pages ready, you'll be the first to know."

"Then we shall not delay you further," Emerson says, touching his fingers to the brim of his cap before offering me his arm. I take it, happy to be moving on from this exchange, relieved that this man will not be joining us for luncheon. Hawthorne nods and then looks at each of us in turn, his green eyes narrowing as he says: "But I shall come to Concord soon. As soon as I can escape this place."

"Please do, Hawthorne," Emerson says. "You'll always find a ready welcome at Bush for writers and friends."

"I know that to be the truth," Hawthorne says. His features tilt upward with the slightest trace of a smile. "And if Miss Fuller is there, why, it makes the trip all the more enticing."

We take our leave of Mr. Hawthorne and walk for a few minutes, settling on a bench overlooking the sea for our picnic. I am glad to be away from that encounter, relieved, and a bit quiet as my thoughts churn. Emerson, on the other hand, is ebullient with energy.

He chatters away over our luncheon, telling me that Nathaniel

Hawthorne is the scion of one of Salem's oldest families. "His great-great-grandfather John Hathorne was a judge during the Witch Trials. Judge Hathorne played a large role in putting all those girls to death."

I swallow my mouthful of food, my throat feeling dry.

"That's why Nathaniel has changed his family name. Now they are the Hawthornes."

"How dreadful," I say, feeling the shiver across my skin, even beneath the bright June sunshine. I would not want that man, those cold emerald eyes, condemning me to the gallows.

"Indeed," Waldo agrees. "And Nathaniel loathes this town. You heard him, calling his family home that he shares with his sisters 'Castle Dismal.' I think he still feels the stains of his family when he walks these narrow old streets. He's always telling me he wants to get out as quickly as he can. As soon as he makes some money. He's plugging away on a book. But he has to remain with his sisters in the family home until he does. Of course, I imagine it's not *all* bad—from what I hear, they wait on him as if he's their king."

I nod, absorbing all of this. "And you mentioned that this Mr. Hawthorne is not married?"

"Only to his writing." Waldo pops a handful of blueberries into his mouth.

I look down at the bread roll in my hands, but I find I have little appetite remaining. My stomach feels coiled and my mind is listless—and I know that is entirely thanks to my brief, curious exchange with Mr. Nathaniel Hawthorne.

Chapter Thirteen

Summer 1837

"YOU AREN'T PLANNING TO LEAVE WITHOUT JOINing me for one final walk, are you?"

Waldo has caught me at my writing desk. I look to him, sitting back as I massage my cramped wrists. My bags sit beside my bed, packed and ready. I push my chair away from my desk. "A walk would do me a fair bit of good right now. Where to?"

"Walden Pond," he suggests.

I stand up, stretching my back. "I do like the sound of that."

We walk down the lawn, past the barn, and follow the narrow trail that takes us into the woods, the earth a carpet of soft mud hemmed by skunk cabbage and fiddleheads. The birds are riotous in their songs, well fed and warm as they are in high summer, and warning one another of our approach.

We cross the rickety wooden footbridge over the Mill Brook. Waldo and I walk side by side in companionable silence, as we've done so many times this summer. I note, with a silent twinge of sadness, how much I'll miss these walks. And the company of Waldo, as well.

"Did you enjoy yourself?" He throws me a sideways glance and I feel, not for the first time, as though he's seen my thoughts.

I meet his eyes. "Very much, Waldo. Thank you. My soul feels revived. After, well . . ." I know that Bronson Alcott is a friend of Waldo's. But there is something on the topic that I do need to say now, on the eve of my departure. "I would never wish to disparage a friend of yours. I'm very fond of Abba, and I care deeply for the girls. Especially Louisa May. It's only . . . well, I would never again put my faith in Bronson Alcott. Particularly not when it came to my livelihood."

"And I cannot say I blame you." Waldo's voice is measured. "Not after what you've been through. I do believe your time at Greene Street School will be entirely different. Hiram Fuller will be a very different sort of employer. I think you'll learn much from him. And your pupils will be bright and curious—they'll be most fortunate to have you."

"As long as he pays his teachers," I say, throwing Waldo a rueful expression. But I am thankful to Waldo for helping me to secure this position—and the thousand-dollar salary Mr. Fuller has promised me.

The trees begin to change, the maples and elms that surround Bush giving way to the paper birch and white pines that fill the thick woods around Walden. The air here smells of sap and pine needles. When at last we descend the steep hill and come down to the clearing, we see the pond. We pause our steps and stand on the sandy shore, looking out over the serene blue, reflecting the ring of trees around it on the surface like a looking glass.

"It really is lovely," I say. "So wild." I will miss it. I will miss all of this.

Waldo glances toward me, then back out over the water. "Thoreau keeps threatening to leave Bush and move out here. He says he's tired of the town, that he wishes to live among the pines and whippoorwills."

"I can't say I entirely blame him."

Waldo is studying my profile. "But, Margaret, you aren't one to come live alone in the woods. You need company. Community to entice you into the lively conversations that your mind craves."

I breathe in, filling myself with the clean scents of the pines and pond water. And then, exhaling, I answer: "I suppose you're right." Though I'm not sure I'll have much community this year; I know no one in Providence.

Waldo walks toward a nearby birch and peels a thin strip of its white bark. "What are you doing?" I ask.

He looks down at his fingers, at the curl of birch bark between them. "Do you remember when you made me my crown of clematis?"

I do. Of course I do. I answer him with a silent nod. My eyes glide upward, toward the broad blue sky. Then back to Waldo at my side. "That feels so long ago," I say.

He offers me a lopsided smile. "Perhaps it's my age, but a year does not seem all *that* long to me."

"No, you're right. It's only that . . . so much has happened since then," I answer, gazing out over the water, at the ring of pines that holds the pond like a bowl.

"It feels like it was just yesterday to me," Waldo says. His voice is quiet, soft, and it is joined by the mournful call of a loon that sounds in the distance, from the far side of the pond. "But perhaps that is because I've thought of that moment nearly every day since it happened."

I look to him, and our eyes lock. I can see the pines and the water reflected in the blue of his stare. Then he blinks, looking away. When he speaks, his voice sounds full of feeling: "You'll come back to Concord, won't you, Margaret?"

My stomach rolls, a churning entirely at odds with the serene, glassy surface of the water before us. After a moment, I answer, "If I'm invited, I'll come back."

Waldo nods. A small, tight gesture. I force myself to walk forward, down to where the water meets the sand. Just at that moment a family of ducks appears, skimming the surface on a swim from one shore to the other. One long line: a father and a mother, then a parade of four little ducklings. A family.

I feel a pinch in my heart. And it strikes me, yet again, just how alone I am.

Chapter Fourteen

Providence, Rhode Island
Autumn 1837

"IT'S ALL THE SAME STOCK—I SUSPECT IF ONE WERE to go back far enough, we'd find some connection between our two branches of the Fullers." Mr. Hiram Fuller, my new employer, stares at me, and I see that he is a man with small, dark eyes and straightforward, earnest opinions. I like him. Or, at the very least, I feel as though I can trust him.

After a brief tour of the school, which is built in the Greek Revival style so popular for places of learning, Mr. Fuller brings me into my classroom and sets forth the facts of my new situation. I'm to be his assistant teacher. I'll be in charge of sixty female pupils beginning at age ten, while he'll have sixty lads in the room next door. He's arranged a rented room for me on the top floor of a boardinghouse in the city, and I'll walk to and from the school each day. He'll pay me a thousand dollars for my work. This, at last, gives me some peace as I think of Mother and my siblings at home in Groton.

We begin in September, and my life takes on a rhythm that unfurls around the school day. I rise before the sun, changing from my flannel nightgown into my day dress and taking a few hours to work alone in my bedroom. Trying, while the air still holds the last lingering warmth of summer, to read and write by candlelight alone, saving the precious firewood I have.

I prepare for the day's lessons before taking a quick breakfast of toast and coffee in the boardinghouse dining room. I'm often the first one seated at the long wooden table, and done with my meal before most others have risen from their beds. Then I set out on my three-mile walk from the boardinghouse to the Greene Street School. The trek is long, but it's pleasant enough in the autumn, and the city is quiet in the early mornings.

My pupils bring me joy. Sixty young girls, sixty bright minds that are eager to absorb learning and facts. Ready for original thoughts and arguments. I fill their hours with Latin, history, ethics, composition, recitation, and elocution. I am fair but demanding, and I know that, within a short time, I've acquired a reputation as being more exacting than their previous teacher.

"It's because I know these girls can meet the high standard I wish to set," I tell Mr. Fuller, who seems to approve entirely.

"We must *think* as well as *study*, and *talk* as well as *recite*," I remind my girls, time and again, as I stand before them in the classroom. Mr. Fuller agrees with me on this, and it makes me respect him all the more.

I send money home to Mother regularly, and this serves as my reminder as to why I must keep this job. Despite the punishing three-mile walk to and from the school, despite the darkness of my cramped, dreary room. Despite my loneliness in Providence, a city where I have neither friends nor family. The work is trying, the hours long, and my eyes feel strained and sore by the end of each day, as I squint in the quivering candlelight to read my students' papers and prepare for the next day's load.

By the deep of winter, after I've returned to Providence from a brief Christmas visit to Mother and the farm, I feel the tugging of melancholy. The days are dark and cold. In spite of the fact that I'm surrounded by my pupils all day, I feel a loneliness of spirit that aches like a bruise. I'm busy all day, but nothing I am doing is stoking any real fire in my soul.

I write to Emerson, letting on how my spirits are flagging. He responds, and his words do serve to bolster me. *"My Dear Margaret, You are guiding them to be all that they can be, to aspire to true nobility of the heart and the mind."*

It is true. I can see that these girls are bright and capable. They do deserve an education just the same as the sixty boys in the classroom next door. *"Each of these girls deserves to live for more than simply the fate of debutante and then bride. They should aspire to more than merely to dress and go visiting, to gossip over tea and dinner parties. They should improve themselves, and do good, and live for their highest nature."* I write all of this back to Waldo, and, feeling a particular barb of loneliness, I sign: *"Always yours, Margaret."*

And I need the salary. As I make my miles-long walk each cold morning, and then again each evening, I look out over the gray, frozen ground of Providence. Winter is a fallow time, I remind myself. Or, rather, the earth *appears* to be fallow. And yet, I must have faith. I must remember that, under that icy and unyielding ground, there are the seeds of new life. Waiting, preparing, and soon they shall be stirring. Life is unfolding as it should, even when the ground lies hard and frozen. Even when I cannot see it happening.

Looking up at the winter sky, an endless wall of hard, marbled gray, I tell myself: somewhere behind that shines warm and golden sunlight. Even if I cannot see it, I know that it is there, and someday soon, I will see it again. This season, like every other before it, shall pass, making way for the new, the fresh, the fertile. And life, for me, as well.

IT'S A SPRING morning, and the first hints of warm sunshine have lifted all of our spirits. The windows in the classroom are open, and the breeze has lost its knife edge. The birdsong sounds louder even than last week. Soon we will see the bright colors of the daffodils, and then the lilacs.

I have designed the day's lesson around Wordsworth's "Lament of Mary Queen of Scots." The work strikes me anew as I read the poem aloud to my girls in the classroom. They are the words of a woman crying out for help, and finding none. A woman who, because she has dared to do bold things, great things, finds herself entirely alone. *"Great God, who feel'st for my distress, / My thoughts are all that I possess, / O keep them innocent!"*

Her thoughts were all that she possessed. I pause, the words reverberating through me like the plucked strings of a harp. I look out at my girls, hoping that they can appreciate Wordsworth's meaning. That they will always fight to preserve the integrity of their own minds. But then our quiet is broken by an urgent rapping at our classroom door.

"Yes?" I lower the book, irritated to be interrupted in the middle of such a powerful reading.

"Pardon the intrusion." Mr. Fuller peeks his head into the doorway. "News!"

I look out over my class and then walk toward my employer. "What news?"

"It's all right, they may all hear it," Mr. Fuller says, stepping into the classroom. "In fact, they should hear it. News from England. The king has died."

"Oh?" I cross my arms, as I hear gasps pop up from the girls around the room.

Mr. Fuller's features are bright, animated, as he says: "Victoria is to be queen. England shall have a young woman on the throne for the first time in almost three hundred years."

I rock back on my heels, allowing this news to sink in. A young woman, younger than I, to rule the most powerful empire on the globe. I write to Waldo that night, sharing with him how enthused I feel, how inspired all my young pupils were when they heard the news. That I hope it may usher in an era in which other girls and women look to a queen's example and find the embers of their own inner strength stoked.

And it's in that moment that I finally admit the truth to myself: I must leave teaching. It is not the path for me. I love the girls, and I love seeing their minds at work, but I do not feel called to the daily grind of recitation and penmanship, of algebra and geography. In fact, I feel that it is slowly chipping away at my life's energy, perhaps even pieces of my soul. Providence is small and lonely for me. The work feels more like drudgery. I yearn to be a writer, a thinker. I long for more.

"*I long for Concord*," I admit, writing it to Waldo and posting the letter before my nerves can falter. Waldo writes back almost immediately, telling me how happy he is for England that they have a woman at the helm. And then he writes that Bush is too quiet. He ends his letter with a statement—"The Red Room is empty."—followed by a question: "Can you fill it for the month of July?"

Chapter Fifteen

Concord
Summer 1838

I T'S A SEASON FOR PLANTING. A TIME FOR LAYING ROOTS into the earth. For Waldo, this means adding to his orchards, his garden, his vegetable beds. He spends many mornings with Thoreau, tending his tomatoes, weeding around his squash and lettuces, inspecting his rhubarb and lavender. Little Waldo and I wander out into the garden together and watch the Sage of Concord wage war on the bugs that wish to nibble his herbs. Waldo is enlivened—he's thinking about the improvements to Bush, and to Concord, as well. For some time now he's wanted to create a place here of meaning, a place where thinkers will gather and do their great work. This summer is to be the season when Waldo brings forth fruit.

To that end, he sends out invitations. He calls the Alcotts home from their wanderings, reassuring Bronson that it will be safe to return to Concord. Anticipating Bronson's chief hesitation, Waldo offers to help with the rent if the Alcotts will take up residence at Orchard House once more. I'm not in any hurry to see Bronson again, but I do feel excitement at the thought of seeing Louisa May and the other Alcott girls. Of meeting Abba's new baby.

And, Waldo tells me, he's invited someone else to Concord, as well. "Do you remember meeting Nathaniel Hawthorne on our trip to Salem last summer?"

I notice the way my heart tips sideways at the question. Yes, I remember meeting Nathaniel Hawthorne. I remember the tall, top-hatted figure with flyaway dark hair and a plain suit. I remember the rich satin of his voice. Mostly I remember the way he looked at me, that intense, green-eyed gaze that seemed to slice through all casual pleasantries.

But I offer simply a nod, attempting to keep a neutral expression on my face, and Waldo goes on: "He's always calling Salem a dismal place and referring to Concord as some sort of present-day Eden. So I've told him he must come here. It will make his work better, to feel that his soul is being nurtured."

So we will all be here together, this summer. Each one of us in some way or another the recipient of Emerson's beneficence. And all our great Sage seems to want in return is that we think and write and inspire one another to create. For my part, ensconced downstairs in the Red Room, at liberty to read and write, and to enjoy the rambunctious jollity of little Waldo and even the anticipated return of the Alcott girls, I am all too happy to oblige.

Emerson's long-awaited gathering happens late one night in early summer. The Alcotts have returned and taken up residence down the lane once more, and Emerson invites them over for a visit after supper. "Hawthorne will come, as well. He'll be staying nearby—I've got him a room at a farmhouse just a short walk from here. In the fields, as he wanted."

I step out of my bedroom that evening to the sounds of laughter and lively chatter coming from the parlor. I stand at the threshold and see them gathered, a colorful assembly of many ages scattered across Emerson's scarlet-upholstered chairs and sofa.

Our hostess, Lidian, sits on the sofa holding little Waldo in her lap, his eyes growing heavy even as he fights to stay awake amid the excitement. Abba holds her littlest one in her lap while the three older sisters hurtle around the room, prompting the occasional scolding when they step too close to the hearth. Bronson is sitting in one winged armchair beside the fire, Emerson in the other.

Thoreau is sprawled on the rug beside Bacchus Bacon, who has grown even fatter and is now snorting his way through a bowl of apples. The Alcott girls are in giddy hysterics as they take turns hopping over Thoreau and petting his pig. And there, too, is Nathaniel Hawthorne. He stands beside the hearth, leaning on the mantel. I look at each guest in turn, feeling my heart flutter in my chest.

Emerson notices my entry into the parlor and fixes his gaze on me. "Ah, Margaret is here."

I smile to him, throwing back my shoulders and striding into the room, affecting what I hope is a look of casual confidence, even if I am cowed by the size and makeup of this crowd.

"Now we can truly begin," Emerson says, clapping his hands together.

"It looks as though you already have," I say.

Emerson waves me deeper into the room. He is our Socrates, and we, here at Bush, are his school. Thoreau rises from the rug and pours me a cup of tea, for which I thank him. I take my seat on the sofa beside Abba and give her a hug. "How wonderful it is to see you," I say, noticing that her smile is a bit hesitant. But I mean it— while I may have little patience for her husband, I still care deeply for Abba and her daughters, and I am delighted to see their faces again.

"Thank you, Margaret. It's nice to see you, as well. Meet our little May," Abba says, smiling broadly at the plump, sleeping baby in her arms.

"Precious girl," I say, looking from the baby to Abba. "Roses and cream, she is the picture of health."

Emerson's voice is loud, and he pulls me from our private exchange to the larger conversation happening beside the fireplace. "I know Margaret shares my beliefs on this, because we've been talking about this for quite some time. The fact is that we are far more likely to meet the divine in the mind and the heart of a striving human than we are in some cold, hard church pew."

I look up, toward Emerson and then Thoreau. They both return my stare, their faces expectant, and I see that they wish for me to speak, to offer some answer. So I do. "Yes, and I would also add that one is far more likely to feel one's soul stirred out of doors, among the wildflowers, the birds, the trees, than in that same cold, hard church pew."

"It is blasphemous to say it"—Emerson nods—"but I agree with you."

"I don't see why it should be blasphemous," I reply.

"Because it is not the word of the church elders." Emerson's tone is wooden.

"I'll offer another blasphemy, if that's all right," Thoreau pipes up.

"Please do," Emerson says. "That's why we are here. Not to be blasphemers, per se, but to be free and brave thinkers."

Thoreau tents his dirty fingers before his face and says: "It is the spirit, not the physical body, that really matters."

"True," Alcott interjects, tapping the arm of his chair, and I have to force myself not to grimace at the sound of his voice. Alcott goes on: "For that reason, we must strive for transcendent experiences. Experiences that speak to our souls. We must not consume ourselves with our base physical desires."

At this his wife rises, May bundled in her arms. "To bed for us," she says, looking to her husband. "You'll bring them home?" Her eyes glide to the bigger girls.

"Yes, dear," Alcott answers his wife.

"I've got a dilemma with my soul," Thoreau interjects. "For the longest time I've felt it. But perhaps it's not a dilemma with my soul—perhaps it's more of a rebellion. The truth is that my soul cannot heel to a master. Whether it's the priest at church, the professor at Harvard . . . even the strictures of the workaday, of what I'm told is life amid *modern industry*."

Thoreau says this last bit with a peppering of scorn, but I nod, understanding what he means about his soul being rebellious. I've known this feeling, too, many times. Ever since I was a young girl, really. If I felt something to be true in my soul, I'd rather trust in that, following that authentic conviction—even when it meant going against a rule I was told to heed. Like hiding with the Shakespeare book when the words pierced my soul. Or speaking out for educating girls, even when the idea is considered vulgar by so many.

"Margaret, you look deep in thought," Emerson says, his gaze searching my face.

"Oh," I say, shifting in my seat. "I was just thinking about what Thoreau said. About having a soul that cannot heel. You see, I feel that way about my mind. . . ."

Emerson arcs an eyebrow.

"I have a mind that insists on expressing itself," I admit. It's likely why I've never married.

"Yes," Emerson says, nodding slowly. "Expressing itself. But it's more than simply self-expression that one needs. What I've always admired about you, Margaret, is the rugged independence of thought." We've spoken about this before. He's playing with this idea of self-reliance, and I can see the thoughts turning in his mind now.

Lidian gets up to leave, with little Waldo asleep in her arms. The Alcott girls tiptoe out with her, making a fuss over the baby. And now I am the only woman here, seated with Emerson, Thoreau, Hawthorne, and Bronson. Just then Louy and Anna come bounding back into the room. "What's this?" Alcott asks, surprised by the sudden reappearance of his daughters. "Time for bed?"

"Not for bed." Louisa stomps a foot. "Mr. Thoreau promised!"

"Promised what?" Bronson throws a look toward Thoreau.

"The giraffe!" the Alcott girls chime together.

"What giraffe?" I ask.

"There's a traveling circus troupe, up from Boston," Hawthorne says. "They've got a giraffe. I told the girls about it and then Thoreau promised he'd bring them to see it."

"Well, I want to see this," I declare, rising from my seat.

"Don't go, Margaret," Emerson says from his chair. "Stay here with us. This ship will go frightfully off course without the ballast of your practicality. You'll leave me with only Bronson to steer?"

I pat down my skirt, looking to Waldo. "You may remain here discussing how your souls can aspire for great heights. I'll step out into the world to witness something that already knows how to reach great heights."

Waldo makes a face. "Like a giraffe?"

"Yes, a giraffe," I say.

In the front hall I'm settling my shawl over my shoulders and preparing to leave when Hawthorne steps out of the parlor. He lopes toward me, a sheepish grin on his features. "Hello."

"Hello," I say, pausing before the front door.

"Would you mind if I joined you?" he asks. "I got the girls all excited, and now I wish to see the thing, as well."

"It's not *my* giraffe," I say, a touch defensively—Hawthorne's presence puts me slightly off balance. Then I force a smile, adding: "I'm only along for the journey because you got me excited, as well."

We walk down Lexington Road toward the village, Hawthorne on one side of me and Thoreau on the other. The three girls trot excitedly between us. Louisa tugs on my hand and I look down at her. "Yes, my dear?"

"Can I tell you a secret, Miss Margaret?"

"Of course you can. I love our secrets."

She grins at this, and I notice that several teeth have grown in where last year there were gummy pink gaps. She waves me down, so that my ear is level with her mouth, and she whispers: "I missed you and Mr. Thoreau the most."

I return her grin, then take her hand in mine as I whisper back: "I missed you, too, Louy. I'm glad you're here." I'm glad we are all here.

We spot a large crowd ahead on the village green, illuminated in a puddle of light seeping out from the street lanterns. They are huddled around the old oak tree, the place where the village was first settled. And there, secured to the ancient oak with what looks like a webbing of long rope leashes and a leather harness, is a mammoth of a creature. I pause, frozen midstep. I have heard of giraffes before, I've read about them in tales for children. But I was in no way prepared for what I now see before me.

I hear Hawthorne gasp beside me as he, too, stares ahead. The Alcott girls have gone uncharacteristically silent, and Louisa squeezes my hand in hers as Anna slides behind her sister. The fact that it's night, that we are seeing this creature through flickering candlelight and shadow, only adds to the majesty of the being before us. Its body is covered in tawny patches of darker hair; its eyes are up impossibly high at the top of its long, slender neck.

"Why, it's as tall as the tree," Louisa gasps.

Throughout the village square, other performers are putting on shows of their own as part of this traveling circus. A cluster of painted clowns are juggling and making several children laugh. But I am enraptured by the giraffe. By its stunning height. Its lengthy eyelashes veiling big, soulful eyes.

"It's something, isn't it?" Hawthorne sidles up to me.

"It's something . . . unlike anything I've ever seen," I reply. "It's remarkable."

The night gets ever darker around us; the folks in the square flow around me like a river. I remain standing there beside the oak, transfixed, staring up at the creature, not needing to see anything else.

Eventually, it's Hawthorne who says he's ready to retire, and the Alcott girls agree. We plod back toward Bush in contemplative silence. I feel as though I've witnessed something holy. Something humbling, really. I've seen something that has reminded me of how small we are.

Hawthorne brings the Alcott girls home to Orchard House, as he's staying there for the night. "Too late to traipse back to the farm in this darkness," he says. We bid our farewells and Thoreau and I turn toward Bush.

The house is quiet as we enter, its occupants asleep. The hour is late, well past ten o'clock. Thoreau glides noiselessly up the stairs toward his alcove bedroom. I go to my room, but I'm not at all tired. I slip into my nightgown and under the cool sheets, but as I settle into bed, I find that sleep evades me.

After a few hours of tossing and turning, I rise from bed, giving up. I cross the room and peel back the window curtain, looking out at the night. The moon is a coin overhead, cold and white, attended by shards of scattered starlight.

I feel thirsty. I look across the room; I forgot to fill my pitcher, so now I pad barefoot out of my bedroom toward the kitchen. I'm groping my way through the darkness toward the soapstone sink when I am startled to find someone else already standing in the kitchen. "Oh," I say, my voice like the squeak of a mouse.

"Margaret?" It's Waldo. He holds a lone candle and he smiles, looking not nearly as surprised to see me as I am to see him. "How was the giraffe?"

"Remarkable," I answer, pouring a glass of water from the pitcher I find beside the sink. I take a long sip, feeling the cool liquid travel down my throat, and then I ask: "And how was the rest of your evening?"

"Unremarkable, after you left. I should have gone with you to see the giraffe."

I take another sip of water, noting that I am standing before him in nothing but my thin muslin nightgown. Waldo is quiet, and then he says: "I can't sleep. I was going to take a walk."

I lower my empty glass. "At this hour?"

He gives a quick shrug of his shoulders. "Why not?"

"Because it is dark out."

He looks to the window on the far wall. "It'll soon be dawn." And then he stares at me, saying: "Join me."

"Where?" I ask, surprised by myself, that I'm even considering it.

Waldo's eyes flicker in the dancing light of his candle. "Let's go watch the sun rise over Walden Pond. Will you come with me?"

"Yes," I say, my heart thrumming in my throat. I can see that he's surprised—pleasantly so, but surprised nonetheless. I explain: "I've seen a great number of sunrises, what with the early hour at which I often rise for work. But I've enjoyed far too few of them. Yes, I will join you. Let me change out of my nightgown. I'll meet you outside."

We walk side by side, in silence, though the night around us pulses with summertime noise. Peeper frogs call out to one another; an owl sounds from within a tree hollow.

We arrive at the clearing just as hints of pale purple are beginning to tinge the horizon. We stand in silence, surrounded by the pines and the water and the birds, the air smelling of marshy earth as a thin lacing of early morning mist curls up over the water. A loon calls out across the pond. I breathe out, feeling the first rose-gold beam of sunlight on my face. I shut my eyes, and I smile.

Here, in this very moment, standing beside Waldo at the end of this night, my soul does feel as though it could touch the divine.

Chapter Sixteen

Summer 1838

I AM CROUCHING IN A CLUTCH OF MILKWEED WITH Thoreau and Louisa May. Thoreau points a dirty finger, and Louy and I watch in delight as a lone monarch butterfly flutters to a landing on the plant before us. When she lingers for longer than a few seconds, we suppress our urge to squeal, knowing what is to come, and knowing that if we make too loud a fuss, we might prevent its happening.

"See there," Thoreau whispers, once the butterfly has flitted off. Louisa and I lean close and look to the place where he points; the butterfly has laid its eggs, a silky white purse stuck to the underside of the milkweed's green leaf. "Four days from now, caterpillars will burst forth," Thoreau says, his tone almost reverent.

An hour later, when we return to Bush and Louisa May has run home to Orchard House to see to her chores, I am still giddy, almost in a state of rapture at having witnessed the beautiful, fragile gift of new life. I walk happily toward the kitchen to pour myself a glass of water, almost bumping into Lidian in the doorway. "Oh, hello." I pause, pulling my bonnet off my head.

"Margaret, good morning." Lidian's hands are full—she's holding a pile of freshly laundered napkins, and she has a busy, purposeful air about her. "How are you?"

"I'm delightful," I answer. "I've just been with Louisa May and Thoreau to watch some of the monarchs laying their eggs."

Lidian arcs an eyebrow, makes an audible sound in her throat, but offers no words in reply. "And you?" I ask, looking to the counter behind her, where canned foodstuffs and linens of various sizes are in a state of disarray before a row of baskets. The kitchen smells of fresh-baked bread.

"I'm making food baskets for the church," Lidian says, meeting my eyes with her pale stare. "I was just going to ask Thoreau to ready the carriage." Lidian Emerson is a woman of good works.

"I'll help," I offer, tossing my bonnet onto the nearby chair.

"Oh? All right." Does her voice sound a bit tenuous? Perhaps even begrudging?

"Put me to work," I declare, pushing my sleeves up to my elbows.

"I've baked two dozen rolls," Lidian says, pointing toward the counter, where the plump mounds are cooling. "You can wrap them in this cheesecloth. Put two in each basket."

"Very well," I say, grabbing a spare apron off a hook and wrapping it around my waist.

"I'll go and fetch Thoreau," Lidian says, eyeing me with interest. "Once we've finished all the hampers, he and I can make the delivery."

I nod my understanding and get to work as Lidian leaves me in the kitchen. I'm tearing squares from the cheesecloth when I notice a piece of paper, like a pamphlet, on the table. I pick it up. I don't want it to get mixed up with the food, and as I push it off to the side, I glance at it. I recognize Lidian's handwriting. I read just the top, noticing, with a slight start, that it's a list.

"*The Transcendentalists' Ten Commandments,*" it reads. Curious, I smile and read on.

"*Loathe and shun the sick. They are in bad taste, and may untune you for writing the poem floating through your mind.*"

I lean back, staring down at the words. I read the next item on the list:

"*It is weak to seek or give sympathy.*"

I cock my head to the side, frowning.

"*The great never value being loved.*"

I peer over my shoulder, confirming that I am alone in the kitchen. I read on:

"*Aspire only for perfection.*

"*If perfection is not attained, then at least talk about perfection all the time.*

"Never confess a fault."

The paper begins to quiver in my hands. As I lower it I notice, with a start, that Lidian is standing in the doorway once more. She is staring at me, her pale face blank. Her eyes dart to the paper in my grip.

"I see you found my list," she says, her voice brittle.

"Oh, yes, I was just—" I replace the paper on the table, embarrassed to be caught reading it. Lidian flashes a quick, joyless smile, then she walks toward the table and takes the paper, folding it and stuffing it into her apron.

I swallow. "It was on the table. I only saw—"

"I don't mind that you saw it," she says with a shrug, a quick shake of her head. She turns back to the food baskets, continues ripping the cheesecloth into neat squares. I watch her, unsure of what to say.

"It is admirable . . ." I say. "All that you do for the poor."

Her hands work steadily, and she's not looking toward me as she wraps the rolls, one after the other in quick succession. After a moment she speaks. "I follow a different set of commandments than do you and Waldo."

The words land like cold stones. I consider them for a moment, my hand curling the apron string between my fingers. And then I ask: "What do you mean by that?"

Lidian pauses in her work, turning to stare at me. The flesh between her brows ruts into a lone, deep groove. She looks tired. Lidian heaves a sigh and then says: "Your . . . the constant quest for rapture, for experiences larger than yourself . . ." She has a dusting of baking flour on her cheek, but I resist the urge to wipe it off.

She goes on. "*I* am the one who in fact lives my life for something larger than myself. These midnight walks to watch giraffes. To see the sunrise over Walden. Or a butterfly laying eggs—I am the one raising the young of our own species. I am in fact working to make the world a more beautiful and—more important—a more just place. And, well . . ." She throws her hands up, then she turns back to the table, saying nothing more.

She doesn't need to. The words she speaks—and especially the words she *doesn't* speak—have already landed like a blow. I nod once, slowly. I see what she means. Or, at least, how she sees me.

She's here, taking care of her child, giving her energy and her time to the service of the poor. I'm living in her home, staying up late to speak with the men, taking midnight walks with her husband, marveling over the beauty all around us. But in fact, what am I doing to make the world a more beautiful place? I'm nothing more than a siren, in her eyes. Some young, itinerant, unwed and unwelcome annoyance. A disruption to the good and noble work that she, Lidian Emerson, is endeavoring to accomplish in her family and her domestic circle.

"I've finished in here," she says, her tone curt. I see she's wrapped all the rolls. I didn't even manage to do that. "I'll be off to the church," she declares, taking the parcels in her arms. "If you see Waldo, you can tell him I'll be back once I've delivered these. Not that he'll ask."

And with that, she's gone. I stand alone in the kitchen. Stunned, I forget the glass of water I came in search of, and I walk out of the house, back into the garden, meandering until I've reached the grape arbor, the one Thoreau built. A moment later I hear the carriage, and I know that Lidian and Thoreau are riding off toward the church. I remain there alone in a thoughtful, troubled silence.

I'm pierced by what she's just said. By seeing the way Lidian sees me. Rather than my being here in Concord to enjoy the companionship of these rich and deep thinkers, to work on my own pieces, to write and create—Lidian thinks I'm a dilettante. A nuisance. Even a hypocrite.

I'm so lost in my unsettled thoughts that I don't hear him approach, don't notice Waldo until he's standing just beside the arbor, asking me: "What is bothering you?"

My body is coiled so tight that I spring at the sound of his voice. Then I remember myself, and I pull back my shoulders and offer a quick shake of my head. "What makes you say something is bothering me?"

"Margaret." Waldo flashes a rueful grin. "Your face does not hide your feelings. One of the things I love—er . . . *appreciate* about it."

I feel wretched. I know that Lidian's paper, her remarks, are just as much a result of her feelings toward Waldo as toward me. If she felt loved, if she felt secure in her marriage, even *noticed* by her husband, I doubt she would see me in such an unfavorable light.

But still, he is her husband. He belongs here, with her. They have very real impediments between them, to be sure, but they both have a place here. This is the home, the family, that they share together—however fraught or cold the state of things between them may seem. I am the interloper. And worse, I've come to realize that, as seen through Lidian's practical and pious lens, I'm an imposter.

But I don't bring up Lidian to Waldo. It is not my place. That is for them to sort. Instead I voice only the other part of what's bothering me: that I'm living here, enjoying my time and my friendships, but I have nothing, truly, to show for my time with the great Sage of Concord. I have not in fact created anything original or beautiful.

"All I do is read other people's writing." I hear how sour my voice sounds. "Teaching it to children. At best, translating the work of other scholars, other thinkers, other writers. And it's almost entirely the work of *men*, at that."

Waldo listens, saying nothing. I go on: "I long to do something beautiful and entirely new, something of my very own." Something to show Lidian Emerson that I am more than just a dilettante. To show *myself* that I am more than just a dilettante. To show all those who find my passion or my ambitions unnatural—all those who question or judge my choice to work and travel rather than simply wed and give myself up to some husband's kitchen and parlor. My heart clamors in my breast as all these thoughts fly through my mind.

Waldo's reaction, when he finally speaks, surprises me. I've just unleashed a deluge on him, but his response is brief. Just a few words. "Then do it."

I narrow my eyes. "I beg your pardon?"

"You want to do something original?" He offers a quick shrug. "Then do it."

I shift on my feet. "Well, it's not as though—"

"You have the intellect, Margaret. You have thoughts worth writing. So write them. Put pen to paper. Why not?"

"I can think of a number of reasons," I say, my voice low and throaty.

"Such as?"

"My position as a woman, for one," I say. "And the many private burdens . . . duties which have filled my life." Such as earning enough money to provide not only for myself, but also for my mother and siblings. "It is difficult to earn a living in a life that is devoted primarily to thoughts." I swallow, thinking of, but not saying, the many other reasons. I have neither a dead wife's fortune, like Waldo, nor Bronson's utter disregard for the practicalities of life. I don't have an inherited family home and a bevy of unwed sisters ready to tend to me and care for me, as Hawthorne does. As a woman I can't live like Thoreau, earning room and board as an unwed handyman with time enough to write my great thoughts.

I can come here to Bush for brief stays, when I'm invited, but even these weeks are fraught and tense. Emerson is happy to have me as a houseguest, but I'm increasingly certain that his wife is not. Moreover, I have a widowed mother and a brood of younger siblings to provide for, as well as the need to feed myself.

Lidian was right to point out that the activity here is so largely devoted to appreciating beauty and seeking rapture. And I relish my time while I'm here. It is a paradise for thoughts, and it nourishes me like water for my parched soul. But beauty and rapture will not feed me. Thoughts and transcendental experiences will not put firewood on my family's hearth. For all of these reasons, I cannot give myself up to these philosophies, this Concord creed of Transcendentalism, wholeheartedly.

"Take a walk with me," Waldo says, trying to pull me from my brooding. "We do our best thinking when we walk. Let's walk together."

I'm too unsettled to argue, so I groan and then fall into step beside Waldo. We set out down the lane. I'm quiet, and so is he. It's Waldo who eventually breaks the silence. "I have something to tell you, as well."

I throw a sideways glance toward him, noting the knot in his brow. "What is it?"

He looks straight ahead at the lane. "You know the piece I recently published?"

"'The American Scholar,'" I say. "Yes, of course. It was bold and brave. I loved every word of it."

But Waldo frowns at my mention of the title. "Not all have agreed with your views of my work."

"I suppose it's to be expected, Waldo. You are calling on people to think for themselves. People who are in charge, why, of course they would find your rallying cry a bit frightening. The storm will pass."

"I fear you are overly optimistic. Harvard has declared open war on me."

His beloved alma mater. And one of the most powerful institutions in American thought. Harvard was a traditional place, to be sure, founded as a place to produce Puritan clergymen. But they'd always been proud of Ralph Waldo Emerson as one of their own. Until now, apparently. "They have?"

He nods. "Harvard's leadership has declared that I shall never set foot on campus again."

"But . . . that's preposterous."

"Oh, there's more. They've said I'll never speak there again. My work will never be read there again. And they've urged *all* publications—in Boston and beyond—to shun me."

I heave a sigh, absorbing this. It is a blow, indeed, and it would sound foolish to suggest otherwise. Emerson would effectively be blacklisted from American scholarly life and publishing, if this called-for boycott takes root.

We've left the lane and are walking through wooded sunshine now, the shade and light flickering in a dappled patchwork around us. It is a splendid scene. Nevertheless, as beautiful as the world appears, we are both heavy-laden with our troubles.

Waldo goes on: "How dare I state that a true scholar must have self-trust? That man must learn to think for himself?"

"How backward," I declare. And I mean it. "Why, it's the very same message I told my students. How can they critique you when all you've done is call for independent thought?"

"Some of the Boston newspapers are calling me a blasphemer, others are calling me a subversive. Members of the clergy are considering charges against me. Saying I'll never publish again."

I heave an audible exhale, staring at him. When I speak next, my voice is thin. "Oh, Waldo. My friend." I lean forward and take his hand. I give it a squeeze. It's a gesture not of an unmarried woman making an attempt on a married man, but of a friend comforting another friend in a moment of need. And a friend who has also faced the fire of critics.

Lidian was wrong about me—I'm not merely some dilettante and poseur. I truly understand her husband; I understand what Ralph Waldo Emerson hopes to achieve in this place and this moment in time. It's the very same mission I myself feel called to pursue.

"I won't be cowed," Waldo says, and his voice has a defiant edge now. "I must be free and brave. I know that what we are doing here is pure and good. And *needed*. The critics can call us radical Transcendentalists. Heretical mystics. They posit that our aim is to insult religion and threaten the domestic harmonies of the family."

Threaten the domestic harmonies of the family. In that accusation I can see an arrow well fixed on me, as I am the unwed woman in the bunch, the female voice that dares to call for education for girls and equality between the genders. The brazen bluestocking who has eschewed marriage well into her twenties and sought to earn a living by publishing her own work.

"I don't wish to harm a single person," he says. "All I wish to do is heed the call of my own active soul. And encourage others to do the same." Waldo flashes a rueful smile, and I return it. I am heartened by Waldo's fortitude. By his belief in the power of free thought and the importance of fighting for it. If he can be strong, if he can defy Harvard and the newspapers and the clergymen of New England, then I can put aside my own petty injuries over Lidian's judgment. Rather than complaining that I have yet to do anything original, I can cease lamenting my lot and instead I can devote my thoughts and energy to writing, to creating.

. . .

THE NEXT MORNING I decide to dedicate the day to just that, to writing. I'm still working on my long piece on Goethe, and knowing that American readers have not yet been exposed to all of his writings, I'm making my way through translations of his original German *Conversations*. I love Goethe's work, and this feels worthwhile.

I sit down at my desk, only to notice that I cannot find my inkwell. I smile, suspecting little Waldo. I always welcome him into my room, where he likes to scribble notes at my desk. He often appears at my door and looks up at me, his big eyes hopeful as he asks if he can carry letters from my room into his father's study. But now that my inkwell has vanished, I have an idea whose tiny hands may have moved it.

I cross the front hall and knock on Waldo's study door. No answer. The door is ajar, so I peek in, hoping to spot my inkwell. I walk into the empty study, tiptoeing. There, instead, I see a paper and immediately recognize Lidian's "Commandments."

Ah, so she's given them to him. I wonder if he's seen them yet, or if she's left them here for his return. I won't bring it up. It's not my concern. Poor Waldo has enough on his mind, what with the entire intellectual and clerical establishment of New England speaking out against him.

As much as Lidian Emerson loves her husband, I can't help but suspect that her own personal beliefs probably fall somewhere in between my wholehearted support of his radical freethinking and the condemnation of these censorious clergymen.

As I stand in Waldo's study, looking for my inkwell, my eyes travel toward his bookshelves. What a beautiful, rich collection. An entire wall of the leather-bound words of Rousseau, Locke, Voltaire. If only his critics could see what I see—that this is a man who just wants others to think. He's not against learning, not at all. He's against blind adherence. Ralph Waldo Emerson wants others to study, but *also* to search for meaning. To read for more than recitation and rote memorization. To think, to dream, and to *act*.

I close my eyes and breathe in, slowly. This room is so filled with

Waldo's spirit. Just as much as his chestnut trees and his elms. I understand what he is doing, just as he understands me. I know what we have. *But he is not mine,* I remind myself, with a chiding voice in my head. *He never can be.*

And then I hear another voice, this one *not* in my head, and my blood stills in my veins. I blink my eyes open. I turn to see Lidian standing at the threshold of her husband's study, while I stand in it. "Ah, Lidian." I try to sound light, but I succeed only in sounding flustered. "I was looking for . . . my inkwell."

"And I was looking for my husband."

"He's not in here," I say, and I regret the words as soon as I've said them, hearing how silly they sound. I shift on my feet, desperate to leave the room.

"I see that," Lidian replies, not budging from the doorway.

I shrug, force a smile that feels tight.

"I have good news for Waldo." Lidian folds her hands together before her waist. "I could not wait to tell him."

"Oh? That's nice. I'm sure we could all use some good news right now."

"Yes, well, not right now. He'll have to wait. I believe eight or so months." She places her hands slowly to her belly, her eyes locking with mine. I nod once, slowly. She smiles, then looks down with a beatific gaze toward her flat middle. "Little Waldo will be so excited, as well."

"He will be an excellent big brother," I say. I return her smile. "I'm happy for you."

And I am. Of course I am. But I can see from the expression on her face that Lidian doesn't know whether to believe me. And I can also see that my welcome in Concord, in her home, has run its course.

Chapter Seventeen

Groton
Fall 1838

WITH THE FUNDS I HAVE MANAGED TO SQUIRREL away from my tutoring and my year of teaching at the Greene Street School, and with Mother's assurance that we will find a way to manage on her annual allowance and my savings, I give myself permission, for the first time ever, to be merely a writer. *Merely* a writer. A full-time writer.

The project is one I've been working on for some time, the full-length English translation of *Conversations with Goethe*. I have never had the time to see it through. Now I throw myself fully into the venture with the goal of producing a finished manuscript that I can publish to become a book. My very own book.

To save money, I move back in with Mother and my siblings, into the cramped farmhouse in Groton. It's not all bad. I've been lonely so often in recent years, but being with my family allows me to enjoy their companionship as I haven't had the chance to do in so long. I sleep in my childhood bedroom, in my narrow wooden bed, and I find sleep easier than I have in many months. In the early mornings I bundle my younger siblings under piles of scarves and cloaks and bring them outside to milk the cow. On snowy days we don snowshoes and go tromping through the woods. In the evenings I play the old piano that Father bought for me when I was a girl, while Mother and I sing together.

The Christmas season comes and the earth locks in under the hard, crispy frost. My youngest sister and brother, Ellen and Richard, are in desperate need of education. We cannot afford to pay for a formal school, so it falls to me to take them in hand, which I willingly do. We debate man's free will through the words of Milton. We consider heredity through the words of Chaucer and coming-of-age through the words of Shakespeare.

Less pleasant is the task that falls to me from my father, whose papers have never been sorted by my mother, even though he's now been gone for years. As agreeable as I've found certain aspects of being home, this is not a chore that brings me joy.

I'm in Father's study, wrestling with his ghost, when Mother comes to find me one cold evening. A single candle casts only a dim, shadowed light over the disordered space. My eyes are sore. Mother enters, watching me work, her shawl hugged tight around her narrow shoulders. After a while, she speaks: "I am glad that you've found a bit of a reprieve here."

I look up. It's an odd thing to say in that moment, considering the sprawl of Father's tedious papers that surrounds me. But, overall, she is correct. This home has been far more comfortable than a rented room in a boardinghouse. And having the time and space to write, and the absence of the long walks through the bitter winter to and from a classroom, *has* offered me a reprieve.

"Thank you, Mother." And I needed this. I've made good progress on my Goethe book, and I think my time with my siblings has been as beneficial for them as it has been cheering to me. We've managed, even without my bringing in a salary.

When Mother exhales, I see the mist of her breath. I'm not prepared for the blow that her words bring when she says: "But we can't keep this place."

Her tired eyes flicker in the shadows. She goes on: "The farm. The home. It exceeds my annual allowance."

My stomach tightens. "So, what does that mean?" But I already know what her answer will be. She confirms my suspicions with her response: "We have to sell."

The words pierce me. In spite of all I've done, the thankless work for Bronson, the exhausting schedule in Providence. My tutoring work. My race to finish this book on Goethe. None of it was enough. "When?"

"As soon as the earth thaws," Mother answers. "We must be out by spring."

I nod, looking back down at the piles before me. Father's papers. His personal items. This won't be the only room that needs packing up. I breathe out slowly, the fatigue pulling on my frame like a too-heavy cloak. I've had my reprieve. I stole this brief moment in time. But now the time is up.

THERE'S MUCH TO be done before we can sell. There is packing: clothing, linens, kitchenware. Desperate for funds, we decide to sell the furniture before the farmhouse. We put anything of value up for auction—including my piano, all of our beautiful books, the nicer pieces of furniture, my bed. Mother will settle in a rental home, and we'll find a place with furniture. All that we can part with must now be sold for cash.

In the meantime, the most important matter I must take care of is the completion of my book. I need the money that might come from its publication. We all need the money. The sale of the farm will allow Mother to rent elsewhere for now, but what about going forward?

I labor that whole winter as the days lengthen and the sound of birdsong returns. Usually I look forward to the turning of winter, to the promising signs of the coming thaw. But now it is my deadline. *We must be out by spring*, Mother has declared. Therefore, I must be done with my book by spring. Before I am without a home.

I devote every hour that I can spare to my work. I develop chilblains from writing in the frigid nighttime hours, when firewood is a luxury we cannot afford and I can squander only the dull light of a lone candle. One hundred pages, then two hundred. Black ink stains cover the angry red and violet sores on my hands. I take a break only for the household chores—the milking of the cow, the gathering of the eggs. Then it's back to work. Three hundred pages and then four hundred. My head aches from the strain on my eyes, and my shoulders feel like they could curl in on each other.

And then, I've done it. I've completed my book. I've translated Goethe's *Conversations* and written my own preface and conclusion to the manuscript. The papers pile up, and as I look at the stack, I see that they could in fact make a book. My very first book.

Spring comes, the earth ripens into colorful fullness once more, and it is May, the day of my birthday. The final year of my twenties. I wrap a cord of twine around the thick pile of my manuscript and prepare it for the post, thinking: *Nothing would make a better gift than to see these pages turned into a book.*

At Waldo's insistence, I will be sending my work to his friend and publisher, a Mr. George Ripley, who has expressed his interest in seeing my manuscript. Though Mr. Ripley knows who I am, I sign my work *M. Fuller.* I frown as I do so, but I know it must be done, so that readers won't take offense or be put off entirely by the thought of a book written by a woman.

M. Fuller. It will be my work, my creation, even if the world cannot yet know my name. If Mr. Ripley accepts this work, I will be a published writer. I will have a book, and perhaps even a check. And with that, I hope, I will have a new freedom to travel into the world. And perhaps, someday, the power to change that world.

Chapter Eighteen

Concord
Summer 1839

"LOOK! OVER THERE. IT'S A VIXEN."
My eyes follow the direction of Thoreau's finger, and I see a flash of orange, just a fleeting streak against a backdrop of wild green.

"I saw her!" Louisa squeals in delight, and Thoreau immediately presses his finger to his lips, reminding her of the need for quiet.

"What is she doing?" I ask in a whisper, looking for the mother fox.

"Hunting." Thoreau narrows his eyes, fixing them on the thick wall of undergrowth. "Her little fox kits are getting bigger, and hungrier."

And then right before us, between the skunk cabbage and the river birches, we catch another glint of amber. The mother fox darts like a flash and then she's gone. "Ah, she's smelled us. Or seen us. She's off now," Thoreau says, his quiet voice tinged with admiration. As I stare at him, I get the suspicion that, were it not for Louy's and my presence here in the forest, the vixen might have strolled right up to him, even let him scratch her behind the ears, so at home is Henry David Thoreau in this wild wood.

"Good for her," says Louisa, rising from her crouch. "If I'm ever a mother, I hope to be like a vixen. Still able to be out in the world."

I exchange a glance with Thoreau and then look to Louy, studying her for a moment. I can't help but think of her mother. Abba Alcott must be exhausted in both body and spirit, and I cannot decide whether she's a saint, or a martyr who facilitates much of her own torture.

My own mother is in much less dire straits, now that we've sold the Groton farm and she's settled in a modest rental in Jamaica Plain. With the sales from my book, I'm able to send her some money each month, and I even have enough left over to rent a small room of my own in Boston once more, where I will soon be moving in order to apply myself to the writing and publication of my next book.

But first, a brief moment of joyful respite: summer in Concord. I was invited by the Emersons, in between my travels from Mother's rental in Jamaica Plain to my own rental in Boston, to stop over for a stay. When pressed, Waldo assured me that Lidian, now happily delivered of her second healthy baby, a little girl named Ellen, had given her blessing for my visit. And so I accepted the invitation. It was precisely what my spirit needed.

Here, I'm spending as much time as I can out of doors. Lidian, now with two little ones, is so preoccupied that I try to keep out of her way. I pass much of my time with Louisa May and her beloved "Mr. Thoreau." And Thoreau is never lacking in ideas for some country jaunt. We pick blueberries and we scout for birds. He takes us floating on his *Musketaquid* down the river. Today it is columbines we are on a mission to gather.

My soul is enlivened by the out-of-doors adventures, by the sunshine, by the clean air and greenery, and very much by the lively company. I'm riding high from the publication of *Conversations*, from the success the book is enjoying, and even the warm praise it has won from my host. "It was a gift to our nation," Waldo declared upon my arrival at Bush, proudly brandishing his copy of my book in greeting.

"You're the first writer to bring Goethe to our American readers. Now you must speed the pen to make more. You are a writer, Margaret Fuller. Enough of the self-doubts and quandaries." I appreciated Waldo's hearty support. Even the suggestion he made to push my success further: "Next you should write a full biography of Goethe, so that Americans can understand the man behind the work."

The task, though intriguing—and one I myself had considered—struck me as daunting when Waldo suggested it. "Why do you hesitate?" he asked, seeing my doubt.

"I fear such an undertaking might be beyond my capabilities."

"But why would you fall short?"

"I don't know . . . what if . . ." The usual self-doubts skittered around in my mind.

"Margaret, please." Waldo looked at me like a patient but exacting schoolmaster. "You could not possibly write a bad book, or even one dull page."

So, that's what I'm spending the summer doing. I'm working on my next book and I'm enjoying this small band of companions who have come to feel like my second family. Here, in Concord, in this place where I come in the liminal moments of my life, the place where I feel most fully alive.

We settle into a harmonious rhythm that summer. In the mornings, after breakfast, I work. In the afternoons I walk to the river or out to Walden. Waldo is busy, too. Now that he's officially banned by the New England intellectual establishment—Harvard, the Boston newspapers, the unforgiving leaders of the clergy—he seems possessed by some feverish need to make his own way. To prove that he needs neither the patronage nor the permission of the fusty old guard.

We all seem to be giving one another space this summer. I don't wish to upset Lidian. I wish to respect her place as Waldo's wife, as the lady of the house. Waldo's pride in my book, his urgings that I hasten to write a second, they ring with a sort of paternal pride, that of a mentor and wise friend. For as much time as we've spent, the pair of us, speaking about the Greek ideals and the gods, I can say that our relationship now feels platonic. It's for the best.

I'm thinking on all of these things as Thoreau, Louy, and I traipse through the woods, gathering columbines. Louisa interrupts my reverie when she declares she'd like to go hunt for some wild blueberries deeper in the forest. Thoreau glances to me, lifting an eyebrow.

"You go with her," I say.

"And you?"

"I'll stay here," I answer him. I wish to remain by the river, in the sunshine.

"You're certain?" Thoreau asks.

"I know my way home." I throw him a reassuring smile. And the pair of them are off, Thoreau whistling like a bobolink as they go. I stand alone and look out over the river, breathing deep of the clean, loamy air. There is a massive boulder closer to the Old Manse that I've come to think of as my favorite spot. It's often my destination when I take my afternoon walks to the river, as I like to sit atop its warm surface and soak up the full sunlight.

I go there now and settle atop my perch, right beside the water. Entirely alone, I slip off my shoes and stretch out like a most happy lizard in the nourishing light. I pluck the pins from my hair and allow my long, dark waves to tumble around my face, over my shoulders. I feel my skin ripple ever so gently as a breeze skitters over me, and then the goose bumps calm as the gentle sunshine seeps into me. I roll up my sleeves and roll down my stockings, and feel the warmth all over my body. *We are all one, under one sun.* It's something Waldo, Thoreau, and I have repeated, in some form or another, so many times.

I give thanks for the sun, storing up this golden warmth for the winter that I know must inevitably return. For now, I tell myself, it is summer. I close my eyes and bask in this fact, in this moment. I'm in such a state of calm, so deep in peaceful and free thought, that I don't realize that I'm not alone—not until I hear a familiar voice close by. "Do mine own eyes behold a sea nymph, right here on the Concord River?"

I startle, opening my eyes, and then I blink, dazed by the bright and direct sunshine. I scramble up to a seated position, rearranging my skirts, unfurling my sleeves. Someone has seen far too much of my flesh. And then I see the pair of them, and I smile, in spite of myself. Nathaniel Hawthorne stands on the riverbank beside Waldo. I answer: "If I'm the sea nymph, then you are . . . ?"

Hawthorne stuffs a hand into his pocket, considering my question a moment, then he answers: "I suppose in this, I am Odysseus. And you are thoroughly distracting me on my journey."

He kicks off his shoes, then leans down to peel off his socks.

When he hitches his trousers up to his knees I realize that he might actually intend to step into the water. "I'll consent to be detained on your island for a period of fleeting but delicious exile, if you'll consent to be my Circe." Now Hawthorne is splashing in the river around me, leaving Waldo on the dry shore. I laugh, dangling my own legs over the rock and dipping my bare feet into the water. Hawthorne lowers his hands into the river, then flicks a small spray of water in my direction, prompting me to laugh in surprised delight as the cool drops land on my sun-warmed skin. It feels like we are a pair of naughty youngsters beside Waldo, our watchful and disapproving chaperone.

"So I'm Circe, the witch of Aeaea, then?" I scoot to the side of the boulder to make room for Hawthorne, who is splashing toward me. "I'll accept that, as long as you don't call me Medusa or Charybdis."

Hawthorne clambers up onto my boulder and leans toward me. "Hello, Miss Fuller."

"Hello, Mr. Hawthorne." Our eyes lock, and I feel that familiar tremor that always comes when I stare into those green eyes. I look away, glancing out over the river, but I can feel how close his body is to mine. "I didn't realize you had returned to Concord," I say, managing a breezy tone.

"I've only just arrived. I'll be staying out at the farm again. And you are in residence at Bush?"

"While they will have me," I reply.

"Well, if Margaret is our sea nymph and Hawthorne is our Odysseus, then I'm Aeneas," Waldo calls out, still remaining on dry land. "And I must be off to found new empires. Hawthorne, I thought you wanted to come see about the Old Manse?"

"I do!" Hawthorne looks dolefully toward Waldo, then back to me. "You present entirely too distracting and enticing a tableau here, Margaret, atop your rock on the river. But I do have an appointment with Waldo at the Old Manse."

"Oh? That sounds intriguing," I say, throwing him a sideways glance.

"He wants to convince me to rent the place."

"Well, then, that *is* intriguing."

"I'll come by Bush later. To see you." Hawthorne's eyes slide downward now, toward my shoulders, my bare neck, then to the wild sight of my unpinned hair, the dark waves loose and catching the sunlight. I resist the urge to fidget under the intensity of his gaze, to sweep my hair back into its more modest, appropriate chignon. My cheeks have gone warm and rosy, and I know full well that this sudden flush is due to more than simply the sunshine.

A sigh, and then Hawthorne slowly slides his body away from mine, slipping off the boulder and loping up the riverbank, his shoes and socks in his hands. He turns back, giving me one final wave. I return it, and then he and Waldo are off.

Alone once more, I settle back down on top of my rock, shutting my eyes, savoring the sunshine as I did earlier. But unlike earlier, the feelings of calm and placid contentment are entirely gone, replaced now with an agitated feeling similar to that of some deep and gnawing hunger.

LATER, BACK AT Bush, I sit alone with Waldo in the parlor. I'm being a quiet post-dinner companion, and I know it. It's because I am thinking of Nathaniel Hawthorne. Are these feelings that I have for him of a romantic sort? I am in a muddle. I cannot deny the frisson that ripples through me whenever I see Nathaniel. The way my nerves coil when he looks at me—and oh, the way he looks at me. Those green eyes like hot, bright embers. The way he says my name.

I've never had a formal suitor. A gentleman caller who made plain his intention to court me. Is that what is happening now between Nathaniel and me? My mind can puzzle out Goethe in the original German, but with these matters of the heart, I feel as though I am grasping beyond my depth.

"How was your visit to the Old Manse?" I ask, masking—I hope—just how agitated I am.

"It was fine," Waldo says. He's looking into the fireplace. "Nathaniel seems eager to take it. Of course he can't afford it, so I'll likely loan him the funds."

This strikes me as odd. "Hasn't he been writing these past years?"

"Oh, he hasn't earned enough for a home yet. Not a home the size of the Old Manse. But I am willing to bridge the gap, until he can afford it on his own."

I sit back in my armchair, ruminating on this. I know Waldo has helped Bronson Alcott with rent and other expenses on multiple occasions. Thoreau lives here at Bush on Waldo's generosity. Now Waldo appears willing to support Hawthorne in renting the Old Manse. Is that all I need to do—simply to ask Waldo? And I may stay here in Concord, as well?

No. I hear the voice in my mind, clear and decisive. No, I cannot. I would not. For two reasons. The first is my pride: I would not wish to live entirely dependent on someone else's provision. What if Waldo and I were to fall out? Or Lidian and I? It would create an imbalance in our friendship, a debt I would carry with me at all times and in all interactions. No, I'd much rather work and live within my own means in order to maintain the self-respect and dignity of my own independence. It is a promise I made to myself long ago.

And the second reason, I bristle to acknowledge, is that I am a woman. Nathaniel Hawthorne may not yet be able to afford the Old Manse on his own, but he is acknowledged as a young man of talent, a promising writer, and thus the assumption is that he should have a household of his own. His money will come in time. And until then, Waldo is happy—as he said—to bridge the gap.

I am a woman, and a single woman at that. Though I might be every bit as talented, though I *know* I am every bit as hardworking, no one assumes that it is my right to have a household of my own. The common view would be that I should marry, and then I may live in my husband's household. But it would be presumptuous— even unnatural—for me to brazenly seek money from a wealthier friend like Waldo in order to settle in a grand home all by myself.

"He'll need a house of his own soon enough." Waldo's words cut short my musings. Perhaps he has even guessed my thoughts. I look back to my friend, and he goes on, saying, "He'll soon be going to the executioner."

This I was not expecting. I swallow, feeling a catch in my throat. I guess Waldo's meaning, and I raise a brow. "Marriage?"

"Yes."

"You think so?"

Waldo nods.

My heart is thumping. Nathaniel Hawthorne, getting married? "Who?" I ask.

I am glad I am sitting, because what I hear next might have knocked me off balance, had I been standing.

"Sophia," Waldo answers. "Miss Peabody."

The sickly younger sister of Eliza Peabody? The pale, retiring, mercury-poisoned invalid? But I don't say any of that aloud; instead I ask only: "Nathaniel Hawthorne is to be married to Sophia Peabody?"

"Yes," Waldo says, tapping the arm of his chair. "Of course I think a much more exciting choice would have been Eliza. And of course he will always carry a torch . . . or, however you wish to call it, an *infatuation*, for you."

I'm certain that now I've gone pale as birch bark, and Waldo must see my disquiet. "Come now, Margaret. Surely you've known. Nathaniel has always been taken with you. But Sophia . . . well, we know what Sophia is like. I suppose . . . if you and Nathaniel, well—it would mean one too many bright stars in the Hawthorne constellation."

I glance toward the fire so that he can't read my thoughts, though I'm sure he's guessed them already. A man like Nathaniel Hawthorne may be infatuated with me. He may love to hitch up his trousers and splash into the river to join me in the sunshine on a rock, calling me his sea nymph, staring unashamedly at my loose hair, my bare shoulders and neck.

But a man like Nathaniel Hawthorne is never going to marry me. Margaret Fuller. What did my father call me? *The Much that always wants More.* I am a woman who is too unapologetic in my desire to write, to think, to work. I am a woman who is unafraid to speak with the men and support my own life. I want too much.

Waldo is looking at me, but I keep my eyes determinedly turned away. I can't keep a mask on my face when my thoughts surge like this, and Waldo, knowing me as he does, would likely be able to read all my inner questions, such as: *Shall I ever have a partner? A family of my own?* Just because I am not married, it does not mean I don't long for love and union as others do. In fact, the total opposite is true; I yearn for a relationship where I can know the other's soul and feel that my soul is known, as well. But is there a man in this world who can offer that to me? A man for whom I won't be too much?

Waldo allows me to remain silent, at least in voice, and for that I am grateful. After a few moments I hear the clock strike on the nearby mantel, and it reminds me of the fact, the immutable fact, that my time here can only ever be brief. That my stay in Concord is just what Hawthorne teasingly called it today, on the river. A *fleeting but delicious exile.* Bush can never be my home, just as neither Waldo nor Hawthorne will ever be my husband.

I need something more. Something else to pour myself into—my passion, my mind, my energy. And now I understand that I must leave Concord in order to find it.

PART 3

Chapter Nineteen

Boston
Fall 1839

"YOU KNOW IT'S NOT LEGAL, DON'T YOU?" MOTHER is looking at me with her features stitched tight, and I can hear the worry dripping from her words. This irritates me.

"What?" I arch an eyebrow, affecting an air of casual indifference.

Mother frowns. And then, as if the words are too offensive to even speak aloud, she tips toward me and whispers, "For a lady to be *paid* for . . . you know, public speaking."

"Mother." I take her hand in mine. "I'm not lecturing from a podium in some lyceum. I'm merely conversing in a comfortable room . . . with my friends."

"That's exactly it," Eliza Peabody interjects, not the least bit daunted by my mother, and all too willing to come to my defense.

"But where shall you find such a comfortable room? With enough space?" Mother glances around at my own cramped quarters, little more than a garret, really, that I rent on the top floor of a boardinghouse in Boston. I sigh. She does have a point. While the room is perfectly fine for me, more comfortable than past lodgings I've had, outfitted with a stove and a window that allows in pleasant afternoon sunlight, I can barely fit my two visitors in here for this afternoon tea; it would hardly be spacious enough to host the lively salon I am envisioning.

But I'm spared from having to admit that. "She'll have free use of my place," Eliza declares, placing her teacup down and offering a decisive nod. "At Chauncey Place. It's a perfect setting—an easy walk from the Common, in the center of town. I have space enough."

I look to my friend, darling Eliza, my features lifting in delight and then appreciation. Mother seems less sure of the idea. "You're really going to pursue this, Margaret, dear?"

I turn from my friend, an outspoken champion of women across Boston, and look toward my mother, her face lined with the many cares of her life, framed by her thinning gray hair. I soften my tone as I answer: "I really am, Mother. For women. There will be nothing indecent or improper about it, I promise you. We will be gathering to ask questions. We will strive to stretch our minds."

"But, my dear . . ." Mother glances into her teacup. "It's not . . . that's not something that is done."

"And that's precisely why I must do it," I reply, refusing to be discouraged by her reluctance. In fact, I feel more fortified in the face of her maternal concern and dissuasion. "Why should women not be allowed to think, as men do? To learn, to ask, to speak? Are our minds any less capable? Any less worthy?"

"Hear, hear," murmurs Eliza in enthusiastic support.

I go on: "We will take up the great questions that far too few have deemed fit to ask us: What are we born to do? How shall we do it?"

Mother shifts in her seat, rearranging the folds of her ample skirt. "Do you think . . . only, do you not worry . . . that perhaps you might . . . offend people?"

I look at Mother, tilting my head to the side. I'm no longer irritated by her genuine care, her questions; I'm saddened by them. And I'm affirmed in my decision as I answer: "If a thinking woman is offensive, then yes, I might offend a number of people. And I'll be happy to do so."

I DO NOTHING by half measures, and so I throw myself into this exciting new venture of a ladies' salon with all the pluck and enthusiasm at my disposal. For years now I've longed to pour myself into something larger than myself, something that will allow me to think and create and grow, and now I cannot wait to share this idea with other like-minded women. I'll open up twenty-five spots, I decide. Women only. I'll charge them each ten dollars and plan for a thirteen-week series of Conversations.

"It's a steep price, I won't deny that," Eliza says when I meet her for luncheon in her spacious apartment to survey the space and plan out the program for our first meeting. "Ten dollars is no nominal fee."

"And yet it's far less than what men charge for their own conversations," I answer. "Anyway, it *should* be more than a nominal fee. For a woman to be able to form and then express her own thoughts—what could be a more worthy investment? And besides, these women can afford it."

And they can; my participants will likely be the wives, sisters, and daughters of Boston's upper crust. This won't cost them more than their usual outings to the dressmaker, or a lineup of new gloves and shoes for the season. It's only a shame that most of them can't earn the money for my conversation series themselves. But these meetings will put them one step closer to the day when that might be an option for us all.

Let people pinch their brows over my exorbitant fee—I know that my ten dollars is far below the fifteen that Waldo is charging for his own series of Conversations in Boston this autumn. People barely batted an eye when he announced his price. And I guarantee no man, not even Ralph Waldo Emerson, is working as hard as I am to make sure that a salon is worthwhile and enriching for those who attend. Yes, these women can afford it indeed, and it's high time that they—and their male patrons—see the female mind as worthy of the investment.

I settle on Wednesday mornings, because I know that Waldo has scheduled his salon series for Wednesday evenings this fall, and this way we can support each other's efforts, as we will likely be drawing from a very similar pool—me from the wives and daughters, Waldo from the husbands and fathers.

The morning of my first meeting arrives. I dress with care, selecting a sensible poplin of dark purple, a cream-colored fichu tied around my shoulders. I pull my dark hair back into a modest bun. I glance at the clock as I finish my toilette: twenty-five fine ladies across Boston are now dressing for the same reason, to attend my first conversation.

I'm barely hungry for breakfast, since my stomach feels tangled in knots. As I sip my coffee I look down over my list of registered attendees. Mary Jane Quincy, whose husband surely nurtures political aspirations like the rest of the Quincy-Adams clan. Sally Gardner, from an old, prominent New England family, her father claiming some distant connection to a British peer. Mary Greeley, wife of the celebrated New York newspaperman Horace Greeley. I glance at this one twice, crinkling my face in confusion; does this mean that Mrs. Greeley is planning to make a weekly trip up from New York, just to attend my Conversations? I carry on reading: Elizabeth Cady Stanton, a name with which I'm not familiar. A Mary Adams, surely related to our former presidents. There's a Hosmer on the list, a name splashed across New England with streets and buildings celebrating her male antecedents from the American Revolution. A Mrs. Priscilla Henley, wife to a prominent attorney who manages the estates of some of Boston's wealthiest families. Twenty-five names—I've managed to fill each spot and even had to open a waiting list. I'm relieved—and thrilled—that my suspicions were correct, that there are indeed twenty-five women out there willing to pay and work to expand their minds.

My aim is to encourage these women not only to think, but also to feel and grow and support one another. A sisterhood, a chance to find allies and friends as we put aside this notion that we must always behave as the gentler sex. But in spite of the feelings of friendship I intend to foster, I will not mince my words. The first topic I've settled on is deficiencies in female education. And I won't be giving a lecture. Not only because it's forbidden for a lady to earn money by public speaking—as Mother has reminded me on more than one occasion—but also because it's not the format that will suit my purposes. I wish to host thirteen true conversations, not one-sided lectures. "*I* already know how to speak," I've told Eliza. "The aim of this is to encourage others to do the same."

. . .

"FAIR WARNING, LADIES, there shall be no passive listening here." I study the gathering of women as they crowd into Eliza's gracious parlor, filling the space with their wide skirts and beribboned hats. They clutch their teacups and take their seats with prim upright postures, looking to me, reminding me of my pupils in the classroom on our first day together.

"We shall have a casual and natural format," I go on, "but each one of you will be called upon to throw your hat into the ring." Their eyes dart about nervously; their spines straighten even more under their tight-laced corsets. Eliza, who has been serving tea in the back of the salon, strides to the front now, a full cup perched on the porcelain saucer in her hands. She selects a seat on the empty settee right before me, fixing me with an attentive stare, a decisive nod. She's ready. So am I.

"And now, we begin." I start with a general, sweeping idea for the first week: the topic of educating females. I want the ladies to think on any assumptions or prejudices they might be bringing to the conversation. I declare, boldly, and can see the shock on some of their faces as I state: "I don't believe we should discourage the 'feminine' in a man, nor should we rail against the 'masculine' in a girl."

Murmurs of discomfort ripple across the room. Mrs. Quincy's eyes widen with alarm. Mrs. Adams stares at me with evident skepticism as Mrs. Henley clears her throat. I lock eyes with Eliza and my friend gives me a wink, steeling me to go on. And I realize, in that moment, just how sheltered—how very privileged—I've been in my conversations with people like Waldo and Thoreau, even Hawthorne and Alcott. People who are willing to entertain the idea that a woman has as much right to think and learn as a man does. My friends in Concord may agree with me, but they are the exception.

Here, in this Boston parlor, even among women bold and defiant enough to enroll in my series, a gathered crowd cannot accept this premise outright, that women need not be treated as different from—and beneath—men. I have much work to do.

I carry on, as though I'm making a first set of footprints into deep, unyielding snow: "Women need not be only sentimental, governed solely by feelings. Told that they are the docile and tender helpers of the men in their spheres. Women can *think*. Why, a woman has a right to judge. Each one of you in here has a right to consult not only your heart, but your mind, as well."

My ladies are sitting rigid in their chairs, some even leaning back, as if to put distance between themselves and my radical ideas. And yet some, I notice, with a twinge of satisfaction, are leaning forward. Angling toward my words like plants toward the sunshine, absorbing my meaning, perhaps even agreeing with me.

AT THE NEXT meeting I take up the topic of the Greeks. I am eager to begin here, to show the women that great thinkers of the past dared to look at the masculine and the feminine in ways entirely different from our staid New England beliefs: that the ancients saw power and potency in not only their male gods but their female goddesses, as well.

"Look at the character of Atalanta," I declare, sitting before the group. "She told her father she did not wish to be married off, and she bested the physical strength of all the men in order to prove her own."

I hear a rasping noise, like a small cough, and my eyes fly toward the sound. Mrs. Henley sits toward the back of the salon, her body swathed in a gown of rich emerald green, her face pinched in a look of apparent discomfort. "Is everything all right, Mrs. Henley?"

She lowers her teacup to the small table at her side, clasping and then unclasping her hands in her lap.

"Would you like to speak on the topic?" I ask, offering an encouraging nod.

And then, with unsmiling lips, she says, "I would not wish to interrupt."

"It's not an interruption at all, Mrs. Henley. I would relish the opportunity to hear from you. As this is intended to be a conversation, your voice is most welcome, as are all of yours," I say, my eyes sweeping the crowded salon.

Mrs. Henley rearranges herself in her seat, her frothy skirt swishing against the plush upholstery. And then, with eyes slightly narrowed, she says: "I only wonder, Miss Fuller . . ." Am I imagining it, or does she hit the word "Miss" with a noticeable emphasis, as if to remind me, and all in this room, that I am unwed? And then, taking her teacup back into her hands, Mrs. Henley asks: "Is it not vulgar to speak about the pagan Greeks as though they have something we ought to emulate?" She throws a pointed look toward Mrs. Quincy, and then toward Mrs. Adams, as ripples of noise skitter across the room.

I take the thought that Mrs. Henley has just lobbed and run with it, raising my arms. "Ah, yes, the Greeks. The pagan Greeks. I urge you all to consider the fact that the Greeks held up Athena as the goddess of wisdom, rather than some male figure." My gaze touches every pair of eyes in the salon in turn as I forge ahead. "Consider also that the Romans prayed to Minerva as their goddess of the arts and justice, and even war. And I ask you to reflect on the fact that Venus was so much more than the beautiful temptress we speak of today, that in fact she also presided over prosperity and even victory, that her bloodline founded Rome through her son Aeneas. Even the great Julius Caesar claimed the goddess Venus as his ancestor in order to bolster his authority."

Mrs. Henley's features look even more pinched now, but I keep my own face earnest and open as I speak to the crowded room. "Let us also consider the fact that men in our present-day society look to the ancients for examples of the highest achievements in law and architecture and philosophy and enlightened government. Even theater and music and the arts."

The side whispers have stopped. I continue: "The ancients knew that their women held power over the battlefield, over the choices of the individual, even on the ground of the Roman Forum. But we women today are not permitted to look to the examples of the many strong women from within their stories and culture?"

The room is now draped in alert and attentive silence. I draw in a deep breath and carry on. "We do a great disservice to all people, male *and* female, when we relegate a lady's talents only to the hearth and the home," I declare. "The question was one of vulgarity.

We have established that the Greeks are considered, in so many areas, to be the opposite of vulgar. In fact, they are seen as the arbiters of high thinking and achievement.

"Well, then, is it *vulgar* for a woman to lead today? To think for herself? To learn? To live up to the talents with which she was born?" I pause for a moment, drawing in another deep breath. And then, looking out over the room full of women, I say: "I am not going to tell any woman in this room what she ought to think. I ask only that you not allow any man—any person—to do that for you, either. And I very much hope that, after our weeks together, each one of you will have the desire to answer these questions for yourself."

AT OUR THIRD meeting I bring up the idea of character, and how the choices that we make define our character, and therefore, our destiny. "How, then, can we ever claim that to be passive and meek is the right path for a woman?"

Sometimes I have my ladies prepare written thoughts beforehand, as I find that this helps them to feel more confident in sharing. I like to be spontaneous, and I want to encourage them to think with agility and flexibility, but I also recognize that I've been practicing since the age of five, at Father's knee. For most of these women, it is different; I am shaking them from years of conditioning and the comfort that they seem to find in quietude and self-effacement. If preparation and some work beforehand help them to stride into my salon feeling more assured, more willing to share their thoughts and ideas, then so be it.

We do not always reach a consensus. And sometimes our hour is up with more of the women disagreeing with me than otherwise, but I want them to know that is not a problem. As women, we should feel comfortable expressing ourselves, even disagreeing with others. We are entitled, each one of us, to our own thoughts and opinions. We need not fear that it is unseemly to disagree or hold to a conviction of our own. We must learn to be comfortable in debate and discourse. We must shake off these shackles that are placed upon us by those who say a woman's only job is to make a man feel respected and affirmed. What of our own self-respect? What of the affirmation of our own thoughts and characters?

The weeks pass, and I see my companions growing more comfortable in our gatherings. I see their confidence unfurling, like springtime buds ripening under the nurturing forces of sunshine and fertile soil. I can hear it in the way their voices are less wobbly, in the manner in which they meet one another's eyes. They are learning to speak, to react. To *think*.

Each Wednesday they come, trooping into Eliza's parlor. While in the first weeks so many of them would cluster toward the rear of the room, looking as if they'd like to seep backward into the walls, many of them now opt for the chairs and sofas closer to where I sit.

Autumn ushers in cooler winds and the changing colors of the leaves. Their late-summer dresses and light shawls make way for thicker wool gowns and fur-lined cloaks. And then, somehow, twelve weeks have passed. On our thirteenth week I sit before them with one final question: What is inspiration?

I've asked each woman to prepare her own essay on what inspiration means to her, and now each of them will share how and where she finds inspiration in her own life. I wish to send them out into this world, at the conclusion of our meetings, with a determination to catch that inspiration. To keep thinking and questioning and talking.

We each take our turn reading aloud. We each comment on the thoughts of the others. I notice, with a deep feeling of satisfaction, just how much more confident and thoughtful they have become. "It is as if we've trained together, ladies, and now you are all fit to run a race. Atalanta herself would approve," I declare. To my delight, twenty-five faces smile, understanding my meaning.

Goodness, I think to myself, *if thirteen weeks in a parlor can bring this much improvement to the confidence of a woman, how formidable would we ladies be if we were entitled, as men are, to four whole years in the nation's universities? If only the men would let us in. Why, we'd be unstoppable. But perhaps that's precisely why we aren't allowed.*

At the end of our final meeting, after all of my ladies have read from their essays, Mrs. Greeley raises her hand. I call on her. "Yes?"

Mrs. Greeley is a stout woman, with a strong voice and even

stronger opinions. She has always sat close to the front of the room, and she speaks loudly now as she declares: "Miss Fuller, I must admit something: I was hesitant to come. It was no easy trip for me to manage from New York each week. But it was my Horace who encouraged me to do it. 'The Most Well-Read Person in America,' that's what he called you. And so I came, that first week, to try it out. And I loved it. So I came back. And then I came back again. And now I'm devastated that it is over. Your series has been a rare gift for us all, intellectually and morally."

The lady seated beside her, Mrs. Henley, pipes up now: "I had my reservations at first, Miss Fuller. To venerate the pagan Greeks as you do . . ."

I can't help but smile at Mrs. Henley as she goes on. "I worried that when I returned home, if I were to tell my husband what you had said, he'd tell me it was most indecent. But now I see that you were showing us that we are allowed to think in new ways. To think for ourselves. To open the book of life, and read for ourselves. And so, I'm most grateful to you for expanding my mind and my sensibilities."

"Too true!" Mrs. Greeley leans forward in her seat. "You told us in the beginning, Miss Fuller, that a genius is one capable of inventing, someone who creates something entirely original and new. I feel that's what you've done here. And so, won't you please tell us when you'll be scheduling your next session?"

Chapter Twenty

"HOW CAN I COMPETE WITH YOU, MARGARET Fuller?" Emerson sits in the ground-floor parlor of my boardinghouse the next day, the morning after both he and I have given our final talks.

I was pleasantly surprised by his appearance this morning, but surprised just the same. Now we sit across from each other, beside the fire, drinking coffee. Christmas is just a few weeks away and the room is chilly, as outside a light snow is falling, sugaring the windowpanes with thin flecks of white.

"But, Waldo," I reply, "I was not aware there was any competition between us?"

He stirs his coffee and looks at me. "I gave my talks the same day as yours, but I have no illusions—too many of my gentlemen have told me that yours were more entertaining. The husbands were raving each Wednesday evening, telling me that their wives would come home enthralled by you."

I lower my eyes in a gesture of modesty, even as I thrill to hear this—that the wives of some of Boston's most educated and powerful gentlemen are raving about me. That they found the venture as edifying as I did. "It is affirming to hear that my series was so well received."

Waldo stares at me a long moment. "Yes. I'd say it was." Then he lowers his cup, patting down his trousers as he goes on: "So I've decided, rather than try to compete, I'll instead attempt to convince you to join forces with me."

I lean back in my seat, throwing him a confused look. "You don't mean . . . a mixed series? Ladies and gentlemen in conversation together?" Waldo has no problem breaking new ground, but this seems radical, even for him. And I very much wonder how my ladies would feel about this.

"Even better," he replies, sitting forward. "Even bigger. Not twenty-five of us gathered in one parlor for one hour. But what about reaching every parlor in New England? Perhaps even America?"

Now I'm truly puzzled, and the crinkle in my brow must show it. But Waldo's features are alight as he declares, "Let's start a newspaper. Our very own newspaper. They mock us, calling us the Transcendentalists. Well, then, let's take that and use it. Let's start a Transcendental journal."

Waldo continues his pitch, his tone bold, even a bit defiant: "I've been banned from ever setting foot on Harvard's campus again. No New England newspaper will dare publish anything of mine."

I peer at him through narrowed eyes. "So now you are determined to go forward alone?"

"Not alone," he says, folding his long fingers in his lap. "I will go forward with you."

As I sit there, taking this all in, he goes on: "Hear me out, Margaret. I want to support, even foster, the free expression of thoughts and ideas. Rigorous thought. Uncompromisingly independent thinking. And I know that you share this mission with me, don't you? Enough of this Puritanism that forces a dogmatic rigidity over everything and everyone. I wish for self-trust. Freedom. Self-expression."

"Why . . . why me?" I'm certain that he hears the layers of hesitation beneath that question, even if I do not voice them all: I am without money, without helpful connections. I have a bit of renown as a writer, to be sure, but that does nothing to change the one large and fundamental impediment that lies before me: I am a woman.

"Why *you*?" Waldo repeats my question with a lopsided smile, then answers: "Because there is no one more worthy. No one more capable of beautiful and original thoughts, nor more qualified to share those thoughts with others. If I want to encourage freedom and self-expression, then I must have you as a partner. I want you to be our editor."

I let out a long exhale, tapping the arms of my chair with my fingers. I look away from Waldo, into the fire, my mind awhirl. This visit caught me entirely by surprise—but this proposition, even more so.

The free expression of thoughts and ideas. Even a female editor's thoughts and ideas. And one of the fruits of more independent thinking would be a greater role for women in our society, I do believe that. One of the results of throwing off this rigid dogma against which Waldo rails would be a willingness to allow women to think, and write, perhaps even someday to lead. He is right that we share this hope, this purpose.

Most of the current newspapers that circulate do not share this desire—Waldo is right in that, as well. And they won't publish Waldo, not now that he's stepped out of their confines. They certainly won't publish any work of mine that strays from their narrow scope. It would be liberating—not only for him, but for me, also, to have a new paper circulating. It could be liberating for a great number of people, many of them women.

"You'd be making history, Margaret." Waldo stares at me, his pale eyes ablaze, revealing the intensity of his hopes. "A female cofounder and editor of a newspaper in America."

He knows what this point means to me. For Waldo, ostracism was a matter of choice and rugged individualism. For me, it was simply a fact of birth. For that reason, this mission is even more important to my liberty than his.

"I'd pay you, of course," he adds. "Two hundred dollars."

"Yes," I say, my voice low.

He leans toward me. "Yes?"

"Yes, I'll do it. I'll be the editor of your newspaper."

"*Our* newspaper," he says, clasping his hands as he flashes a triumphant smile. "Very good. Then come to Concord. We will sort out the details of how to make this thing work. And besides, you need to celebrate with us. There's nothing quite like Christmas in Concord."

THE FOLLOWING WEEK finds me stepping down from the stagecoach, looking up at a snow-covered Bush, its front door trimmed in cheerful sprigs of fresh holly and fragrant pine. I enter to a blast of warmth on my cold cheeks, and the air smells like cinnamon and stewed apples. Someone—my guess is Thoreau—has clipped boughs of pine and decked the mantels, the banisters, the doorways with greenery. Pinecones are strung together with holly berries like garland, and a fire warms the parlor.

It's in that parlor that we gather later that day, Bronson, Thoreau, Waldo, and I. We are to be the founders of this Transcendental journal, this venture that Ralph Waldo Emerson has conceived. "Not only the brilliant but the brave will make this venture," Waldo declares. His mood is ebullient, his words uncharacteristically proud. "We shall be the best club that ever made a journal."

"What are we to call it?" Thoreau asks.

"How about *The Dial?*" Alcott suggests.

I turn toward him. "Why *The Dial?*" Even after several years, I am still reluctant to accept much of what comes out of the mouth of Bronson Alcott.

Nevertheless, when he speaks next, even I have to admit, begrudgingly, that Bronson makes a nice point. "Because, like a sundial, we shall be an instrument of the light. Like a sundial, we are taking the measurement of our days."

"I like that," Waldo says.

"As do I," Thoreau agrees.

Waldo looks thoughtful as he muses aloud: "We will be bringing the light of language and thought to many."

Bronson beams, his face flushing to the roots of his blond hair. The title works, we all agree. "To *The Dial,*" Waldo declares to our gathering in his parlor.

"To *The Dial,*" we echo. And, with that, our magazine has a name.

. . .

WE RING IN the New Year together at Bush, filled with cheerful enthusiasm for our new venture. It's not just any new year; it's a new decade, as well. And with the dawning of this new decade, we friends from Concord will be giving America its newest literary journal. And I will be editor.

I spend much of January, that month full of fresh beginnings and promise, writing to potential contributors from my guest room at Bush. I'm explaining the purpose of our project, and asking the brave thinkers of our circle to contribute. *"We will provide a voice for the freest expression of thought on all the questions which interest earnest minds in every community."* I write that over and over again, posting my letters and then awaiting the replies.

The replies do come. Hawthorne agrees to contribute several essays. Thoreau as well, a poem and an essay on the Romans. Alcott declares he will contribute a poem. Waldo will of course write several pieces for the paper. Eliza Peabody will write something. And so, of course, will I.

I RETURN TO my boardinghouse in Boston and throw myself into the work. I write feverishly as winter gives way to spring. I work on my own pieces for the paper and I check in with our contributors to ensure that everyone is proceeding apace. Waldo and I exchange letters almost daily. My birthday comes and I, too, enter a new decade. I am now thirty. I'm not married, which is a shocking fact to many, but I am a cofounder and editor of a newspaper. Also a shocking fact to many. But a fact in which I allow myself to feel deep pride.

As the days lengthen, we prepare to go to print. The pieces have been written. They have been edited—by me. They have all been approved by Waldo. The printer takes the pile of papers from my hands and gets to his work. The pale pages fill with dark text; the wet ink dries. *The Dial* is ready to fly out into the world and into the hands of our readers. I only hope that there will be many.

Our first issue opens with a lengthy letter from Waldo, and I thrill as I spread the crisp pages before me. Though I've read the essay many times—as its editor I could practically recite the piece from memory—it feels entirely new to see it set forth on the front of my newspaper. Waldo writes that our work in *The Dial* is to be "an antidote to all narrowness."

One of my pieces, which I've titled "A Dialogue," expresses some of my own deep feelings. My yearning to enjoy life, to someday find love, but the pressing need to always be working, creating, providing for myself. It's written from a safe distance, however, modeled as a conversation between a flower and the sun overhead.

A more critical essay of mine takes up the topic of literary critics themselves, and the relationship that a writer or poet has to the tradition of literary criticism. I look over this piece and all of the pieces that I've written, at the other sections I've edited, at the whole newspaper, which feels simultaneously so familiar and yet entirely fresh in my hands. I smile with broad and sunny pride. Mine is the lead article. I read it through again, all the way to the end, where I've concluded with a lone initial: "F."

I've done this, and Waldo understands, because even though it is well-known that I, a woman, am the lead editor of this paper, we all agreed it might be shocking to have too many of the submissions written by women, as well. Not to us, the creators, but to readers. Many people still do not wish to read a woman's thoughts.

It is evident that we still have a long way to go. But, as bitter as that realization tastes, I find great comfort in knowing that *The Dial* will help us to get there.

Chapter Twenty-One

Boston

"'THE VERY BEST MAGAZINE PUBLISHED IN THIS country.'" I beam as I read the words, printed by Horace Greeley in his review of *The Dial*. I can imagine that a similar smile upturns Waldo's features, noting that Mr. Greeley's approval means our work is being well received as far as New York.

I'm not entirely surprised; while New England's intellectual elite has scoffed at Waldo—and all of us Transcendentalists—for some time now, the New York literary and scholarly world is more diverse, more welcoming of a broader array of voices and arguments. Our paper is intended for more than just New England, it is for any reader in America who values self-expression and individual thought.

I dash off a note to Waldo in Concord, including a clipping of Greeley's review in the *New-York Tribune*, in case Waldo has not yet seen it. But there is no time to rest in triumph, for the second issue is already slated for only a few months away. Our plan is to put the paper out every three months, an issue for each quarter, and the pieces need writing.

As editor of our newly minted journal, I am busier than ever. Summer gives way to fall as I throw myself into soliciting and then editing our next slate of pieces. Emerson sends me a steady stream of his own writing, as does Thoreau. Hawthorne and Eliza contribute, and of course I plan to write a number of the pieces myself.

By the time the cold weather returns, I've published our third issue and I'm hard at work on our fourth. For this edition I've completed two original pieces, which I've titled "Magnolia" and "Leila."

Since I edit for everyone else, Waldo edits my submissions, and he's just written back to me that he feels my work is ready.

I can't recall a time when I've been busier or more passionate about my work. I feel enlivened by *The Dial*, by the mission of a free and independent journal. And yet, it's not all positive. As I prepare to bundle our fourth edition off to the printing house, I am growing unsettled. Increasingly so.

There is one large, primary reason for my disquiet: I've yet to receive a penny for my work as writer or editor.

I draft several different notes to Waldo, alluding to my promised salary. I try explaining that I need the money, but my words don't look right. I craft a different letter, not explaining myself, but instead asking outright for my wages. But I don't mail that one, either. Next I draft a note setting out the plan for the fourth edition, explaining that since we've now completed four issues of our quarterly paper, I hope to receive my two hundred dollars in full. I crumple the paper and toss it toward the hearth.

What is wrong with me? I wonder. If I were speaking to a friend, I'd have no hesitation in telling her to demand what is rightfully hers. So then why can't I ask for this fair compensation for myself? But none of these notes feel right.

I look around at my small, drab room—a space so modest, and yet one I can barely afford. My savings from my first book are dwindling, with no new money coming in. I've put my next book project on hold because *The Dial* devours all of my time and energy. How many more months of rent will I be able to afford?

I bristle at the unfairness of it. And yet I know what Waldo's response will be, which is why I have such a hard time posting my letter. He will point out that our paper has yet to break even, much less earn a profit. *He* is doing this for free because he believes in our ideas and in the importance of a new journal that promotes our values. Of course I believe in these ideas, as well. I share his passion and his purpose. But I also have to eat.

Once again I feel as if the men around me do not understand. I am the sole breadwinner in my life—without wages, I will have no bread. I don't have an inheritance, nor do I have some husband's financial support.

And there are other practicalities that weigh on me. By the spring, Mother gives me the news that she can no longer afford her rented home. She will go visit my brother in New Orleans, where he, too, is working for a newspaper—one that pays him.

With the spring sunshine returned and a year as editor under my belt, I must face the realities of my life in a stark and revealing light. I can no longer pay my own rent. Our *Dial*, now a year old, has found critical support across the Northeast, but it has not reached a place of financial sustainability. As it stands, we have too few subscribers to do so anytime in the near future.

Waldo sees *The Dial* as a passion project, an important investment that he hopes will amplify his voice, and all free voices, and perhaps someday take flight as a financial success. But he will be fine to carry on in his life, even if that day never comes. I do not have that liberty. I cannot wait, with nothing more than hope and passion jangling in my coin purse.

I confess all this to Eliza when she invites me for tea one afternoon that summer. We sit in the gracious, well-furnished apartment that her affluent parents help her to keep. I frown into my teacup, my voice strained as I say: "I love the work, but I cannot do it for free."

Eliza nods, her features creasing in understanding. "You cannot, Margaret. Nor should you."

I sit in silence for a moment, weighing my words. I have a question, one I am loath to pose. But I have to. "What will Waldo do?"

Eliza cocks her head to the side, considering this. "You mean, without your unpaid labor?"

I nod. Eliza replaces her teacup in its saucer, leaning forward and taking my hands in hers as she answers: "Waldo will have to find someone else to work for free. Or he shall have to edit his own paper. Only then will he fully understand just how much you've been doing."

WHEN I RETURN home, back to my rented room and ready to draft this long-overdue note, I'm surprised to find a letter already awaiting me. From Bush, in Waldo's handwriting.

As I open the envelope and begin to read, all concerns of the newspaper fly from my head. As I take in the words of my friend's familiar hand, the paper begins to quiver in my grip. Then the letters blur, as a scrim of tears makes Waldo's handwriting dance before my eyes. I no longer have a single thought for money or my work or the newspaper. Every concern flees as I read the devastating words, absorb the shock of their meaning.

Little Waldo has died. Waldo's precious boy, so plump and healthy, so bursting with rosy life, is dead. Scarlet fever. At age five. Those chubby little hands will never steal my inkwell again.

"I will never love another being," Waldo writes to me. I shudder, picturing him at his desk, declaring this. Putting this vow down on paper. *"I will never love again."*

I dash off a reply, posting it immediately. My response is short, because words fail in a moment such as this. All I write is: *"What can I do? —Yours, Margaret."*

Waldo's reply comes quickly, before the week is out.

> *Come to me, Margaret.*
> *I beg you.*
> *Come to us, and make the bright days brighter,*
> *and the gray ones tolerable.*

I pack up my room, telling my landlady farewell, thanking her. "I'm going for a visit," I tell her, "to comfort a dear friend facing a most grievous tragedy."

"And after that?" she asks. I do not know. But right then, it does not matter. That morning, I'm on the next coach out of the city, headed to Concord.

Chapter Twenty-Two

Concord

I ENTER BUSH LIKE I WOULD A MAUSOLEUM. WHILE IN some ways it feels like a homecoming—the familiar smells of books and flowers, the familiar face of Thoreau at the door, my friend greeting me with a somber nod, a squeeze of my gloved hand—in another way, it feels like a place entirely foreign. I've never walked into Bush and felt the immediate and heavy weight of deep mourning.

At Thoreau's suggestion, I go first to Lidian, who can only receive me upstairs in her bed. I step quietly across her threshold, summoned to her bedside by her quiet voice. I blink; the curtains are drawn and the room is enveloped in shadow, filled with the various stale smells of a human body that has not left the space for days. We really should open a window.

I pad softly toward her large bed. "Lidian, my dear friend," I say, finding no other words at the ready. And then I see her. Even though I'm prepared to find a stricken mother, a woman heartsick and bereft with the loss of her beloved babe, the reality stuns me. Lidian's frame appears impossibly frail, her skin whiter than bone, her pallor set off by the hard black of her mourning dress. Her hair is limp, likely not washed in days, perhaps weeks. But most unsettling of all is the fact that, while Lidian's frame looks shrunken and thin, her face is swollen, her cheeks puffed out so that they nearly close her sunken eyes.

"Oh, this." Lidian has seen my reaction; she's read the horror on my face before I can manage to pull my features back into a look of composure. Now she lifts a hand, stroking her swollen cheek in a weary, absent-minded gesture. "I had to have some teeth pulled," she explains. "I would imagine I look a fright."

"No, it's simply—I hadn't realized you'd had an operation," I say, attempting a bright tone, placing my hands on her bedcovers as though to tidy her bed.

"Yes, well. I haven't looked in a mirror in some time," Lidian says, her voice hoarse. "I don't wish to." She yawns, pulling her mouth wide open. She takes no care to cover her gaping jaws with a hand. "So tired," she mutters, pulling the covers up to her narrow shoulders. "So very tired."

"Shall I leave you to rest?" I shift on my feet. And then, seeing the vial of laudanum on her bedside table, its liquid contents nearly emptied, its stopper tipped against a cloudy water glass, I frown.

"Waldo," she says. My heart seizes—I'm not sure whether she refers to her husband or the boy she's lost. "Waldo will be comforted . . . it is good you've come, Margaret." So then she must mean her husband. I've yet to see him.

"Oh, Lidian." I put a hand lightly on top of the bedcovers. "It's so, I'm so . . . I'm so very sorry."

"Yes," she says, nodding, her hollow eyes staring off toward the far side of the dim bedroom. "As am I. And now . . . I shall rest."

"Of course you must rest," I say, looking toward the chair nearby. "Would you like me to sit by you? Until you fall asleep?" She makes a small movement in response, but I can't read whether she's nodding or shaking her head. It doesn't matter: within several minutes she's shut her eyes and I hear a steady, rhythmic breathing. She's drifted off to sleep. That, at least, is a small mercy. I step slowly from the room, trying not to disturb her, closing the door softly on my exit.

I startle when I turn and see Waldo, standing at the bottom of the stairs. I press my hands together in front of my heart. And now the tears come. I fly down the stairs, whispering, "Oh, my dear friend, I am so sorry."

We embrace at the bottom. I feel his frame shudder, and then he's weeping, too, his tears moistening my shoulder. I hold him, like I imagine I might hold a child in need of tender comfort. I know his wife has not been able to console him, ravaged as she is by her own deep grief. Waldo weeps, saying nothing for several minutes, and I allow his tears to come.

Eventually, he does pull back, lifting a handkerchief from his pocket and dabbing at his red-rimmed eyes. When he speaks, he says only: "Margaret."

I take his hand in mine. "My friend."

He looks at our entwined hands, gives mine a squeeze. "You're here."

"What can I do?" I ask.

"Just be here. All right?" Now his light gaze rises to meet mine, and I see the pain behind the glistening water of his tears. "I'll never weep like this again. But just . . . be here."

So that's what I do. I stay in their home. I keep mostly to myself, as they do the same, but I'm there. In the mornings I write, returning to my efforts on Goethe. In the afternoons I walk, occasionally knocking on Waldo's door to invite him to join me.

He rarely accepts, but at least he knows that he can. That I am there. I sit by the fire in the evenings, and often Waldo does join me in that. He's reading, mostly, not writing. But sometimes he will let me read aloud to him, so I share passages of my work. He offers no critiques, like he has in past visits, but he nods as he listens and sometimes even offers a feeble smile or word of approval.

One evening in the middle of summer, Waldo does surprise me by offering a piece of feedback. I'm reading him a passage on Goethe's thoughts on marriage. "'Love is an ideal thing, marriage a real thing; a confusion of the real with the ideal never goes unpunished.'"

"It's the truth," Waldo says aloud, lifting out of his daydream state, his voice firmer than it has been. I look up from my page. And then I feel my stomach tighten as our eyes meet. Waldo goes on, saying, "Marriage should be a temporary bond, I've come to see that."

I look back down at my pages, fluttering the pile in my hand, noting how my breath feels shallow. "I would not know much on the matter," I say. I'm not eager to go down this road; it feels wrong, what with Lidian upstairs in a laudanum-induced sleep, her body and spirit diminished to mere shadows of their former selves, and all of Bush draped in a veil of sorrow.

THOREAU AND I are alone at breakfast the following morning, and I take that moment to confide in him, confessing my concerns for Lidian. My friend offers a knowing nod. Eventually, his features creased with his own care, he speaks to me in a low voice: "Lidian was relying on laudanum after the operation, to manage the pain. But now . . . well, now she's taking it to manage pain of a very different sort."

I sigh. From upstairs I hear the muffled cries of little Ellen, the toddler being cared for now almost entirely by a hired maid. "But life does continue on," I say, looking to Thoreau. "And Lidian and Waldo will have to reenter life. Both for their own sakes and for the sake of their family."

"Yes," Thoreau agrees. "And speaking of life continuing on, I think I shall ask Waldo to help me in the garden this morning. I always find that digging in the dirt has a most restorative effect on one's dashed spirit."

I am so glad that Thoreau is here, for both of them. I'd always thought that the Emersons were helping Thoreau, but now I see that the reverse is true. His presence in this house is like a talisman of purity and goodness. "How is the garden coming?" I ask.

"It thrives," he says, laying his napkin on the table. "In fact, I have more tomatoes than I can keep. I wanted to bring a bushel over to the Hawthornes today."

The *Hawthornes*. Nathaniel, and now his wife, as well. My heart squeezes. I draw in a slow breath and force some calm into my voice when I speak next: "How are the Hawthornes?" I think I've succeeded in masking just how much the mention of Nathaniel Hawthorne has rattled me. I haven't seen him since he married Sophia.

"They seem well enough," Thoreau says. "They've taken up residence at the Old Manse. You know Hawthorne married Sophia Peabody recently?"

"I did hear that, yes." My tone sounds wooden, but I keep my face neutral. "I've yet to see them since I've arrived."

"The married state appears to suit them," Thoreau says, his tone guileless as ever.

"It'll be good to see them happy," I answer, offering a tight smile. "I am friends with Sophia's sister Eliza."

"Oh, yes, we've had her out here," Thoreau says. And then, his head leaning to one side, he adds: "Well, Sophia is not much like Eliza."

I clear my throat, as Thoreau goes on: "Waldo had me put in a garden for them, as a sort of wedding gift when they moved in."

Waldo's wedding gift was probably a good deal more than simply a garden, I think to myself. But I don't say this aloud, instead answering only: "That was kind of you both."

"It was kind of Waldo," Thoreau corrects me. "His idea. He's always doing those sorts of things."

"Yes, he is." It's true. Waldo is the friend who makes everyone feel so welcome, who does all he can to nurture others. I reflect on this with a pang, feeling guilty for my bitterness of just a moment earlier. Waldo, who is so shattered now, even as he's always done all he could to make others feel happy.

"I want to see how their garden does." Thoreau is rising from the breakfast table. "And to bring them some of our tomatoes. But I'm reluctant to leave today. I want to bring Waldo outside with me. And . . . and . . . well, I don't like to leave Lidian. Just in case she has need of me."

I press my hands on the table, pushing my chair back. "Allow me to help."

Thoreau lifts an eyebrow.

"Let me bring the Hawthornes your gift of tomatoes," I offer.

"But don't you have work?"

"I can do it later," I assure him. "It'll be good—it will allow you to stay here with Waldo. And with Lidian. And besides, I have not yet seen Hawthorne, nor Sophia. It will be nice to visit the Old Manse."

WHEN I ARRIVE half an hour later, I stare admiringly at two rows of gracious black ash trees that frame the lane up to the house, which looks like it's had a fresh coat of pale taupe paint. The trees in the orchard grow with small summertime apples, and the vegetable garden appears lively and well tended. The entire place appears tidier, less ramshackle and overgrown, than I remember it being. Perhaps it's the clear sunshine that's pouring down. Perhaps it's the backdrop of a perfect blue sky with just the occasional puff of white clouds. Or perhaps it is the fact that a happy pair of young lovers now lives within, changing the place from an abandoned old rectory to, well, a family home.

And the new husband is outside as I walk up. *Nathaniel Hawthorne.* I see him in his garden just an instant before he spots me, and that is a mercy, as it allows me to collect myself, to pull my frayed nerves back into a bearing of calm and friendly composure. *Nathaniel Hawthorne is married,* I tell myself. And I remain, as before, his friend.

"Does Margaret Fuller approach?" Nathaniel looks at me, smiling at my sudden appearance in his garden. He holds a shovel and seems to be planting a small bush. His hair flies dark and unruly about his rosy face, and his sleeves are rolled up to his elbows, showing the tanned skin of his forearms.

"Hello," I say, offering a restrained smile. I remain a few paces back, pausing my steps, feeling grateful for the broad brim of my sunbonnet as I try to keep my face calm. The sun-kissed flush of his face makes his green eyes glow even more than usual—more than I remembered. "It's nice to see you."

"And you," he says, leaning on his shovel. "It's been some time."

"Yes," I say.

His eyes travel to the parcel in my hands. "You come bearing gifts?"

"I do. From Thoreau." I glance around the garden. "For you and Mrs. Hawthorne. Congratulations, Nathaniel."

"Ah, thank you." He jostles the shovel at his side.

"A married man," I say, forcing myself to meet his eyes with a look that says I am happy for him.

He lets out a slow exhale. "I did my Christian duty."

This comment strikes me as puzzling, and I frown. Nathaniel notices my expression, because he hastens to add: "In matters of the heart, I think a young man fancies himself on stilts in the beginning of his journey. And by the time he's wed, he's limping about on his knees."

This does nothing to clarify things for me. And were I Sophia, I think I'd be less than happy to hear my new husband speaking of our union thusly. I clear my throat. "Yes, well, I've not yet had the honor of meeting your bride. Though I am very fond of her sister Eliza."

"Ah, Eliza." Nathaniel nods. "Yes. Everyone loves Eliza."

And yet Eliza, robust and spirited Eliza, like me, has never had a man love her enough to marry. I bite my lip, keeping this thought unspoken, instead asking: "And . . . is Mrs. Hawthorne at home?"

"She is. She's resting," Nathaniel says, an upward dart of his eyes toward the house. "She was . . . tired."

My eyes follow his toward the row of windows on the upper floor of the old home. *A bed case.* That's how I've heard Sophia Peabody—now Sophia Hawthorne—referred to.

A frail slip of a woman when Nathaniel Hawthorne likely could have had any number of young ladies for a wife. Why, could he have had . . .

No, I tell myself. I pull back my shoulders, forcing myself to stand upright. I will not allow my mind to wander toward daydreams or pointless questions. Possibilities that I know shall never come to pass.

"For me?" Nathaniel asks, his silky voice invading my disordered thoughts.

I meet his eyes. "Pardon?"

Nathaniel gestures down, toward my waist. And then I realize he's pointing toward my hands. "Oh, this. Yes." I fidget with the sack. "Tomatoes. From Thoreau."

Nathaniel leans forward, extending a hand toward the bag. As he does so, his palm comes to rest on top of my hand. Our eyes lock, and I suck in a quick breath. I'm not wearing gloves, I realize. Neither is he. His flesh is on mine, and a current of something warm courses through me. I feel very strange, suddenly. As if I'm not entirely in control of my body. My heart is hammering so loudly in my chest that I can't believe he doesn't hear it. "Delicious," he says after a long moment, his face angling toward mine.

"Yes," I say, pulling my hand away. He has the sack in his grip, and I take two steps back. "I'm sure they will be."

That vibrating feeling, that tight pulsing of warmth from a moment ago, has snapped now that Nathaniel is no longer pressing his skin on mine. I exhale, feeling as though I'm in command of my body once more. I blink, pulling my sunbonnet just a bit lower over my eyes. And that's when I look up, back toward the house once more.

And there, in the window, is something new, something that I did not see before. Or, rather, *someone*. A pale moon of a face. I see white on white on white—Sophia Hawthorne stands looking out, her flesh the color of mist beneath a colorless nightgown, a draping of pale curtains nearly concealing her from view. How long has she been standing there at the window, watching? And then she raises a white hand, offering a slow wave. My breath catches in my throat. Nathaniel notices me staring and his eyes glide up in the same direction, toward the window and his wife. He returns her wave, saying, "Ah, Sophia, my dear."

I wave, as well. I send Sophia Hawthorne a smile, but it's wobbly and fragile, like a sparrow with a broken wing, and I'm not entirely certain it makes its way to her at the window. And then I can't help but wonder to myself: *Why do I always feel like a bane before these Concord wives?*

Chapter Twenty-Three

WHEN I RETURN TO BUSH IN THE EARLY EVENING, after a long walk along the Sleepy Hollow hillside to clear my head, the house feels somehow different. As though the air inside it has brightened ever so slightly, like the clear air that remains after a storm. Perhaps it is simply that I feel an odd but undeniable sense of relief to be back from the Old Manse, far from the ghostly woman in the window and the coil of nerves I'd felt beside her husband. Or is it simply that there's a delicious aroma swirling through the rooms?

I peek into the dining room and see Thoreau setting out a lovely spread—candles, fresh-clipped flowers, and a number of steaming dishes. Thoreau looks up when he notices me. "Ah, Margaret, so glad you returned in time for supper. Lidian will be joining us, so we'll be four. Quite a party."

I rush to my bedroom to change out of my mud-caked clothes and then reenter the dining room to help Thoreau. In an effort to lift the spirits within, he has run to the fish shop and returned with mussels. He's prepared them in a delicious sauce made from the herbs he's grown right here at Bush. The table is set with the Emersons' silver, the warm bread is brought out, and the colorful spread offers itself for a festive gathering. I give thanks, yet again, for the presence of Henry David Thoreau. He's so kind to all of us. Especially to Lidian. And I marvel that he's somehow convinced her to leave her bed and join us for dinner.

. . .

AND YET, AS we sit down to the table and begin to tuck into the savory meal, though Lidian's body is there, her soul seems entirely absent. She barely touches her stew, even as I try my best to conceal how delicious it tastes to me.

By the time we've cleared our dinner dishes and Thoreau reappears with a warm cobbler, Lidian begins to weep quietly at her place. I lower my spoon, looking to her in concern. "Lidian?"

All three of us watch her. She doesn't speak for a long moment. And then, closing her eyes, her entire body curling forward like a wilted plant, she whispers: "I'm so . . . very tired."

Thoreau makes to rise. "No," I say, pushing myself back from the table. "I'll help her. You . . . stay. Enjoy this delicious dessert you've made."

I fly to her side, helping her from her chair. Lidian leans on me and we walk out of the dining room, leaving Thoreau and Waldo in silence. Waldo, the only person, I note, who did not leap to help his wife.

As I'm tucking her into bed, settling the covers over her shoulders, Lidian grips my arms, pulling on me with a strength that surprises me, her face twisting as though in fear. "What is it?" I ask, alarmed.

Her voice sounds choked when she asks: "Did you not see?"

"See what?"

Tears seep noiselessly from the creased corners of her eyes. "The way . . . he can't even look at me."

I know she means Waldo. I *have* noticed. Of course I have noticed. I only hoped that she had not, and it infuriates me now to see that she has. But I force a brightness to my tone as I answer: "My dear, he barely spoke to anyone. Now, some rest will do you good."

"Thoreau makes himself so useful here. And you . . . well, you are his high priestess. His goddess. His muse. I'm only taking up space."

"Lidian." My stomach hardens. "You must not say such things."

"Perhaps he blames me."

Hearing this, I can't help but shiver, in spite of the summer warmth. I sigh, raising my hand to Lidian's face to give her forehead a gentle, soothing stroke. "My dear friend, he could never. Why, anyone who ever saw you, well, we all saw what a loving, devoted mother you were . . . *are*. You are still a mother," I say, wishing with a pang that she would pull herself out of this strangling melancholy in order to be a mother to the little girl tucked into her bed just down the hall.

Lidian leans her head back, melting into the pillows as though she wishes she could vanish. And then, looking to me, she says: "Help me to my medicine." My eyes glide toward the bedside table, where I see the pitcher and glass, and there beside it, the small bottle with its little black stopper. I swallow. My hands feel heavy as I pour her a glass of water. Then, when she insists again, I drop the medicine into the cup, watching as it turns the clear liquid into a small storm cloud.

Is it in fact medicine? I wonder. *Am I* helping *her?* The droplets swirl and curl, dissipating, leaving the water a bruised gray. Lidian drains the entire cup and tips back her head once more, shutting her eyes. Within just a few minutes her body is limp, stilled by a deep and unnatural sleep. As I pad out of her bedroom, throwing her one final glance, I can't help but wonder whether her sleeping mind will be filled by dreams or nightmares.

SHORTLY AFTER THAT, fresh storm clouds gather on the horizon. Rain, sheets of it, slapping the windows and carving the vegetable beds into rivulets of dark mud. It rains for days without pause.

Inside, Bush feels stormy as well. The air is crackling and unsettled, silent but thick, as though we are all walking along the edges of swords. Thoreau, irritable because he cannot escape out of doors to work and putter, grumbles that his tomatoes will get root rot. After a few days, when he can stand the walls no longer, he throws a hood over his head, slaps boots onto his feet, and troops out into the storm. I watch through the window as his frame lopes across the flooded lawn, thinking yet again that his blood must be at least part forest faun.

Thoreau remains outside for hours, busying himself over the roses. "Lidian's roses," he calls them, as though ministering to them can assuage the ache he feels at not being able to heal her. When he's soggy and the roses don't need him anymore, he retreats to the barn, where he tinkers with pieces of furniture. I know that he's removed many of little Waldo's items from the house—the rocking horse he carved, the small wooden bed—tucking them away so as not to have them in front of Waldo and Lidian. I wonder if he's doing something with them out there now.

No one gathers at the table for luncheon that day. Lidian remains in bed, the laudanum ever at her side. Waldo is irritable and keeps to himself, largely closed in his study. Several hours later I knock. A beat, and then his muffled voice sounds from within. "Yes?"

I lean against the closed door and ask him if perhaps he ought to go visit his wife. I'm not certain when the last time was that they spoke. Waldo grunts a noncommittal reply, so I walk away, back to my bedroom. I don't see him emerge.

And it's for that reason that I am surprised when I nearly bump into him later that same afternoon. I'm descending the stairs, having just checked on Lidian myself. "Waldo, hello." It's as though he hasn't seen me. He pauses, finally meets my eyes. "I've just brought Lidian some toast and milk," I say.

He nods, his expression vacant. He says nothing. "She's resting now," I go on, disheartened by the fact that he does not ask of her. "She's quite melancholy. I think a visit from you . . . I think it could be good for both of you."

Now he narrows his eyes, and I can read from his expression that he's confused by my suggestion. "The pair of you," I say, swallowing, choosing my words with care before I go on. "The two of you are unique in the world in knowing this pain. Perhaps if you could come together in your grief . . . even if you could share a small moment. Perhaps it might help you both to—"

When he speaks, it's a tone I'm not at all expecting, his voice sharp as gravel as he says, "Why must you harangue me like this?"

I'm startled by the interruption. By the hard edge in his voice. "Harangue?" I put my hand on the stairway banister. "I'm only giving you a report on your wife."

His eyebrows tilt toward each other. "You disturb my peace."

"But, Waldo . . . think of Lidian. There's no peace for her. I think if you were to go to her, it would mean so much."

"You are bogging me down." He taps the side of his head with his finger, an angry frown rutting his features. "This is beneath you, Margaret, to meddle in domestic trivialities. Why would you encourage me to go in there when it will only lead to discord. . . ." He darts his eyes up toward his wife's bedroom, the closed door. Then he shakes his head, as though trying to throw off a dousing of water. "No. I have bigger things to think about."

I'm stunned by this. What could be bigger than the well-being of his family? "Waldo, please, I was only trying to—"

"Enough."

I wince. But he says nothing more. He merely turns and walks away, down the stairs, back to his study, where he shuts the door with a decisive thud.

Now the house is quiet, a gnawing, foul silence. I remain on the stairs, shocked and unmoving. I wanted only to encourage him, both of them, but Waldo would have me feel as though my presence is doing more harm than good. This is vexing. I make two balls with my fists and march down the stairs to his study door, where I offer a quick series of raps. "What is it?" he growls on the other side of the door.

I step in, speaking before I lose my nerve: "It's me. I only ask . . ." But then my words taper off. In truth, I don't know what to ask. I sigh, my righteous indignation withering in the face of his desperate heartache. "My dear friend, I was only trying to help. I thought that perhaps you and Lidian could be a small comfort to each other, as you go through this together."

He's leaning on the back of his chair, and his eyes smolder but do not meet mine. "Have you not listened to anything I've said?"

I feel a twist of disappointment at this. Of course I listen to him. I sound almost childlike when I answer, stung: "I *do* listen to you."

"Listen to me, perhaps. But *hear* me?" He lets out a bitter rasp of a laugh.

I feel wretched. Wounded and angry, but also completely unable to help. After a long moment I answer with a question of my own: "Should I leave?" My presence at Bush is not providing any comfort to Lidian. And since Waldo is the one who invited me here, and I'm only bothering him, it seems like the right thing to do.

But Waldo frowns at my question. "Leave?" He says it like I've insulted him by suggesting it. "Why would you leave me?"

Now I'm confused. "Well, because . . . you asked me here, but it does not seem you want me here. And Lidian, well . . ."

"What do you want from me?" he asks, stuffing his fists into his trouser pockets.

"Want from you?" I shift on my feet. "I don't want anything from you. I was only trying to help."

He peers out the window for a long moment, then back toward me. "We can't walk, as it's raining."

"I know that," I answer.

"I don't much feel up for writing."

"That's fine. You are entitled to one day's reprieve."

"Nor do I care to dance. I barely have an appetite to eat. What do you want from me, Margaret?"

I look at him through narrowed eyes, feeling a sting beneath my eyelashes like I could weep. He's half-mad with grief, I can see that. And I feel for him, knowing that he's not entirely right. That I cannot take his words too straight to my heart. But I'm not expecting what he says next: "What, do you want me to take you to your bedroom?"

I feel the blood drain from my face. I remain silent, as he offers only a bitter, strangled laugh. "See? The very suggestion disgusts you."

There's a thrashing in my head, my veins swelling as if they might overspill. I have no words with which to reply. We've never before spoken like this to each other. "Excuse me, Waldo, I'll just . . ." I fumble, but I can manage no answer. So I know I must leave. He lets me go, neither of us saying anything more.

I STEP OUTSIDE, into the rain. I've hastily pulled on a hat and gloves, but they do little against the downpour. I don't much care. I'm not sure where I'm going, but I'm certain I can't be in Bush right now. Orchard House is just up the lane, where they will be dry and cozy inside. But no, for as much as I'd relish Louisa May's and Anna's company, I can't stand the thought of Bronson in this moment.

I stomp my way to the river, which is swollen from the days of rain. I'm not thinking so much as I'm trying *not* to think. I'm trying not to repeat Waldo's words in my mind. I march resolutely forward, unbothered by the wet earth through which I trudge. My feet are soon soggy, the hem of my skirt caked in brown.

By the time I notice the old taupe house perched by the river, it has stopped raining. And there is a man, also by the river. Not just any man. Nathaniel Hawthorne. I've walked so far that I've approached the Old Manse.

Hawthorne is down the hill from his house, hunched over beside the river, where the surface of the water roils with debris, raised to a level much higher than usual. His small rowboat bobs in the dirty water. He turns and sees me, waving one hand as he holds on to the boat with the other.

I approach. "Hello," I call out.

"Hello," he replies. Somewhere nearby a bird sings, perhaps alerting the others that the storm has passed. Or that I've approached.

I know I won't breathe a word of Bush, of Waldo, to Nathaniel. Or to anyone, for that matter. I pause my steps a few feet from him. He has a stripe of mud up the front of his shirt and his hair is wild. He looks toward his boat, saying: "I was checking to make sure she fared all right in the storm."

"Ah. Yes."

"But I won't really know unless I take her on a quick trip."

I look at the boat, then to him.

"Will you join me?"

This request surprises me. "Oh, no, I was only walking—I don't love the water."

"You go with Thoreau all the time."

"Yes, but that's—"

"Do you know how to swim?"

"Yes," I answer, my tone wary.

But Nathaniel takes no note of my hesitation, saying only: "Good. Then we will be fine."

"I was going to keep walking."

"It'll only be a few minutes. Please? I promise to deliver you safely back to shore. But I really could use a hand."

I let out a breath. "Very well." I see his features brighten.

I slip off my gloves and hat, tossing them onto the riverbank, and then I climb into the rowboat. Nathaniel paddles us out into the river, skimming a surface cluttered with sticks and leaves from the days of rain and wind. The sun is just emerging from behind the thinning wall of clouds as we approach the ruins of the Old North Bridge.

I tip my face up toward the golden light and close my eyes, relishing the warmth after days of damp gray. When I open my eyes, I see that Nathaniel is staring at me. I shift in my seat. He doesn't look away, doesn't seem at all abashed that I've caught him staring. He offers half a grin, then says: "Interesting day for you to take a walk." A beat, and then, "How is everything at Bush?"

"It's . . . they are doing as well as one could expect." I don't say more. Rather, I change the subject. "And how are you? Days of rain; you and your bride have had plenty of time together."

At this, his face looks as though its own curtain of clouds has slid across his features. He says nothing; instead, he looks down the swollen river, and I follow his gaze. There, before us, is a massive boulder. The massive boulder. My rock.

Nathaniel sees it, as well—I know that, because he says: "I remember once coming upon a sea nymph, sunning herself on that very rock."

I let out a quiet puff of breath. I nod. He goes on: "I remember that her dark hair was unpinned and tumbling around her shoulders. But most of all, I remember how she smiled when she saw me, and that she slid her body over to make room for mine beside her."

I sit up a bit straighter, clasping my hands together. "Your boat seems just fine," I say. "Shall we turn back?"

But Nathaniel doesn't move to paddle. At least, not right away. Not until after he's held my eyes in his green gaze for a moment, perhaps even a moment too long. "If that's what you'd like, Margaret," he says, his voice low. I nod. "Very well," he says, and with that, he lowers the oars, dipping them into the water to row us back toward the home he shares with his wife.

I wrest my eyes from his stare. As I look forward, in the direction of where we are heading, I see the looming gray-brown bulk of the Old Manse. And then my heart dips. Because there, standing on the riverbank toward which Nathaniel now paddles, is his wife. And beside Sophia stands Waldo.

Neither Nathaniel nor I say anything, but I know that he sees them. The pace of his paddling stays steady, and a few minutes later our boat drifts up out of the water onto the soft, damp bank. Sophia, in pale muslin, a shawl wrapped around her impossibly narrow shoulders, glides forward. Her step is tenuous, but at least she doesn't look as though she'll tip over.

I've not yet met her. I'm expecting some introduction, but instead she launches into a flurry of words that are entirely unexpected, her slender frame tilting forward like she might intend to hug me. "Oh, Margaret, thank you." Her voice is thin as a river reed, but her manner is warm, warmer than I would have expected, as she carries on, saying, "Thank you so much for agreeing to help my Nathaniel."

I'm so confused. Then Sophia throws a sideways glance toward Waldo, before looking back at me. "He asked me to accompany him, but I was too afraid of the river. I'm not a strong swimmer. Thank you."

"Aren't we all just so very helpful?" Waldo pipes in. I turn to him and feel a hardening in my gut. I blink, trying not to remember the words with which we left each other just an hour earlier at Bush.

But Waldo appears entirely recovered, composed, and he even smiles as he says: "I did not like the thought of you walking in the foul weather by yourself. I felt bad, Margaret. You left Bush without telling anyone where you were going."

"Good guess at finding me," I reply. We are all here, speaking to one another. And yet, taking such pains to keep so much unsaid. Waldo carries on: "Night will be here soon. I did not wish for you to walk home alone. But I see perfectly well—" Waldo's eyes dart between mine and Hawthorne's, and then, flashing a joyless grin, he says, "You didn't need me here, not at all."

Chapter Twenty-Four

I WAKE THE NEXT MORNING TO THE UNSETTLING REAL- ization that I've left my gloves and hat at Hawthorne's. I was in such a flustered state as I departed that I left a trail of personal items and now, I suspect, Nathaniel will bring them by. He'll come here, to Bush. I groan, rolling over in bed and wishing I could avoid the day.

I decide it's better that I be out of the house, so that Nathaniel might leave my gloves and bonnet when he calls. I dress hastily, helping myself to a quick slice of toast and coffee and then grabbing a different bonnet and stepping outside.

The weather, unlike the recent days, is fine and clear. I'll retreat to the woods, I decide. A few hours out of doors, alone, in the fresh air will do me a fair bit of good. I need a break from Waldo. From Nathaniel. From almost all of them.

The air is cool, cleansed from so many days of rain. Now the earth is warming with the return of the sun. I make my way to the nearby grove and pause, looking up at the patchwork of limbs overhead. A ring of hemlocks encircles me like a meeting of giants, and in front of me, through the clearing, is a lovely view of the river.

I sit down in a carpet of scarlet columbines. *Louisa May would love these*, I muse to myself. I begin to pick them, my mind drifting back to yesterday. Then I shake my head, not wanting to think on yesterday. Waldo, and then Nathaniel, and then Waldo again. No. This will only make me brood. I pick up the blood-red flower petals that I've plucked and I arrange them into an *M* on the earth's soft brown floor.

I lie back, closing my eyes. I will my strained muscles to soften. To allow the cool, yielding floor of the earth beneath me to hold my weight. To my relief, my breath begins to come a bit easier. The sun feels gentle on my skin, but I have a headache. Probably from a night of troubled, fitful sleep. I reach up and begin to remove the pins from my hair, shaking the weight of it loose. Almost immediately my headache has lessened.

The sound of birdsong lulls me into a pleasant, easy reverie. I am just beginning to feel calm, at peace once more, when I hear another gentle noise, a lapping sound. I open my eyes and sit up. And then I pull in a quick intake of air. It cannot be. Nathaniel Hawthorne is there before me, paddling down the river in his rowboat, and he's staring at me. "Oh, hello." I scramble upright, rearranging my skirts so that my legs are not on display. Then I quickly tuck several pins back into my hair, fashioning a loose, modest bun. I glance down and see the *M* I've formed with the scarlet flower petals beside me and I feel silly, girlish.

"Margaret, what a lovely happenstance." Nathaniel is staring at me, the hint of a smile turning up his lips. "I was just on my way to Bush . . . to see you."

As I expected—but I did *not* expect he would come by way of the river. Nathaniel halts his boat now, heaving it up onto the bank as he hops out, my personal items in his hands. He drops them and the oars to the earth. So then, he intends to join me here.

"You left so quickly last night, you forgot your gloves and bonnet," he says, lowering himself to sit at my side. He glances at my *M* on the ground and flashes me a smile.

I look away, shaking my head as I reply: "Yes, thank you. And . . . oh, it was nice to meet Sophia."

Nathaniel narrows his eyes, studies me a moment. "Yes, she was happy to meet you, as well. 'Course she felt like she knew you already, the famous Margaret Fuller, from everything she's heard. From your legions of admirers."

"I'm friendly with her sister," I say, staring out over the river.

"Yes." He dips his chin. "Exactly." He grazes his hands over the grass. Then he lifts a fistful of the red petals that I've not yet used and sets to work, fashioning himself a letter, and I see that he's making an *N* beside my *M*. I don't say anything, but he does: "And from me."

I swallow, looking from our scarlet letters up toward his face. "Pardon?"

"She's heard much about you from me, as well." He lifts his eyebrow.

Am I imagining it, or is he tilting his body toward mine? I swallow, force a casual tone as I say: "Well, I hope to see Sophia again. For a proper visit."

How must Sophia Hawthorne feel? I wonder, not for the first time.

"You are welcome anytime," Nathaniel says.

"It was quite an impromptu gathering on your riverbank last night." I throw him a sideways look. "Wasn't it?"

"Not like now." He glances down at the columbine petals that color the earth before us. "Now we are alone."

I need to rise. To walk. To do something. Just then a cardinal flies low before us, a sudden flash of crimson against green, and my nerves are pulled so tight that I start.

Hawthorne notices me flinch. "Just a bird," he says, his voice low. But then I hear the sound of a whistle; it does not sound like a bird. An instant later I see a familiar figure striding through the woods, toward us. "Waldo?" I sit up taller. "Hello, Waldo! Over here."

"What?" Waldo pauses, his voice revealing his surprise at stumbling upon us. He looks at me, then to Nathaniel, then back to me. Nathaniel rises to stand as Waldo, lifting a hand to lean on the nearest tree, says: "I keep finding the two of you together."

"Yes, Nathaniel was just returning my gloves and bonnet." My words come out like nervous chatter.

"Isn't that some fine chivalry?" Waldo flashes each of us a searching smile, then his eyes settle on my personal items discarded on the ground nearby. "You know, both of you, that in a great number of stories, a glove is left behind in order to force a second meeting."

My face burns with heat, but I force out a laugh. "Perhaps in the Arthurian court."

"Yes, that's good. So this is our Camelot. And you are our Guinevere. And that must make you our Lancelot, Hawthorne. And I am . . . ? Oh! Am I Arthur?"

My throat is dry, but I manage a steady tone as I declare, my eyes fixed straight on Waldo's: "I am Margaret, only."

"You're the farthest thing from an *only,*" Waldo says, then lifts his hand and waves around the grove. "But is this not a lovely day?"

"Glorious day," Nathaniel agrees. Waldo looks at Nathaniel's boat. The three of us remain there, silent, the birdsong clamorous all around us. I gather the folds of my skirt, rising to stand, scattering the spray of red flowers as I do so. "I've been out for some time, and I would like to—"

"Yes," Waldo strides toward me, extending an arm, his eyes on Nathaniel as he puts himself between us. "Shall I escort you home?"

I look to Nathaniel, giving him a nod of thanks as I pick up my gloves and bonnet. And then I look to Waldo, accepting his outstretched arm. I will walk back to Bush with him. But it's not my home.

IF THE WORLD assumes that we Transcendentalists hold any keys to sorting out the quandaries of the world, that we have any particular brilliance or insight, then all they need to do is visit Concord this summer. Here they might see just how far we are from having any answers, particularly on the matter of finding happiness. Because, as it turns out, even we Transcendentalists are making ourselves miserable.

There is a problem that occurs in planting, Thoreau has told me. When a plant is placed in a pot of soil and its roots burrow deep, eventually the pot becomes too small and the plant becomes thwarted. The plant needs new earth, and more of it, in order to grow and flourish.

This summer, at last, helps me to realize that I need new earth, and more of it. I do not wish to be here, a guest in another family's home, adding to the disharmony between a husband and wife. Nor do I wish to cause strife for Sophia with her new husband. I do not wish to stay here in Concord and, in doing so, dwell in daily discord.

I wish to find freedom, to feel it both within my soul and out in the broader world. I long for fresh soil in which to grow and flourish. And I no longer believe I can accomplish that as a houseguest of Ralph Waldo Emerson.

PART 4

Chapter Twenty-Five

New York City
Autumn 1843

M R. HORACE GREELEY GLANCES AT MY LETTER OF introduction, recognizing the name of Ralph Waldo Emerson scrawled in his friend's familiar script, and he shoos it away with a busy hand. "No, no. No letters of introduction required for you, Miss Margaret Fuller. Waldo can speak however highly he'd like, but it's my Mary who's been singing your praises for years now. It's high time we met. Come in, come in. Please sit."

I take the offered seat in the office of Horace Greeley, a place strewn with papers and books, his wire-rimmed glasses perched atop one particularly precarious-looking stack of documents. The entire space hums with an air of purpose and industriousness. The famed New York newspaperman and publisher sits down at his desk, across from me, and I steal a quick opportunity to study him. Horace Greeley, founder and editor of the *New-York Tribune*, outspoken critic of slavery, friend to our Transcendentalist philosophies—and self-avowed reader of my work. He wears a rumpled, loose-fitting jacket. His hands bear the telltale ink stains of a committed writer, the same markings that hide underneath my own gloves now.

On the other side of his windowed office door, Mr. Greeley's newsroom thrums with activity; in here he picks up his wire-rimmed glasses and slides them back up the bridge of his nose, his face framed by thinning hair so pale it appears white. He offers me an earnest smile as he peers across his desk and asks: "First time in New York City, Miss Fuller?"

So then, he's noticed my stolen glances toward his window. He's noted the stunned expression I must wear as I gaze out at the city teeming below, the intersection of Nassau and Spruce streets clogged with horse and foot traffic. Beyond that rises the imposing monolith of City Hall. The view is a sprawl of mazelike streets, throbbing with horses and humans, striated by borders of trees and fencing. Just before Mr. Greeley's office is a tall, gracious fountain around which gathers a crowd comprising all ages and varieties of humanity. I spy a little boy tossing a fistful of breadcrumbs into the air, as a scrum of pigeons descends. Does one ever truly acclimate to such a world of noise and activity? Can one truly ever adjust to the rush and bustle that is New York City?

"I remember the feeling." Mr. Greeley is staring at me over the top of his glasses, and I pull my focus from the window back toward him. "Boston is a great city, but New York is a modern Babylon. I'm a New England transplant, myself."

I fold my hands before me, hoping to project an air of composure, perhaps even sophistication. "Is that right?"

He offers a curt nod. "From New Hampshire."

"I'm from Cambridge," I say. I've spent time on busy city streets; I'm not a total country bumpkin. Do I wish to make that point to Mr. Greeley—or myself?

"Yes, I know you are." Mr. Greeley flashes me a wry smile and adds: "I know a great number of things about you, Miss Fuller. Like I said, Mrs. Greeley relished every one of your Conversations. And I have relished every one of your pieces in *The Dial*."

I allow myself to grin. Mr. Greeley's body tilts forward as he asks: "What are you working on now?"

I light up at this question, more than happy to speak about my current work. "I'm finishing a new book, in fact."

He raises an eyebrow, and I go on. "I spent this past summer traveling."

"Where to?"

"A great number of places. I started not far from here, the Hudson River Valley. From there I traveled out west to Niagara Falls."

"Ah. They are something magnificent to see, those falls. Are they not?"

"Indeed." I blink, trying to maintain a composed demeanor, and trying to push aside the memory that now floods me—the over-powering gush of fear I'd felt on first seeing them, in fact. That much water, all in one place, falling at such a pace and volume, had overwhelmed me. I wasn't so much *impressed* by the sight of the famous Niagara Falls as horribly *frightened*. I stepped back from the vista as quickly as my trembling legs would allow.

But yes, they were something to see. Mr. Greeley is eyeing me with an expectant stare, so I pull my shoulders back and sit up just a bit straighter in my chair. I carry on: "Then I took a steamship across Lake Erie. I traveled by boat from Cleveland to Detroit."

"Quite a trek you made, Miss Fuller!" What is that look Mr. Greeley now flashes at me—the look of one who is surprised? Perhaps even a bit impressed? His face is earnest and attentive as he asks: "And what did you think of our wild western lakes and lands?"

I take a moment to consider this question, to wrangle my many thoughts on all that I have seen and experienced. "The mountains, the nighttime stars, the lakes and the streams . . ." I pause, letting out a whistle of breath. "Why, Mr. Greeley, I found that the rugged and natural beauty out there did nothing short of speak to my soul."

"Indeed," he replies after a moment, his voice quiet, even a bit reverent. "Quite a bit different from New York City or Boston, eh?"

"Entirely," I agree. "I spent ten days in Chicago." My mind is un-spooling with the colorful memories of the many stops along my journey. "'The Land of Wild Onions,' as the Natives call it. It might as well be another world. Those tribesmen from the Great Plains, the Pawnee, why, they would walk right into town to trade their goods, carrying buffalo pelts and sweet grasses. These new western cities are springing up from out of the plains. Out there all is rug-ged and wild in a way that our old cities here in the East have not been for centuries."

"Remarkable." Mr. Greeley's features crease in concentration, making evident his sincere interest. "And did your travels end at Chicago?"

"Oh, no. I carried on. I went up to a northern place called Mack-inac Island."

"How was that?"

"Equally remarkable. I rode the rapids in a birch canoe around Sault Sainte Marie with guides from the Chippewa Tribe."

"My word. You are certainly a bold lady, Miss Fuller."

"Oh, but I had to be. There was no other way to drink in all of the adventure. Why, there was one evening—it was the Fourth of July, and I was out on the prairie in a place known as Eagle's Nest, fittingly enough. I was traveling by covered wagon with a larger group, and when we stopped for the evening to make our camp, I climbed up onto a bluff to watch the sunset.

"The milkweed wildflowers at that time across the plains were a bold bright red—a shade I'd never quite seen before. The grass rippled like the sea, and the sky was in its final moments of brilliant blue, as beneath us the Rock River curled around the bluff. I realized in that instant, as I looked out over a scene of such wild and untamed splendor, that our nation is in a truly remarkable moment. This moment, right now . . ." I press my gloved hand onto the desk between us, as if to emphasize my meaning. I'm droning on, blabbering in a way that is most unladylike, but I can see that Mr. Greeley hangs on my words, eager to hear what it is I have to say, so I allow myself to press on.

"Soon, the buildings and the industry of our East Coast will make their way out to our West. One can already see it happening. One can smell the felled timber and smoke. But for now, out there, it's still raw and wild. And what is to come, why, it could be truly great. I believe our nation can surpass the Greeks, the Romans, the great empires of the past. If we will build our country with beauty and goodness, if we will allow *all*, our men *and* our women, even the children of those now enslaved, to seize the promise that is offered by our rich and bountiful lands, then America can truly live up to its promise of greatness."

I reach the end of my soliloquy and sit back in my chair, spent, the room now enveloped in silence as, on the other side of the office door, dozens of newspapermen carry out their work. I cringe a bit as I note just how long I've rambled on, practically hearing aloud Mother's chidings that I need not lecture men on all that I think and feel. Mr. Horace Greeley of the *New-York Tribune* asked after my summer travels, and somehow I've managed to turn my answer into a lecture that includes the ancient Romans.

And yet, as I steal a glance at Mr. Greeley's expression now, at the forward tilt of his body, at his brow, creased in thoughtful attentiveness, he does not appear to be put off by my overenthusiasm. Or even bored.

In fact, Mr. Greeley looks entirely interested, and he says, "That's all quite good. Quite good indeed." Then he plops an elbow onto the desktop, resting his chin atop his palm as he goes on. "I must ask, is it not unusual?"

I swallow, lean my head to the side. "I beg your pardon?"

"Only that . . ." He waves his hand. "That you made this journey on your own?" He flutters the hand between us. "As a lady?"

I sit back, my shoulders flush with my chair. I hear no judgment in Mr. Greeley's question. No hint of censure. I believe that Mr. Greeley asks this question with only genuine curiosity and sincere interest. Folding my gloved hands in my lap, I offer a quick grin and answer him. "Mr. Greeley, I've always done things that were considered . . . *unusual* for a lady."

He smiles at this. And I see, with relief, that in fact Mr. Greeley did not intend judgment or chastisement. In fact, it might even be admiration I see in his expression. And this suspicion is confirmed when he slaps the top of his mahogany desk and declares: "Well, Miss Fuller, I think it's all quite good. Poetic. And important for our people to read. I agree you ought to write this down."

"*Summer on the Lakes*," I say, floating the title I've been considering.

"Have you only just returned from these travels?" he asks.

"Yes. That is why I am here in New York City. Only the day before yesterday, I came back down the Hudson River by boat."

"And where do you go next?"

"Back to Cambridge," I answer. "To finish this book." I've rented a room for the autumn, hoping that the publication of this work might bring me some respite from my financial concerns.

"That's fine," he says, as if my plans awaited his blessing. Then he presses his palm to his cheek, tapping the side of his face as he goes on: "But then your next work must follow quickly thereafter."

I tip my head, slightly amused by this. "Oh?"

"Yes. It's what will come *after* the publication of your travel journals that interests me."

I feel the fluttering of my heart. "What is that?"

"I read your piece in *The Dial*. What was it titled?" He snaps his fingers. "Ah, yes, 'The Great Lawsuit.' That one. That is to be your great work, if you can expand on that."

The fluttering of my heart has become a thumping. Of course I know the piece to which he's referring. In all my time at *The Dial*, of all the scores of pieces I wrote, 'The Great Lawsuit' is one of the works of which I am most proud, to be sure. And it is the closest to the topics I hold so dear in my heart, as it has to do with the education and work of women. It was the first time I'd written a full-length essay on so many of the thoughts I've had for years, specifically when I declared that women in America ought to enjoy rights equal to those of men. It was bold, a bit scandalous, even for our *Dial*.

And Mr. Greeley might be the only other newspaper editor in America who would celebrate a column so audacious as to state that girls have a right to education, just like boys. But Greeley is of a like mind to me and Waldo, even Alcott, in calling for equality for women.

He goes on now: "What you and Waldo and the rest of your friends are doing out in Concord, that's all well and good." He scratches the top of his head, thinking for a moment, and then he carries on. "But here in New York we need more than poetry. Let us leave those fireflies out in the country. Here we need labor and toil to bring about the beauty that we all envision in our minds."

I am a bit surprised by this sudden tack, and I consider his words for a moment. I don't disagree with him. Not at all. In fact, what Mr. Greeley is saying touches on why I've never felt fully satisfied during my stints in the idyllic greenery of Concord. It's a balm to my soul to converse with my friends up there, to be sure. It's a joy to walk the meadows and listen to the birds. And yet, I've always felt the need to take action after all the thinking and talking.

Here, in this busy office of the *New-York Tribune*, I sense that there is real action afoot. Greeley doesn't want merely to think about ideals and to talk about thoughts—he wants to work at turning those thoughts into meaningful progress. More than simply speaking about a world that is just and beautiful, Mr. Greeley wants an active hand in making the changes that are needed to bring about that just and beautiful world.

"You know my Mary has been telling me that I need to meet you. And Mary is a determined woman." Mr. Greeley clears his throat, and I bring my focus back to what he's saying at the desk across from me. "She's also determined that we will get you to move here to New York."

I let out my breath; I hear the audible exhale. *This* I was not expecting. But while I'm silent, Mr. Greeley goes on: "I want you to come work for me, Margaret Fuller." Then he raises a hand, pointing his finger toward the ceiling as though he's had a spark of thought. "No, not *for* me. *With* me. Come and work with me. Here at the *Tribune*. I know you believe in our mission. So help us to see it through."

I adjust myself in my seat, pretending to busy myself with rearranging the folds of my skirt, really so that I can buy a moment to think on it. Move to New York? To come work here, with Horace Greeley? Leave Cambridge and everyone I know behind and plunge myself full-time into the maelstrom of life and labor in this dizzying metropolis? Eventually, I manage only a question in reply: "Can I think on it?"

"Of course you can think on it. As long as you promise that, after your thinking, you'll write me and tell me your answer is yes."

I TAKE MY leave of Mr. Horace Greeley and step outside of the *Tribune* offices, opening my parasol over my head as if it were some piece of needed armor as I walk out into battle. I'm a bit stunned, not only by the strong September sunshine and the busy street, but by all that I've just discussed with the zealous newspaperman. By the fact that Horace Greeley has offered me a job as a writer at his *New-York Tribune*.

I'm collecting my bearings, trying to figure out which direction will take me back toward my room at the City Hotel, when I hear a familiar voice. "Margaret Fuller? Can it really be?"

I'd know that voice anywhere. Even here, in the last place where I'd ever imagine hearing it. A jolt of surprised delight courses through me as I turn and see Henry David Thoreau. And, somehow, Bronson Alcott at his side. "My friends!" I am so overjoyed to see their familiar faces here, in New York City, in this sea of strangers, and especially after so many months away. I'm even happy to see Bronson Alcott.

"Returned from your travels through the wilderness?" Thoreau offers me his arm, and I gladly take it, falling into step alongside my friend beside the busy street, just as I've done on so many country paths and dirt lanes before.

"Returned from one wilderness to find that Manhattan offers a wilderness all its own," I answer. "I've just come from a meeting at the *New-York Tribune*."

"And coming back up toward our Concordia soon, I hope?" Bronson asks.

"As far as Cambridge, at least," I answer. "I've taken a room there for the autumn. But I am all amazement—what brings the pair of you to New York?"

"We've just come from a meeting at the Union Church," Bronson says, pointing in an indeterminate direction toward the warren of buildings and streets that bustle before us.

"Oh? And why is that?" I ask.

"We are attempting to raise funds for a new venture," Thoreau says. Do I hear hesitation in his voice? I know how Thoreau dislikes all talk of money—I cannot imagine fundraising would be an activity he'd enjoy.

Bronson goes on, blithe as ever: "We are calling on the great circle of New York thinkers who share our values. Whitman and Melville, these great minds will heed our battle cry." Bronson speaks of Walt Whitman and Herman Melville, I surmise. Fellow stars in the constellation of new American writers and thinkers. They are the New York set, while Waldo and Thoreau—and I—shine from our Massachusetts literary sphere.

But what new venture Bronson speaks of, I cannot guess. "Well, then," I go on, "were Misters Whitman and Melville supportive of your petition?"

"Too soon to know," Thoreau answers. "But we are hopeful, are we not, Bronson?"

"Ever hopeful," Bronson replies.

"Pray tell, what is this new venture?" I ask.

"I wish to start a group farm near Concord," Bronson declares.

I stop walking. Bronson Alcott, a farmer? Thoreau throws me a sideways glance. Surely he sees my surprise; does he even throw me a hint of a wry smile?

Bronson does not. As Thoreau and I continue our walk, Bronson chatters on beside us. "More than a farm. A community. A utopian community. The finest corner of America, it shall be. Where all may live as one, joining our hands together in wholesome labor and enlivening play. Where all may enjoy the fresh fruits of our most generous earth." And then Bronson turns to me, his pale features brightening as he asks: "Would you join us, once we have established our utopia?"

I cock my head to the side, looking down at the path before us as I choose the words for my reply. "Bronson, you are kind to invite me. But . . . well, the truth is, I don't see a future with my hands put to farming." The words of Horace Greeley are still pinging about in my mind as I go on. "I see my hands getting dirty, but with the ink of my writings. My toils will likely lead me to the city, where humanity has so many great needs."

"Oh dear, Mr. Thoreau," Bronson says, frowning, perhaps even displaying a rare bit of perceptiveness as he says: "I believe that the great Horace Greeley has gotten to our Margaret before we could."

"That may be," I say, and I can't stanch the smile that now tugs at my features. Perhaps Mr. Greeley *has* gotten to me. Perhaps New York has gotten to me. Perhaps I will be coming back here, to Manhattan, to put my hands to work.

Chapter Twenty-Six

Cambridge
Winter 1843

B UT FIRST I HAVE AN APPOINTMENT AT HARVARD
University. Harvard's Gore Hall, to be precise. The largest library in America and, until today, a place forbidden to me. A place forbidden to all women.

I stand before the imposing Gothic structure on a cold winter's morning, a day of low iron-gray clouds and a wind that stings the cheeks. I pull my wool cloak closer as I stare up at the vaulted arches and soaring spires of Harvard's library. The thick walls of stately granite match the wintry sky. After a long moment I pull my gaze back down, staring determinedly at the doorway before me. I draw back my shoulders, standing up just a bit taller. Then, taking the folds of my heavy winter skirts into my hands, I stride forward out of the cold and into Harvard.

The space into which I step is cool and shadowed, with high ceilings and a hush of faintly muffled noises that speak of busy industry and quiet, purposeful study. Candlelight dances along the stone walls. My footsteps sound clamorous as my heeled boots click against the floor and I pause, midstep, to look anew at my surroundings. It is a hallowed sanctuary, a cathedral; in place of jewel-encrusted chalices, there are books. In place of pews, there are desks. In place of priests, there are pupils. All male pupils.

I stand motionless for a moment longer, closing my eyes. I pull in a slow breath, drinking deeply of the scents that permeate the space. Beloved scents: old leather bindings, tight-pressed paper, dust that lines the thousands of bookshelves. It is enough to make me a bit dizzy.

Then a soft sound pulls me from my reverie, and I turn to see a bespectacled man staring at me, his expression wary as he clears his throat. I stride toward him.

"Good day," I offer in greeting, and immediately regret that my tone is too loud—I am in a library, after all. He says nothing in return, his features bemused. I lower my voice and go on: "My name is Miss Margaret Fuller of Cambridge, and I've been granted permission to study here." I reach into my bag and rifle through my stack of notes and papers, eventually finding the prized ticket that will allow me to pass by this dubious gatekeeper. I hand it to him with a bridled but expectant smile.

He studies the paper with leery interest, his eyes lingering on the stately Harvard letterhead, the seal of the office of Harvard's president, Josiah Quincy. I resist the urge to fidget as his eyes fly from the paper up toward me, then back down to the paper. A minute later, apparently finding no actionable reason to object, the gentleman lowers the paper to his desk and slides it back in my direction. A slight nod, the muttered words, "Very well," and I take the prized passport back into my gloved hands. I am admitted. I stride forward, clutching my bag, my steps brisk as I plunge deeper into this hallowed temple.

I follow signs for the main reading room. With each step, I thrill a bit more over the fact that I am the first woman to ever walk the path that I now tread. I am the first woman ever admitted to Harvard's library to study, work, and write. How Waldo must have laughed when I wrote to him with the news, even though he is still banned from his alma mater. Is this the first time that I, Margaret Fuller, have been admitted to a place that would not allow in Ralph Waldo Emerson? Surely it must be. I am no longer attempting to bridle my happy grin.

It is all to be self-guided, of course—I have not been granted the privilege of joining the young men in lectures or seminars—but I have access to the great riches of Harvard. Its books and texts and maps are at my disposal. It is precisely what I need. I am deeply satisfied that President Josiah Quincy has granted my request to plumb Harvard's resources as I work on my manuscript for *Summer on the Lakes*. I will be the first lady, he informed me—I only hope I will not be the last.

As I glide into the main reading room now, I notice the dozens of eyes that dart toward me. Several Harvard gentlemen temporarily forget their manners, some even craning their necks, so stunned are they to see that a woman has breached their fortress. I stand there a bit stunned myself, pinned in place by the shock so apparent in their eyes. I blink, and my mind swirls with memory: I am a young girl, standing before Harvard's gates, staring longingly into a courtyard of brick and stone. A courtyard into which I have been told I may not enter. Squinting as if, with only enough effort, I might be able to see what lies on the other side. And then I blink again and there I am, a young lady, standing in Harvard Yard, tempting any young man who ambles by to engage me in debate.

Now here I stand, inside their building. A woman who has likely read more than any man in here. Surely I am a woman who has published more than any man in here. I have a right to be here, to study here, to take my place at a desk as one of their rank. I glide forward, passing several of the long wooden desks, choosing one that is empty. I pull back the chair and slowly take a seat, my movements measured and controlled. I am unruffled by their stares. Or, at least, I hope my movements will make it appear as though I am.

I hear a loud cough from nearby, followed by titters and whispers. I ignore the disturbance, reaching into my sack and pulling out my note from the university president. I set it before me like a talisman, in case anyone might require my proof. And then I pull out my papers, the scores of pages I have already written. These pages that shall soon be my book.

I've taken up another season of my popular Conversations with women in order to pay for my rent and expenses, but my main work at the moment is to finish and publish this project, *Summer on the Lakes*. The reason I petitioned Harvard for entry is that I need access to their archives to ensure that my writings on the American Midwest and the tribes who live there are accurate. I need the maps, the histories, the primary sources written by travelers other than just me—all male, of course. To my delight, and a fair bit of surprise, President Quincy agreed. I can't help but suspect that perhaps his wife, enrolled in my first series of Conversations, put in a good word.

I'm just settling in, sorting my papers to find the spot where I've left off, when a gentleman approaches my seat. I glance up at him, noting just how young he looks now that he's so close. He shoves his hands into his pockets, then pulls them out as he whispers: "Excuse me, miss?"

I lean back in my chair, offering him a measured smile. "Yes?"

"Begging your pardon, but I think there's been some mistake."

I stiffen. "Has there?"

He throws a glance toward his small cluster of pals, some of whom are barely concealing their giggles, then glances back down at me as he says: "You see, the tea parties aren't held here."

I cock my head to the side, assuming an expression of befuddlement. "Is that so?"

"Afraid so," he says, sharing a look with the observing crowd at the adjacent table. He wears a smug grin when he leans back down toward me, and speaking very slowly, as if I require the extra time to understand, he adds: "This is Harvard."

"Gore Hall, I believe?" I lift my paper, raising it toward him.

He looks at it for a moment, eventually mumbling, "Yes."

I pull the paper back, lowering it to the desk before me. And then, sitting up straight as can be, with my best schoolmistress posture and a clipped tone of authority, I answer him: "Then this is precisely where I am meant to be. I'm only sorry it took so long for me to get here. Now, if you'll excuse me, I have work to get to before even thinking about my tea."

The young fellow walks back to his group of friends, offering only a quick shake of his head. I hear them erupt in shocked whispers, but I pay them no mind. I turn my gaze down to my papers. My heart is pounding in my chest, the blood thrashing in my temples, but I force myself not to look toward them. I know everyone in this hall is watching me—I can feel each pair of eyes.

But I raise my pen and read over my words. As I said, I have work to do.

EVERY DAY THAT week I report to Gore Hall in the early morning, taking the same seat in the reading room and spreading my pages before me. Of course I notice that the space around that seat stays empty. The lads who trickle in and out of the reading room continue to stare, but by the end of the week, they seem to have accepted my presence there with a resigned sort of apathy. The stares are less stunned, less lingering. Eventually I learn to ignore them entirely. I settle into a routine, writing for six hours each day, with an hour's break for midday luncheon, which I take out on the yard.

I pull the books and maps and atlases from the shelves with glee, like a child plundering a forbidden toy shop. I curl my body over the books and pages, my mind so utterly consumed in my reading and writing that the hours pass quickly. Oftentimes I look up from my work and notice, with a jolt of surprise, that night has darkened beyond the tall Gothic windows. My shoulders ache, my hands look bruised by the ink, but my mind and my spirit are enlivened with the work.

In the evenings, in order to uncurl my hunched body, I walk. The Cambridge winter is cold and the wind off the Charles needles my eyes, but I amble for as long as I can take it. I breathe in the sights and sounds as darkness envelops the city. I make my way back to my rented room and by the time I climb the stairs I feel hungry for dinner and eager for bed. Eager to sleep so that, tomorrow, I may walk back to Harvard and begin my work again.

The book that takes shape in my hands is in part a travel memoir, in part my journalistic accounting of the places I visited and the people I met. But it's also much more. It's a work of female adventure, written by a woman who went on her own into parts unknown. It's a philosophical pondering of what we carry with us from our own natures, and what we take on from the society around us and the conditioning of our circumstances. It's a treatise on finding religious sustenance and spiritual experiences in the mystical wilds of our American frontier. It's a glimpse into our nation's landscapes and character at this fragile point of our history, a crossroads of rapid growth, massive change, and staggering potential.

It's also, I hope, a rallying cry. A chant for female expression in the place of repression. It's an invitation for readers, both male *and* female, to take on the hard work of adventure, of wandering, of self-exploration and expansion. There's a call to action that I've issued to each reader who takes up my pages: be bold and daring.

Just as I have been bold and daring.

As spring returns to Cambridge, as the lilacs and cherry trees around the Harvard campus begin to bud and then to flower, I have a stack of pages that looks very much to me like a finished book. I send my manuscript to Emerson, who has informed me that his publisher wishes to see my work.

Several weeks later, as I'm concluding my final Conversation, I receive word from Waldo that I have a good deal on the table. Little and Brown wishes to offer me not only a contract to publish, but also royalties of ten cents for every book that sells. It's a promising proposal, and one I should take, Waldo advises. If the book does well, then I shall do well.

THE DAY OF my birthday dawns mild and clear, with spring ripening into her full glory. I open the window of my room to allow in the gentle May sunshine and the cheerful sound of nearby birdsong. I stretch, breathing in the scent of the breeze. I am entering my thirty-fourth year of life feeling strong, feeling that some deep energy has been kindled inside me, stoked by both my travels and my writing. By the promise that might come from this work.

I spend the day of my thirty-fourth birthday outside under the shade of a cherry tree, reading the final draft of my work. Knowing that, after this, I will send these pages back to my publisher and then out into the world. Into the hands of readers. It's the story of an adventure that I took, and now I suspect that its publication might lead to countless further adventures ahead. I feel as though I'm stepping not only into a new year, but into a new and important moment in the journey of my life.

Chapter Twenty-Seven

T HE SURPRISING SUCCESS OF *SUMMER ON THE LAKES* gives me a deep and joyful satisfaction, and also a respite from my financial worries. It sells well, my book. Seven hundred copies, which is hundreds more than Waldo's first book sold.

My work also enjoys the sunshine of widespread critical acclaim, and that is perhaps the greater prize. No one's approval makes me smile more broadly than Horace Greeley's; he writes to me from New York with his fulsome congratulations: *"Miss Fuller, it's the first truly original American book to be published this year."* And then he reiterates his request that I come to New York and work for him: *"I'm looking for new content. And a new voice. I see both in you."*

Emboldened by my new acclaim, I respond to Greeley in kind. *"Make me a formal offer,"* I write. I can be enticed to consider his invitation; in fact, I'd relish the prospect of charting a bold new course that would take me to Manhattan and the full-time work of the newspaperman. Newspaper*woman*, rather. If Mr. Greeley can set forth enough incentive to pull me from Boston to New York. My days of working for a newspaper for free are over.

In the meantime, there's another invitation I readily accept. Waldo has also written with his congratulations from Bush. In his letter he includes a most lovely request: Might I consider a summer visit to Concord?

A summer visit in Concord sounds like just the thing. I set at once to packing.

. . .

I ARRIVE BY coach and immediately see that the village of Concord has changed in one dramatic way: there's a busy new train station. It now runs from Charlestown in Boston directly out to the country, meaning that for the price of two quarters, Bostonians are offered a one-hour trip into the heart of our rural village. They come by the hour, disgorged from out of the train onto the new stone and wood depot, walking at their brisk city pace, carrying their city cargo as they troop out into our quiet lanes.

A train has arrived at the same time as my coach, and so I stand a moment and observe the colorful crowd, the people stepping down off the platform; I can't help but fear, as I watch, that the wider world might soon overrun our precious, peaceful little corner.

I arrive at Bush and I soon discover that no one is more disgruntled by this new development than Thoreau, who rails against "the belching iron horse" and declares that this might be the final push he needs to leave village life altogether. "But if Concord is now too much the metropolis for you, where will you go?" I ask my friend.

"I'll retreat to the woods," he answers. "To the shores of Walden Pond."

"You aren't really leaving, Mr. Thoreau?" Louy, who is sitting with us in the garden under Waldo's old tulip tree, flashes her beloved tutor a look of disbelief. "You can't very well live on the *Musketaquid.*"

"I could indeed, if I needed to," Thoreau replies, winking at the girl. "But I will not need to. I'll build myself a home."

Louy looks dubious. "With what tools?"

Thoreau raises his dirty hands. "With these two tools that our Creator gave me."

THERE IS SOME happy news at Bush, also. Lidian is eagerly awaiting the arrival of another baby. I wonder: Does she hope for a boy? To replace the beloved son who left them far too early? But how could anything ever heal the heartache of little Waldo's absence?

No, perhaps another little girl would be better, so as to invite less temptation for comparison.

Emerson is hard at work. He's nearly finished with a series of essays that he plans to publish as a collection under the title *Second Series,* and he expects the great triumph of the work to be an essay titled "Experience." He spends every morning closeted in his study, rarely emerging even for luncheon. When he does, his mood is mercurial, his manners aloof. He prefers now to take his walks alone, slipping out the front door before I hear that he's gone.

I tell myself that it's work that occupies his mind, and I should not push my way in. Of course he wishes to finalize this series before the baby comes—he must feel a sense of urgency that spurs him on and leaves little time for our free conversations and visits of summers past. Our relationship has weathered enough at this point for me to understand that Waldo and I have our seasons, the natural ebbs and flows of any close kinship. Whatever the current state of things between us may be, it, too, shall shift. He would not have invited me here unless he'd wanted me to come.

But why *did* he invite me, only to shun me and avoid my presence? As the weeks pass, I can't help but wonder. In truth, I do begin to suspect that there may be something more to this chasm between us. There is some hardness to him now that I see with more frequency.

Is it the passing of little Waldo? As if the slicing pain of losing that boy, and the scab that formed as a result, has caused a hard casing to thicken around his heart. After losing his beloved Ellen and then his brother, perhaps the loss of the babe he adored made a burden too great to carry on top. I begin to wonder whether Waldo will ever be willing to open his heart again.

If he does, it certainly won't be to me. That is what I come to see, as the days of the summer pass slowly by. Waldo has become all cold and steady intellect. I, Margaret Fuller, *the Much that always wants More,* I am too much passion. Too much feeling.

But it should not be me, anyhow, I remind myself. If and when Waldo does once more soften his heart, it should not be me who stands as the recipient of all he has to offer.

And so, while I pine for my close friend of visits and years past, while I miss his unrivaled conversations, his smiles, his interest—I force myself to find diversion elsewhere. I console myself with the wild countryside of Concord. I chase Louisa May as she drives her hoop down the shaded lane. We take a picnic out to our beloved Fairyland Pond. Thoreau and I help the girls as they stage a production of *Jack and the Beanstalk*, and we laugh to see Louy's performance as the reluctant milk cow.

ONE SUNNY AFTERNOON, Louy and I float with Thoreau down the river toward the Old Manse, where the Hawthornes are still in residence. Their family is growing—they, too, have baby news. Sophia has given Nathaniel a little daughter named Una, and I am eager to meet the baby.

I sit at the front of the *Musketaquid*, looking out over the water as dappled sunlight filters through the leafy trees. I close my eyes and draw in a deep breath, relishing the smells of river mud and grass. This visit to the Old Manse shall be only joy, I tell myself. A reunion with Nathaniel and Sophia and a chance to meet their little girl. None of the awkwardness of past summers. Whatever once passed between Nathaniel and me, it has subsided. The Hawthornes do enjoy a happy marriage, from what everyone tells me, and I'm sure they have settled into a lovely harmony now that they are three.

And that is precisely what the visit is. It's a happy meeting, a domestic pandemonium in and around the Old Manse. Una toddles across the sun-warmed grass in just her diaper, taking turns chasing Louy and Thoreau, who prance around on all fours like ponies. Sophia and I sit nearby on the lawn, enjoying the gentle breeze and the peaceful view of the river, sipping lemonade as Hawthorne toggles between our two groups. Motherhood suits Sophia, who sits in loose white muslin, a contented smile upturning her lips as she relishes Una's playful squeals of delight.

On the boat ride back toward Bush I am in a quiet, contemplative mood, my thoughts unspooling as we glide across the river. Once we reach Thoreau's favorite maple and tie off the *Musketaquid*, I slip off to my bedroom and open my journal. *"Life here slumbers and steals on like the river,"* I write. *"It's a very good place for a sage, but not for the activist. Life here in Concord is lacking in Discord."*

Perhaps it's the taste of success I've enjoyed following *Summer on the Lakes.* Perhaps it's the realization that Waldo and I, for the moment, have reached a plateau in what we can offer each other here on these warm summer afternoons in the country. Perhaps it's the glimpse of domestic contentment I've just witnessed over at the Old Manse, noting—not with bitterness, but certainly with a pang of melancholy—that I am so far removed from that sort of life with a husband and a household. Whatever the reasons may be, I now feel, more than ever, the need for change. A tugging feeling toward something new. The struggle to grow, to learn, to challenge myself through a new adventure.

I know where that could be found. If I were to accept a position at the *New-York Tribune* working with Greeley, I'd have new challenges and opportunities for adventure in abundance. New York City is the opposite of Concord.

But, troublingly, I have heard nothing further from Greeley this summer. Not since I arrived in Concord. No formal offer has materialized. Perhaps he has had a change of heart. Perhaps he's filled the position with someone else, someone who accepted more readily.

That night, after our hours on the river, I drift into sleep with visions of water swirling before me. I'm not sure how much later it is that I awake with a start, convinced I've only just saved myself from drowning. I bolt upright, looking around as I gasp for air. The bedsheets cling, wet, to my skin.

I blink, and the shadowed room materializes before me. My heart is an angry hammer in my chest. I blink again and remember where I am. I am in my bedroom. At Bush. Not on a ship. Not struggling to keep out of the water as the ship goes down into the roiling waves. I breathe out an audible exhale, willing my heart to slow its pace. I am safe. I am not drowning, I tell myself again. Yet as I lie back down in bed, sliding over to the other side where the sheets are less damp with sweat, I know that sleep will evade me for the rest of the night.

I am in a wretched state at breakfast the next morning. I sip my coffee but I have little appetite. Waldo does not come down, nor does Lidian. It's just as well, I tell myself. I'd make for poor conversation this morning. But when Thoreau ambles in with the morning post, he places a letter before me. I glance at it, a bit stunned, then I sit up straighter in my chair. Horace Greeley. I stare at his handwriting on the envelope for a moment, then I tear it open.

> *Margaret,*
> *Please come be my literary editor, and the first lady to*
> *work for me. Come here to make history, and then, carry on by*
> *helping us to shape its arc. There is much work to be done.*
> *I shall pay you ten dollars a week. That's three dollars more*
> *than the last writer who had your job, a gentleman.*
>> *Yours truly,*
> > *Horace Greeley*

ON MY FINAL night in Concord I sit in my favorite red arm chair in my bedroom, unable to sleep. I've packed. I've said my goodbyes—to Nathaniel and Sophia and Una, to Louisa May and the Alcotts. To Thoreau. I'll say my farewells to the Emersons in the morning before I leave by the new train.

But though I'm ready to go, my mind churns with thoughts. Thoughts of all that is to come in my new life in Manhattan, so much of it unknown. And thoughts of so many Concord evenings of summers past—the blooming of the Night Queen in the fragrant garden, the impossible glimpse of a giraffe in the town square, the scattering of stars over Walden Pond just before sunrise.

That's when I hear a coughing noise, from out in the garden. I take my lone candle and go to the window, which is open, the curtains fluttering in the breeze. I blink and look out into the night. The garden is silvered in moonlight that seeps through the leafy chestnuts. There's a shape, a darkened silhouette, and I know it immediately. Waldo.

He must see me looking out because he speaks, his voice traveling across the night and through my open window. "I was just thinking that tomorrow, if I take a nightly walk, I will see no candlelight in your window." From the tenor of his voice, the willingness of his words, I can see that Waldo is different than he has been, less closed off.

I lean on my windowsill, glancing out at him. "Come now, I've taken my leave of Concord a great number of times."

"But this feels different," he says, his voice low as he walks toward my window.

I nod. He is correct; it does feel different. This parting will take me farther afield. To work that will make demands on me in ways I do not yet even fully understand. And I don't know when I shall return.

I look up at the night sky over Concord, the vast bowl of stars and moon, and then back down at my friend. In this moment he is here. He is open in a way he has not been all summer. All is restored between us because our friendship, though in many ways built on words, has also always been a union that does not need words. At least, it does not need them to be spoken aloud.

Waldo reaches up and I take his outstretched hand, giving it a squeeze. "Waldo, my friend. You have been my steady star, while I've been a constantly flowing stream."

I see the flicker of his smiling eyes, as he responds in a way that is so perfectly Waldo. "If you've been the constantly flowing stream, then never forget my steady beam." And with that, I see, it is poetry between us once more. And the perfect time for me to go.

Chapter Twenty-Eight

New York City
Fall 1844

"MARGARET FULLER, IS IT REALLY YOU?" HORACE Greeley looks up from behind his hulking wooden desk, slipping his wire-rimmed glasses down the bridge of his nose, as if he does not quite accept the fact that I've finally answered his invitation.

"It is I, Mr. Greeley."

"It took you some time."

"Well, there was this to see to." I stride toward his desk and place a bulky, heavy parcel before him.

Greeley stares at the mountain of pages a moment, then lets out a slow whistling sound. "You tarried on the Hudson River all autumn to work on it. And now . . . may I?"

"You may."

"It's long," he notes, taking the pages into his grip.

"Yes, three times the length of 'The Great Lawsuit,'" I say, mentioning the original essay I wrote for *The Dial*, the piece that Greeley admired and urged me to expand into a book, the very book I now place before him.

"Please, Margaret, sit. I am hoping you'll stay awhile."

I take the offered seat across from him.

"Do you have a title in mind?" Greeley asks, riffling through the pages.

I *do* have a title in mind. After much thought, I have settled on one particular idea. "I was thinking *Woman in the Nineteenth Century*."

Greeley considers this a moment, eventually offering a nod. "I like it. It's clear. It says what we are endeavoring to say."

I like how he puts it: what *we* are endeavoring to say. Horace Greeley has made me feel as though we are two members of the same team from the start. In truth we are: in fighting for the expanded rights of women, in speaking out for the freedom of the enslaved populations of the southern states, in calling for decent treatment of day laborers, protection for children, widows, prisoners—in short, those who are most often let down by our society. Those who have not yet had the full chance to prosper in our land of opportunity. Greeley, like me, wishes to fight each day to help make America a more perfect union. And not just for wealthy white men.

"How did you make it so much longer?" he asks. "'The Great Lawsuit' did not cut corners."

"Prostitution," I answer.

Greeley's mouth falls open. His eyes meet mine as two rounded orbs, and I see that I've flummoxed the great, unflappable Horace Greeley. He clears his throat, muttering: "Excuse me?"

I sit up in my chair, glancing at my pages in his hands. "I covered female prostitutes in my research and writing this time."

Greeley's pale cheeks flush, but he nods now in understanding—and relief—as he surmises my point. "Ah, yes, I see. Yes. And that was why you were spending so much of your time up at the prison on the Hudson?"

"Yes, Sing Sing, precisely. I did not think it was fair, or right, to write a book on women but only speak about the women among us who have enough to eat. Or who have a safe home to sleep in at night. What of the many women who do not have that comfort and security?" I shift in my seat, rearranging the folds of my skirts, my mind sifting back over the hundreds of women I've spent the past few months meeting and interviewing in my efforts to glean their stories.

I sit for a moment in thoughtful silence, then I go on. "A woman does not end up a prostitute or a prisoner by her choice, or because she is born with an evil nature. Yes, a woman should be permitted to divorce a cruel or abusive husband. Yes, a woman ought to own her own property and not merely give it over to her husband as soon as the marriage vows are uttered. And I argue all of those points, but what of the women who do not have the privilege of owning property in the first place? The woman who does not have a man to marry after she becomes pregnant with his child?" My voice is thick now with the deep feelings stirred by these topics, and I can see from Greeley's features that he is listening intently. I carry on, saying, "Some of the lowest in our female ranks, why, that 'lowness' is but an accident of birth. Whether we are born paupers or princesses, we have no say in that. And yet life will be entirely different, depending on those circumstances at birth. I needed to share with readers a more full picture of womanhood."

Greeley is quiet for a long moment. "Quite right," he says eventually. He begins once more to flip through the pages. He halts on a page, then reads aloud: "'But if you ask me what offices women may fill; I reply—any. I do not care what case you put; let them be sea-captains, if that be their calling!'"

I flush as I hear Horace Greeley reading my words aloud: I know the exact section from which he's pulling now. My argument that a woman ought to be free to pursue her own passions. That there really ought to be no such thing as a *woman's* job and a *man's* job. That looking at the world in such a narrow way does a great disservice, not only to men and women but to society as a whole. A woman is a human, and as such, has a right to know her own worth, to pursue self-realization and satisfying work, same as any man.

"You speak here about a woman's 'fullness of being'; I like that. Mary will like that," Greeley says, fingering the page in his grip.

"Thank you," I reply.

"It's long," Greeley notes. And then he places the full stack of my labor down on his wooden desk with a loud thump, sending a slight breeze across the air that makes my hair flutter. When he looks at me his face is a bit flushed, his features creased in earnest thought. "Yet you didn't in fact take all that long. Just a few months to get all these pages."

"Yes, well, I found that these words, having resided in my heart and soul for so long, were eager to come out. And thus my inspiration kept spinning out from my hands."

"And we are most fortunate that it has." Greeley dips his chin in a quick nod. "Most fortunate indeed. I think that in this you shall be giving women everywhere the single best argument they've ever had for living their lives with freedom." He riffles to the end and presses a finger onto the page, pausing on the last lines. I've written there, very candidly, that I do not regret that so many see me as an "old maid," useless to society because I do not have a husband or children. Instead, I have forged a path for myself that feels natural and full of meaningful work. I don't see my life as a waste or a failure, even if others do.

Greeley heaves an exhale, and then he reads aloud, as if I don't already have the words memorized: "'Let my life be a beautiful, powerful, in a word, a *complete* life in its kind. Had I but one more moment to live, I must wish the same.'"

"What do you think?" I ask, my voice quivering slightly.

"What do I think?" Greeley props an elbow on his desk, staring down at the page. When he looks up at me, his eyes are two flames. "I think I've been trying to get you to come work for me for some months now . . . and, well, it was all worth the wait."

I braid my fingers together in my lap, smiling a moment before I say: "You mentioned you might wish to publish it."

"Yes." Greeley leans back in his seat, throwing me a pointed stare. He rolls his sleeves up as he says: "I'll be publishing it, Margaret. I only hope you are ready for what is coming your way."

Chapter Twenty-Nine

Spring 1845

WHAT COMES MY WAY, IT REACHES BEYOND MY WILD-est hopes. When *Woman in the Nineteenth Century* pub-lishes that spring, all fifteen hundred copies sell out in just the first few days. Apparently my name holds some interest for readers, of which there are many. The readers and critics are in agreement—mine is an important book and a worthy book. Not only for women, who are my immediate audience, but for all Americans.

There are detractors, to be sure. Some scoff at me, saying that as an unmarried woman I have no standing to opine on marriage or anything else having to do with a woman's experience in society. Some call my assertions unnatural. One particularly offended critic points out that many ladies have been committed to insane asy-lums for ideas and thoughts less bold than mine. But those shards of outrage do little to pierce me, and besides, the whiff of scandal only fuels further sales of my book.

Greeley appears even more elated than I do. "They're comparing you to Mary Wollstonecraft," he proclaims, citing the name of the celebrated English writer, one of my heroines. "Really, Margaret, I had hoped we'd sell a few hundred, perhaps a thousand over the course of the book's life, but, my friend, you've already sent us scrambling back to the presses."

We are seated at breakfast, Greeley and I. When I'd accepted the editorial position at his newspaper, he had very kindly invited me to take a room in his large farmhouse, as well. He and Mary live just a couple of miles to the north of the crowded Manhattan neighborhood where his *Tribune* offices are located. The Greeley estate, "the Farm," is tucked up on a bluff overlooking the East River in the rural region called Turtle Bay. It is a lovely place, even if a bit run-down, but I find that the unruly state of things simply adds to its charm. The home is an old white wooden farmhouse, with a porch wrapped in climbing vines and roses. I don't know Mary or Horace to be particularly concerned with pruning or weeding, but they tell me their garden is quite productive in the summer nevertheless. Thoreau would approve.

Nestled into a dozen leafy acres with a warren of old trees and the river as its border, the Farm sits back at the end of a long dirt lane. My quarters are upstairs, a comfortable bedroom with plenty of light, thanks to a row of windows that open out over a lovely willow tree and views of the East River. It is a living situation far preferable to renting a cramped room in a New York City board-inghouse, and it had helped that the invitation by Greeley immedi-ately put Mother at ease with my accepting a job in New York City. To know that I would be safe in a home and enjoying the compan-ionship of the respected Greeleys had softened some of Mother's reluctance over my leaving New England.

"I won't hear otherwise. Mary would have my head," Horace had said, when I'd politely demurred at first. "We can't have Margaret Fuller alone and at large in Manhattan. It wouldn't do."

And in fact, the Farm is a most agreeable spot for my new work and life in Manhattan—close enough to the center of things, but far enough to feel as though I have the peace and greenery of a coun-try abode. Most days Horace and I take breakfast together and then either walk down to the *Tribune* offices or, if pressed for time, catch the Harlem omnibus down Fourth Avenue.

As much as I enjoy the friendship and support of Horace, it is especially lovely to also have time with his wife, Mary, who has become a fast friend, as well as the companionship of their darling little toddler, Arthur. And it is Mary and Arthur who come trooping into the dining room to join us at the breakfast table this morning.

"Good morning, Mary, Arthur." I shift in my seat, happy to see them, but also bracing for what I suspect is to come: I'm drinking coffee at the table, and Mary does little to hide her scowl when she sees. I try to conceal my good-natured smirk as I take a sip. Mary throws a pointed look toward her husband, who offers only a non-committal shrug; Horace and Mary are faithful adherents to the diet and teachings of Sylvester Graham, that health prophet who advocates a strict regimen of his bland "Graham crackers," along with vegetables and water. Tea, and especially coffee, are flatly forbidden.

"Good morning," Mary answers, apparently deciding against issuing a scolding. "And how are you both?" She settles her little boy at the table, where he immediately begins tapping his spoon against the wood.

"Morning, my dearest ones." Greeley pats the corners of his mouth with his napkin. "I was just telling our Margaret here what a sensation she has become. Both famous and infamous, depending on whom you ask."

I glance down at my toast, attempting a look of modesty, even as I feel my cheeks grow warm. I know that it's true, what he says about my burgeoning reputation; I see the way people sometimes look at me on the street, while I ride the omnibus, or while I sit in the newsroom. I have name recognition now that I've published several bestselling books, and particularly now that I'm writing for a newspaper that has more than fifty thousand readers, its circulation extending as far as the Middle West and beyond.

But even more than the wide circulation and recognition of my words, it's the subject matter that gives me the deepest satisfaction—the fact that it's interesting and worthy work for which I raise my pen each day. My assignments as a newspaperwoman allow me to drink deep of all that New York and its half-million souls have to offer. Why, just the week before, I attended the New York Philharmonic to review a concert featuring works by the German virtuoso Ludwig van Beethoven. The week before that, I reviewed the new poetry of the great Englishwoman Elizabeth Barrett. This week I'm assigned to review pieces by two up-and-coming writers named Frederick Douglass and Karl Marx.

Greeley takes a final bite of his Graham cracker, pushing his chair back from the table. His mind, too, is on our work. "How is the piece on Douglass coming along?"

I tap the side of my coffee cup with my fingers, collecting my thoughts to answer. My assignment—which Greeley gave me—is to review the book by Frederick Douglass, a former slave, titled *Narrative of the Life of Frederick Douglass, an American Slave, Written by Himself*. The truth is that Mr. Douglass's work has pierced me, the blades of his truths and arguments landing in my heart and my gut in a way I have never before experienced. Mr. Douglass has laid bare the lies and falsehoods of any person who would dare to claim that an individual with dark skin is inferior to one who is white. Mr. Douglass has put a human heart and face to the fierce arguments that are currently gripping our nation on the question of slavery. I say as much to Greeley now.

"Reading the words of Mr. Douglass, I cannot fathom how any person might credibly contend that a Black individual does not have the same soul, the same potency of mind, the same spirit, as a white individual. Why, Mr. Douglass himself stands as a refutation to anyone who would dare try."

Greeley nods heartily, rising from the table. "Amen," he says. Striding across the room, he pauses an instant to plant a quick kiss atop his wife's head, and one on his young son. And then, looking to me, he adds: "Much as you do, Margaret, for anyone who would dare claim the same argument against a woman."

What I've come to love most about Greeley's newsroom is that there he considers me a trusted partner. And it is to that newsroom that we now make our way. I rise from the table, slipping my shawl over my shoulders and then inching my fingers into my leather gloves. Mary Greeley, who is crumbling up bite-sized pieces of cracker for her son, throws me another scandalized look. Then, pointing to my leather gloves, she lets out a beleaguered gasp. "I can hold my tongue no longer. Why, Margaret, that's the skin of a poor beast!"

I raise my hands in apology, but then realize that the leather gloves on my hands are precisely what have caused the offense, so I lower them, folding them behind my back with a look of contrition. "I know, Mary, I'm sorry." But I need my fingers in order to write, and I need gloves in order to keep my fingers warm on our long trek to work. These spring mornings can still be chilly. Mary can keep her offenses and opinions; it's a price I'm willing to pay for her friendship and her hospitality.

I LIKE IT when time allows and we set out for the *Tribune* offices on foot, gradually watching the meadows of Turtle Bay give way to the dirt lanes of Peter Cooper Village, before we reach the roiling bustle of southern Manhattan. There, in the lower corner of the island hemmed by rivers, humanity and human activity reach their colorful crescendo, through the busy neighborhoods of Washington Square and the Bowling Green.

It's a world apart from the Farm, down here where the priests and nuns serve the hungry of the Five Points slum and the business-men march like soldiers to Wall Street to serve their general, the dollar. The broad avenues narrow into the older, mazy cobblestone streets that teem with horse and human traffic. Greeley and I, side by side, dodge carriages and pedestrians as we tromp down in the direction of New York Harbor, where an endless flow of ships stream in and out on the tides. They bring goods from every corner of the globe, these vessels, but I feel that their most fascinating cargo is the people who arrive each day from countless distant countries—Ireland, Germany, Sweden, Italy, Hungary, even as far afield as China and Japan. New York City, like our nation, is in the throes of a massive and undeniable change.

We keep up our brisk pace as we walk through City Hall Park, past the splashing fountain, eventually arriving at our office build-ing. Outside, several of the young newsboys are back from their early deliveries and they rest, sitting on their bottoms beside the doorway. We greet them and then step inside, out of the chaos of a New York City morning and into the chaos of a New York City newsroom.

We climb the three stories to arrive at the large, crowded offices of the *New-York Tribune*. Inside, the space is brightened by rows of windows, and dozens of wooden desks and bookshelves hulk under the weight of paper, books, and journals. The newsmen still look up as I enter, and that's only in part because I'm walking in just before their employer. It's mostly because I'm a woman in their midst.

The fact of the matter is that these are some of the most forward-thinking men in America, and they *have* gotten subtler with their stares, but I do feel how the energy in the room shifts as I enter. I could be back at Harvard again, the only woman penetrating the sacred space of men.

I bid farewell to Horace, who makes his way to his private office, and I walk past a long row of unruly bookshelves, then a seating area with sofas and tables, arriving at my very own desk. It's tidy, filled with books and magazines, carved of a sturdy, gleaming pine. I take my seat, slipping off my shawl and gloves. I thrum with energy after the long walk and my eager anticipation for the work of the day. But before I begin, I take a moment to stare out the windows that show lower Manhattan, the same landscape through which I've just trooped to arrive here.

America is changing, and nowhere is that more visible than in New York City. Here, in Greeley's newsroom, I am on the front lines of that change, working toward something that feels most meaningful. As I sought to do when I held my Conversations for women in Boston, or when I marched into Gore Hall at Harvard, or when I visited Sing Sing prison to speak with the women whom society wishes we'd all forget, here I am working to challenge. I am planting seeds with my words, in the hopes that my writing will burst into new life in the minds of my readers, in the form of independent thoughts and important questions.

I told Greeley, when I began my work for him, that I would be guided by three principles. The first is that I wish to tell the truth. The second, I wish to write what the public needs to know. And finally, I wish to write stories that will help us to bring about a better day for all.

I look down at my task for the day: The book that has held me in its thrall this week as I've devoured the words of Mr. Douglass. *Narrative of the Life of Frederick Douglass, an American Slave, Written by Himself.* A brilliant man who will show Americans a truth that far too many do not know, and too many more do not wish to know. Mr. Douglass will humanize the enslaved masses, pulling their pain into the light after far too many years concealed in shadow. Will Mr. Douglass's words help lead us to the truth? Yes.

Will Mr. Douglass's words offer something that Americans need to know? Yes. And, in supporting his work, am I helping to bring about a brighter day? My most fervent hope: yes. This is just the sort of work that needs to be done, and there is no one who is more determined to do it than I.

Chapter Thirty

Summer 1845

"DO MINE EYES DECEIVE ME? OR ARE YOU *NERVOUS*?"
I stand with Horace outside the gracious brownstone of
Miss Anne Charlotte Lynch, a poet and fixture of the New York
literary circles. And our hostess for this night's gathering.

"Not nervous." I press down the folds of my purple poplin dress.
"Only . . ."

"No need for further explanation." Horace gives the ground a
decisive rap with his cane. "You like to have a firm grasp of things.
And yet we don't know what we are walking into. But never fear—
you've walked into thornier vipers' nests than this one."

"I suppose you are right." But I am to present to the crowd gathered that evening in Miss Lynch's elegant Waverly Place parlor,
what promises to be a glittering and artistic assembly. And yet it's
my fellow presenter, my fellow honoree that evening, who is giving
me my greatest worries.

The writer Edgar Allan Poe has just recently published a scathing critique of me in his paper, *The Broadway Journal*, mocking the
very work that I am to present this evening. Poe, no doubt thinking
himself quite clever, has made a play on my name and called me
"Margaret Fooler." I would ignore his jibes just as I've ignored so
many others throughout my thirty-five years, but for the fact that
his success is everywhere. His new poem "The Raven" is the current
favorite of all New York literary reviews and journals, and we are
scheduled to be speaking in the same parlor this evening. No mat-

ter how spacious and grand Miss Lynch's home may be, I doubt it will be big enough for the two of us to occupy it entirely peaceably.

And it is the words of "The Raven" that I hear as I step out of the noise of a Manhattan evening and into Miss Lynch's hushed, elegant foyer. A butler greets us with a polite, quiet nod, leading us into the packed parlor, where Poe is already well into his recitation, a king holding his court in thrall. I slip into the room, noticing the eyes that dart toward me to note my entry. I suppress my instinctive urge to scowl as I hear Poe droning on about his *"bleak December."* Unsurprisingly, the colorful audience gathered there is rapt. I see how they hang on his words, as his deep southern drawl intones, making his words *"Once upon a midnight dreary"* seem even drearier.

I meet the eyes of a few familiar faces. The writer Walt Whitman is here this evening, standing beside the far window, his clothes worn and rumpled, his face fixed in attention. He's beside his friend, young Herman Melville, whose mahogany beard is as wild as his thick bramble of hair. Our hostess, Miss Lynch, glides over with a warm smile. She looks every bit as elegant as the home over which she presides, dressed in a taffeta gown of bright salmon, festooned with tasteful gold trim and embroidery. She moves without making a noise, holding a tray of shortbread cookies, which she extends toward us now. Behind her is a table heaped with samovars of tea and tidy rows of porcelain cups and saucers.

Poe, up front, notices the small flurry of activity that my entrance has elicited, and he throws me a passing scowl as he carries on with his performance. We are tardy, but it's because I had an interview just this afternoon at the Bloomingdale Insane Asylum, and the nurses and governors of the place were generous enough to give me hours of their time. During a most thorough tour I had the chance to speak with a handful of the inmates, to observe them taking the air and their exercises in the yard. I didn't want to rush out of there, nor did I wish to be rude to them, even if it meant that I was now being slightly rude to Mr. Poe. But something told me I did not need to worry all that much about Mr. Poe's robust ego.

I glance around the room but I don't see Mrs. Poe, a young lady and Poe's cousin who became his child bride at age thirteen. They are an odd pair, the Poes. She's a beribboned southern belle who has weathered years of ailments following a lingering case of tuberculosis. He's a well-known philanderer; in fact, even as far removed as I am from the New York ladies' gossip and sewing circles, the scandals have reached my ears. Whispers of how flagrant Poe is, how little he does to hide his assignations with various and sundry lovers. Poe is no advocate for the rights of women.

Nor do I like the fact that Poe, who was raised in a Virginia household with slaves, goes to little trouble now to hide his odious belief that slavery ought to continue in our country. With a character as deficient as that, Poe is hardly the man I need critiquing my work. I hear the famous concluding lines of his poem now, droned through Poe's slow, sonorous drawl: *"And my soul from out that shadow that lies floating on the floor, / Shall be lifted—nevermore!"*

There's a beat of silence, a pulsing, pensive pause as all in the room absorb the final words, and then, a crash of raucous applause. Poe throws up his hands in a theatrical display of magnanimous appreciation. He is a sensation. He performs well and he writes even better, I will not deny that, even if I don't like the man. Nor do I particularly relish the prospect I now face of having to present my own work on the heels of his smashing success.

Nevertheless, as our hostess introduces me, I step brightly to the fore, nodding at the ladies and gentlemen as I wade through their crowd. I hear pockets of whispers; I notice the way their eyes scan my figure from head to hem. I take my place in the front of the parlor, pulling back my shoulders and drawing myself up to my full height. I clear my throat, smiling out at the attentive assembly, and I say, "Good evening, ladies and gentlemen."

They respond in kind, many of them leaning forward in their seats. I offer my hostess an appreciative nod, a word of thanks. And then, drawing in a slow, fortifying breath, I begin.

"I thought I might devote my time here this evening to speak not only of the book I've already published, but of a rather important piece on which I'm now working, and a matter that affects each one of us gathered in this lovely home. And that is: the many necessary and vital charities of our city." I can tell that this lands around the room to mixed reactions. Some perch on the edges of their seats, eager to hear what it is I feel compelled to say. Others, Poe very much included, look less than enthusiastic. He whispers something to the lady at his side, and I recognize her famous face. She is Frances Sargent Osgood, another poet, and rumored to be one of Poe's lovers.

I launch my talk by telling the crowd that the reason for my tardiness this evening is that I have just come from a visit to the Bloomingdale Asylum. I see their heavy glances, their quick-whispered exchanges, as I describe my walk through the facility, known as one of our city's busiest madhouses. Then I tell them about my recent visit to the Bellevue Almshouse beside the East River, just a few days prior. Another recent stop has been at the Farm School Orphanage, where I met, in particular, the little children of our city.

"Picture the poor little dears," I say, "their bodies thin and stooped. It is not their fault they've been abandoned. But let them not be abandoned, a second time, by us." I tell the small crowd that I've visited, also, the Asylum for the Insane and the Blackwell's Island Penitentiary, where more than one thousand poor souls wallow in what I can only describe as a most bleak and hopeless pit. Poe can speak about his dreary midnights all he likes—I have in fact been to places as macabre and desolate as anything in his wild imaginings. And they are right here in our city.

And yet, though one could suspect that the grisly subject matter of my speech might pique his interest, I can see now that he's anything but interested. In fact he's still whispering to Mrs. Osgood, and something he says makes her chuckle outright.

"Mr. Poe," I say, throwing him a pointed look. "I can see that you have a question. Would you like to pose it to me directly?"

"A question?" Poe meets my eyes with his, and I can't help but notice the shiver that runs over my skin. Then he hitches his facial features into a slippery, mocking sort of smirk, his thin dark mustache hovering over a row of stained teeth, and he adds: "I've got a great number of questions, in fact."

I fold my hands before my waist, holding his dark-eyed stare with a direct look of my own. I won't be daunted by Edgar Allan

Poe. My tone does not betray even a hint of hesitation as I ask: "Any that I may answer?"

He turns his gaze away. His neck appears squeezed by his high, tight cravat. "I doubt it," he mutters.

"Very well, then." I look back toward the crowd, noting that the rest of them appear perfectly polite and attentive, even interested. "All of us should visit these places and meet these souls," I declare. "All of us have an obligation to care for these most unfortunate of our ranks. To see them not merely as sinners but as people. Why, take up the matter of the women who are imprisoned for their prostitution. . . ."

Several ladies squirm in their seats, busying themselves with the folds of their costly, elegant gowns. Some even exchange scandalized glances. I force myself to press on: "Why is it that only ladies pay for the crimes of prostitution, when the men do not? When I met the women of Sing Sing prison, I could not help but ask: How am I all that different from these women?"

Now there are titters of astonished laughter throughout the salon. But I shake my head, refusing to be cowed. "Hear me on this, please." I raise my hand. "I work to earn my daily bread. How is that different from what these women must do? I do my work with my pen, because I have been fortunate enough in my life to gain the knowledge that allows me to do so. But these women who were not given a single day of schooling—how are they to earn their living? To feed themselves and their children? Is it right that we punish them with judgment, rather than extending to them mercy? These women who have been trampled in the mud to gratify the brute appetites of men?" I fix my gaze on Poe as I deliver these words, then I press on. "And if we are to help, ought it not to be done by more than merely giving of our coins, but also in giving our time and our opened hearts in service toward them?"

It's then that I hear him again, the unmistakable words, spoken in a whisper but one that is loud enough to ensure that all gathered in the room can hear. "Insufferable busybody."

My eyes fly once more to Edgar Allan Poe. My heartbeat is an angry thumping in my throat. I'm not one for wielding a dagger, but my words can be every bit as effective as a weapon; I've come to know that over these recent years. And my anger is now sharpened to a point that I am ready to unsheathe, just as Poe has volleyed his words as weapons toward me.

"Mr. Poe, I thank you for your opinions. I've heard plenty of what you have to say on the topic of my work. And now, like any freethinker, I wish to issue my response, which is this: If writing my front-page piece for the *New-York Tribune* on the charities of New York makes me a busybody; if the fact that I've written more than one hundred articles so far this year, with a plan to write a hundred more, if speaking up without concern for your whispers or your insults, makes me a busybody . . . well, then yes, you are correct, Mr. Poe, I am quite busy. So busy, in fact, that I have little time or inclination to contend with you further. But since I suspect that you, like me, prefer to have your information correct—even in your opinion pieces—so that you do not come off looking unintelligent in the future, I must correct you on one thing: the spelling of my name is F-U-L-L-E-R."

Chapter Thirty-One

Spring 1846

I'M LOUNGING ON A BLANKET ON GREELEY'S LAWN, LIT-
tle Arthur curled up at my side. It's a fine Saturday in Turtle Bay,
a day of gentle sunshine and new buds, and I'm taking a rare respite
from work. It's the first day that feels as though spring has returned
to New York; the forsythia bushes have just begun to burst with
small pops of yellow, joined by the brave early crocuses and daffodils. With the Farm perched as it is atop a bluff overlooking the
East River, Arthur and I have immediate and continual entertainment as we sit and watch the boats, wondering aloud where they
might be headed. Just now a small sailboat glides before us, on a
pleasure cruise, I suspect, and I raise my hand. "Oh, I know! I know
what that one is!"

Arthur glances up at me, his light eyes kindled with earnest interest beneath his downy curls.

"Shall I guess?" I ask. He nods. "I believe that is the Peppermint
Fairy."

Now his eyes swing back to the small boat with even greater
interest. "You do?"

I nod, appearing solemn. "Bearing its cargo of sweets to Mount
Peppermint."

"Where's that?"

I point out at the water. "Why, just up the river, that way."

Little Arthur cranes his neck and squints, as though he might be
able to make it out on the northern horizon. It's all I can do not to

take my hands to his head and tousle his precious pile of perfect little curls. He turns back to me, asking: "Is it filled with peppermints?"

"Indeed. And hotcakes, as well. Drizzled with honey."

"I'd like to go there."

"As would I, my dear."

Then his little face crumples, a look of thoughtfulness. "Say, Aunt Mags?"

"Yes, Arthur?"

"Why is it that you're not married?"

This question hits me with a thud. I toss my head back onto the blanket, looking up at the willow branches that sway overhead, and I consider his question. It's a perfectly natural question, and to be expected, given his age and his bright, earnest curiosity. And he's certainly not the first to wonder it, even if he is perhaps the youngest. While his inquiry does fill me with an undeniable tug of melancholy, I assume a bright tone, and I answer Arthur with an equally earnest candor, saying: "Because, my dear lad, I've not yet met the gentleman who is supposed to be my husband."

But Arthur does not appear satisfied. He cocks his head to the side, placing a chubby hand on my stomach in a gesture of childish unself-consciousness that turns my heart into a seeping puddle. Then he asks: "Will you meet him?"

I swallow. "That, I do not know."

"How will you know . . . if you *do* meet him?"

I'm working hard to keep my features neutral. "That I do not know, either, my boy."

"But, Aunt Mags, I thought you were supposed to be the cleverest woman in America?"

At this, now, I cannot help but laugh. Dear little Arthur has put a finer tip on this question than anyone else has ever managed to do—my detractors, my supporters, even myself in moments of solitary wondering. I don't know whether I'll ever marry. Do I wish to marry? Why yes, I suppose I do. But that's because I would like to meet the man who is meant to be my husband. I would like to find the man who sees and knows my soul. It's not that I wish to marry simply to be married; it's that I wish to find a love so overpowering that there's no choice but to join myself with this other person. Until that happens, I can't see any reason to become a wife.

And until I've become a wife, I don't see how I shall ever become a mother. This realization, perhaps more than anything else, fills me with a deep and aching sadness, a hole that refuses to leave my stomach. Though many have called me *unnatural* in my quest for learning and achievement, the truth is that I *do* experience what feels like the very natural and overpowering love of children—their guileless goodness, their earnest, thoughtful questions, their ability to see adventure in any place and any time. I've cared for many children in my life; I would love to hold a child of my own. I daresay I do love little Arthur here at my side, not to mention Louisa May and the Alcott girls. Little Ellen Emerson. And little Waldo, of course. Little Waldo, perhaps most of all. My throat thickens now, just to think of him.

But then a ruckus interrupts my sad daydreaming. Through an open window I hear the plunking of piano keys, then a moment later Mary begins to sing. She's not a great talent, but she sings with the jaunty confidence of one. It pulls me from my brooding, bringing a small smile to my lips, which I now offer to Arthur.

The door of the farmhouse opens, and out walks Horace, armed with top hat and cane. He spies us on the lawn and strides toward us. I feel a moment of guilt at my employer catching me in such a state of relaxation, but then I remember that it was Horace who was just telling me that I work too much, and ought to find moments of rest and leisure.

"Margaret, Arthur!" Horace marches toward us, his voice upbeat. His eyes are on mine as he says: "I was hoping we might speak a moment."

I sit up on the blanket. "Of course."

"Perhaps if we could . . . would you take a walk with me?"

So much for my afternoon of leisure—he must have some urgent story that needs writing. Arthur pipes up, saying, "I'm hungry, Father."

"Run inside and ask your mother for something to eat."

I rise to stand as the boy trots off toward the house and the jolly sound of his mother's piano. I fall into step beside Horace and we walk down toward the river. I'm intrigued. "What is it that you cannot say in front of Arthur?"

Horace looks out on the water. "I did not wish to upset him."

A knot of dread coils in my belly. "What is upsetting?"

Horace's face is draped in shadow, his broad top hat pulled low over his brow, but his features do not look grim. Not at all. In fact, I think I see the hint of a smile tugging his lips, and when he turns to me, the smile reaches up to his eyes. He says, "The thought of you going away would be most upsetting—not only to Arthur, but to all of us."

My body stiffens. I swallow, then ask: "Am I going away?"

"Well, that decision resides only with you."

"I do not understand."

Now his gaze glides back out over the silver-blue water. "I'd like to offer you something, Margaret. And even while, as your friend, I'd love for you to decline . . . well, as your employer, I have to hope you'll accept."

"Accept what?" I ask.

"I am wondering how you would feel about Europe."

I am stunned by this, and my mouth falls open.

"Ah." Greeley looks at me with an expression of amusement. "Have I managed to do something most remarkable? Something that no other person in New York City has done—not even the great Edgar Allan Poe? I've made Margaret Fuller speechless."

I can't help but laugh at this, a quick sputtered exhale. Greeley presses on: "You've reviewed the poetry of Elizabeth Barrett and Shelley in England. You've covered the writings of George Sand and the music of Frédéric Chopin in Paris. You've written about Italian politics and art. I'd like to see if you'd go there. More than a tour. It would be for the *Tribune*. As my—no, not my . . . *America's* first full-time foreign news correspondent."

"Europe." My voice is thin with disbelief. I can't manage to say more. He goes on: "I'd like you to file stories for me from England. And France. But really, I'd like you to be based in Rome."

"Why Rome?" I ask, barely able to mask my delight and surprise. Why, I've studied Latin and the Romans since my youth. To go there, to see the sights, such as the Forum and the Colosseum, and to do so with no purpose other than to observe and think and write? Can this be a real offer?

Horace's tone is all thoughtfulness when he answers, and his crinkled features match that tone. "There's something big stewing over there on that Italian peninsula. You know the Italian movement?"

I nod. Of course I know of the nationalistic movement of which he now speaks: after centuries of division and warring, the Italians want a country of their own. Enough of being carved up and occupied by the Austrian army, the French army, the Prussian army. Even the pope's army.

Horace says: "Pretty soon I think we might see a country called Italy . . . and I'd like you to tell us what that's like."

Chapter Thirty-Two

ON A STIFLING HOT DAY IN LATE JULY, THE TRAIN bears me north from New York up toward Boston, where I plan to stay for a brief, final visit with Mother before crossing the Atlantic. The steamship *Cambria* will leave from Boston's port for Liverpool in just a few days' time, and I will be on board, set to chart a course that will take me farther than I've ever gone before. Perhaps farther than any American newsman—or news*woman*—has ever gone.

To help fund my travels and my time abroad, I've published another book, titled *Papers on Literature and Art*, which is a compilation of my many essays from my tenure as an editor and writer at both *The Dial* and the *New-York Tribune*. God love Greeley and Waldo for their blessing of this work, which, though thrown together hastily for the printing presses, was a product of years of my work that oftentimes felt thankless and went unpaid.

The book is yet another success that helps to put wind in my sails before my planned departure. I couldn't help but chuckle as I read the reviews that circulated upon its publication. Of course there will always be those critics who find my voice too forward, too bold, who find me *unnatural* in my assertiveness as an unwed woman. And yet, one critic of seasons past has flipped into the camp of supporter this time around: Edgar Allan Poe. He even published what, I daresay, reads as a sort of compliment: "Humanity is divided into men, women, and Margaret Fuller."

I laugh now, thinking of Poe's words, staring out the train's window as the mountains of the Hudson Valley form a green summertime wall along the banks of the Hudson River.

Mother greets me at the depot, and it's just a short ride by hansom cab to her small rented home in Cambridge. With the funds that my siblings and I are now able to send to supplement Father's annuity, Mother can finally afford a home of her own without crushing financial woes. I'll pass my last few days on American soil in this home with Mother. We deposit my luggage and take some tea, and then I ask my mother to join me for a walk.

"Where to?" she asks.

"I was thinking along the Charles," I suggest, and so, in the cooling hours of the late afternoon, we set out. Cambridge is a city of summer activity, smelling of horses and grass, even a hint of the salty water of the nearby harbor. I breathe in deeply of my hometown, suspecting that I'll miss this place, even if I am overjoyed at the prospect of my upcoming departure. I'll miss New York, as well, a city that in many ways also felt like home during my years there.

"In truth, each place has felt like a home in a different way," I explain to Mother as we walk side by side along the Charles. "Concord did during many seasons. Cambridge at times, Boston as well. And New York."

We are strolling past Harvard now, and I look at the stately brick buildings, largely draped in leafy shadows and a quiet stillness during this summer recess. In the fall it will become a hive of learning and activity once again—for all its young men students. My mind whirls with memories: The many hours spent huddled over the desk in Gore Hall, writing my book. The lads throwing me their dubious, questioning glances. It is Mother who speaks, interrupting my reverie. "The thing about it, Margaret, is that perhaps there is too much in you to ever feel truly at home in just one place. How could one place speak to the many layers of your being?"

I absorb her words in silence as, all around us, Harvard's campus dozes in the haze of the summer warmth. *The many layers of your being.* Rather than the gentle censure she's so often expressed over my roaming and my pioneering in times past, this feels like a rare acknowledgment from Mother of my true nature, perhaps even tinged with a hint of admiration.

I turn to her now, taking her hand in mine. "I've always been your daughter who challenged you, Mother," I say, my voice thick with feeling. "The Much that always wants More."

Mother sputters out a laugh of recognition at the mention of my childhood nickname. "You know that, in spite of all that your father did and accomplished . . . with his law career. His education. His public service, the offices he held . . . all of it. Well, do you know the single thing in his life of which he was always most proud?"

I shake my head. Mother tips toward me and says, "It was that he was your father."

This hits me in a deep place. I don't say anything, but instead walk silently beside Mother. She goes on after a moment: "He was hard on you, Margaret. The fact is that I think he was looking for himself in you. Or himself, improved. I think that's why he took you in hand so young and poured so much into you. I know it was not easy."

I nod, as the threat of tears needles my eyelids. Mother gives my hand a squeeze. "But look at you now. He'd be so proud. Just as I'm so proud. Like the strongest of wildflowers, you thrive in fresh earth. Our Margaret, the Much that always wanted More. I want more for you, as well. I am happy you shall have it."

WHEN WE ARRIVE back at home, I see a lone figure lingering outside Mother's front door. Tall and slender, dressed in a tidy three-piece suit and hat. He turns at the sound of our approach. I come to a standstill, pulling in a quick inhale. "Waldo," I say, my surprise evident in my tone.

"Hello, Margaret. Hello, Mrs. Fuller." Waldo nods to my mother.

"This is a surprise," I say, throwing a look from my friend toward my mother. She welcomes him warmly, then excuses herself to step into the house, offering something about getting a drink of water. In truth, she doesn't appear all that surprised by Waldo's sudden appearance at her doorstep. Certainly not like I am. I can't help but wonder if perhaps this has been prearranged, and with her help.

I stand before Ralph Waldo Emerson outside my mother's door. My dear friend. My mentor and greatest supporter at times, at other times my chief tormentor. The man who has helped me to realize so many of the moments and developments of my most unusual life.

"You've come to my home so often," Waldo says. "I thought it was high time I paid you a visit."

"And not a moment too soon," I say. "I sail in just a few days."

"I couldn't let you go without bidding you farewell."

We step into the back garden, where an old elm casts its rippled shade over the space. Dusk is lowering around us, and we sit on Mother's wooden bench. There, as the birds hop and warble their evening songs, as the last gentle spears of sunlight land on the lawn, we pass a few moments in thoughtful, companionable silence. The silence of old and dear friends. The silence of two people who can communicate with so much more than words. Eventually, it is I who speaks. "How are you?"

He heaves a slow exhale, answering: "In good health and good enough spirits."

"And everyone else at Bush? In Concord?"

"Life is much the same, and also very different."

"How so?"

"Well, Louisa May is practically blossoming into a woman before our eyes. She's showing great talent as a writer."

I smile at this, not surprised. "You tell her I said to keep writing."

"She says she wishes to be like her friend, the great Margaret Fuller."

"To which I say: she should strive to be the great Louisa May Alcott."

He grins and promises to deliver my message.

"How is Lidian?" I ask.

"Much improved," he says, nodding. "And busy. The children thrive. You know that Ellen is now the big sister to Edith and Edward. And Lidian is back to teaching Sunday school in the church each week."

"That is wonderful," I say. I mean it. "Will you give her my warm regards?"

Waldo assures me that he will, so I ask: "And the Hawthornes?"

"They are fine. They've left the Old Manse and returned for a time to Salem."

"I can't imagine that Nathaniel is happy about that."

Waldo flashes a smile. "I'll leave that to Sophia to sort. And you know Thoreau is no longer staying with us? He's made a one-room cabin for himself out on Walden Pond."

I lean back on the bench, clasping my hands in my lap. "So he finally did it," I say, nodding with admiration.

"Indeed. He tells me it's where he can write the best. Out there on Walden, where he may have his evening conversations with the whippoorwills and the owls."

I take all this in, my mind's eye seeing my friend beside that deep blue pond, his wreath of dark hair growing ever thicker around his ruddy, suntanned face. "Well, then, I wish him all the best out in the woods. Will he still help Louisa May to find the butterflies as they hatch?"

"Oh yes," Waldo says. "It's my land that he's on out there. He comes into the village to visit often."

"Then that is good."

"But, speaking of butterflies—" Waldo pauses, shifting in his seat. He reaches into his pocket. Then he removes a small parcel wrapped in tissue.

"What's this?" I ask, throwing him a look as he extends the parcel toward me.

"For your journey," he says. I tear the tissue paper slowly, pulling it apart to find a pair of silver hair combs; carved onto them is a set of delicate, colorful butterflies wrought of pearl and ivory. I can't help but gasp. "Waldo!"

"Butterflies," he says, his voice thick, as though he's holding back some deep well of emotion. I meet his eyes, and I see that they glisten. Is he crying? He blinks, an effort to stanch the tears.

Now my eyes begin to sting. "Oh, my friend. Thank you." I put my hand gently on his and he takes it in his fingers, his grip closing around mine. I give him a squeeze.

The garden is dark now, the crickets roused to their nightly performance. No words are needed between us, as we sit side by side in the cooling, silvered air. Just as we've done on so many occasions before. Only, this is to be our last vigil of this kind. For how long? I do not know.

Eventually Waldo pulls his hand loose and reaches for one of the combs in my lap, which he takes in a gentle grip. Then, lifting it, he leans toward me and tucks the butterfly into a wave of dark hair beside my face. He settles it in just so, with a softness and precision that surprise me. Our eyes meet, and I see the way a glint of light glimmers in his pale gaze. When he speaks, his voice is tender. "You are flying on once again, dear Margaret. And this time, to a place far beyond my reach. I am filled with joy to see you fly. I only ask that you bring this small piece of Concord—and me—along with you."

Chapter Thirty-Three

Boston
August 1846

A CRUSH OF GULLS MAKE THEIR LOOPS OVERHEAD AS I brace myself on the railing of the steamship *Cambria*, staring out over what will be my final glimpse of American soil for quite some time. When will I next see these shores? I do not know. It's a warm day as we bob in Boston Harbor, a late-summer sun pouring down on us. I narrow my eyes as I turn and look out over the softly rolling blue that unfurls to the east. The water appears calm enough. I whisper a quick prayer that the Atlantic will remain this clement throughout our entire two-week crossing, until we arrive safely to Liverpool.

All before me the busy docks teem with people—those who will go, and those who will remain behind. Passengers hand over their trunks and luggage to smartly uniformed porters, young lads who scurry about to see the mountains of cargo sorted and loaded into the belly of our vessel. In the melee of the docks I spot Mother, waving. Her figure looks so small, a slip of white. I raise my kerchief and wave back to her. Her eyes are cloaked in shadow beneath the broad brim of her bonnet, but I suspect they are moist with tears, just as mine are.

I cannot help but think to myself, here, at the outset of the longest journey I've ever undertaken, of the many other trips I've made. Especially those trips I've made on the water in recent years: Floating down the Concord River on Thoreau's *Musketaquid*, Louisa May laughing at the calls of the birds. The time spent perched on Hawthorne's rowboat, Sophia and Emerson standing on the shore before the Old Manse. I think of the canoes on the rapids in the Middle West, and then the softly gliding sailboats alongside the Farm, the happy hours watching them pass with Greeley and little Arthur. My final stroll along the Charles River with Mother.

And now I sail away from America, to parts I've only ever spent my life reading about, places I've conjured in my mind's eye with a yearning to see. I give Mother one final wave, then I raise my gloved hand to my hair, where, under my sunbonnet, I feel the wispy bones of the butterfly combs from Waldo. I will wear them as I go. I'm a butterfly once more, and now I'm flying off.

"Did you spot her down there? Your mother?" I turn to glance into the sun-kissed face of my new friend, Rebecca Spring, a young wife who has stepped to the railing at my side. Rebecca Spring's friendship has been yet another gift of the incomparably generous Horace Greeley, who, knowing of my plans to travel to Europe, introduced me to the Spring family, a party of three who had similar travel plans. Rebecca and her husband, Marcus, are sailing for Liverpool and ultimately headed to Italy, just as I am, and so Greeley recommended me as the tutor they sought for their nine-year-old son. Delighted to have found a companion for their little Eddie throughout the ocean crossing and then the trip from England through France and on to Italy, they've paid for my passage aboard the *Cambria* and have also agreed to cover my lodgings and travel expenses until we all arrive in Rome.

In sponsoring me like this, the Springs have not only removed much of the financial burden of my trip, but have also helped me to navigate around the other, thornier impediment of my planned itinerary: the problem of traveling alone as an unwed woman. It was all very well and good for Horace Greeley to hire me as his first-ever foreign news correspondent, to advance me a portion of my salary in exchange for the promised columns on European life, politics, culture, and news. And it was all very well and good for me to accept the job, becoming the first American reporter ever to undertake an assignment like this. I was quite willing to make this trip and relocate my life to Europe. But conventions being what they are, it is not yet an entirely acceptable thing for me to make the move alone, a woman without a chaperone or husband. The

Springs have made it all much more acceptable, as now I am making this trip not as a spinster on my own but as a governess, traveling in the company of a most respectable family of three.

And so here we stand, Rebecca and I, as Eddie and his father dart around the upper decks in eager exploration. When the *Cambria*'s horn lets out its final low, doleful bellow, the ship's propellers begin to froth the water, driving us away from the docks. Rebecca and I wave frantically to the crowds cheering below. Overhead the seagulls screech in reply. I send my mother one final kiss, then I grip the railing to steady myself. Rebecca turns to stare at me, studying me a moment. She asks: "How do you feel?"

The roiling ocean cleaves before our bow as the land recedes behind us. I breathe in deep, the breeze whipping my bonnet, the air smelling of salt and steam. Eventually, turning to meet Rebecca's earnest expression, I answer: "I feel as though we are at the start of something quite grand."

Rebecca smiles at this. "Indeed, Margaret. We most certainly are."

Just then another figure approaches, an older gentleman. He pauses before us. "Excuse me, begging your pardon, misses?"

Rebecca and I turn to meet this newcomer, who looks at me with an expression of eager interest as he speaks over the din all around us. "May I be so presumptuous as to ask, are you Miss Margaret Fuller?"

"I am," I answer, taken a bit by surprise as I stare into a ruddy face bordered by thick sideburns. There's a stiff white cap atop his head—what appears to be a captain's hat. I pull my shoulders back to stand up slightly straighter.

The man gives me a tip of his hat, then he does the same to Rebecca. "Captain Charles Judkins at your service, ladies." So he *is* the captain, indeed.

"Captain Judkins, well, it's an honor. Please meet my traveling companion, Mrs. Marcus Spring."

"Mrs. Spring, pleasure to meet you." The captain greets her cordially, then fixes his gaze back on me. "Miss Fuller, the honor is entirely mine. A great honor indeed. I have read your work and I have admired it so very much. '*Let them be sea-captains,*' eh?"

I feel the smile bursting across my features at this as, at my side,

Rebecca turns to glance at me with a look of thrill. Captain Judkins goes on: "If I may be so bold as to say, I had the honor last year of bearing Mr. Frederick Douglass from America to Europe on this same route. I believe you are familiar with the work of Mr. Douglass?"

"Indeed I am, Captain Judkins. I am a great admirer of Mr. Frederick Douglass."

Captain Judkins replies with loud animation, his voice carrying over the chaos and noise of the steamer as he says: "As am I, ma'am. And I have to say that it was my honor to offer Mr. Douglass full rights upon my ship, the very same as that of any other gentleman."

I like this, I like this very much indeed. I offer a full smile as I reply: "I take it as a most auspicious occurrence that I now have the privilege to travel to Europe with you, Captain Judkins, just as Mr. Frederick Douglass did."

The captain raps the ship's railing with his knuckles, staring out over the shifting blue horizon through which he will bear us. Then, after a moment of thoughtful silence, he turns back to me, his fingers lightly touching the brim of his cap, and he says: "Mr. Douglass is urging our nation to grow into its promise for the members of his race, just as you are doing the very same for the members of your gender."

"Hear, hear," Rebecca agrees at my side.

"Captain, thank you." I lower my eyes, looking out over the water, seeing a distant seagull plunge into its swells, emerging a moment later with a sliver of silver in its beak. I turn back to Captain Judkins and say: "I am most grateful to be in your hands, sir."

At this, Captain Judkins taps the brim of his cap once more and bids us farewell, making his way back to his work. I remain at the ship's railing in silence, turning my gaze out over the ocean. My hands glide upward to the butterfly combs tucked into my chestnut waves, and I look forward, as though I can already see the promise of all that lies ahead. All that will soon be within my reach.

Chapter Thirty-Four

The Lake District, England
Summer 1846

WILLIAM WORDSWORTH, FAMED POET LAUREATE OF the English people, celebrated writer the world over, steps out of his old stone cottage and walks up the lane at my side. At nearly eighty years old, the man moves slowly but with a healthy and spry step, taking his time as he glances from side to side to inspect the unruly flower beds that overspill his lush garden in its high-summer splendor. After a pause, the celebrated father of the Romantic poets, the friend and confidant of Samuel Taylor Coleridge, the man who served as the creative inspiration for William Blake, turns to me and asks what I think of his hollyhocks.

"Well, Mr. Wordsworth," I say, admiring the pink petals that perch atop their long, thick greenery, "I think they are grand."

"Yes, my dear Miss Fuller! Nothing grander than a summer bloom. You see?" Wordsworth gestures with a sweep of his hand over the acres of his colorful garden, his swath of fertile land that stretches down toward the lake of Rydal Water, and beyond that the rolling fells of his beloved Lake District. "It's no longer the pen for me, but my petals. Why, when the prime minister offered the prize of poet laureate, he assured me that I need not write another word. 'That's all well and good,' I told him. 'For I don't intend to.'"

At this Wordsworth gives me a playful shrug, and there's a slight twinkle in the eye, and I can briefly imagine the virile young man who once rhapsodized about running across this green English countryside, the adventurer who once traveled the Continent with Coleridge, giving birth not only to his beautiful poetry but to an entire movement of thought. And one that directly impacted our lives as far away as Concord.

In that sense, this afternoon visit to William Wordsworth carries the significance of a sort of pilgrimage. We Transcendentalists might not have ever come into being without our predecessors in England, the Romantics, who wrote about their own rapturous and transcendent experiences in nature. And the Romantics would not exist but for this man, this giant, who now stoops before me to inspect another lush pink hollyhock.

I docked in Liverpool the month before, along with the Springs. From there we made our way toward Manchester and on to Scotland with its waterfalls at Dungeon Ghyll Force, a striking landscape of crumbling stone castles, crystalline lochs, and the highlands stippled in pale heather. From there, in our baggage-laden coach, we wound our way through the narrow roads of Edinburgh, with its ancient castle perched on the hill, before traveling on to Glasgow. In just these past few weeks, I've witnessed the windswept moors and the sooty coal mines of Newcastle, taking dutiful notes on all of it to send word back to Greeley and my American readers.

But it is here, to Ambleside in the Lake District, to Wordsworth's country retreat of cottage and gardens, that I have been most eager to come. Of course Waldo smoothed the way and made the introduction from afar. And to my delight, Wordsworth was willing to host the afternoon visit.

And the great poet stands before me now, dressed all in black, set off by the shock of white hair that crowns his famous head. He leans forward and breathes deep of the flowers that brighten the scene around us. "These fuchsias," he says, his voice like that of a proud papa as his fingers flip over the petals. "Ambrosia, if ever we mortals could claim it."

I am moved in this moment, so struck by the scene that I can't help but speak aloud the words that fly to my mind, reciting: "'Therefore am I still / A lover of the meadows and the woods / And mountains; and of all that we behold / From this green earth; of all the mighty world.'"

At this, the old poet looks up from his flowers and throws me a coy glance. Wordsworth has a glimmer in his eye, a ruddy, youthful smile. "I wrote that, didn't I?"

"And in doing so," I say, nodding, "you changed life for so many."

"Well," he replies, his voice turning soft, "that may be so. You are most generous, Miss Fuller." A moment of thoughtful silence settles between us, pierced only by the gentle trill of a bird overhead. And then Wordsworth perks up his features, changing the tack of the conversation, asking: "And what about you, my dear?"

I fold my hands before my waist. "Pardon?"

"Are you a lover of the woods?"

"Indeed I am," I reply.

"So what shall it be next for you? Woods or city?"

"London," I answer. A city where he seems to have little interest in traveling, given how happily ensconced he is here in his rustic hideaway. But a place where I imagine there will be no shortage of news to report back to America. "Mr. Greeley has given me all manner of topics to investigate," I say. "What with the outrage over the Corn Laws. And the scandal of Elizabeth Barrett and Robert Browning running away to Italy."

Wordsworth arcs a pale eyebrow, then stares off toward the far corner of his garden. His reply, when it comes, is a perfunctory: "Is that so?"

I press on, trying again to engage him on some of the news of the day—the news of his nation. "Or what about the news from Giuseppe Mazzini, the Italian revolutionary, now living in London?"

Wordsworth is curled over, his eyes fixed on a cluster of fuchsias, distracted.

"Giuseppe Mazzini," I repeat the name. "The Italian exile? Leader of the Young Italy movement?" I've read everything I can find about Mazzini. I've become an admirer of his, as is Greeley, and I hope to make his acquaintance in London. It is the story that Greeley is most eager for me to chase once I arrive in Rome, this movement to form a free Italian republic from all of the many divided city-states, kingdoms, and principalities currently pocking the Italian peninsula.

Wordsworth, for his part, appears entirely disinterested. I try once more, hoping to jostle some reaction from the great thinker. Even just an opinion on the question of a free Italy. "Mazzini is calling for one Italy. A republic. It would be momentous if the Italians were finally unified and able to throw off foreign armies, free to form their own republic. It seems Mazzini has supporters in England. Or, at least, he's working to rally some."

Wordsworth finally meets my gaze. "Yes, yes, all that . . ." He lifts a hand, his fingernails trimmed in brown from his hours of gardening. "Do you know what my neighbors say of me?"

I'm caught off guard by the question. I shift on my feet, answering, "I can imagine that they, well, that they admire your brilliant work."

The old poet shrugs. "Perhaps." He stares down at his flowers, then looks back to me. "But do you know why they are fond of me? Because I am a good neighbor, they say. You see, this . . . all you are saying"—he waves his dirty finger through the air—"I don't much concern myself with all that. The more I've learned of the land, the more I've come to see that this has always been a place where people fought. Why, go back to the Romans. The Saxons, the Scots, even the Danes. Now it's the Whigs and the Tories. There is nothing new under the sun. But, my dear, you see, here, for this brief moment, this land offers me peace. Here, tucked away in my gardens, I am quite content. I am happy to leave the fighting to the young soldiers. I'll wage war on the blights and the weeds."

I take all this in, absorbing it for a moment in thoughtful silence. Looking around, at Wordsworth's hollyhocks, his fuchsias, his distant views of water and hill, I can't help but think how much Thoreau would love roaming the greenery of this Lake District. And I cannot help but think how much Emerson would love roaming the wilds of Mr. Wordsworth's mind.

I look back to the great poet, offering him a polite smile. I am glad to have come here to Ambleside. To have met the great William Wordsworth. To have ambled at his side through his lanes of hollyhocks. But I cannot agree with what he says now. I have had enough of walking and talking my way through gardens. I am eager to throw myself into the melee. Because I believe that my words have a power that I cannot waste.

Chapter Thirty-Five

Paris
February 1847

I T'S THE CHILLY SORT OF FEBRUARY EVENING THAT CAN feel romantic only in Paris. Here I sit in the elegant Rive Droite neighborhood off Place d'Orléans, once the haunt of France's kings, now a gathering place for artists and their cadre of bohemian friends who have little use for kings or anything that reveres the old aristocratic ways. I'm in the even more elegant apartment of the world-famous pianist and composer Frédéric Chopin. I'm enthralled, as is the rest of the crowd gathered around me. And I'm entirely alone.

My pupil, little Eddie Spring, was not feeling well earlier this afternoon, so Marcus and Rebecca have elected to remain with him back at our hotel. "Probably not the best night to be trooping about in the cold and damp," Rebecca had declared, when she'd told me of her plans to send our regrets to Monsieur Chopin. Then she'd seen my crestfallen face; this private recital was an invitation I did not wish to decline. "Of course, you may still go, Margaret, and give Monsieur Chopin our regards."

So here I sit, chez Chopin, staring at the small man with wild silver-brown hair, his body writhing over his piano as if in the throes of some sort of ecstatic prayer. I watch him intently as his fingers fly up and down the gleaming ivory keys; it's as though his entire frame is a part of the performance that's now happening—indeed, even his very soul.

Monsieur Chopin announced to our private assembly, before sitting down to play, that this was perhaps his favorite piece, Étude

No. 3. I can see why he would feel such a fondness for it. As the notes rise and fall, Chopin's music pulses into the very core of me. "The reviewers like to call this one *La Tristesse*," he announced, scowling as he pronounced the nickname, "The Sadness." As I listen, I can see why this name came to be. But all of Chopin's music has an underpinning of melancholy, I think to myself. But also triumph, as well, and always deep feeling.

When at last Chopin does finish, his body hunched and spent, his eyes shutting, the packed salon pulses in silence. No one moves, no one speaks, no one even dares to exhale; we are still humming with the final melting strains of Chopin's overpowering performance. And then, all around me, people fly to their feet.

"*Brava!*"

"*Formidable!*"

"*Magnifique!*"

These hearty shouts of praise and applause burst across the room as I remain in my seat. I don't need to move, I don't need to speak. In fact, I shut my eyes and feel my body tremble with a frisson of deep feeling, perfectly content to pulse with the stirrings that Chopin's beautiful music and virtuosic playing have pulled from me.

I open my eyes a moment later, still motionless in my seat. I see that a knot of admirers has crowded around the small musician, who can barely rise from his piano. And then I see a figure slip out of the crush of people, sauntering toward me. A woman. At least, I believe it's a woman. She is unsmiling and unusually short, with thick dark hair forming two stark curtains down a long, unattractive face. She moves like someone accustomed to conquering. I marvel as I watch her approach, her small figure somehow taking up so much space, as though she carries some intangible force that overspills the diminutive dimensions of her bodily frame.

Up closer now I see she has a large nose and intense eyes, and she pauses before me in a most curious attire of black pants and a dark velvet cape. She places one hand casually on her hip as the other raises a cigar to her lips. She stares at me, unapologetically, but before she says anything, she takes a slow pull from her cigar. As she exhales a cloud of smoke, out just the right side of her mouth, she arcs a dark eyebrow. Then she says: "Is it really you? *La Dame Américaine?*"

The American woman. But am I *the* American woman to whom she refers?

"Margaret Fuller," I say, extending a hand, and then I immediately pull it back in regret—with a stab of mortification—as I recall that the French do not greet one another in this way, but rather with kisses, one on each cheek. A manner that feels both unnervingly intimate but also so very French, and thus so very sophisticated.

"*Enchantée*, Mademoiselle Fuller," the caped lady replies, the cigar poised between her thumb and pointer, its smoke wafting on her breath as she leans toward me to brush her cheeks against mine. "George Sand."

So then, this is George Sand! Frédéric Chopin's famous lover. Or, rather, *infamous* lover. Chopin's muse, his torment. I know of George Sand, of course. Her writings and her speeches are known across Europe and America. But I'm a bit stunned at beholding her before me like this, cape and cigar and all. Nevertheless, I pull myself to my full height and manage what I hope is a bright, poised tone as I say: "Thank you for having me this evening, Madame Sand."

A small dip of her chin, a playful smile, then she takes another draw from her cigar. I hope I sound worldly and sophisticated as I go on: "I admire both your writing and your . . . and Monsieur Chopin's music." I was thrilled when the invitation arrived at our hotel. But as I think about it, Rebecca was quite willing to decline, seizing on Eddie's slight complaint of a cough. And now I believe that I understand why my modest friend was hesitant to come to a recital chez Monsieur Chopin—she supposed his scandalous lover might also be here.

A development that delights me now. Madame Sand gives me a quick full-bodied scan with her dark brown eyes, taking in the sweep of my modest navy dress, my simple chestnut bun and unadorned face. The only jewelry I wear are Emerson's butterfly combs tucked behind my ears. I had this new dress fashioned at the modiste when I first arrived in Paris—thinking I should indulge in something fashionable and chic for my Parisian outings. But now I feel utterly simple before Sand's bold figure. A cape, and black pants!

Grazing her cigar against her lips, Sand replies, her voice low and husky as she says, "If you admire my work, I imagine you must be very much alone in feeling that way among American ladies."

I feel myself wince at this. It is true that Sand is reviled by some—by many of the same people who decry my outspoken advocacy for women. But while critics may furrow their brows over my unwed state and my willingness to interview fallen women, they rail in outright horror over Sand's unapologetic enjoyment of her many lovers and her sartorial panache.

"But you are kind to say it, *ma chérie*," she adds, her lips forming a coy upward curl. Then, with a flutter of her dark eyelashes, she goes on: "The feelings of admiration are mutual, Mademoiselle Fuller." I love the way my name sounds on her lips, wrapped in her thick French accent. It sounds not entirely unlike how Poe had pronounced it when he'd called me Margaret Fooler. And yet, it is entirely different. It feels as though I've stepped into quite a different world.

In fact, I'm a bit stunned by all of this. By the fact that I'm standing in Frédéric Chopin's Parisian salon having just heard his private concert. And now the world-famous George Sand is standing before me, telling me that she not only knows my work, but admires it.

My hostess cuts her gaze toward her lover for a moment, then back to me as she says: "Chopin is always a friend to foreigners. He remembers what it was like to come to Paris." She refers to her lover's Polish origins, his immigration to France in his youth, I surmise.

"It was a gain for Paris that he came," I answer.

Sand's body angles toward mine, as if I'm the only person in the salon with whom she wishes to speak, as she asks me: "And what about you? Are you enjoying yourself here?"

"Oh, very much," I say. And it's the truth. Compared to London, Paris thrills me: its elegant buildings, the silver vein of the Seine, the smells and sounds and tastes of this unashamedly gorgeous capital. Even the bridges in Paris seem more beautiful than anywhere else I've ever seen.

"Where are you staying?" Sand asks through a mist of exhaled cigar smoke.

"Hôtel Rougemont," I answer. "Not far from here, on the Boulevard Poissonnière."

"Yes, of course," she says. I imagine that this woman knows every neighborhood of Paris. "Well, when you write back to America— for that is what you are doing, is it not?"

"That's correct. I'm writing a weekly column for my paper, the *New-York Tribune*."

"Greeley," Sand says with a knowing nod. "He's a good one. Well, you must be sure to tell them all the scandalous truths of Paris. I think it's time the Americans got a bit shaken out of their comfortable little lives. Tell them how you came here to our den of iniquity. *Voici*—" She reaches her hand into her pocket and pulls out another cigar, which she now extends to me. I take it in my hands, unsure of what else to do. But before I can demur, Sand leans toward me and I smell the smoke on her breath as she throws me a devilish smirk. Then she says, her voice deep and conspiratorial: "I will corrupt you first, in the hopes you'll take the mantle and return home to corrupt many more *dames américaines*."

I look around at her so-called den of iniquity, the chic Aubusson carpet and parquet floor, the tastefully upholstered sofas and chairs arranged in small clusters, perfect for facilitating small exchanges of witty barbs or delicious morsels of scandalous gossip. An impossibly large gilded mirror that tosses the candlelight across the crowded room. A wall of graceful floor-to-ceiling windows draped in rich crimson, with doors that open out onto a string of terraces overlooking Paris. I marvel to myself: Sand lives here with her lover in their unwed state, and unapologetically so.

And even more shocking: Sand has a husband. The Baron Dudevant, making her the Baroness Dudevant. She's left all that behind, changing her name and pursuing her passion as a writer and a great thinker. Pursuing, also, her bodily passions, living as the unrepentant paramour to the great musician—and others. Even, if the rumors are to be believed, some lady lovers. It makes my head pitch like a ship just to think of it; this is another world, indeed. I don't speak any of this aloud, only saying: "I have no intention of returning to America anytime too soon."

"Ah. Where do you go next?"

"Rome," I answer, barely hiding my delight.

"*Fantastique*. You've never been?"

"No," I say.

A coy smile brushes her features. "Do you know what Goethe said about Rome?"

Of course I know what Goethe said about Rome. "That 'only in Rome can one prepare oneself for Rome,'" I reply.

"*Exactement*," Sand answers with an approving nod. "So then, you are prepared."

"As prepared as one can be, I suppose."

Sand returns her cigar to her lips. Meanwhile, I still hold the unlit one she's offered me. I have little interest in actually smoking it. She goes on: "And you've been on something of a tour, have you not? For Monsieur Greeley?"

"We were in England and Scotland before France."

"*Eh bien*. What did you think?"

I hesitate, only for a moment, but she sees it. Her dark eyes narrow. "You did not enjoy London?"

"I would not say that."

"Then what?"

"London . . ."—I consider my words a moment—"surprised me."

"How so?"

"Well, the museums, the gardens, the palaces, they were lovely, of course. Fascinating, even. London is very much the glittering capital of a great empire."

Sand's cigar hovers a few inches from her lips. "But?"

"But all of that I was expecting, you see. It was the poverty I had not expected."

Sand is listening intently. I go on: "And not only London, but all over England. Really, from the instant we disembarked in Liverpool, I was overwhelmed by the amount of destitution I saw. Children begging in the streets. And the women . . . the women in Manchester, Glasgow, Scotland . . ."

I had expected more from the great Queen Victoria, in all honesty. She rules the most prosperous, powerful empire in the world. She, a mother, speaks openly about her love of family, and the virtues of the happy home and domestic sphere. Yet her land is filled with starving children and downtrodden women working in factories, begging in grimy alleyways, peddling their starved and broken bodies on so many of her kingdom's crowded streets.

Yes, London was most impressive. Scotland was beautiful. The sparkling lochs and rugged highlands were unlike anything I'd ever seen before—anything I had ever even imagined. And the tour of the Lake District was an experience I will never forget, having the opportunity to meet Mr. Wordsworth, the great father of the Romantics. But, after all that, I was ready to move on from Queen Victoria's dominion. And I say as much to Sand now.

She tosses me a cheeky wink. "I like your candor. You know that we French are always happy to hear an insult to the English. Centuries of war will leave a bad taste in one's mouth, even worse than the taste of their English *cuisine*—if one can even use the word."

We exchange a smile, and then I say, "As a matter of fact, I would say the high point of my time in England was a meeting in London with an Italian revolutionary."

Her body tilts closer toward mine. "Oh?"

"Giuseppe Mazzini," I say.

Sand raises her cigar aloft, her eyes rounding. "You met Mazzini?"

"I had the privilege of attending a lecture he was giving in London." I blink, recalling the raven-haired man. "On his efforts to rally the Italian people." I could wax further on the topic of Mazzini, happily so. On my passion for his idea of throwing out the Austrian and French armies in order to allow the Italian people to govern themselves. But just then my host, Monsieur Chopin, approaches, having finally broken free of his clutch of admirers.

Chopin joins our tête-à-tête, weaving his arm around his lover's waist as she turns to greet him with a kiss. I can't help but flush at this bold display of affection between them, right here in this crowded salon. George Sand and Frédéric Chopin—locked in a most intimate embrace. And yet, to my further astonishment, no one in the crowded salon seems to care in the least. No one even looks askance. I cannot imagine a display such as this in a Boston parlor. Even a New York one.

But Sand, rather than being reviled for her libertine choices—her freedom with her love, her outspokenness, even standing here smoking a cigar, wearing men's pants and a most curious velvet cape—here in Parisian society, these are not marks against her. None of this appears to stoke scandal or even disapproval. No one in the fashionable set shuns her invitations or cuts her while out in public. In fact, it seems to be quite the opposite. Here, in Paris, Sand is celebrated for the way she lives, for her audacious and un-inhibited choices. Her salon is always full, her ideas shared and re-vered.

Now Sand pulls herself away from her lover and catches me star-ing at her. A playful grin tugs on her lips. Then she angles her body back toward me and says, "Margaret, my dear, please meet Frédéric. Frédéric, meet my darling friend, *la Dame Américaine*, Margaret. I think she was summoned here as if by magic to inspire my soul and make me fall in love with America, since it produced a woman such as her."

Chopin offers a broad smile as he leans toward me. "Mademoi-selle Fuller, *enchanté*." We exchange two quick kisses in greeting, and the room sways a bit as I smell his thick eau de cologne, as my cheeks brush against his. But Chopin goes on, all warm and com-fortable hospitality: "Thank you for coming this evening. George has not stopped speaking about you since she read in the papers that you were coming to Paris. She simply had to meet you."

"Oh, Frédéric, now you are revealing my secrets," Sand chides, giving him a playful swat on his world-famous hand. I stand before the pair of them, speechless. Stunned by all of this. Chopin chuck-les and then fixes his gaze back on me as he asks, "Did you enjoy the recital, my dear Mademoiselle Fuller?"

"Oh, very much," I answer, and it's the truth. Almost as much as I've relished my conversation with George Sand.

"I think Margaret here has some French in her," Sand says, putting the cigar to her lips. Her long inhale sets its ashy tip aflame.

"Ah, *oui?*" Chopin looks at his lover with unbridled adoration. Exhaling, Sand presses a hand on mine and I feel the warmth of her palm. I smell the smoke of her breath. I notice how my heart begins to race, my body's instinctive response to being so close to her electricity. Then Sand whispers to me: "I think it's quite good that you've come to Europe, *ma chère*."

"I agree," I say. I do. Sand licks her lips, tossing a look to her lover, and then back to me as she adds: "And I'm not surprised you liked Mazzini."

"Why is that?" I ask.

Sand offers a quick shrug. "You speak and act like an Italian. I suspect you are going to love Rome."

I nod at this, glancing at Frédéric Chopin, then back to his lover. I hope George Sand is correct. I, too, suspect that I might love Rome.

PART 5

Chapter Thirty-Six

Isle of Capri, Bay of Naples
Spring 1847

"Now, Miss Fuller, close your eyes and open your mouth. No peeking." My little pupil, Eddie, has a playfully stern tone, and I bite back my smile as I obey his orders. A moment later, I feel a small orb land on my tongue, and I close my lips and take a bite. An explosion of flavor bursts across my mouth: salty, velvety smooth, the most rich and savory bite I've ever taken. I open my eyes, and I'm certain they are rounded in delight as I demand: "What is *that*, Eddie?"

"That, Miss Fuller, is called an olive. I've removed the little stone from its center. Is it not tasty?"

"It's divine, is what it is," I offer in reply, savoring the last few bites as I swallow the grape-sized morsel.

"Olives were the food of the gods," Eddie says, and I cannot help but smile at what a little pagan my young pupil is becoming in just our first few days on this Italian soil. I have to say I agree with him—this is ambrosial.

"Now, one more for you, Miss Fuller, close your eyes."

I obey, and this time a larger bite is placed into my mouth. I chew slowly, enjoying the flood of sweetness. A gummy texture. Not overly sweet like a cherry or a plum—this tastes earthy, loamy. "What is this, now?"

"That is called a fig."

"A fig. I quite like it. May I open my eyes?"

"Oh, yes! You may."

I open my eyes, and my, how good it is to do so—to see the view that sprawls before us. We are staying in lodgings on the isle of Capri, and at the moment, my ward and I are sitting on the terrace, a stunning expanse of the Bay of Naples shimmering under a sky of perfect blue. In the sun-soaked distance, Mount Vesuvius climbs up out of the sea, that ancient volcano that tormented the great legends of antiquity. Closer to us, the picturesque cities of the southern coast perch atop the cliffs—Pompeii, Sorrento, Naples, Positano. I've read about these places, but nothing I have read could have properly prepared me for the beauty of the Amalfi Coast. "The gods themselves must have walked on earth, here in the Italian springtime," I say, and Eddie nods as I help myself to another olive.

AS OUR TRAVELS take us north, toward our destination of Rome, I can't help but fall further under the spell of enchantment. "Italy suits you, Margaret," Rebecca says to me, noticing my flush of delight. I agree with her. For so many reasons. It's not only the ambrosial food and the sweeping views—it's the sunshine, the rolling hills, the way the people speak with passion and abandon. I love it. I feel as though I've come at last to soil where I may thrive and flourish.

Things remain joyful like this—that is, until we arrive in Rome in the darkness of evening. Exhausted from a long day of travel, we settle into our rented suite on the Via del Corso. I am eager for bed and a good night's sleep, eager for the Roman sunrise and the chance to explore the Eternal City in the daylight. But the night brings with it a terror I could never have expected.

I awake to black, blinking against the darkness. Consciousness washes over me, and with it, the realization that I am in my bedroom. In Rome. Our new lodgings on the Via del Corso. Not, as my nightmare had me believing only a moment earlier, on the deck of a ship, the waves roiling beneath me. I had been soaked, the boat pitching, the sea an angry swarm of grasping waves, ready to drag me into its maw.

I shudder as I sit up in bed, pulling my knees to my chest and wrapping my arms around them, needing a comforting embrace, but having no one but myself to offer one. Outside, on the street, I hear a shout, then laughter. It sounds as though a crowd has gathered, but only in a celebratory way, nothing threatening. My breath is still ragged but I tell myself that I am safe. I am on land. I can rest. Sleep will mean the start of my adventure in Rome.

I JOIN REBECCA and Eddie the next morning for breakfast. "How did you sleep?" my friend asks.

I clear my throat. I decide against telling her of my nightmare, the shipwreck, and instead say: "It sounded as though there was quite a crowd gathered in the street last night. Did you hear it, as well?"

"We did," Rebecca answers, and she slides an Italian newspaper across the table toward me. "I believe this might have something to do with it."

I look down and read the words splashed across the Italian journal.

SPERANZA!

"Hope," I say, translating it aloud.

Beneath that: *RISORGIMENTO!*

"Hope and Resurgence," I read, taking a sip of my coffee.

Speranza and *Risorgimento*. I quickly realize, in our first few days in Rome, that those two words have become the rallying cry of our new city. They are all over the newspapers, uttered on the lips of the Romans we see in the streets.

"The resurgence of what, precisely?" Eddie asks me one morning as we sit down to his lessons. I open our atlas to a map of the region around Rome, then I explain: "Since the early part of the century, the Italian people have been divided and separated, purposefully so, by foreign occupiers who wished to prevent a feeling of Italian unity. All so that they might keep their city-states and principalities, their thrones and footholds in this prosperous land."

Eddie's face crumples in thought as he looks at the map. I go on. "You see, the Spanish have their Bourbon king on the throne in the

Kingdom of the Two Sicilies. The Austrians hold tight to their vast territories in the north. The House of Savoy holds Piedmont and Sardinia. Even where we are, this area around Rome in the Papal States, is ruled as a miniature kingdom unto itself, and our ruler is the pope."

Eddie flashes me a thoughtful look. "So why now all this *Speranza*, hope, in Rome?"

"Because we have a new pope. And with that new leadership comes new hope. A resurgence of hope. You see, the unyielding Pope Gregory XVI has gone to meet his maker, and now the Romans have Pope Pius IX. He is known affectionately by his people as Pio Nono."

"Why do the Romans love this Pio Nono?" my pupil asks. "What if he's as tough as the other one?"

"That's a great question. I think they have good reason to hope. In just his earliest days in the Vatican, Pio Nono has shown himself to be a man of kindness, setting free many prisoners."

"Why were they in prison?"

"They were men and women who had called for Italian unification, who had done nothing more than demand an end to foreign despots and occupying armies."

"Oh. Well, then, that's good."

"I agree, my dear. And Pio Nono has even given hints that he might be willing to allow a constitution, or an elected governing body that comes from the people." A thought occurs to me. "Do you remember when we saw that Italian gentleman give a speech while we were in London?"

Eddie scrunches his face. "You mean Signore Mazzini?"

"Precisely, my dear boy. Well, perhaps now Giuseppe Mazzini might even be able to return from his London exile, to live among his own people once more. The people who love him and want him for their leader."

Eddie nods, absorbing all of this, and I see the wheels of his bright mind turning in thought. A moment later, his features perking up, he looks at me and says: "Miss Fuller, I can see why the Romans have this *Speranza*."

. . .

AND I SEE it, as well. I see it later that same morning, when Rebecca, Eddie, and I set out on foot to explore. We begin by climbing the Spanish Steps. We make our way toward the Villa Borghese, where Cardinal Borghese once built himself one of the grandest estates in all of Rome, transforming his vineyards into an enchanting sprawl of gardens, temples, lakes, and grottoes. We stroll happily through the tree-lined lanes, little Eddie running ahead, giggling in peals of giddy ecstasy as he glimpses the nude statues.

"I suppose it's something we shall have to adapt to." Rebecca sighs. She, who declined the opportunity to see Chopin in concert because of his unwed state. Here, in this city, every statue is nude.

"We shall embrace it as part of the Roman experience," I say, though I'll admit, it's easier said than accomplished.

Next, Rebecca is eager to see Michelangelo's Moses statue, so we trek together to the Basilica di San Pietro and gawk before the behemoth of smooth white marble. After a break for gelato, we make the short walk to the Colosseum. By that point, little Eddie's legs are tired and Rebecca herself is eager to rest. But I myself feel enlivened. Not only do I wish to keep walking, I wish to keep seeing and experiencing.

Most of all I wish to see the statue of Saint Teresa of Avila, the Bernini masterpiece of the female saint in the throes of ecstasy. It's in the Church of Santa Maria della Vittoria. Since we have to walk north to return to our rented rooms, it's not far out of the way. And in fact, I suspect it might be the sort of outing I would prefer to undertake alone, without the chaste bashfulness of Rebecca or the flighty distractions of little Eddie. "You go on. I'm not far behind," I tell my companions. "I wish to visit one more church."

Rebecca's eyes widen. "You don't mind going alone?"

"Not at all," I say. "You forget that I've lived alone in Boston and New York."

"But this is Rome."

"And I speak Italian." I suspect that perhaps it's Rebecca who does not wish to walk alone with Eddie. But I give her a bolstering nod. "I'll meet you back in our rooms."

I make my own way, arriving half an hour later and stepping out of the warm Roman sunshine into the cool, quiet church. Inside it's a feast of marble and gold. Frescoes soar overhead, with chubby angels flying about as I pass the remains of dead saints. I pause for several minutes to admire the painting of the great patriarch Joseph, from the Old Testament.

And then, when I behold the object of my visit, I come to a standstill, overwhelmed. Santa Teresa is forged in white marble and situated up high, elevated over me in a niche in the wall. She leans back, reclining, her face twisted in a look of rapturous ecstasy, while an angel pierces her with a golden spear of celestial light.

Saint Teresa was known for her mystical experiences of God's grace, her transportive visions that set her body aglow. But this work feels overpowering to me in ways I had not even imagined. Teresa appears like a woman in the throes of a spiritual experience, to be sure. And yet, there's also something undeniably sensual about her. As if she's a woman in thrall to a great physical ecstasy, as well.

How interesting, I note, that this city is filled with nude and erotic statues, and yet this work strikes me as the most sensual, the most seductively inviting, seething with passion. And it's housed here, in a church dedicated to Mary, the mother of God and perpetual virgin. As I stare up at Teresa, I notice how my breath has become shallow and quick. I can feel that I'm flushed. I notice the lovely ache that gnaws somewhere deep within.

That's when I turn, and nearly bump into the gentleman behind me. "Oh, I'm so sorry. *Mi scusi*," I say, fumbling to recall my Italian, so flustered am I, so overwhelmed by the whorl of feelings and passions that this statue has stirred within me. I look up into the man's face and am caught completely off guard by the kind, large, brown eyes. I freeze. He smiles at me. I smile back. Then I remember myself, and I lower my gaze. "*Mi scusi*," I repeat, turning to leave the church. Not glancing backward, and yet knowing that the man watches me.

I walk at a brisk pace back toward the Springs and the Via del Corso. I remind myself to pull in deep, steadying breaths as I go.

Yes, it was good that Rebecca did not join me to view this statue. Rome is stirring feelings and longings within me that are entirely new and even, at times, overwhelming. Perhaps even a bit dangerous. Because I can't help but wonder: Will these longings soon be too powerful for me to control?

Chapter Thirty-Seven

Rome

ROMAN PASSION AND PAGEANTRY ARE ON FULL DISplay during Holy Week, the days leading up to Easter. The Springs and I join the throngs of thousands gathering at Saint Peter's for Holy Thursday, in a service celebrating the night of Jesus Christ's Last Supper with his disciples. It's one of the holiest gatherings and we are here in the holiest of places. Rome is flooded by thousands, many of whom have traveled even farther than we have. They speak all languages, they wear silks and satins in every variety of color.

We move as if carried by a sea, streaming from the colonnaded court into the sacred inner sanctum of the Sistine Chapel. The musical notes of vespers soar around us. After a wait that whirrs with anticipation and excitement, in comes the pope, Pio Nono, carried aloft by his men on his pontiff's chair. Silk drapes over his head like a canopy, his face turned out in a beatific smile. He's a monarch of celestial and earthly power, and the people love him. The pilgrims form a line following after him, calling out to him, reaching up for him.

We follow Pio Nono's floating chair out. Many of the worshippers carry candles, and we move now like a river of flames. I am swept up in it all, in listening to the music, admiring the rich art that swirls all around. I am so engrossed that I don't even notice as I somehow become separated from Rebecca and her family.

That is, until I am outside once more, back in the darkened piazza, where even more people are gathered now. Some women are weeping, others are on their knees, overcome by the moment, prostrating themselves before the retreating figure of the pope. "Rebecca?" But as quickly as I cry out for her, my voice is swallowed, absorbed, a drop of water in the vast ocean of voices all around.

An old woman with a black veil approaches. "What's the problem?"

I shake my head with a quick smile, declining what I believe is her offer of assistance.

"*Signorina!*" A trio of men—they appear younger than me—come close. Too close.

"*Scusi.*" I stride off. Next I try to approach a small cluster of nuns, but they are consumed in prayer.

That's when I hear a deep, quiet voice. "Pardon me, my lady?" I turn and look into a pair of dark eyes, almond shaped and full of expression. The tall gentleman asks: "May I help you?"

"*Grazie, no . . .*" I'm about to decline, just as I've done with the other men who have foisted their attention on me, but something gives me pause. "Wait," I say. I narrow my eyes, raise my hand. "You're—it's you. I've seen you before." It dawns on me. "You're the gentleman from yesterday, at Santa Maria's. The statue of Santa Teresa?"

"I thought that might be you," the man replies, an easy, earnest smile brightening his handsome features. It's so loud in the square that he takes one step closer, so that I can hear him speak, but his posture is entirely formal, respectful, as he says, "Please allow me to introduce myself. I am the Marchese Giovanni Angelo Ossoli."

Marchese? He's a count, an Italian nobleman.

I pull back my shoulders. "It is nice to meet you. I am Margaret Fuller." I flinch; it sounds so plain. I have no aristocratic title, no endless series of florid Italian syllables to my name.

But his smile is so sincere, so unaffected and warm, that my worries seep away as he says: "You looked like you might be in need of assistance, Signorina Fuller."

I let out my breath, scanning the teeming piazza. Still no sign of Rebecca. "Indeed, I think I may be."

"I can see farther." He gestures to show me he's taller, which is a point so obvious that it makes me laugh. He's not only tall but well built, his slender physique turned out in an elegant suit complete with walking stick and hat. With his rich mahogany hair and olive-toned features, he looks every bit the Italian nobleman.

We search for a quarter of an hour, the count and I, but we catch no sight of the Springs. "I am sorry to say it, but I do not believe you will be able to secure a carriage at this time, not with—" Marchese Ossoli gestures at the swarm of people still filling the square, and I know he's right. Any coaches would have been waved immediately.

"It's no matter," I say, attempting a bright tone. "I can walk. I've walked all over this city."

"Not alone, surely?"

"You saw me yesterday at Santa Maria. I was alone then."

Marchese Ossoli's features crease in a look of concern. "But not at night, Signorina Fuller."

He must see my self-assurance wobble, because he hastens to add: "You shall not be alone tonight." The count offers me his arm. "Please, signorina, may I escort you safely?"

I shift on my feet, leaving his outstretched arm dangling. "It's really not necessary, sir."

"But of course it is. Have you not heard of Italian chivalry?"

I remain in my spot, unmoving. The count tips his head to one side. "If you do not allow me, signorina, I will not sleep a wink tonight over concern for you. You don't want that on your conscience, do you? Not right before Easter. Please, allow me to see you safely home. Home is . . . ?"

"Via del Corso," I reply. "Where I am staying with my friends."

"Then we must get you back, as I am sure they are eagerly awaiting your return."

"Oh, very well," I say, and I take his arm. We set off together, wading through the crowd, which remains thick all the way through the piazza and out onto the street. Marchese Ossoli guides us toward the Tiber River.

I can feel my heartbeat, hastened by this walk on the arm of a stranger in a new city. But Marchese Ossoli appears entirely at ease. Happy for this evening jaunt. Even striking up conversation as he asks: "Well, then, Signorina Fuller, what brings you to Rome?"

"Work," I answer. I see from the look he throws me that he's intrigued. "I'm writing for a New York newspaper. And also tutoring. Hence the family with whom I travel."

"New York," he says, his deep voice tinged with what sounds like awe.

"Have you been?" I ask, throwing him a sideways look.

"No. I've barely left Rome."

We approach the Ponte Sant'Angelo, that ancient marble crossing over the Tiber, which is lit up with torchlight. Arches curl beneath us, carved angels hover above us, and the river slips by, mirroring a thousand glimmers of torch- and starlight. I pause, taking it all in. After a moment, I speak: "I really cannot imagine ever becoming accustomed to this."

Marchese Ossoli nods, looking out appreciatively over the Roman night. "As someone who has been here my whole life, I can tell you: you don't."

"You were born in Rome?"

"Like my father, and his father, and his father."

I throw him a playful look. "Does your family go all the way back to the she-wolf?"

His dark lashes flutter as he smiles. "Ah, yes, she was my great-great-great-great-grandmother. Or something like that."

We laugh at this, and I glance back out over the Tiber River. I notice that my body feels less tense. Marchese Ossoli gives me no reason to be on edge. I speak: "You know what Goethe said of Rome?"

He arcs an eyebrow, throwing me a questioning look. I can see he has no idea.

"'Only in Rome,'" I say, "'can one prepare oneself for Rome.'"

He listens to my words, taking them in. "I don't know Goethe," he says. "But I know Rome. My family, the Ossoli family, has been here for centuries. My older brother is in the Pope's Guard." He says all of this with an earnest, touching trace of pride, not a whiff of arrogance or conceit.

"And what do you do?" I ask.

"I'm a sergeant in the Civic Guard here in Rome."

I tap the railing with my hands. "And your parents?"

"My father serves in the pope's administration."

"How wonderful," I say. "I admire Pio Nono tremendously." But then I catch myself. Marchese Ossoli is an aristocrat; perhaps his politics are not for reform.

But his face is alight. "Yes," he agrees. So then, he shares my fondness for Pio Nono.

"And your mother?" I ask.

"She is . . ." His words taper, his eyes glide upward. "She was always an angel. And now she is with the angels."

I feel a twist of sadness at this. "I'm so sorry to hear it." Marchese Ossoli makes the sign of the cross at his front, and then he offers me his arm again. I take it without a moment of hesitation, and we resume our walk, over the Ponte Sant'Angelo and toward the Via del Corso. Eager to fill the silence between us, I tell him about my own family—that my father is gone, as well. I tell him about Boston and New York. For some reason—why, I'm not entirely sure—I don't tell him about Concord and Waldo and Hawthorne and Thoreau. It all seems like such a different world as we walk away from the Tiber and through the ancient streets.

The count points to a faint mark on his cheek, just below his eye. I hadn't noticed it, but now that he's shown me, I see the groove in his smooth, warm skin. "A dog," he says, his finger grazing the flesh.

"How terrible," I say, my eyes fixed on his face. His strong, lovely profile. My stomach feels as though it could tip sideways.

"The same year my mother died," he says. "I was six."

I blink, taking this in. So then, Marchese Ossoli bears scars both visible and invisible. I study him just a bit closer, thankful for the darkness of the evening, which makes my stare less obvious. He looks to be in his late twenties, perhaps. A few years younger than me. But I don't ask his age.

We walk for just shy of an hour, and yet the entire time is enjoyable. Even when we slip into quietness, it is a pleasant, companionable silence. I notice that our pace is easy—neither of us seems to be in a hurry, even though the hour is late. "I hope your home is near," I say, as we approach my street.

He offers a slight shrug.

"Is it?" I ask.

"I live with my father and brother, near Trajan's Market."

"Marchese Ossoli!" I gasp. "I may not know Rome as well as you do, not by half, but I know well enough that Trajan's Market is nowhere near here. You've gone far out of your way."

He meets my eyes, his dark gaze warm and friendly. "And I've enjoyed every minute of it."

We have reached my door, and we pause before it. Like he promised, he's seen me home safely. "As have I, Marchese."

He remains a step back as I walk to the threshold, his body language entirely gentlemanly. I pause, turning to him, my hand on the doorknob. "Thank you again, Marchese."

He offers a playful flourish of a bow. "The pleasure, Signorina Fuller, was mine."

I hover a moment longer before the door. But then, realizing that there is no more reason for my delay, I smile and I step inside. As soon as I've shut the door, I glide to the window, looking out at the street, watching Marchese Ossoli's tall, strong figure recede into the Roman nighttime. Thinking, with a pang, that I've had the good fortune to bump into him twice in as many days. Which means I'm not likely to see Marchese Ossoli ever again.

Chapter Thirty-Eight

B UT I DO SEE MARCHESE OSSOLI AGAIN. THE NEXT day, in fact.

I've slept late, fatigued by the previous evening's excitement and long walk home. I rise from bed and move through my toilette. After a quick breakfast I glance out the window. There, in the street just below, I spot a familiar figure—tall, lean, with beautifully thick dark hair. I know instantly that if the gentleman were to tilt his face upward, I would see a pair of warm brown eyes. Marchese Giovanni Angelo Ossoli is just outside.

I check my appearance in the mirror, patting down my gown of rich crimson, then I step out into the warm Roman springtime. The marchese is still there on the street, but now he's marching away from my door, and I realize that he is pacing; for how long he's been at it, I do not know.

When he wheels back toward me, I see that his face is entirely consumed in thought. Unlike last night, when he appeared relaxed and at ease, today his body seems coiled. Also unlike last night, when he wore a fashionable dark suit, this morning he appears dressed in some sort of uniform—a dark tunic coat with red cord embroidery and slacks. A soldier's uniform. He had told me he was an officer in Rome's Civic Guard.

The marchese sees me and immediately halts his pacing, his expression turning almost bashful. "Ah." He raises his hand in a wave. "Signorina Fuller."

"Marchese Ossoli. Don't tell me you stayed here all night?"

He smiles at this, his stiff posture softening slightly as he strides toward me. "No. But last night, it was such a long walk for you. And your friends, being separated . . . I wanted to make sure that everything was all right this morning."

I'm so touched by his earnest attention. "Italian chivalry indeed," I say, lifting an eyebrow. "As you see, I am quite well."

"Good," he says. He folds his hands before his waist. "But . . . I also wonder . . ."

"Yes?"

"Do you have any more time, for just one more walk with me?"

I had not expected this. I look around at the street, biting my lip to stanch the smile that tugs my features. The morning is washed in Rome's golden light. He thinks I'm hesitating, so he adds: "I promise, it will be shorter."

I fix my gaze back on him, stepping forward from the door. "I would love another walk with you."

He gives me his arm, just as he did last night, and I allow him to guide me south along the Via del Corso. True to his word, it's quite a short walk—not that I would mind a longer one. Only a few minutes later we are gliding through the busy Piazza Colonna. And then we pause before a stately white palazzo with a grand arched doorway and four stories of large windows. In a city where every street hides some priceless and historic building, I do not know which one this is.

"Where are we?" I ask, angling my gaze upward to look into the count's face.

"This is the Palazzo Ossoli," he says, staring at the grand building.

"Your family's palace?" I study the splendid structure.

"*Sì*," he says, cocking his head. "The Ossoli Palace."

"But . . . you told me last night that your family lives near Trajan's Market."

"Correct," he says. "This was my family's palace. For hundreds of years. But my father could no longer . . . well, we've lost it now." He shifts at my side. "But we can still go inside the Ossoli Chapel," he says, gesturing to the adjacent building tacked on to the corner of the sprawling palace. "Would you like to?"

"I'd love to."

We step inside together, where the air is cool and dim. Candle-light from hundreds of votives skitters off countless marble columns, the whole place colored with the most vibrant blues and reds. A quick glance around tells me that we stand alone in here. This is so scandalous, even if it is a holy site. A young man and a young woman together, alone, without a chaperone. But I don't care. I plunge farther into the holy space and take in the luxuriant setting. So many painted panels and scenes—so many Ossoli ancestors who prayed here and hoped that their generous patronage of this beautiful church would guarantee a spot in heaven.

At the altar I pause before a stunning rendering of the Virgin Mary. I'm realizing that the Romans love the Virgin Mother in a way we New Englanders do not. Beside her is a saint. I study the image. He holds what looks like wheat in his outstretched hands.

"That is Saint Nicholas," Marchese Ossoli says to me, following my gaze. "He was our family's patron saint. He was always feeding the hungry. My ancestors honored him hundreds of years ago because the first Ossoli to attain great wealth, and a noble title, was a baker here in Rome."

I nod, trying to listen to his words, even as I find his closeness entirely distracting. He smells of lemon soap and wool, perhaps the trace of coffee.

"Even though we Ossolis no longer have great wealth, though this palace and this chapel no longer belong to us, I feel the connection. The sense of duty. To serve others."

I turn to face him, struck anew by how close we stand to each other. By the fact that we are alone in this chapel. I can feel my heartbeat in my throat as I say: "That is beautiful, Marchese Ossoli."

He offers me a timid grin. When he speaks, his voice is low, smooth like the marble all around us. He asks: "Would you please call me Giovanni?"

After a moment, I answer only: "Very well." But I do not offer him the same invitation to familiarity. He extends his arm and says, "*Signorina*, shall we?"

I nod. We should go. We've pushed our luck far enough. We step out of the cool Ossoli Chapel and back into the warm Roman morning, where the sunshine lands on our skin. I feel as though it carries with it the promise of beneficence and blessings.

GIOVANNI BECOMES A daily visitor after that, and I introduce him to Rebecca, Eddie, and Marcus as my friend. "Your deliverer from Holy Thursday?" Rebecca asks, her tone inviting further detail.

"Yes," I answer, saying nothing more.

Soon he is back at my door with an offer to escort me to Easter Mass at the Vatican. "But don't you wish to attend services with your family?" I ask, surprised—but delighted—by his offer.

"They all work for the pope," he says. "They will be there. And I would be sitting alone."

So Giovanni joins us, and we manage to stay all together this time, even as the crowds throng around the service presided over by Pio Nono. There is one moment during the service when we both reach for the same hymnal, our hands brushing against each other, and my entire body fills with warmth. It's the most holy day of the year for these devout Roman Catholics, and my body pulses with the power of it all.

In the weeks that follow, I fall in love with Rome as Giovanni opens his city to me. I drink deep of the myriad sights, tastes, and smells of this Eternal City, this ancient capital with more layers of rich history than I can even fathom. Though Rebecca, bless her, most certainly disapproves of my stepping out with a gentleman unchaperoned, she does not voice her concerns aloud—at least, not to me. And in truth, she need not worry. I never invite Giovanni to call me Margaret, and he never tries anything more than extending his arm as an attentive escort through the crowded Roman streets. He does not even attempt a kiss on my cheek.

Is he my gentleman caller, or, as I've told Rebecca, just a friend? And do I wish for him to be more? Giovanni walks me to the Colosseum at night, where the torchlight dances off the ancient arches and I close my eyes to imagine the roars of the thousands. And then I hear something else. "Owls," he says, his voice dangling in the shadows like the last strains of some beautiful song.

"Roman owls," I say, smiling, thinking of Concord and Walden Pond. And how far I've come. I would not wish to be anywhere else, nor with anyone else.

With Giovanni as my tour guide, Rome unlocks itself to me like some wondrous labyrinth. He knows where to go and when. He takes me to stroll the streets of the Forum, old stone pathways now covered in new grass. He hasn't read Ovid or Virgil, he doesn't know their ancient texts the way I do—and yet, he knows the roads that they walked. He brings their writings and worlds to life for me in a way that no one else ever has. Together we imagine the colorful stalls once overflowing with jewelry and books, oils and lambs, all the treasures that were bartered and sold. We pause before the ruins of the temple where the Vestal Virgins lived and worshipped. "It's funny," I remark. "For a people as passionate and sensual as the Romans, you certainly do love your virgins."

Giovanni considers this, his eyes crinkling into a thoughtful smile. "I think it is a case of, how would you say it: Do as I say, not as I do? Perhaps Roman men—artists—love virgins so much because they do not know any?"

I flush scarlet at this. The topic of virginity, his quip about the virility of Roman men, of which he is one—and virgins, of which *I* am one. But then he looks at me and together we break into shared laughter.

IT'S INTERESTING TO me that Giovanni and I speak together only in Italian; he does not have any other languages, and I'm entirely comfortable operating in his tongue. This means that he is the only man with whom I've ever been close who knows nothing of my writings. Not my newspapers, my essays, my books. I tell him about my work, I tell him when I'm filing a column for Greeley, but he cannot read my work for himself.

And I've never met his family. He does not offer it, and I don't press it. Though he speaks of them with a certain pride, I know that his brother and ailing father are conservative Roman Catholics who serve the pope. I'm American, I'm Protestant. I'm an unwed woman in my midthirties who has made a career as a writer. The older Ossoli men would never imagine me as a suitable companion for their youngest son.

But what sort of companion am I? I wonder. While none of those differences seem to hinder our connection or the warmth and ease between us—not in the least—I still don't know what exactly Giovanni believes the state of things between us to be.

And yet, in so many ways, I do feel as though I truly know Giovanni. And he knows me. Better than any of the other men with whom I've been close. As we walk side by side along the meandering streets of the Trastevere quarter, or through the crowds of the Piazza del Popolo, we talk about everything we see. I never cross a street without Giovanni at my side, offering his arm to help me through the traffic. If ever I pause for a moment in my step, Giovanni offers a rest at a nearby café, suggesting that we take a cold drink or gelato. Or he slips his soldier's coat over my shoulders if the sun dips behind a cloud or he suspects I might feel even the slightest chill. There's a warmth to him, a softness to his eyes that makes me feel more *seen* than ever before. An openness to his manner, all the hints that his thoughtful and tender gestures are just the prelude and that, underneath, there lies a deep pool of love and feelings. It's a place I long to know.

When we do break from each other, me to return to the Springs or to complete my work for Greeley, Giovanni to report for his duties with the Civic Guard, it's always with a feeling of sweet and shared sadness. As soon as we've bid farewell, I long to see him again. Luckily, he always comes back. Nearly every day, he comes back.

FOR THAT REASON, I dread our imminent separation. The separation that is to be far greater than simply our nights apart. As the Roman spring marches steadily toward summer, with June only a few weeks away, I look to the calendar with increasing desolation.

At the end of this month, the Springs and I will be finished with our time in Rome, and we will be taking off by carriage for Tuscany and the north. Our tour of the Italian peninsula will continue and our itinerary will carry us away from this city, from this Roman soldier whom I never expected to meet.

I had been eager for the remainder of our travels, particularly through Tuscany and into Florence. I had looked forward with great delight to seeing the many cities made glorious by the Medici gold and the Italian Renaissance. I had thought several months in Rome would be sufficient, as they were for London and Paris. But now, as the date for our departure draws irrevocably toward me, as Rebecca begins to speak about packing our trunks and Marcus begins to make arrangements for the coach that will carry us north, I don't wish to go. I haven't had nearly enough time here. I haven't had nearly enough time with Marchese Giovanni Ossoli. And then the question bubbles up in my mind, like the gurgling and frothing waters of the fountains that fill each one of these Roman piazzas: Would *any* amount of time be enough time, here, in Rome, with him?

Chapter Thirty-Nine

Rome
Spring 1847

"**H**APPY BIRTHDAY, SIGNORINA FULLER."

He remembered. I had mentioned it only once, in passing, that today would be my birthday. I had not expected Giovanni to take any special note of the day, had not even been entirely certain that he'd heard me say it. But of course Giovanni had heard me. And now here he stands on the Via del Corso outside my door, a hamper on one arm, his expressive eyes crinkled in an eager smile as he asks, "Join me for dinner? How does the bank of the Tiber sound?"

"*Perfetto*," I say in reply.

"*Andiamo*," he says. "Let us go together."

So we set out. Rebecca is entirely preoccupied with packing the last of Eddie's trunks, and they treated me to a delicious birthday dinner at midday, so the Springs barely notice my departure, and they certainly won't mind my absence this evening. *Our final evening in Rome.* I notice the twist of sadness that the thought brings on.

But I force that melancholy aside, at least for now, determined to enjoy this gorgeous evening and the companion at my side. The gentleman who has prepared this private celebration with such thought and generosity, just as he's prepared so many other lovely outings. We walk side by side, as we've done nearly every day for months. He asks me what my birthday wish is, and I answer, truthfully, that I have not yet settled on one. In this moment, I don't feel as though I want anything more—only to be with him, here, like this, but I do not speak that part aloud. Giovanni guides us and we make our way to the Tiber, to one of my favorite spots, right beside the Ponte Sant'Angelo.

As Giovanni spreads a blanket and unpacks the hamper—bread, cheese, ripe melon, olives, slices of prosciutto—I look out over the water, and beyond that, to the soaring dome of Saint Peter's Basilica on the opposite bank. "We've walked all over Rome," I say, settling in on the blanket beside Giovanni. "But this is the place where we first walked."

Giovanni breaks the loaf of bread and serves me a piece, along with a scoop of olives. Then, looking to me, his eyes warm in the evening light, he says: "I thank God every day that you got lost in Saint Peter's."

I laugh at this, popping an olive into my mouth.

"I suppose what I thank God for is . . ." He pauses, and now something more serious has crept into his tone. "That I was able to find you. In spite of the crowds, I came right to you. Do you know, Signorina Fuller, that I—"

"Please, Giovanni." At this I cannot help but interject; it's our last night together, after all, and he's shown more kindness and care for me than any person in recent memory—perhaps ever. "You may call me Margaret."

He arcs a dark eyebrow and I nod, my small reassurance that it is indeed all right for him to take this liberty. Then, slowly, as if whispering a sacred prayer, he says: *"Margherita. Mia cara Margherita."*

Margaret. My dear Margaret.

My name is made so much more beautiful on his lips. And in this place, where the waters of the river lap like a quiet song against the bridge, blending with the notes of the doves that nestle in its crevices to coo their nightly vespers. I feel my body lean toward Giovanni's, a flower craving his sunshine. And now I know my answer to his question: What is my birthday wish? I would like a kiss. A kiss from Marchese Giovanni Ossoli. Here, on the banks of the Tiber, beside our favorite bridge. It's something he's never tried, even though we've walked all over this city together and there have been occasions enough for him to do so. But now, on my final night,

I would like to depart from Rome with the parting gift of that memory, that experience with him. This seems like the right place for it, after thirty-seven years of never knowing the feeling.

But Giovanni is looking at me expectantly, and I force myself to come back to what he's saying. He is in the middle of asking me a question: "Do you know that I've never taken a lady to my family's chapel?"

This surprises me. "Oh? Why not?"

He glances out over the river. "I made a promise to my mother, before she died." Now he turns back to me, and I meet his gaze. "I promised Mother that I would only ever bring my wife there."

I swallow. A mouthful of salty olives, but I taste nothing. Giovanni goes on: "I knew, Margaret, when I met you. I knew that it was you."

"Giovanni, this is . . ." Only an instant ago I was wondering whether he wanted to kiss me. Now is he saying he wishes to *marry* me? "We've only known each other a few months."

"And when I brought you to the chapel, I'd only known you one day. What does that matter? I knew. I *know*."

"But . . ." I wave my hands between us. "It can't be."

"*Perchè no?*" he asks with a shrug.

Where to begin? "Well, I'm American. I'm not Catholic. I'm older than you." And then I pause, frowning. "In fact, I don't even know how old you are."

"I am twenty-six," he answers, both his tone and his voice entirely unruffled.

"Well, that further proves my point," I say, drawing my shoulders back, my posture a stiff upright line after my tilt of a moment earlier. "I am *far* too old for you. No, no. We are not well suited, not in any way."

He leans his head to the side, a puzzled expression on his face. "How can you say we are not well suited?" A wave of his dark hair falls across his brow, grazing the corner of his eye, and it prompts something in my stomach that feels like an ache. I wish he didn't have to look like that. Not in this moment. Nevertheless, I force a hardness into my tone as I answer: "I'm being reasonable here. How can you say we are?"

"You know that we are." He says it as if it were the most basic, most knowable of facts. As if I'm the one not seeing the plain and obvious truth. And then he goes on: "Our souls could not be more well suited, Margherita." There it is again, that aching feeling in my gut. I exhale, a beleaguered sigh, but he goes on. "We've walked together all over, and our steps have never been anything but in perfect harmony."

It's beautiful, how he says it. And perhaps it *is* true, the bit about our being in lockstep together. But no, it is preposterous that he is proposing! It cannot be. We have never even kissed, though I don't voice that aloud. Instead, I remind him that there's one even bigger impediment, one immovable obstacle that makes his hopes entirely impossible. "Giovanni, I'm leaving Rome tomorrow."

"So you'll come back."

"No," I answer, my voice hard now, my throat feeling tight. "I will not." The plan is Siena, Florence, Parma, Venice, and then out of Italy altogether, toward Germany. Goethe's homeland! How is it that somehow, now, I'm not even excited to see the birthplace of my favorite writer?

Giovanni, for his part, remains unruffled. And his words catch me by surprise when he says, simply, "Yes, you will."

Now I'm slightly piqued. At his unwillingness to hear me, to see reason. At least allow me to feel this sadness at our coming separation, rather than insisting on this impossible and irrational reunion, one that we both know can never happen. "Why are you saying that?" I demand. I expect that the sharpness in my tone might, at last, put him off. But when he speaks, he holds me in a gaze that shows only tenderness and care. That warm, brown-eyed gaze that first held me in the Church of Santa Maria, beneath the statue of rapture and ecstasy, and then found me again in the crowds of Saint Peter's once I'd lost my way. His tone is all patience, even peacefulness, as he says, "Because I know you. Just as I know myself. And I know that we will be together. You will return to Roma, Margherita, *amore mia*, and when you do, I'll be here. Remember, my dear, our word here in Roma is *Speranza*. Hope."

Chapter Forty

Venice
Summer 1847

VENICE IS A FAIRYLAND, AWASH IN NIGHTTIME lights, as I stare out over the Grand Canal. Behind me, the balconied terrace of Caroline, Duchesse de Berry, is filled with string music and laughter. The duchess herself looks like a colorful fairy queen as she mingles, gliding among the hundreds of dinner guests who swarm her waterside palazzo. She's festooned in coral jewels this evening, her French profile almost birdlike in its noble sharpness, her hair piled atop her head like a puffy pastry. The Springs and I avail ourselves of her gracious hospitality, feasting on the duchess's lavish dinner spread of lobster and *baccalà mantecato*. I even take a few sips of the prosecco, then I watch gamely as Marcus and Rebecca twirl across the ballroom with her other guests.

But after only a short while of this, I have had my fill. I slip out, craving fresh air and a break from the stifling smells of so many bodies and syrupy perfumes. I need some time alone. Some time to hear my own thoughts. More than anything, I need a chance to frown—perhaps even to cry—without worrying that someone will notice.

I stand before the balcony, looking out over the Grand Canal. The water is a teeming thoroughfare, an endless procession of gondolas, the men in striped shirts singing to their passengers as they ply the liquid road. From the massive palazzo across the way I hear pops like gunfire, then I see the bursts of orange and red light that brighten the sky; someone is setting off fireworks. Ripples of delighted laughter and applause follow.

My dress feels too tight. It's a chic enough dress, one of the new pieces I commissioned in Paris, and yet it feels all wrong. Perhaps it's just a stomachache from the too-rich food. Everything here feels decadent—the jewels, the palaces, the banquets. Yes, Venice is a fairyland. Why, then, can I not enjoy its magic?

It's been this way for much of the time as we've traveled north through the Italian peninsula. Stunning views, incomparable opportunities. And I've relished so many of the moments, to be sure, experiences like reading Saint Francis's writings while visiting his home in the mountains of Assisi. Appreciating the staggering jut of the Alps that rise up from the deep blue of Lake Como. Touring the rolling green vineyards of Tuscany. The art of Florence and the cathedrals of Milan. I've dutifully visited it all, recording it and filing it for Greeley and my readers of the *Tribune*. I've written on everything from the food and the views to the stirrings of political unrest in a populace that seems ready to throw off its occupying armies.

And yet, Rebecca is the one who says it right when she finds me on the terrace that night in Venice. Appearing at my side, unbidden, she voices aloud the very thought that I have not yet allowed myself to express: "Margaret, my dear, you're not with us."

I look at her, frowning. Startled by the deep cut of her perception. And surprised, too, by the certainty of her tone. "Ever since Rome," she says, her fingers tapping the limestone balcony before us, "it's felt like you've been gone. With us in body, but not in spirit."

I break from her gaze, staring back out over the water, no longer hearing the music or the laughter or the chatter within. The truth is that I miss Rome. As I look ahead to our itinerary continuing on north, toward Berlin and Frankfurt and then Vienna, it fills me with no excitement or eager anticipation. I know how odd that is, considering Frankfurt is the birthplace of Goethe, but it's the truth. Rebecca has seen it; perhaps it's time I acknowledge it, as well. Perhaps it's time that I admit to myself that I've been grieving ever since we left Rome.

And what's more, I've come to realize that I'm ready to part ways with the Springs. I traveled here under the acceptable coverage of their chaperoning, but now that I'm here, I feel less of a need to stay on their lead line. I wish, instead, to live for myself, without answering to Rebecca's well-meaning but maternal monitoring. Here, in Europe, many women live with a freedom and boldness that stirs something within me, calling out to me with an invitation to try to taste it for myself. In the face of Rebecca Spring's pious philosophies, I've been wrestling with a persistent and mounting longing to embrace these ways. I no longer feel the need to voluntarily wear the shackles that, for more than thirty-seven years of my life, I've accepted. If George Sand can write and speak and love without fear of condemnation, why must I live in fear of offending?

Here, so many thousands of miles away from the Puritans who raised me, I feel myself expanding. Things that would have seemed out of the question only months earlier are now entirely possible. Enticingly so. I'm in a different place, not only in body, but also in my mood and my inclinations.

Standing on this terrace overlooking the Grand Canal, I finally admit to myself, and to Rebecca, the thought that will no longer remain unspoken within me. "I don't wish to leave," I say, my voice resolute. "I feel that Italy is the soil that at last suits my soul. The garden in which I may flourish and thrive." And not just Italy, but one place in particular: Rome. Yes, I long to return, unchaperoned, to live in Rome. And, once there, to see a certain pair of warm, brown Roman eyes.

Chapter Forty-One

Rome
Fall 1847

"NOW I SEE AND FEEL THE REAL ROME." I STARE DOWN at the words, my words, that I intend to post to Greeley for the *Tribune*. In this dispatch I've written about my return to the golden, glorious light of the Roman autumn, where I am living once more—happy, enlivened, and entirely alone.

I'm renting a suite of rooms on my beloved Via del Corso, but my new neighborhood puts me at an even shorter walk to so many of my favorite places: the Spanish Steps, the Borghese Gardens, the Ponte Sant'Angelo. *"The very same neighborhood where Goethe lived while in Rome,"* I write to Greeley. Though I did not make it to his German home, I am in the place where he felt most alive. And where I feel most alive as well.

And now I wish to be truly myself, open and free, and I plunge headlong into my new Roman life. In addition to writing for Greeley, I savor everything I can about my independent days in the Eternal City. I decorate my new apartment with fresh flowers from the markets, also shopping for artichokes, olives, figs—foods that only a few months ago I had never even tasted. Another touch of décor in my new room is a framed print I mount over my writing desk: the Greek muse of love poetry, Erato. It feels right to celebrate her here. To call on this goddess for inspiration and guidance, she who charted a course that was free and full of passion.

"I am not the same person," I write to my mother. *"Nor have I ever been happier. I only wonder how I might ever consider living anywhere else."*

My work for Greeley makes this new life possible, so I apply myself with renewed focus to my writing. The bulk of my columns are on Italian politics, as that is the topic I found most captivating on my travels, and seems to be where Greeley's interests are fixed, as well. The north felt restless—the people there want freedom from the Austrians. The south, too, trembles with the rumblings of volatility; they crave freedom from the Bourbons. Here in the Papal States, Pio Nono has allowed for an elected council of representatives, almost like what we have in America with our Congress. Might Mazzini return to Rome and the people who call for him? I write about all of this, hoping that American readers will find this thirst for freedom in their Italian counterparts to be both relatable and undeniably inspiring, just as I find it to be.

Once I've finished my work for the day, I walk to my beloved spots. I visit Trastevere and the Forum, the Colosseum and the Fontana di Trevi. I walk along the Tiber, crossing at the Ponte Sant'Angelo. I walk not only to see these cherished places once more but also, *more so,* in the hope of seeing him.

Remember, my dear, our word here in Roma is Speranza. *Hope.*

I cannot write to him directly to inform him that I've returned, nor can I visit him at his family's home. That's been clear from the start, that Giovanni does not wish for his brother—and even more so, his father—to know of our relationship just yet. But I think back to Giovanni's words on my last night in Rome: That I would return. To this place and to him. He knew I would, long before I did. And he said he'd be here, waiting for me, when I did. So I trust that, as well. I have faith that he will find me, just as he has done before.

The days pass, one after the other, stringing together like the beads of a necklace to form a week, and then two. I see no sign of Giovanni, but I do not give up. I continue to walk all over the city. I even visit the piazza beside the Ossoli Chapel several times, in the mornings, when I suspect he might be there for his prayers. But each day passes, and still he does not appear. I begin to wonder: Is something amiss? Has he left the city perhaps?

No, I chide myself. Giovanni has been in Rome his entire life, he told me that himself. Just like his father before him, and so many Ossoli fathers before that. I simply have to keep my hope.

Speranza. The faith that, in this massive, teeming city, we are meant to find each other, and so we shall.

The Advent season begins with a clamor of church bells across the city. When I hear that Pio Nono is to give a service at the Church of San Carlo, a short walk from my apartment, I am eager to attend. I love the services by Pio Nono, and, knowing that Giovanni's brother and father serve in the pope's administration, I suspect one or more Ossoli men might be in attendance. I'd love to catch a glimpse of either of his relatives, even if from afar, hidden behind my veil. Perhaps *he* might be there, as well.

I file into the stunning church along with the hundreds of Christmas worshippers. I am in a long gown of midnight blue with a veil, the look of a pious adherent, though my wardrobe choice is as much for the freedom it affords me to be an observer as it is for piety. I stare at my surroundings in awe. The ceiling soars heavenward, a dome of burnished gold, anchored by gleaming columns of alabaster marble.

I take my seat as the sacred music fills the space, reverberating through me until it feels as though it sets my soul to thrumming. Several minutes later Pio Nono is swept in, raised aloft on the shoulders of his attendants, who bear his pontiff chair. His gleaming robes of gold thread and creamy white satin match the interior of this church. He extends his arms to all as he passes, showering the crowd with his blessings like tossed coins, his smile that of an adoring father. This is when I begin to weep, so happy to see Pio Nono again. So happy to know that he has allowed his people the chance to vote and elect a governing body. *Speranza.* It is a season for hope.

And there, several steps behind Pio Nono, walks a tall, dark-haired man. I know that profile, those features, even if they've been painted to a slightly different effect. I narrow my eyes and confirm my suspicions: it must surely be an Ossoli. My heart begins to thump. I pull the veil closer over my face.

The service begins and I try to immerse myself once more in the feelings of worship and devotion. I close my eyes and listen to the prayers of Pio Nono. I clasp my hands and try to pray myself.

But now all I can think about is where, in this crowd, *my* Ossoli might be.

Later, as the service is reaching its conclusion, I feel a flutter of hope. It is a time to kneel; as the crowds lower themselves to pray, I see a man's head go down just a beat after those around him. My heart clenches.

It is him. It's Giovanni. I'm sure of it. He does kneel, and I lose him in the colorful sea of bowed heads, but I don't lose hope. *Speranza*. At least I know that he is in here. And I have an idea.

When the mass is over, I race to the doors. I don't even care that I'm being embarrassingly rude as I weave my way past the worshippers and hurry up the aisle. I leave the church and post myself like a sentry, standing out front, unmoving. My eyes fix on the open doors, combing the face of every person who exits. Several minutes later I see him filing out. It is Giovanni. He walks alone. I charge through the crowd, pushing against the current of their steps, composing myself only a moment before I reach him.

There, I put my hand softly to his elbow. Like he did to me, in the crowd after a service with Pio Nono, so many months earlier. Back in a different life, when I felt like a different woman.

He looks at me askance, startled to be touched, and then I slide my veil ever so slightly to the side. For an instant my heart stops beating. I wonder how he will respond to seeing me.

It's not until his face breaks open in an expression of pure, unadulterated delight that I allow my own smile to burst across my features. And then I begin to laugh.

He says nothing, throws his eyes across the crowd. Pio Nono's pontiff chair is visible atop the heads of the pilgrims as they stream through the piazza. His brother, perhaps even his father, will be there with the pope. I replace my veil across my features.

Giovanni leads me into the crowd without a word, and I follow. We walk quietly toward the gardens that border the church, the space teeming with worshippers. My breath is quick, but I don't think it's from our brisk walk. We continue past the Piazza of Apollo. We don't stop until we arrive before the Trevi Fountain, one of my favorites of the city. I look at the churning water for a moment and then up at Giovanni. I can see from the rise and fall of his chest that he, too, is panting.

I brush my veil aside, staring up into his eyes. "How long have you been back in Rome?" he asks.

"A few weeks," I reply. "I returned in October."

"So long," he says, his voice thick. "I had no idea you were back."

"I had no way of telling you." I had only my faith that we would find each other. That this, between us, is strong enough that he would feel my presence in this city, the same way I feel him on every street, in every place I visit. And I had been correct.

"No matter," he says. "I've found you now."

I throw him a bridled smile. "I believe it was *I* who found *you*."

His happy expression clouds for a moment, just for a beat, then he looks away, into the fountain. A moment later, still staring into the water, he says: "The ancients called this place the Virgin's Water."

I angle my body toward the fountain, along with my gaze. "Again, you Romans with your virginity."

He laughs, a quick, throaty laugh. "The legend is that this place was where the roads of Rome came to an end. A virgin helped find this point, where the purest water was."

I nod, taking this in. When he turns to me he asks, "Will you walk with me?" He extends his arm, and I do not have to think before I take it.

As we walk, side by side, the sun begins to set over Rome. It's a chilly night, with clouds grazing the moon at regular intervals, shuttering her light for just a moment before she returns. We walk and we talk, Giovanni and I. We walk for hours as the church bells ring at their regular intervals. We become reacquainted after more months apart than we have ever had together. I tell him of Assisi and Lake Como, of Florence and Venice. Giovanni tells me of his time in the Civic Guard, that the men are growing more restless by the day for a free government. He tells me, also, that his father, ailing for so long, has passed.

"Oh, Giovanni, I am so sorry," I say, my heart aching for him.

"He was a devout man who spent his life in service to the pope.

He met his end with great faith. And in the end, death came as a sort of blessing. Now, at least, I know he is at peace."

But, sadly, there has not been peace for him in the Ossoli household. Now Giovanni's older brother is managing the estate and what is left of the inheritance that is intended to come their way. It won't be much when it finally does come through, Giovanni's share as the younger, but it will give him a bit of security. He longs to move out of the cramped quarters of his family's home and be free from his overbearing brother.

The way he lays all of this out for me, it feels like a suitor telling the object of his affections that he has a plan, and good intentions.

I look at him as we walk, relishing the sight of his features after so long. After so many days of seeing him only in my mind's eye. I forgot, in fact, how handsome he is. I forgot how expressive his eyes are, how gentle and kind he appears as he listens.

Giovanni Ossoli has been educated not at Harvard, but by life. He serves his homeland. He honors his family's history. He has faith and a true nobility of spirit. He is tender, honest, authentic, and good. He is truly living a life of self-reliance. And he loves Rome the same way I do. He leads me all over his city, *our* city, in these dark hours as the Christmas season begins. Along the Tiber, walking across our beloved bridge. In spite of the hours and the miles, I do not grow tired. After weeks of searching for Ossoli, coming to these places to find him, I am now finally returning to these places with him.

After a long while he leads me to a place I do not know, past the Vatican. "Where are we going?" I ask.

"The Janiculum Hill," he tells me. It is still dark, but I can feel that dawn is not far off. We don't stop until we come to the top and what appears to be a courtyard, hemmed by tall cypress trees and stone markers in rows. "This is the Santo Spirito Cemetery," he tells me. The birds up here are singing the arrival of morning, and the bells below begin to chime.

The darkness is thinning as he guides me to a path that brings us, eventually, to an overlook. When we pause there, I cannot help but gasp. The sun is now purpling the skies over Rome. Through the

lifting darkness I can see the countless close-packed rooftops terraced into the city's hills, the bell towers of her ancient churches,
the broad sprawl of her piazzas, even the wooded pathways of the
Borghese Gardens. All the places where we have walked, and been,
together. It is both timeless and eternal.

"Oh, Giovanni." I turn from the view to meet his eyes, two deep
pools that glow with the gold of the sunrise. "It's beautiful."

It sounds silly, what I say. It is not nearly enough. But he offers a
nod, answering, "Yes, it is."

Before I can think to do otherwise, I lean forward and press my
lips to his. I feel his quick gasp, his intake of breath. I'm afraid I've
startled him. Or worse, offended him. His lips retreat for a moment, but then I feel his entire body exhale and he leans into me.
Our lips meet with a fresh and pressing ardor. I wish to take all of
him in; his scent, his taste, his touch. His hands find my waist, then
my lower back. I press myself forward. Now I want not just his lips,
but his whole body against mine. I am on fire; I need more of him.

But that's when he pulls back.

My breath is coming in ragged gasps as I meet his eyes, and I'm
sure he can read my confusion. I cannot stop; how can he? I need
his body to come back against mine. But when I step forward, he
shakes his head. It's a small gesture, barely perceptible, but it's
there. And then he takes a pace backward, putting a distance between us that, though it's only a foot, feels like a chasm.

I would have lain down with him, here on the grass, with the
cypresses over us and Rome beneath us. I would have allowed him
so much more than just this one kiss. I had felt the desire rising up
in his body. I can see the way his eyes smolder, even now. I had
thought he wanted the same. But he doesn't. Giovanni had told
me, before I left, that he wished to marry me. But now, it seems, he
does not even wish to kiss me.

Chapter Forty-Two

I AM WRETCHED FOR THE NEXT FEW WEEKS, AND ALONE. Giovanni does not come to me, nor do we walk. I don't see him again until Christmas Eve, when he appears outside my door. I am just preparing to attend Christmas Mass at Saint Peter's, hoping to find a much-needed lift to my spirits by being in the presence of Pio Nono, in the place where Giovanni and I were happy together. I tell him of my plans. "I cannot linger," I say, my tone curt.

"I will come with you," he says. "If you will have me."

I sigh. Hearing him say that, seeing the softness in his expression, I find myself softening, also. "I would like that," I answer. It's the truth.

We walk in silence toward the Vatican. The sky is iron gray and the air has a damp chill. He slips his coat over my shoulders without my mentioning that I'm cold. Inside the packed space, the air is warmer and smells of incense and perfume. Giovanni and I sit side by side in a pew near the back. I don't wear a veil; I do nothing to conceal my face. I try my best to follow the service, to allow the welcome feelings of worship and elation to engulf me, but having Giovanni beside me proves entirely unsettling, as though I'm sitting too close to the hot fire.

At the high point of the mass, as the voices of thousands are raised, proclaiming the return of joy and hope to a world blanketed in darkness, he turns to me and our eyes lock. I feel the way my heart tips. Does he offer a slight nod?

We say nothing as the mass ends and we leave the basilica. Or as we weave our way through the crowds of the piazza and he walks beside me, back toward my apartment. The skies begin to drizzle and once more he drapes me in his coat, but we keep our pace steady. And then, as we arrive at my door, I push it open and step in. When he steps in behind me, I feel my entire body begin to quiver. We walk, without a word, up the stairs. I say nothing, because I have far too much to say. I try to steady my hands as I fumble with my brass key, unlocking my door, and together, we enter. It is night, it is dark, and we are alone. I feel as though I should offer him some coffee, or at least some water.

I turn, and as I am about to speak, Ossoli steps toward me, closing the distance between our bodies. I tip my face up toward his. Our lips meet. And this time, unlike on top of the Janiculum Hill, he does not pull back. He presses closer, and I welcome it. We shuffle across the room, unwilling to wrest our bodies apart for even a moment, passing by the image of Erato and eventually landing together on top of my bed.

I lie flat on my back, and when Giovanni presses his body against mine, I can feel how fully he longs for me. It is the same longing that I myself feel. I remove his damp coat from around my shoulders. When I fumble with the buttons of his shirt, he helps me, and then I return the favor by helping him to unravel the layers of my dress and petticoat. When our flesh is all that remains between us, I feel no shame. In fact, the way he looks at me, I feel as though I might burst. As his soft lips explore my skin, I relish the way it ripples and aches. I can't help but shudder with the pleasure of it all.

I pull his face back toward mine, craving the taste of his lips once more. Craving his closeness as the only possible cure for the urgent, insistent ache that now consumes me. And when at last his body falls into mine, there's a sacred, wordless tremor in the room, and in my body. The most beautiful, exquisite pain grips me, one that I need more of. I pull him even closer. I think of Saint Teresa in her ecstatic rapture. I think: *How is it that I've waited thirty-seven years to taste this pleasure?* On this holy night, a night of birth, I feel as though I've finally and fully burst to life. As I cry out, Giovanni does the same, and I know that from this moment on I will forever be a fallen woman. Why, then, do I feel as though I'm soaring?

Chapter Forty-Three

January 1848

MY MIND HAS ALWAYS BEEN MY SHARPEST WEAPON, capable of absorbing, interpreting, even anticipating. So how, then, did I fail entirely to anticipate this? To be sure, I *did* anticipate much of what would come from taking Giovanni to my bed. I anticipated pleasure, passion.

But this? This, I somehow failed to see, that my body could possibly betray me in this way.

I brood on all of this as a winter damp settles over Rome with days, then weeks, of bruised clouds and continual rain. There's no escape from the chill. The naked trees outside my doorway writhe in the wind like macabre figures dancing around a bonfire. The bleak scene through my window is one of drenched passersby who hurry to and fro, forgetting entirely their usual sunny Roman joy, and it all suits the dismal mood that's settled over my apartment. I pull my wool cloak tight around my shoulders and seldom leave my fireside. And as the weeks pass, it becomes harder and harder to deny the truth: I am carrying a child. Giovanni's child. A bastard.

My body no longer feels like a place I know or trust. I sleep in heavy but fitful spells, the fatigue like a weight that pulls me under and then spits me back out into the reality I don't wish to face. When I wake in the mornings I barely make it to my pot before my stomach flips itself. Food, wonderful Roman food, no longer offers any appeal. Nor does coffee. I turn to the Graham diet in desperation, opting for only bland rice and bread. The sun still does not appear, but I doubt I could stand its brightness, in any event.

Giovanni visits each day, but I plead the rain as my excuse for my low spirits and ill health. I decline his invitations to walk or visit churches or museums. I can barely hold a conversation with him beside my fire for an hour before I feel the need to empty my stomach again or crawl, wounded, into my bed. He is concerned for me; I can see it in the soft, appraising look of his eyes. But I can't tell him the true cause of my misery, both bodily and spiritual. I can't tell him that his beloved Margherita, once so full of vim and fervor for this life with him, is now a treacherous vessel that will bring him shame and burdens. I've been a fool. I've become a Magdalene.

The truth is that, with all the things I feel, the strongest emotion with which I am wrestling now is fear. I'm afraid to tell Giovanni that my body has betrayed us both. How will he take it, the news that I, an unwed, older American woman, am going to make him a father? He's made it clear that his own father, a staunch and traditional Catholic who devoted his life to the papacy, would never have approved of me, a Protestant, as his marchesa, and now, neither will his older brother. Especially now, were he to find out that we've bedded each other out of marriage. I shudder just thinking about the disaster this would bring to Giovanni in his family. He'd be cut off, disinherited and thrown out, without a scudo to his name. How would that help either of us?

And what of *my* family? I am here, alone, in Rome, thousands of miles and an ocean apart from any of the people who love me—the very people to whom I have not written a single line about Giovanni. How can I now tell them that I have taken an Italian lover and I carry his child? How would Mother take this news? Or Greeley? Or—I grimace to think of it—Waldo?

My mind spins out, spooling and unspooling these dreary and dismal thoughts across these dark winter days. The futility of my situation is a deep rut out of which I cannot find a way to climb. Nor can I seem to find a path forward for me and this poor, damned child.

The only thing that does pull me from my melancholy brooding is a loud noise outside, on the streets. The city has been quiet for so many days now, huddled as we've all been underneath the unrelenting downpours. But now it sounds as though people are taking to the streets. I cross the room and look out the window, where I see a gathering. They are getting soaked, but they don't appear to notice or care. I hear them screaming, and I strain my ears to make out what they are saying.

"Mazzini!" They are chanting for Mazzini. The revolutionary who has been calling, from England, for Italian unification. More people join, men and women of all ages, and soon the streets throb with their shouts. Some wave banners emblazoned with the mottoes of *Risorgimento* and *Speranza*. Someone sets off a firecracker and I wince; it sounds unnervingly similar to gunfire. Fresh shouts erupt across the crowds. I press my hand, instinctively, to my belly. It's still flat. There is no outward sign, yet, of the life that is stirring within. And then there is a pounding on my door and I gasp in shock.

I stride toward the door and peek out. Giovanni stands there, drenched. "Margherita, *cara mia*."

"Yes? Come in. You must have passed through quite a mob to get here."

"And it's even bigger over by the Vatican." He tromps his wet boots into my room, leaving puddles with each step. "They are marching outside the pope's palace. They are calling for action."

"What do they want, precisely?"

"A republic. And they are growing less patient. You see there?"

We stand together at the window and stare out. By now the street is filled. A group of young men are holding a long chain, which they shake. I look to Giovanni in confusion.

"They are saying: Off with the shackles. Down with the tyrants. It is time for freedom for Italians."

Once more my hand presses to my belly and I sigh. I have to tell him. It's been weeks, and he knows *something* is amiss. With the unrest building in the city, who knows what tomorrow will bring, let alone eight months from now? He has a right to know. And I can no longer carry this alone. "Giovanni, I have news of my own."

He's still peering out my window, consumed with the scene before him. But he turns to look toward me, asking, "Yes, what is it?"

I draw in a long, fortifying breath. And then, before I lose my nerve, I declare: "We have made a life. Together."

Confusion tugs on his features, and then I watch as understanding takes hold. His eyes go wide, those big, beautiful brown eyes that I've loved from the start. And then, miraculously, like the sunshine that hasn't appeared in Rome in weeks, a light breaks across his features. He smiles. "Margherita, *cara!*"

"But . . ." I fold my hands before my waist, shifting on my feet. "You aren't cross?"

"Cross? How could I be cross?" He wraps his wet arms around me, and I could weep I'm so relieved. That he's drawing closer to me, rather than pulling away. I breathe in, smelling the damp wool of his tunic and, beneath that, his skin. And yet, it's a relief that I'm not quite able to fully trust.

I press on: "But your family . . . your brother. You've said from the start that he wouldn't approve of me. Older, foreign . . . and a Protestant, worst of all."

"He won't. In fact, I can see him using this to his own advantage. He could seize this opportunity to cut me out of the estate, taking my share to himself. But I am my own man."

"So, what does that mean?"

"I won't tell him. At least, not until my share has been transferred to me. Once I have what is rightfully mine from Father, then we can tell the world. *Cara mia,* are you willing to keep this a secret for just a bit?"

Considering I had no plans to tell my own family or friends anytime soon, this is hardly difficult. "Yes, that is fine." As long as he and I are together, I don't need anyone else.

He pulls back from the embrace, taking my hands in his. "Margherita, I've told you that I knew from the beginning. I've always known you would be my wife. Will you have me?"

An explosion from the street below, another firecracker being set off, and then the crowd answers with uproarious cheers. And so, while war breaks out beneath us, I tell Giovanni Ossoli that I will become his wife, and together, we will bring a child into this mad, uncertain world.

Chapter Forty-Four

Spring 1848

T HEY ARE CALLING IT THE YEAR OF REVOLUTIONS. War is seeping across Europe like a great and unstoppable tide, and every kingdom in Europe wants to topple its king. In Hungary they are rising up to throw off the Austrians. In Vienna they have run Metternich out of the Hofburg. In France they've thrown out another Louis to establish a new republic. The Kingdom of Two Sicilies, long under the rule of the cruel King Ferdinand, has finally thrown him off, and they are now drafting their new constitution. Next the republicans seize power in Milan, then Venice. *Speranza* is closer than it has ever been.

Here, in Rome, the mood is more hopeful than I've ever known it. Pio Nono has shown he is open to the idea of reform, granting us a constitution and an executive body, and now, this winter, he's expanded the rights of the press. Elsewhere across the Italian peninsula, millions of Italians are now crying out for freedom and self-governance. When the cold rains stop and the sun returns, it feels as though God himself is smiling on our hopes.

By the time Rome prepares to celebrate Carnevale, the hopeful mood nearly pulses along the warm spring air. By day the larks sing from branches newly in leaf. By night, the Romans take to the streets to revel and march, to dance and sing. "See that?" Giovanni is pointing to the rows of windows that glow with candlelight along the crowded street. "*Moccoletti*," he says. "Lights of hope. For Carnevale. But now for freedom. For Italy."

"Will Mazzini finally come?" I ask, the hope evident in my voice.

"Perhaps," he says. "But the Austrians will come first. They will not allow all of this to go unanswered. We are too rich a land, and they have held us for too long." I look around, confident that even the Austrians with their soldiers cannot crush the spirit and desire for freedom so evident on these ancient streets.

WAR DOES COME, first to Piedmont and Tuscany. Even the pope is on our side, praying for the revolutionary soldiers who have enlisted to march out to meet the Austrians.

After a decisive battle in the distant city of Goito, the Italians push back the Austrians. The *moccoletti* continue to blaze across the city, and I put them in my windows, as well. Our hopes for freedom in Rome, for a united nation of Italy, have never been closer.

"Now Mazzini will come back," Giovanni tells me one spring morning over breakfast. As my belly has begun to swell, the nausea has receded, and I find that I can once more enjoy bread and coffee. "He has to. After nearly twenty years of exile, he will return home. And the Italians will be ready for him."

It is in this mood of euphoria, of freedom and change and near madness, that Giovanni and I make a private trip to the Church of San Carlo. The Ossoli Chapel is not an option, given the likelihood that one of his relatives might hear word. Nor anyplace near the Vatican, since his brother lives and works there, in spite of how meaningful it is to us. But San Carlo is where we were reunited. It is the place where I decided, finally, to give myself to Giovanni, and where we consecrated our new beginning.

It has been one year since our first meeting at Easter time. What a year. Spring now holds Rome in its glorious grip once more. The birds sing and the people float with hope and joy down the streets. I am ready to become Giovanni's wife.

"Margherita, *cara mia*, Marchesa dei Ossoli," Giovanni says, breathing my new name as we walk out of the church and into the sunshine, back toward Via del Corso. He carries me over the threshold as we enter the home as man and wife. There, we give ourselves once more to each other, to pleasure and passion, to torturous ecstasy that grows and crescendos in rapture. We don't know what the arrival of this babe will mean for our lives. We don't know what the arrival of foreign troops will mean for our lives, or this land, by the time this baby arrives. But for now, in the Roman springtime, in the season of Easter and renewal and *Speranza*, we give ourselves over to bliss.

Chapter Forty-Five

Summer 1848

I STARE AT A PILE OF PAPERS, ALL OF THEM TELLING ME the same thing.

Return home, to America.

Rome is too dangerous.

Leave at once and return to your home.

Notes from my mother, from Eliza, from Waldo. His are the most insistent. He is in London on a trip of his own, and he sees himself as my protector. *"Can you not join me in London?"* he writes. *"We can sail for America together. Return with me, Margaret. Return with me to Concord. Can we not live happily there together?"*

Waldo and the others maintain that Rome is unsafe, with battles breaking out across the land and the Austrians and French making plain their intent to fight for the Papal States and prevent the formation of a free republic. Things have grown even more precarious now that Pio Nono, once our ally, has caved to his hard-line royalist advisors and declared he does not support the establishment of a Roman republic. He cannot condone it, he declares, if it will lead to outright war. He cannot abide a war between Catholics. He may be the governmental leader of the Romans, but he is the spiritual leader of all Catholic nations, and he cannot choose sides.

Rome reacts to this by erupting—riots in the streets and a fresh crush of young men racing to take up arms. Thousands of students become soldiers overnight. Pio Nono has betrayed them. He has abandoned the ideals that we all believed him to share. He is as bad as any foreign emperor. Romans will not let anything—not even Pio Nono—stop their dreams of freedom.

My friends write to tell me that Rome is a powder keg and I will be caught in its destruction if I do not leave and return home. But what my friends do not understand is that Rome has become my home. As much as New York or Boston or even Concord ever felt like home, Rome feels like the place where I am meant to be right now. It has been the work of my life to observe and write about events; I feel that I am meant to bear witness to what's unfolding here.

Only Greeley seems to understand. Yet not even Greeley—and certainly not Emerson or my mother—can possibly know that there is another, even more immediate, pressing, and personal need to remain here. I look down at my belly, now swollen with the incontrovertible signs of the new life within. My baby. Giovanni's baby. The child that will come in the early autumn. There is no traveling to America for me. I will remain here with my new husband and give birth to my Italian baby here, in a new Italy.

I do give my American loved ones some measure of peace, writing to inform them that I have quit the city for the summer. It was at Giovanni's insistence, in fact. He, too, shared their concerns for my safety and the baby's in the coming fight. And there's one additional consideration: Now that I'm visibly carrying a baby, it's too risky. What if someone were to spot us? What if word were to reach the Vatican of the American woman who carries an Ossoli babe? Giovanni has still not received the payment of his inheritance, and a scandal now would allow his brother to ensure he never does.

No, I need to be tucked safely away in the country for the remainder of my confinement. Not only for my safety, but for the future well-being of the child. Rome is a big city, but we know people in every neighborhood. I need to go somewhere no American will recognize me and no Roman will see Giovanni, doting and loving husband, at my side. I write to my family claiming that it is to escape the summer season and the risk of Roman malarial fever.

AND SO HERE I sit, in my ancient little cottage in the rural village of Rieti, where no familiar friends may find me out. It's a beautiful scene of sheep pastures and red rooftops. My companions here are the pigs that wander the dusty streets, tended by the barefoot children who walk beside them. I am in my little bird's nest, tucked into the mountains, a place unvisited by tourists and unpressed by time or politics. Here, where the summer sun shines down on the hills and the medieval monasteries that cling to their curves.

I'm alone, as Giovanni is still serving in the Civic Guard, his position more important than ever before as Rome braces for the coming invasion. But we chose Rieti because, in spite of its pastoral seclusion, he can reach me for visits on weekends. Traveling at night in a coach, my husband can arrive by morning for eggs and coffee. He's the only person who ever visits.

When Giovanni is not with me, I have plenty of time to work, and that is what consumes most of my hours. In addition to my regular columns for Greeley and my *Tribune* readers, I'm now working on a new book, a manuscript on the revolution through which I'm living. Americans, who enjoy their freedoms because of their own hard-fought Revolution, must know about what the Italians are doing. And as the only American correspondent currently living near Rome, I am the person who can tell them this story.

In the afternoons, once my hand has cramped from hours of writing and the baby kicks in restlessness, I take walks. What glorious walks! I can't help but think of Waldo and Thoreau and Louisa May, how much they would love these ambles through the hills and down into the sun-soaked valley. And I miss my mother on these outings, too. Something about the impending birth of a child makes me long for the comfort and wisdom of the mother who bore me from her own body. I long to ask her questions, to hear her stories and reassurances. I long for a woman to tell me that I am up to the task, that I will be able to survive the ordeal that approaches.

These hills become my church, my sanctuary, my haven. The crystalline brooks that feed into the languid curves of the Velino River soothe my soul when I do become worried for what is ahead. The vineyards and olive groves ripen just as my body does, reassuring me that all is as it should be. There is a peace here. A sense that nature is doing what it has always done, and what it is meant to do.

When the church bells ring out from the hillsides, the old monastery calling the faithful into its cool stone embrace, the villagers pass me on the narrow dirt paths. The women in their veils and bonnets look at my swollen stomach with unabashed interest. Some pause their walking and press their hands to my belly. "*Povera*," they say, raising their hands to make the sign of the cross over my head. "*Sola, soletta!*"

The poor thing. She's alone, she's all alone.

And I am. The only contact I have from outside this small village is the visits from Giovanni and, in between those visits, letters. Giovanni sends me clippings from the Roman newspapers, updates from the city, and I include these details in my writings. He's growing increasingly frustrated. His brother remains blindly loyal to the pope, even as Pio Nono has turned his back on the Romans and aligned with the Austrians and French.

The Romans need a leader to rally them, Giovanni says. He hopes for Mazzini. Like so many millions, he waits for Mazzini. But it's still too dangerous for Mazzini to come home from his exile. Not yet. He would never put it in writing in his letters, but as he visits that summer, Giovanni tells me that there are screams in the streets, arrests in the night, the sudden disappearance of people known to be republicans. It is good that I am safely tucked away, he tells me. Even if I worry for him.

The people here, in Rieti, pay attention to the ripening of their grapes, not the political events unfolding miles away. Seeming to have accepted me into their village, having seen Giovanni in his soldier's uniform on his visits, they adopt me as their communal responsibility. The little girls pick me peaches and grapes. The old women bring me figs, explaining that it will prevent the dyspepsia that I am coming to see as a fact of life in the later months of confinement. A local midwife makes regular visits, prodding my belly, massaging my swollen ankles, telling me that red wine will help me to stay calm. For the price of one cent, I get my daily loaf of bread and I savor the freshness of the local cream and cheeses. My daily walks to and from the market, up and down the hills, are getting slower and more lumbering, but my body still feels strong.

But then, as the days grow shorter, as the light shows the slightest shift from white and hot to golden and gentle, as the signs of the coming autumn first begin to blow into our valley, I hear troubling news from the north. The Austrians have escalated their war on the Italians. The free regions begin to fall, and quickly. Austria's troops topple Milan and then Bologna. They enter the Papal States from the north. Rome is surely their ultimate target, which means that Giovanni will soon be at war. It also means that he won't be here with me when the time comes for the baby's arrival.

My physical discomfort grows worse as sleep becomes difficult, and then almost impossible. My indigestion makes meals uncomfortable, as does the fact that I feel there is no room remaining in my stomach. But these pains are nothing compared to the anguish and nerves I feel over Giovanni and the fact that he won't be here with me.

And then I begin to feel a sharpening in my stomach. "The baby is preparing," the midwife tells me. These aren't the pains of the actual labor, but they are the pains to tell me that labor approaches. "*Presto.* Soon. It is almost time," she tells me. It is. It's now September. Why did war have to come the same month as my baby?

For several days the pains build. They aren't unbearable during the day, but they come like a fiendish drumbeat at night. Cramps that force me to curl and writhe in my bed. Sleep becomes an impossibility. And then one night a stream of water drips down my legs. I have been warned this would happen: These are the birthing waters, the midwife has told me. The river that will carry the baby out of my womb and into the world. I lumber out to the yard and cry out to my neighbor, an old woman. Seeing the worry on my face, she dispatches her little grandson to fetch the midwife. I return to my bedroom, leaning against the bed. The pain is coming in waves now, intense and almost unbearable, and then receding. I have no idea how long this will last. I have no idea how long I can survive it.

Dear God, where is the midwife? I groan, pacing my room. Then finally, a rapping at the door. "Yes, come in!" She's finally here.

But it's not the midwife who enters. It's a tall, dark, familiar figure. The beloved face, the warm brown eyes. His clothes are rumpled, layered in a thin coating of dust from his long journey, but I don't ask after his trip. "Giovanni!" I gasp, beginning to weep in both joy and relief. I can read in his expression a good deal of alarm as he takes in the scene and my feral appearance, my loose hair flying wild around my flushed, sweat-slick face. "It's time. The baby is coming."

"My darling." He takes my hands in his, guiding me back to the bed. "I'm here, I'm here."

"You cannot go!" I say, clutching his hand.

"Of course I won't go. I've only just arrived."

"You promise? You won't leave me?"

"Never," he says, his expression almost wounded that I would ask. A moment later the pain grips me again and I squeeze his hand so hard I see his face crumple. But I cannot stop. He can hold it with me. He's here. And soon our baby will be here, as well.

Chapter Forty-Six

Rieti Village, North of Rome, Papal States
September 1848

"WHAT SHALL WE CALL YOU, *MIO CARO*, DEAREST little one?" I stare down into the eyes of my son; his face is brand-new, and yet it feels as though I've always known it. My little boy. I believed it was a girl within, that I would not know what to do with a boy. And yet, now that he's here, a being born of my body, he is as much a part of me as my very heart.

"I was thinking Filippo," my husband says, smiling at the face that is a perfect blend of his and mine. He has the shape of his father's big eyes and perfect lips but my coloring, the blue-gray gaze and the same fair hair I had as a little girl.

"Filippo," I say, repeating the suggestion. My husband wishes to honor his father, the head of the Ossoli family who has just passed. But I have a better idea. "*Angelo* Filippo, to honor your father, but also *his* father." As my husband's full name is Giovanni Angelo Ossoli, this feels right. So we settle on Angelo, and Nino quickly becomes his nickname.

For as much as I dreaded the birth, and feared that I might not be capable as a mother, I take to my new job with a natural joy. Giovanni has to leave quickly, to return to Rome before the Austrian soldiers arrive, so we decide to bring in a young nurse to help. Having given birth to a babe of her own five months prior, and with her entire family in the village, she can help me adjust to my new role as Mamma.

Her name is Chiara, and I immediately take to her youthful energy and attentive ways. "You must rest," she tells me. "Forty days of rest." She cooks me thick broth with bones and vegetables. She walks to the market each morning so that I may stay in bed with Nino. When I'm resting, rather than disturb me, she nurses Nino at her own breast. And so, as autumn brushes the trees of the village a warm and burnished gold, I settle into motherhood, and Nino settles into our little family.

By the time Giovanni returns to visit several weeks later, he cannot believe how much the baby has grown. "He really does resemble you," I say, marveling at our boy. At how overwhelming and primal my love for him is. As if he's always been with us. We were meant to be the three of us. Nino has opened doorways into my heart and my spirit that I had not previously known existed, and he's brought me even closer to Giovanni. With Chiara's care and attention I feel strong, even rested. And I am ready to speak with my husband about our return, as a family of three, to Rome.

That night, after Nino is tucked into his small bed, I ask my husband to begin making inquiries for a reliable young woman in Rome who might help us as a nursemaid. I am even ready to begin thinking about working again. Greeley, like everyone else in America, remains entirely unaware of the baby's existence, and he's asking when my next column will be ready.

But Giovanni barely considers my request before he answers, "No. It's not possible."

I am stunned by this, by how immediate and resolute he is in his rejection. "But . . . why not? I feel strong enough for the journey. Women have made journeys with their babes before."

"You and Nino cannot come to Rome."

I feel a tendril of unease as I absorb my husband's words. True, the threatened invasion is still to come. But even so, I am willing to return. I have faith in the Roman people, the Roman soldiers who have vowed to defend their city. But Giovanni won't consider the idea, saying only, "You and Nino must remain here."

I sigh. My tone is soft, so as not to wake the baby, but girded with a determined bluntness as I answer: "We both know that we need my salary. Greeley wants more information from Rome. That's where my work is. Not here in a rural village, removed from everything."

I don't like the firm set of his jaw. And when my husband speaks next, his tone is just as resolved as mine. "We need your salary, yes. But we also need my allowance. If you and Nino come back, and my brother finds out, what then? It's bad enough I have aligned with the republicans against the pope. All he needs is one more push to cut me out entirely. You and Nino would be that push."

I look to my baby, our baby, the beautiful boy whose existence cannot be known—even by his own family. The baby whom the Ossolis would see as a source of shame, not the beautiful and precious gift that he is. He sleeps in innocence, but now I cannot resist the urge to walk to his bed and take him into my arms. As I feel his soft weight against my body, my heart begins to hurt, a gut-deep feeling unlike anything I've ever in my life experienced.

Giovanni sighs, raising his hands as if to show that there's nothing he can do. "We must do what is best for him. For all of us. How will we survive if we can't feed him?"

These words land like a blow because they are true. My wages, while enough to support my life in Rome, would never be enough to feed all three of us. Without Giovanni's modest monthly allowance, we'd never manage. The great hope is my book on Roman politics, but I need to be in Rome to write it.

"Then how about this," I say, brightened by an idea. "We bring the baby with Chiara," I suggest. My husband looks at me with a creased brow. I go on, undaunted: "We take a room for the two of them, and another room for ourselves nearby. I can visit him. Anyone would guess the babe is Chiara's, and I am just a friend."

"How will we afford two households?"

"We will economize. We will manage."

Doubt is etched on my husband's face. "And Chiara is going to leave her baby here to come with us to Rome, a city about to erupt in war?"

At this I feel my body, and my will, wither. Anguished, I have no choice but to eventually yield to the cold and unbending realities of our situation. My concession, though tortured, is for two main reasons. The first is that Chiara has known the baby since birth and he is as comfortable with her as he would be with a sister. She will bring the baby into her own family's home, where her baby also lives with her husband and parents. Nino will be fed the fresh foods of this region and the milk of a healthy young mother. He will be safe, far away from the threat of war.

The second reason that allows me to agree to this plan is that it is only temporary. Just long enough for me to get settled. I'll file more stories for Greeley so that I can continue to collect my *Tribune* salary, and finish my manuscript. The funds from that will give us a surer cushion to bring Nino to Rome.

We will be only one day's drive away, I remind myself. Giovanni made the trip regularly during my confinement. I'll be able to visit often to see and hold my baby.

And yet, as I load the coach under a gray November sky, pulling my cloak tight around me, my baby bouncing in the arms of his young nurse, I tremble with the enormity of it all. I didn't want this baby, not at first. I didn't think I could care for him. But now, leaving him feels as though I'm leaving the greater part of my heart behind, in these remote Italian mountains, as I ride toward the unknown, and a city bracing for war.

Chapter Forty-Seven

Rome
Autumn 1848

OUR ROOMS, BRIGHT AND SPACIOUS, WITH SWEEPING views over the Piazza Barberini and the Triton Fountain, feel far too quiet. The warbles of the doves outside my window remind me of the baby whose sounds were even sweeter. I miss Nino's gurgles and coos. I miss his milky smell and the weight of his body against mine. Chiara and her family don't read or write, so there is little hope of regular letters or updates from Rieti. I long for news of him; each day feels like an eternity as I wonder what he's doing and how he's changing. Does he forget me? Some days it takes all the strength I can summon not to hop into a coach and ride out for Rieti. No, the only way forward is to finish the work on my book so that I can collect payment and afford to bring my baby here to Rome.

Greeley is excited for the book. And yet, he can't possibly imagine how much more exciting it is to be *here*, in Rome, where the action is unfolding. In the distance out my window, the papal palace is visible across the skyline. And it is there, on a gray morning in mid-November, that I see them gathering. Men, women, children, even the telltale uniforms of the Civic Guardsmen. I wonder, with a stab of concern, if Giovanni is among them. I narrow my eyes and try to bring the scene into clearer focus. What are they doing? I rise from my desk, quickly grabbing my shawl and gloves, and dash down the stairs.

Standing out there, on the crowded street, I get a sense of just how many of them there are. It appears to be some sort of march, though I am not certain whether the assembly is planned or spontaneous. Some of the nearby men and women are carrying banners emblazoned with the slogan *Speranza*. One young lad—he appears too young even to shave—is waving a massive tricolor flag, based on the French symbol that has become a universal sign of republican ideals.

I approach a woman who clutches her child's hand. "What is happening?" I ask.

"Marching to Pio Nono," she answers as I fall in step beside her. "Why?" I ask.

When the mother speaks next, her features are etched with the unmistakable look of anger. "He can't ignore us any longer! He cannot put us under the yoke of foreign armies. We deserve to be free. We want peace, but we aren't afraid to fight, if that's what is needed."

I walk beside her and her child, and countless others, my steps pulled into the current of their river. I look for Giovanni among the many faces; I see a number of Civic Guards, but not my husband. That doesn't mean he's not in this crowd. Many are linking arms; some are singing "The Marseillaise." We walk like this across the Tiber and past the university until the Vatican hulks before us and we reach the gates of the pope's palace. There, we stop; there's nothing we can do but wait. The guards who stand sentry before the gates barely acknowledge the crowds, shouting only, "Keep back!" Several in the crowd resume singing revolutionary anthems. The air crackles all around me, with both hope and tension.

When the gates outside the palace complex do eventually open, someone toward the front shouts, "*Ci siamo!* Here he comes! Pio Nono!" and the crowd erupts in expectant cheers. I feel my heart hammer. What will he say? What will he do? Will he finally hear the cries of his Roman people who long to build a republic?

But it is not the pope who appears. Instead, as the gates yawn open, two columns of his Swiss Guards march out toward us in a tight, swift formation. I hear gasps of surprise and confusion all around. And then, inexplicably, the guards raise their rifles and they begin shooting in our direction.

The crowd erupts with cries and shrieks. My hands fly to my ears against the onslaught of noise. People begin to scatter in all directions. I wonder where the mother and her child have gone. More gunfire from the pope's guards. Several bodies fall to the ground, and I can't help but gasp, horrified, when I see the curling streams of red that begin to color the street.

"Murderers!"

"Tyrants!"

"*Gesù e Maria!*"

People are screaming all around me. Those who are dashing away to escape the bullets must swerve and leap to avoid the dead and mangled bodies. Dazed, I see an older woman holding a limp, bloodied figure in her arms as she wails. More gunfire, more bullets. More bodies fall to the ground. I join the crush of those who are running away and I don't stop until, with aching lungs, I've raced back home and shut my door behind me.

My mind surges as I stand there, alone, thinking of all that I've just witnessed. The pope ordering his guards to fire on his people. People who had gathered before him in peace. Pio Nono; how could he? He who promised to love the Roman people like an adoring father.

But this is the end for Pio Nono; he can never make this right. His people march to him with songs and flags, and he meets them with bullets. All the while, he cowers behind his walls and his hired guards. He's not a father to the people. He's a tyrant who will cling to power by whatever means necessary, even if it means spilling our blood.

IN THE AFTERMATH of the Pope's Massacre, I'm not the only person in Rome who feels this sense of despair. This gaping wound of disbelief and shock, mingled with the gutting facts of grief and fear. Over the next few days, the entire city pulses with a rising tension. Some are crying inside their homes, scared to be out in public, but many others are out on the streets in defiance, enraged, as if inviting the next clash in the conflict we now all see as inevitable. The crowds continue to gather at the pope's gates, too, but he does not acknowledge them again.

And then, just a few days later, I awake to the news that Pio Nono has fled. Under the cover of darkness, dressed like a commoner, the prince of Rome has scurried like a rat through the Vatican's secret tunnels and raced to the south, to the Kingdom of the Two Sicilies and the palace of a brain-addled tyrant.

Giovanni and I sit together at breakfast as we glower at the morning newspapers. "Where he belongs, with another tyrant and fool." Giovanni nearly spits the words out along with his bread.

I can barely keep up with how quickly things are unfolding now, knowing I must record it all for Greeley and the American public. The pope is gone. Rome is without a leader. The French and the Austrians are fighting among themselves as to who can take this city, while the Romans are more determined than ever to establish a free republican government. I feel, this morning, the stirrings of hope as I say: "Rome must name her next leader."

BUT MY THOUGHTS are not entirely on politics, because I have plans to visit Rieti for a much longed-for reunion with my baby, where I will celebrate Christmas. "You are certain you can't come?" I ask Giovanni, as I'm folding the final pair of wool stockings into my trunk.

Giovanni throws me a beleaguered look, his eyes flicking toward the newspaper as if to ask: *Have you forgotten that this city, which I am sworn to defend and protect, is on the brink of war?*

"I know, I know," I say with a sigh. "I suppose I was simply swept up in the spirit of *speranza.*"

"We do have every reason to hope," he says, crossing the room and weaving an arm around my waist. I turn into his embrace, allowing Giovanni to take my chin in his grip and tilt my face upward for a passionate kiss. And then I can't help but laugh as my husband sweeps my trunk aside, clearing space on the bed, as all thoughts of packing flee my mind.

My optimism is met with more good news when I arrive in Rieti to find Nino looking plump and happy. Chiara's milk is clearly abundant and wholesome. He giggles and claps his hands and he appears to be a cheery, bright little boy. I am overjoyed to be re-united with my baby. To my relief, he allows me to hold him in my arms without any protests as I separate him from his beloved Chiara. That night he rejoins me in bed and together, our arms entwined, we sleep a deep and nourishing slumber in an upstairs room of Chiara's modest family home. I awake to his stirrings and coos the next morning. When I look into his eyes, I feel happier than I can ever remember being.

Chiara keeps him wrapped tight in wool all day and night, and I can see why—the Rieti winter means cold mountain air, and her family does not light a fire often, other than in the early mornings and when preparing meals. I want all the news of Chiara but she's often busy and distracted throughout the days leading up to Christmas; she seems to want this time to hold her own baby, and I can't blame her.

"Can I teach you some letters?" I suggest one evening after both our babies are asleep. "So perhaps you can write me?"

Chiara is in the corner of the room, scrubbing a pan from supper. She doesn't look in my direction as she answers: "Marchesa Ossoli, I don't know my letters, and I can't learn now. But you're a rich American woman, no? Leave me more money, and ask the local priest to write for me."

This brusque response strikes me as odd, but I can't hold it against her; her husband has been gone the entire time that I've been here—hunting, she told me with a quick wave of her hand. She's nursing her own baby and mine, all while helping her older parents run a crowded and humble household, and now she has me as a houseguest. No doubt these months have been exhausting for her.

Whenever I ask Chiara when her husband is expected to return, she avoids my question. "Getting us food," she says. Sometimes she exchanges a look with her mother, but she says nothing more. I want him to come back because I get the sense that they need his help around the house, and certainly could use any money he might be able to bring in.

"Will he be back soon?"

"*Si, si*, soon," is all she says, not meeting my concerned gaze.

Christmas morning brings the ringing of the church bells from the ancient stone church on the hill. I think back to all those warm summer afternoons when those same bells would echo across this valley. When the local worshippers here would flock to their summons, passing me on my walks, looking at my swollen belly with pity. And then I think of Giovanni, alone in Rome, hearing the Christmas bells of Saint Peter's, the basilica abandoned by its pope. I wonder what is happening there. I pray that he's safe. I do long to see my husband and hold him once more. But I cannot bear to think of the coming separation from Nino.

When the time for my farewell does come, he cries, and so do I. Nino's chubby arms reach for me, his body straining against Chiara's grip, this time truly knowing me and wanting me. Needing me. As the stagecoach pulls me away from him, up from the valley and into the hills that will form a wall between me and my baby, I swat at my stinging eyes. I try to calm my shuddering breath. I tell myself: this is the last time I will separate from him. The next time I come to Rieti, it will be to fetch Nino into my arms and carry him with me back to Rome, a place that, I hope, will be a free republic. And I will be a woman who is free to be not only a writer and a wife, but also a mother.

Chapter Forty-Eight

Winter 1849

T HE NEW YEAR BRINGS FRESH REASONS FOR HOPE:
Victories for the free forces in the north fighting under the
patriot Giuseppe Garibaldi. New assemblies and constitutions and
calls for unity spring up across the regions of Italy, with Rome at
the center of these hopes. And here we are, in the heart of it.

The mood in Rome is like that of a champagne bottle, ready to
uncork and spill over. If 1848 was the Year of Revolutions, then
1849 is to be the Year of Republics. Only Pio Nono, who remains
in his southern exile with his ill-tempered host, seems disapproving of Rome's march toward freedom. He writes with fury from
within Ferdinand's palace walls, vowing to excommunicate any
Roman who dares to support a free assembly, who dares to strip
any of his powers away. This petulance by Pio Nono only pushes
everyone on, into the final steps of their march toward freedom.

February brings the hoped-for day, at last. I stand outside on my
balcony and look out with rapture as, just below me, on the streets
of Rome, the regiments march by in their colorful uniforms. They
are no longer Pio Nono's Civic Guard but have refashioned themselves into the new Army of the Roman Republic. Giovanni
marches among their ranks, and I strain my eyes to make out his
tall, strong figure. They are an impressive sight, these hopeful
Roman men keeping time with the drums as they march toward
the empty grounds of Saint Peter's.

But it's not for the purpose of war that they march today. It's to
convene the first meeting of the freely elected assembly for the

Roman Republic. I can't help but cheer, calling out in Italian: *Viva la República!* The band plays jaunty marching tunes as the church bells throughout the city join in the uproarious and celebratory din.

I don't think the streets of Rome could get any louder. And yet, several hours later, when the members of the assembly step out of their meeting and read the official proclamation, the roar does get louder. We now live in the free Roman Republic, and Mazzini has been invited back to Rome to take his place as our leader.

I rush down into the streets to join the celebrations. I buy a tricolor Italian flag from a little boy who has set up a stall and I unfurl it from my balcony beside my American flag. Two free nations, established with the overthrow of two despots. My husband has taken the oath to fight for this new nation, and I will keep its records, using my pen to bear witness so that the whole world may join Rome in her beautiful quest. My entire body surges with the significance of it all.

The celebrations last for days, and then it finally goes quiet. Rome goes to sleep after the glut of revelry and dancing. Even the church bells fall silent. Giovanni is quartered at the army barracks, as all of the officers are on high alert during these heady and early days of our republic, so I go to bed alone. I, too, fall into a deep sleep. And yet, I stir when I hear a knock on my door.

It is the dark of night. My first thought is of Nino. Is he all right? Has some accident befallen him? I throw a shawl over my shoulders, my hair in a long braid down my back, and I fumble toward my door.

My eyes can't see well in the darkness, but there is a shadowed figure in a hood. My heart leaps to my throat. But then he steps forward and I recognize the familiar face, and my entire body softens with the knowledge that there is nothing to fear. "Mazzini?" I gasp the name aloud. I glance down the hall, looking each way, and then I beckon him inside, shutting the door behind us.

"My friend," I say, curtseying deeply before him. He is, after all, now the most powerful man in our republic.

Giuseppe Mazzini lowers his hood and looks at me through his large, tired eyes. It's been years since I met him in London, and I see that age has pulled on his dark features, but the effect only gives him a more dignified air. He leans forward and raises me back to standing as he says, "Hello, Margaret Fuller." He hastens to add, "I must apologize. Calling on you so late like this. I'm sure I've disturbed your rest."

"It's . . . no, not at all." We both glance around the room; it's entirely dark and quiet. Clearly he's pulled me from bed. We laugh.

"I couldn't risk coming in the daylight," he says. "Pio and Ferdinand have assassins all over. I'm not afraid for myself, but I'd never wish to put you at risk."

I swallow, feeling how dry my throat is. "But how did *you* know where I live?"

Mazzini points to my balcony. "How many women in Rome are displaying our new tricolor beside the American flag?" He flashes a smile, and I see the fire that coils just behind his eyes. He goes on, saying, "Everyone knows of the famous American woman who lives here in Rome. Who supports our republic. Who will be our faithful friend as we grow as a nation. You will be our champion with your pen, *si?*"

"Of course I will," I declare, my heart fluttering. "I've already been telling the Americans with every column I write."

"I know you have," he says. "I'm more grateful than you will ever know. As is Garibaldi. We've read every one of your columns."

I feel my cheeks flush with heat. Mazzini goes on: "If it were possible for women, I'd ask you to serve as our ambassador."

My heart clenches at this. How much would I love that position? To advocate for warm relations between the nation of my birth and the nation of my heart, the land that has produced my adored husband, the land in which my son will grow, a free man. I have such high hopes for Rome. If only I, as a woman, could play a powerful part.

"Your role here will be more important than ever in the coming days and months," Mazzini says, seeming to see my thoughts. Of course he sees my thoughts—he knows people. That's why he's the leader Rome needs, even after decades of absence. He goes on: "The Austrians and French—and of course Pio, with Ferdinand's soldiers—will not let this go unanswered."

I frown at this. "But we've been peaceful for days now. They've not responded."

Mazzini shakes his head. "It's not a peace that will endure. It's, what do you say in English . . . ? *The calm before the storm*. They will answer. And it will be with blood and bullets when they do."

I feel the hope that's been surging in my body begin to seep out, a wineskin that's been punctured. "When?" I ask, the word barely a whisper.

"Any day," Mazzini replies, his tone hoarse. "They will encircle us. War is coming to Rome."

Chapter Forty-Nine

Spring 1849

THE FRENCH ARRIVE AS AN INVADING FLEET JUST A few weeks later, thousands of them, their ships slicing across the Mediterranean and making landfall north of Rome. Their stated goal: to crush the Roman Republic and reinstate their puppet as pope.

The Romans all around me meet this news with defiance. The assembly votes to stay and fight. The soldiers prepare for war, with Giovanni's regiment stationed just outside the Vatican. The citizens of Rome will join in the resistance. I see the barricades rising up from the narrow streets. Soldiers and volunteers pull together to haul cannons up the ancient hilltops over the city. The tricolor flag of our republic waves from nearly every window, including mine.

Throughout the streets I hear the cries day and night: *Viva la República! Viva Italia!* Mazzini warns us that the French will march on the city any day now. They have moved quickly and are only a few miles from our walls. We must be prepared for a long and punishing siege. The heady days of parades and dancing in the streets are behind us.

Like everyone else in the city, I am desperate to help the cause. To do more than simply take up my pen. As I am a woman, I cannot bear arms and encamp beside my husband. So I march to the nearby hospital, Ospedale Fatebenefratelli, an old stone building nestled on the Tiber River.

The building, when I approach its front doors, buzzes with a mood of nervous and purposeful anticipation. There is a wooden desk set up outside, which appears as a collection place for supplies and donations. I pause before a young staffer, a medical student, and offer my services. "Margherita Ossoli," I say as the young man makes no attempt to mask his scowl. "I am here to work."

But the medical student seems disinterested in my help, even muttering to the young lad beside him, loud enough for me to hear: "We are being invaded by the French, and now we must face an invasion by the women, as well?"

I draw in a deep breath, squaring my shoulders as I lean toward the man and say: "The priests have gone. The men are encamped. The wounded will soon be flooding in, and you need support. I can read, I can write, I can change dressings, or at the very least take dictation and read stories to the wounded."

Begrudgingly, he takes down my name and address and tells me to report back the next morning to begin my service in the Roman Republic.

"Nurse? Nurse Ossoli! Come here, come at once!"

I look up from my list of patient names and fly toward the voice, which comes from an older man, a surgeon, who stands beside a bed, its white sheets streaked with red. "Yes, what is it?" I ask, looking from the surgeon to the writhing patient between us.

"Amputation," the doctor says, his tone matter-of-fact. "We need you to hold his hands. Speak to him. Anything."

I look down at the man—no, not a man. A *boy*. He doesn't even have the hint of a mustache. Likely a student who traded in his books and took up the cause of freedom. Now fired on by French soldiers who claim to serve a republic, even though everyone knows their new leader, Napoleon III, is just as bloodthirsty and ambitious as his uncle, the first Napoleon, was.

The French keep saying that they are here to emancipate Rome, but we are already free. Or we were, before they started this siege. We don't need their emancipation. We don't need their cannon fire, ripping through the ancient, sacred walls of Saint Peter's. Murdering and maiming our civilians and volunteers, like this young lad who now calls out for his mamma as the surgeon takes the dreaded handsaw into his grip.

"There, there," I say, folding his hand into mine and squeezing. "Don't look down, look at me," I say, my voice insistent, but soon overpowered by the shrill and bloodcurdling cries of this poor lad who will never again have use of his foot.

It's not just this lad. It's the hundreds who fill this great hall. And this is just one hall of one hospital. The men, women, and even children of Rome have done all they can to repel this attack as the French encircle our city and fire on our streets. But how long can we hold out?

What the foreign cannons don't manage to raze, time will— starvation, attrition. Rome is being viciously and purposefully destroyed, demolished, one precious building at a time. One valiant young man at a time. And my Giovanni, encamped at the Vatican, is in the direct line of fire.

But I worry about not only my husband but my baby, also. We know full well that the French are ruthless. They would not hesitate to kill anyone in their way. And I've heard that there is fighting all around Rieti. What would Chiara do if her home was fired on or burned? She'd save her baby. Would she save mine? With Rome surrounded, I have no word and no hope of getting to Nino. I can't send her the money that she needs for food and care. Will she continue to care for my baby? Does she even know what is happening here in Rome, the reason why I've stopped sending payments, isolated as she is in her provincial and rural world?

These thoughts drive me mad, and so there's no relief but to pour myself into work. And it's punishing work. The Roman summer is here; the sun is relentless and the air is stiflingly hot. I walk to and from the hospital, my feet blistered from the long hours, my head throbbing from the constant bombardments, the artillery that pounds Rome day and night.

But I forget my own complaints, at least for a few hours, when I walk into the crowded halls of the *ospedale*. As soon as I enter I'm hit by a wall of overpowering smells that fester in the hot, breezeless air: singed flesh, rancid vomit, emptied bowels. The needs of these men are both bottomless and urgent. Gunshot wounds, amputations, blood poisoning, and wound fever drive them mad with pain and delirium. Oftentimes my work is nothing more than holding the hands of a man who is dying, telling him that his mother is on her way. When they mistake me for a mother or sweetheart, I play along. Of course I do.

If I don't keep busy, my hands tremble and my mind roils, so I do my best not to stop. I push through the cloying heat and fatigue as I change bedsheets and wound dressings, I empty waste pots, I sponge off bloodied limbs and sweating foreheads. The best work is when a young man is healing and I can bring fresh-cut roses to his bedside. Or books and paper. When they ask me to read with them or beg me to take dictation while they craft a letter to a parent or a beloved. There is pain and suffering all around, and yet, in these rare moments, there is also hope.

Like the work that I find myself doing one hot morning in early June. I'm helping a young soldier, Paolo, to practice walking with a cane, now that he has only one leg. I was the nurse who held his hand during the amputation; now Paolo is determined to learn how to manage in his newly maimed body. I try not to weep as we inch forward together, each step a fresh agony for him.

Instead I look around the hospital courtyard, reminding myself to take deep breaths in this precious fresh air. Gracious old oaks shield this space with much-needed shade, and many have come out here for a temporary escape from the smells and heat of the inner rooms.

It's not just men we are treating, these days. Women and small children are flooding into our walls daily, as well. They are afraid that their homes will be bombed, or they have already been bombed. Some of them come because they need food. Some come in the belief that they will be safer here, though of course we cannot promise that to anyone. But we take them all in. How could we not? In a city filled with the tombs of countless martyrs and the relics of so many miracles, these are the living martyrs. We are living through the desperate moments of Rome's story, just as the people did thousands of years ago. And like them, I am starting to believe that we need heaven's intervention.

It's pleasant enough in the courtyard this morning. A small cluster of children are playing chase, hiding behind the broad trunks of the oaks, weaving in and out of the adults with the carefree joy that only children can maintain in a time of crisis. The women watch their children with grateful smiles; some of the convalescing soldiers even laugh. I wonder, if these women are widows, might some of these men and women find companionship during this time? At the very least, friendship and comfort?

"I remember that feeling." Paolo's voice pulls me from my thoughts. I turn toward him as he goes on, watching the nearby children: "A summer morning. The way they run . . ." He doesn't finish the thought. He does not need to: His own body is ruined and broken. He'll never run in the grass, laughing, again.

When Paolo turns his gaze back toward me, I see the shimmer of tears in his young eyes. And then he asks: "Nurse Ossoli, how long will you stay with me?"

I swallow, fighting back against the threat of my own tears. Paolo gets to cry now, not me. I can cry later, because in this moment, what Paolo needs is my strength. I angle my face toward him and answer: "As long as you need me. I'm here until—" But I don't finish the thought, because I hear a strange buzzing sound. And then something lands before us, across the courtyard in front of a row of windows. A small dark ball kicked amiss? A stone? No, it's not a stone and it's not a ball. It's still letting off that unsettling droning noise. Then someone in the courtyard yells: *"Bomba! Bomba!"*

Bomb.

And then the air turns red and searing hot all around me. And then, it all goes black.

Chapter Fifty

Summer 1849

I AM ONE OF THE LUCKY ONES: I SURVIVE THE HOSPITAL bombing with just a concussion, but when I awake, the nightmare of the Roman siege continues. Where French cannons and bullets may fail, starvation will succeed. That becomes clear to all of us as we struggle that summer to keep the hospital stocked with supplies and food: we will run out.

We will also run out of able bodies. Women are stepping up, using buckets and pans of water to put out the fires of the bombs, including the bomb that hit our hospital, killing several dozen volunteers and convalescing soldiers. All over the city, as the men are engaged in battles, women are taking up whatever guns they can find. But soon enough we will run out of men, women, *and* guns.

And yet Mazzini stands as firm as the Roman oaks. And so does my husband, who, by a miracle, remains alive. He's promoted that summer to captain. He faces barrages of artillery almost daily as his men die all around him. He writes to me of the bloodstains on his uniform from the men who are hit on his left and his right. *It is the cruelty of the gods,* I think. *One person dies, the other one lives.* But for how much longer? If I am to die in this war, I only hope that death will come as a swift and merciful visitor.

By the end of June, the feelings of optimism from just a few months earlier are gone, evaporated like mist in this scorching and unrelenting summer heat. All of us have held someone who is dying. Most of us have lost many. I'm hungry all the time.

I return to my apartment late at night, after hours of grueling work in the hospital and the long walk home. I'm sweat-caked and weary in a way that I would not have believed possible. I keep myself up for the dying soldiers all day. But when I come home, I cannot pretend any longer. I collapse onto my bed and I weep. And yet, sleep does not come. My body trembles with fatigue, but my mind spins and churns, unable to find a safe and peaceful place of rest.

We will lose. I know that. We all know that. Garibaldi has told the assembly himself that our cause is lost—for now. And then I receive word from Mazzini. *"Dear friend, it is all over."* I read his words through a blur of tears. Mazzini will race north with his men to plan the next steps of the resistance. But the French will take Rome. We have no more men with which to hold it. No more food to feed its people. He warns me: *"Brandish your American flag prominently from your window,"* and then the chilling warning: *"Give the name of Ossoli to no one."*

Giovanni must leave, as well. The French won't harm the women and the children, we hope and believe, but anyone who has taken up arms, they will slaughter. My hands quiver as I lower the page and absorb Mazzini's words. Outside it is black, but I know what I must do. I walk to the door and grab my cloak, setting out in the night. I walk in the dark, as I've done on so many nights before this one. But tonight, Rome lies in a state of eerie quiet. The night before meeting the executioner's blade.

I cross the Tiber and come to the familiar sight of Saint Peter's. The place where our love story began. My love story with Giovanni, and with this place. I look up at the walls and shudder, seeing for myself what Giovanni has described: the ancient walls painted red in the many places where Roman blood has flowed. I walk through the shredded gardens that surround the pope's former buildings. These lush lawns once filled with peacocks and flowers now flicker with the small campfires of the last few soldiers who survive.

Eventually I find him, stationed where he's been for months.

"Giovanni," I say, my voice strangled. When my husband looks up from the small campfire before him, surprise washes over his drawn, haggard face. "Margherita, *cara mia*." He jumps to stand and then pulls me into his arms. Eventually he speaks. "But, my darling, how are you here?"

Before I can answer, I must ask the questions of my own. "Are you all right?" I scan his body. "Are you hurt?"

"I'm fine, I'm fine," he says, his tone almost guilty as he shakes his head. "But how are you here?"

"I just received word from Mazzini," I say, whispering to him, my hands grazing the beard that now darkens his tired face. "I'm sorry if I shouldn't be here. I had to see you when . . ."

He gives my hand a squeeze. "You do not apologize. Not for anything. I'm glad you've come."

Without a word, he guides me toward his camp, before the walls that we both know will not hold. I settle in beside him, and he drapes his bloodstained officer's tunic over my shoulders. We sit in silence—for how long, I do not know—and we look out over Rome. The monuments across the city are ravaged. The ancient fountains look ghoulish, their beautifully carved figures missing arms and legs, as maimed as the bodies of the soldiers that fill the hospitals and new burial sites.

Giovanni and I hold each other for the entire night. Here, where he first found me in the crowded piazza. Where we started out on so many walks along the Tiber and across the Ponte Sant'Angelo. My mind spins with the memories of our many corners of Rome. The Palazzo Ossoli, where he vowed to pray beside only one woman. Our reunion at San Carlo, the look in his eyes when I slid the veil from my face. Taking each other's hand in Saint Peter's on Christmas Eve. Walking up the Janiculum Hill to see all of Rome spread before us at sunrise. And now, our beloved city bleeds and trembles in the dark.

Wrapped in his arms, I realize something. "Tomorrow is July fourth," I say. Not sure that Giovanni knows the significance of the date, I add: "The day of American independence." I think of them, an ocean away. Waldo, Louisa May, Thoreau, the Hawthornes, the

Greeleys, my mother. They will have picnics and parades. They'll listen to music and eat foods fresh from the summer garden. They can't know what we are living through here, on the other side of the globe, where all of us are as hungry for freedom. And yet we now live in a place where the dream of freedom has turned into a nightmare.

Chapter Fifty-One

Rieti
July 1849

W E CRAWL INTO RIETI A FEW DAYS LATER, GIOVANNI
ordered by his commanding officer to leave Rome before
the French entered. Clutching our hastily packed bags, my American passport tucked safely into the pocket of my traveling cloak,
we'd sped by rented coach in an eerie quiet through the *campagna*,
arriving at the village of rusty red buildings and dusty streets at
daybreak.

We see, with relief, that the town seems to have been spared
fighting. The two sides must have met elsewhere, for we see no
signs of bombs or bullets as we make our way toward Chiara's family home. In fact it is hard to believe how peaceful it all looks. Here,
the people wake from sleep not to the sound of bombs but to their
roosters. They have not watched buildings collapse, but have
watched grapes grow fat on their vines. Their church bells ring not
to warn people to take shelter, but to mark the passage of morning
and evening services in the hillside monastery. War has not ravaged
Rieti, and that gives my ravaged soul a large measure of comfort. I
am desperate to take my baby in my arms.

Chiara's house looks squalid, but I breathe a sigh of relief to see
how lived-in it appears—the chickens peck the scorched grass in
the yard; there's a small, skinny goat tied to a post. They have not
fled. They have not had to flee.

And then we see them, two babes in the backyard. The little boy
a few months older than Nino spots us and runs inside. "Chiara's

son," I say to Giovanni. An instant later I hear a noise like someone dropping a pot in the house. The other little child, sitting on the grass, blinks up at us. "Nino!" I gasp. I take my skirts in my fists and run to him.

He does not recognize me, but he does not cry in fear at my picking him up, either. He simply stares at me, his gaze hollow. My heart flips as I take him in; he looks dreadful. His eyes, once such a bright and clear blue, appear blank, looking out from skin that's a sickening shade of yellow. He seems entirely disinterested in his surroundings, as if he does not have the vigor to engage. He is not yet a year, ten months at this point—but he should be more responsive than this by now. I narrow my eyes and study his skin: there are scars on his arms and neck. And he's so thin! Where once he was all soft flesh and milk fat, now I feel the hard jut of his bones.

Just then the sound of footsteps, and Chiara emerges from the door, holding her boy on her hip, a jug of something in her other hand, which she places on the table. She, also, looks too thin. "Chiara," I say, my voice flimsy as a reed.

She's clearly surprised by our sudden appearance in her yard. "Marchesa Ossoli. Marchese Ossoli. I did not expect you. I was just about to give them breakfast."

"The entire trip was unexpected," I say. "Chiara, what are these?"

She looks to where I'm pointing, to my son's neck. "He had the pox," she says. "Almost dead." She makes a sign of the cross. "But it leaves the scars."

"When was that?" I ask.

She shrugs. "Month ago?"

"He's so . . . he's so thin."

"My milk is gone. I didn't have enough."

But her little boy looks robust and happy. Toddling around the yard while my son can barely focus his eyes. "What do you feed him? What is for breakfast?"

"Bread," she says, avoiding my eyes. "You didn't send me money. You're lucky I gave him anything."

This hits me like a punch. How can I even respond? Does this girl know that Rome was besieged? I let out a weary sigh. I, too, am starving and exhausted, and I'd rather save what scant reserves I do have for my son. From the looks of it, he needs me.

"We will put it all to rights," I say, looking to my boy. "We are here now. We will pay you what is owed and we won't impose on you any longer. If we could just stay with you for one night, Chiara, then we will make our travel arrangements and move on."

She cocks her head, throws me an aggrieved look. "One night. You'll want breakfast now, too?"

"Only if you have enough," I say. "We would be happy to pay you for food."

She pours three glasses of wine. My baby in my arms sees the wine and begins to writhe in my grasp, crying, straining to reach forward. I look at Chiara, confused by this reaction of his. It's the first reaction I've seen of any kind since we arrived.

"He wants the wine," she says, as if this clears anything up. I arc an eyebrow. "He knows it's time for his breakfast, so he's impatient."

"Impatient . . . for the wine?"

"*Si.*" She breaks off a small piece of bread, dips it in the wine, and puts the soggy bite in Nino's mouth. He eats it with well-practiced nibbles.

I throw Giovanni a look, then turn back to the woman, asking, "You give him wine?"

"*Si.* That lazy goat makes not nearly enough milk for all of us. The water is not clean. What else should he drink?"

After breakfast, we retreat to the loft above their small barn, where Chiara tells us we can stay for one night. I settle Nino in for a nap, and Giovanni sets out into the village to make inquiries for where we might be able to stay next. Perhaps there is a small cottage we can rent nearby for a time. As my baby sleeps, I look at him and can't fight back the onslaught of silent, hot tears. I'm so relieved to be back with him, so overjoyed to have him here, safe, with me. And yet, I'm also ripped apart by anguish at his condition. By all that he has had to endure already in his short life. I only hope that with our love and care, Nino can heal. That all three of us, together, will be able to heal. As Nino sleeps, I whisper a silent prayer over his head, a prayer for his forgiveness. And a prayer that his youthful strength and spirit can somehow revive and return. And then I step back, allowing him the rest that he so badly needs.

I sit down on what I suppose is to be our straw bed. I rifle through my bag, finding the paper, pen, and inkwell. There's something I must do.

It's been too long that I've felt the need to hide my twin secrets. I've been too ashamed to admit that Nino is my child and that Giovanni is my husband. I feared that my friends back in America would look down on my choice of an uneducated Roman soldier, a Catholic, younger than me, not able to read or write beautifully in his native tongue, let alone in English. And I've been ashamed to admit that Nino exists. At first it was for fear that they'd know he was conceived out of wedlock, because I could not very well admit to having Nino without admitting to Giovanni first. But now it's just a secret I've carried because I was embarrassed that I had not already admitted it, and it seems strange to claim the child when he is nearly a year old. It's no small thing to have "failed to mention."

And yet, living through war, as we've done, is also no small thing. It's the very biggest of things, and it's changed everything for me. I will not hide our family for another minute. We will be together at last, unashamed. We've lost Rome, we've lost our home, our dreams of freedom, but I've finally gained my full family. And in admitting to that, there is freedom of a different sort.

I write three letters: one to my mother, one to Waldo, and one to Greeley. Mother will tell the rest of my family. Waldo will tell my friends in Massachusetts, and Greeley my community in New York. After all this time, after all this difficulty in finding the words, now they come easily. That, at least, is a blessing.

I'm disturbed from my writing, and Nino stirs from sleep, when we hear a loud noise below. A man's shouting, and then a second voice. I take Nino, now awake, into my arms and I go downstairs to see.

Out in the small brown yard stand two men. Chiara is between them, and all three of them are yelling. Their faces are red and the words are so rapid that I can barely make out what they are saying. I remain back, hidden in the doorway of the barn.

When I see Giovanni appear in the yard, returned from his errands, I wave him forward. His face is etched in confusion. They are speaking some sort of dialect that I cannot fully understand. "What is happening?" I ask my husband. Nino fusses in my arms but I bounce to comfort him. Neither Chiara nor the two men take any notice of us standing there watching. They are screaming even louder now, then one of them raises his fists, and I *do* understand when they begin threatening blows. "What are they fighting over?" I ask.

"They are brothers," Giovanni says, his eyes narrowed as he listens to their insults. They both appear to be drunk, on wine and rage. I hear one of them yell the name Pietro. Ah, so this is Chiara's husband. I've not yet met him, he was gone on my past visits.

"They are fighting over money. This one"—my husband points to Pietro—"is accusing that one of stealing." And now the brother hurtles forward and punches Pietro. Chiara screams. She tries to step in, but he slaps her across the face, then shoves her backward. She lands with a thud on the ground. I hold Nino tight in my grip, taking a stride back. Giovanni is ready to step in, but before he can, Pietro is back, ready to answer his brother's blow, only now he's holding a hammer. The brother wrests it from his grip, hurling it across the yard, where it comes within just a foot of hitting me and Nino.

I turn and flee, away from the yard, holding tight to Nino and grabbing Giovanni by the wrist to ensure that he follows me. We climb back up into the loft, where I hand the baby to my husband and frantically begin to organize the few items we've unpacked. "We are not staying here," I say. "They almost killed Nino. If not today, they would have killed him eventually. We cannot."

HOURS LATER, I lie on the lumpy bed of our room at the village inn, knowing that sleep will not come. Not after the day we've just had. Not until we have left this village and put many miles between us and Chiara's family.

Mercifully, Nino has settled, and my husband's snores beside me tell me that he's managed to drift off. But that's when I notice the strange flickering lights in the street below our one dirty window.

"Who are they?" I ask, nudging my husband from sleep, whispering so as not to disturb the baby.

I watch as the drowsiness shakes off of his features and he attempts to focus on where I'm pointing. And then I see the strain that grips his entire expression. "Hunters."

My body feels cold. "Hunters?"

He nods, his jaw set in a tight line. He points a finger. "See the insignia? Papal States. They are hunting for anyone who fought against the pope. They are looking for me."

The dark room lists like a ship. I step back from the window. "Giovanni, we aren't safe here. We don't know the innkeeper." From the looks of his small, dingy establishment, he could use the money that would come from a valuable tip-off to the pope's rich scouts. My throat feels strangled, but I lean close to my husband and go on: "Or Chiara and her family . . . you saw the way they live. Why, if not her, then her husband. Or that terrible brother. They'd sell us to the bounty hunters in a heartbeat."

He nods.

"We cannot stay here," I say.

"No, we cannot." He is quiet a moment. "But we can't leave now, not while they are in the streets. We'll go tomorrow, first thing."

"I won't sleep tonight," I say. I cross the room in several determined strides and rummage through my bag.

"What are you doing?" he asks, the confusion apparent in his voice.

"Writing my mother," I answer. In my haste to flee Chiara's house after that horrific fight, I did not finish my letters. So I'll finish them now. I'll use my writing to fill these anxious hours before the sun rises and we can leave the nightmare in this village.

I conclude my letters in a new way than what I had planned on, explaining: *"Nino is the sunshine of my life. Giovanni is the solid earth beneath me. In them, I have found a home."* It's true. This pilgrim who has filled her life by wandering, this butterfly who never had a place to land, who never had people to call her own, I now have the two people from whom I will never be parted. Giovanni and Nino, they are my home. Now the matter of *where* that earthly home should be—that must be decided.

Chapter Fifty-Two

Tuscany
Autumn 1849

T HE TUSCAN COUNTRYSIDE UNROLLS BEFORE US AS
I peer, entranced, through the dirty windows of the hired
coach. It's a sweeping view: dark cypress trees and bright green
pastures, terraces and vineyards that climb the gentle hillsides, the
thick clusters of burgundy and green grapes dancing on the vines.
We are traveling through this *campagna*, this countryside, in the
weeks just before the harvesting season, which means that the
people of Tuscany are busy, the land overflowing with the riches of
its fertility.

Looking out over these scenes of unspoiled beauty, of a countryside ready to yield its abundance and a people ready to cull that
abundance, I can't help but marvel: these lands are mere miles
from the Papal States, and yet, all is ripe and thriving, unmaimed,
with stories of nearby war and bombs and siege only that—stories.

"*Pecora!*" Nino shouts now, his blue eyes going wide in delight as
he surveys the scene through his window, his soft hand tapping
against the pane.

"Yes, my darling, sheep," I say, taking a moment of maternal delight in his early attempts at language. In his clear improvement
from just a few weeks earlier.

Nino points next at a sprawl of vineyard. "*Uva!*"

"Yes, my darling, grapes, a great number of them." I exchange a
smile with Giovanni over the head of our little boy. I am grateful—
relieved beyond measure—that here my son may gape and marvel
at sheep and grapes, rather than run and cower from soldiers and

cannons. And that is precisely the reason why we have fled to Tuscany, traveling incognito as a family of three, resting for a time at an inn in Perugia before setting out for the final leg of our journey to Florence.

The Florentines did not ever fully join the tidal wave of revolutions led by the Romans. Far from being a republican or a nationalist, their leader, Grand Duke Leopold, is a close ally of the papacy and therefore a friend of the Austrians and French, and he holds the city like a king would. He would not consider us welcome additions to his domain, Giovanni and I being a pair of Roman refugees who fought for the republic, so for that reason we hope to make a quiet entry into the crowded capital of the Tuscan region.

The bustle and intact prosperity of Florence, the indifference and even prevailing disdain toward the disruptive republican movements that played out elsewhere on the Italian peninsula—all of that works in our favor now. We hope to set up a household and live in relative anonymity, and therefore safety, for the coming months.

We roll into the gated city on a mild, clear evening in September and give the name Marchese and Marchesa d'Ossoli. We hope that the noble title, combined with the fact that the Ossoli family has been known to be close allies of the Vatican for centuries, will provide us with a bit of cover, should any of the authorities see fit to make inquiries.

The first and most crucial business at hand is to find rented rooms where we may set up a home for Nino. I have fixed my hopes on the neighborhood of the Piazza di Santa Maria Novella. It's not the crowded, busy heart of the old city, but near enough to it. I love the sprawling grand square, where Nino will have the freedom to walk and run about, chasing the pigeons that gather on the steps of the cream-colored basilica.

Florence welcomes us with her busy and storied graciousness. I have been here before, during my travels with the Spring family, but it is entirely new for my son and even my husband, who has never left Rome. And it's different now for me, as well, seeing the city as a refugee rather than a tourist, settling into the place with the hopes that it may provide us with a safe harbor, for a time, before we must set out on another journey—the destination and particulars of which are not yet clear to me.

We settle on rented rooms in an ancient building up six flights of stairs, which is not ideal when having to carry the bulk of our little son, but we are convinced that it's the place for us when we learn of the building's name: the Casa Libre. "The Free Home," Giovanni says, reading the old plaque.

"It was meant for us," I say, offering him a confiding smile. The apartment is modest but all that we need: a suite of furnished rooms with good sunshine and windows that look out over the square and the tawny rooftops of Florence. From our bedrooms we can hear the bells of the countless churches and cathedrals that ring out from nearly every corner of this city. From my bedroom window I can stare out at the distant sweep of the Tuscan hillsides that rise up like protective arms around this prosperous, flourishing city. I can hear the rowdy chatter of the men who sit below in the cafés, and the negotiations of the women who wind their way past the vendors selling cheese and olives. I hear, even, the laughter of children. Here, at last, in this city, in this home, after months of siege and separation, we hear laughter again. We, too, can laugh. We can breathe out.

In those first few weeks of the golden Tuscan autumn, we settle into a pleasing rhythm as the air turns cool. Nino grows healthier—his skin now appears less sallow, and his body grows softer, as a baby's should be, from a healthier diet and more consistent love and care. His hair fills in, soft and golden, framing a face with the most delightful eyes that light up at all manner of sights. It is my greatest joy to see that his smiles now come easy and often. The trauma of Rieti, I hope, will soon be nothing more than a fading nightmare.

There is much in Florence to distract us and even to delight us. It's quieter here than Rome was in her pre-war glory, of course. But I like that for now. We are easily situated for walks along the Arno River. Nino's favorite outing is to walk to the Ponte Vecchio, the ancient bridge of stones and arches. Together we marvel at the shops and apartments that are built right into the sides of the bridge, perching above the Arno, clinging as though they might slip into the brown water at any point.

We celebrate Nino's first birthday with a small cake that Giovanni brings home from the nearby bakery. Nino claps in delight and relishes the sweetness of the almond frosting. With the final scudi of Giovanni's salary and my modest but steady income from my columns, we have enough to get by, for now, but we do need the money that will come if I can sell my book.

Adjacent to our bedchamber is a room that I declare my writing room, with elaborate frescoes to provide a rich backdrop as I sit and work. After months of frantic worry over both my husband's safety and my child's, after exhausting hours working in the hospital, I am determined to turn back to my book on the Roman revolution. The project has taken on an almost sacred significance for me now that Rome no longer stands as a free republic, now that Pio Nono is ensconced once more in the Vatican. What must he make, I wonder, of the deep red stains that smear his palace walls? Of the pocked landscape of his gardens, where for months, the free young men of Rome lived and camped and fought and died?

This work that pulls on my heart and my pen, it will be a monument to what might have been. To what we fought for. All that we lost. And all that we cannot stop hoping and yearning for.

Greeley has our new address and he writes often. Not only to congratulate me on the news of my child and marriage, but to express his eagerness to read my manuscript on Rome. He's not alone: both Waldo and Mother have written the same. Waldo is excited for my work, and Mother is even more excited for the news of my family life. My secret is out, my shame has been shed from my breast. All of my loved ones in America now know of the two loved ones I hold closest to my heart, right here in our Florentine exile. And so now I feel free—to live, to love, and to work.

IN THE MORNINGS, as Nino naps, I pour myself into my work. I write my columns for the *Tribune*, but most of my hours are devoted to my manuscript. The words come to me like a flood, and I give myself over to their current and power. I take breaks only to look out the window at the lively urban scene before me, or to refill my cup with the delicious dark coffee that this city boasts. When Nino awakes, I hear his sweet voice in the next room. *"Bravo!"* He applauds himself for the triumph of climbing out of his small bed. Giovanni tends to him, dressing him, feeding him, and then if the weather allows, the two of them set out for some adventure in the city. They walk to the Duomo or the Arno River, or else Nino is perfectly happy to toddle about in the piazza in front of Casa Libre. Now that he's a bit older he has become a steady walker, and he enjoys practicing an ever-swifter pace. His favorite activity is to watch the marching of Duke Leopold's regiments as they parade through the city.

We do have to keep a quiet profile, seeing these ever-present signs of the duke's rule across the city; he is no friend to the cause for which we nearly died. But as long as we wear civilian clothes and speak in Italian, no one seems to take much interest in us. When they do, it is only to delight in Nino, who is a charming and adorable child.

We find our favorite spots. In midday, once I have put in hours of work, I walk down to meet Nino and Giovanni at the Caffe d'Italia, where we dine together on bread rolls and cheese, grapes and olives and roasted chestnuts, and Nino relishes bites of salty salami and prosciutto. In the afternoons we stroll along the river, or we walk to the Ponte Vecchio, perusing the sights of the ancient shops. We take Nino to the Uffizi and watch in delight as he marvels at the masterpieces of Michelangelo and Botticelli. We visit the bright stalls of the outdoor markets, where the Tuscans peddle their leather goods and spices.

Of the many sacred sites and holy houses of worship in this rich and thriving city—where every Florentine nobleman seems to have built himself a lavish chapel or church to secure his place in heaven—I like to visit the Duomo the best. In the evenings, after Nino has drifted off to sleep and Giovanni has settled into the worn armchair before the fire with a book or newspaper, I slip on my wool cloak and step out into a city shrouded in shadows.

Inside, the Duomo is quiet and empty, a far different scene from the thick crowds that clog its aisles during the day. The colorful altars glimmer and dance in the glow of the thousands of candles that have been lit by petitioners and pilgrims, but otherwise the space has the velvety softness of night. The air smells of rich incense—I breathe in deep, feeling as though I'm being scrubbed clean, my only company the occasional priest or nun, and the pigeons that coo and flap in the massive dome overhead. The massive dome that, when it was built, was so vast and soaring that it was intended to cover all the Tuscan people in its shadow.

There, with my cloak pulled tight around me in the cool and shadowed interior, I can sit for hours, listening to the haunting, doleful chants that waft across the air, the voices of the priests who are gathered behind the walls, cloistered in their sacred inner confines. Their songs, faint but beautiful, make me feel as though my soul could soar out of my body, floating skyward to reach for the outstretched grip of God.

It is here, in my solitary reverie within the vast but soothing embrace of the Duomo, that I find moments of peace. I stare at the richly painted faces of so many saints and angels, locked for all of eternity in their celestial struggles for salvation. I study the many scenes of Mary, the mother of God, the patron saint of this city of art and money. A woman who knew, better than most, what it was to love—and to weep for the love she lost.

Closer by, to my side, I look up at the stunning painting of Dante as he stands over me. Dante, one of my favorites. The great medieval creator of *The Divine Comedy*, one of Florence's greatest treasures, the man whose beautiful words I've studied since before my memory begins. I stare at the man in thoughtful silence. Dante stands draped in red, his hair capped by the laurel wreath of antiquity, his gaze fixed longingly toward his beloved city of Florence, which waits in its glory on the other side of its closed gates. Dante, too, was an exile, forced from his home. Beneath him swarms the fire of hell; above him, Eden. And there he stands, still, locked in the middle.

I imagine how Dante must have felt. I feel as though I can understand a bit of his struggle. While I am happy enough here, enamored of my son and overjoyed to be united with both my husband

and my child for the first time, inspired by my work and hopeful
for what can come next, I do also know that my husband does not
feel the same hope for the future. How could he? He, like Dante, is
locked in a middle place. A purgatory. Giovanni is far from the
home he's always known and loved, forbidden to return. He's lost
not only his dreams for the place's freedom, but his family and so
many of his comrades in arms, as well. Where can he go next?

Kneeling in the pews of the Duomo, alone at night, listening to
the lulling chants, breathing in the earthy perfume of the incense, I
close my eyes and I allow the feelings of all of this to curl through
me like a cleansing flame. Giovanni, my beloved. He wears a melancholy that I can see, just as I can see the dirty brown soldier's
jacket that he slips on so often at night, when we are alone and our
doors are locked. His officer's uniform, the mantle he wore for so
many days and nights while fighting for his home and for freedom.
Settled in beside the fire, his face crumpled with new ruts that
were not there even a few months ago, he speaks to me of Rome.
Of his childhood days in the Ossoli Palace. Of his nights encamped
beside Saint Peter's. He never speaks of his mother or father directly, but I know they haunt him, as sure as the ghosts of the
bloodied boys and soldiers he held.

Giovanni is a man of deep faith, perhaps a faith even stronger
than mine. And I know that he loves his son, and me. I look to those
truths with hope, praying that they might help my husband out of
this trench of loss and grief. He is relieved that we are safe, and he
knows we cannot be in Rome. But he carries the sadness of the
refugee who has lost his life and his purpose. He is in mourning.
He's only ever been a soldier serving Rome. What can he do here
in Florence, or anywhere?

As the year comes to a close and the darkness of the early evenings settles in, we are warned to prepare for cold and snow. In the
markets, in the museum, in the café—all the Florentines tell us:
"From Rome, *si*? Prepare for winter."

I've lived through snow, of course. It shall be nothing new to me.
But my husband has never spent a winter, a Christmas, any length
of time, away from the warm streets of Rome. How will he fare in
the coming months?

I continue my nighttime visits to the Duomo. Alone, in the ancient pews that have held the tired bodies and the whispered prayers of countless petitioners before me, I seek solace in the space. The holy dome, the glimmer of candles dancing across the painted faces of the angels and saints. It's chilly in here. Now I need gloves and a scarf, as well, on these outings. As I glance up once more at Dante, locked in a purgatory between heaven and hell, I feel a shiver pass through me. I pull my cloak tighter over my shoulders. But even as I do so, I know it's not just the cold that causes me to tremble.

Chapter Fifty-Three

Florence
January 1850

N EW YEAR'S DAY, AND FLORENCE STIRS ON THE FIRST
morning of the year with quiet whispers, its piazzas and
palazzos cloaked in a sugaring of fresh snowfall. The air inside our
apartment is bitter, as the fires have long since sputtered to ash, and
I can see my breath as I slip out from under the warm covers, leaving Giovanni snoring on his side of the bed.

I light a candle and see that there's a thin crust of ice over our
washbowl. My fingers ache as I set to work, starting the fires once
more, preparing coffee. I am careful to be quiet, padding through
the shadowed rooms, stepping lightly to avoid Nino's toys that he's
left scattered on the floor of our parlor, a new stuffed horse and a
drum that he's been playing with since Christmas morning.

I sit down at my desk, relishing the peaceful hush of the room.
The warm mug of coffee feels like a balm to my chilled fingers. I
suspect my husband and son might stay abed for another hour or
so, tucked under their covers, and I savor this time that I have for
myself—to think, to write.

I glance down at the pages before me, finding the place where I
left off yesterday. It's a passage I've been working on that describes
one of the young men with whom I sat in the *ospedale* during the
frantic days of the siege. He had been wounded, this fellow, in
the fighting along the Tiber. Grapeshot to his arm. Eventually the
wound festered beyond treatment and he lost the arm to amputation while with us at Fatebenefratelli. He was eighteen years old.

What I remember most clearly about this young Roman volunteer is his eyes. Rich and dark, but kindled with something that looked like hope, even in the fiercest moments of his pain. While I'd expected him to be distraught at the loss of his limb, at the loss of so many of his life prospects now that both his body and his city were maimed beyond recognition, he showed quite the opposite reaction. In fact, he took a scrap of his arm bone and tied it with a red cord around his neck, calling it a souvenir of "the best days of my life."

Even now, thinking about my conversations with those young men, and my time with the mothers and widows who came to our *ospedale*, frantic to find their loved ones, even my own days working and living with so many Romans who were willing to die for their freedom, I can't help but be overcome. Just traveling back to those memories in order to write them down makes the wounds feel as though they could start bleeding anew.

I know this work is important. Not just for me, and not just to honor the Romans. This work is important for Americans. For all freedom-loving people to see how the Romans fought. To see that freedom is something we ought never to take for granted.

Perhaps because of this, I don't have the angst, the struggles, that I often had when I was younger, attempting to wrestle the muse into place as I wrote about Goethe or Shakespeare. This is a story that has grown up within me, from the moments of my own life. Perhaps it will even help me to heal.

I lose myself to the words as they come through me. An hour passes quickly, and I don't look up from my pages until I hear Nino call out from bed. "Mamma!" he warbles, clapping his chubby hands. I blink, rubbing my sore wrist, stunned to see that morning has brightened across Florence. Through my window, the snow-dusted piazza and the pale backdrop of the basilica of Santa Maria Novella loom in full view. Florence is awake; the Florentines beneath me are darting about on their morning errands and New Year's Day visits. I lower my pen and tuck my pages away.

"Good morning, my darling." I greet my son in high spirits. I am excited for the visit we have planned: the celebrated English writer

Elizabeth Barrett Browning has invited us to tea in the home she occupies with her famous writer husband, Robert Browning. I have accepted with pleasure.

I've longed to make Elizabeth Barrett Browning's acquaintance for years. I love her writing, everything from her shockingly bold and amorous sonnets to the manifestos she's written railing against slavery, and one especially moving piece she wrote, "The Cry of the Children," which made a strong case for new laws necessary to protect children from the horrific conditions they face while laboring in factories and mills. I love that Mrs. Browning is a woman and yet she's prolific and outspoken, and even so, she's popular. I hope, from reading her words, that I will find a kindred spirit in Elizabeth Barrett Browning.

But there's more: for, as much as I admire her writing and feel a kinship to Mrs. Browning's pen, I love her personal story even more. The reason Mrs. Browning was not in London when I arrived years ago, with the Springs, is that she had eloped with her now-husband, Robert, and the pair had fled to Tuscany in defiance of society's—and her family's—condemnation. They've been here in Florence since. And happily so, from the sounds of it.

Mrs. Browning has listened to the passions of her heart. She's ignored the cries of condemnation that her actions have stoked. And here she is, in Florence, much like myself. Also like me, Mrs. Browning has a little boy, the same age as Nino, and she's written that she wants our fellows to meet and hopefully become friends. I suspect that we might in fact become quick friends, Elizabeth and I, and the thought of a friend in Florence fills me with the warm embers of hope.

As I prepare to leave home, tucking Nino into his cap and warmest wool coat, I notice that my husband is not rising from his armchair beside the fireplace. *"Amore mio?"* I prod him with a gentle tone. *"Pronto?"*

Giovanni looks up from the fire, flinching a bit, as though he's only just noticed that Nino and I are in the room and that we are ready to go. I feel a small dart of pain. Then my husband offers a quick shake of his head, explaining that he would prefer to stay at home.

"Why not join us?" I ask. But I can guess at his reasons. He tells me it is because he does not speak English, and that the thought of meeting two English writers makes him feel abashed. "But, my dear, they speak beautiful Italian, I am sure," I reply. "They've been here for years."

Giovanni breathes out slowly, his gaze sliding back toward the hearth, and then, tapping the sides of his armchair, he adds: "But there is more to the language than just the words."

I know what he means. My Giovanni does not speak the language of poetry—regardless of which tongue it is being spoken in. The Brownings are writers, they are people of letters and verse. Elizabeth is so beloved that she is already being spoken of as England's possible next choice for poet laureate, when my dear friend of the hollyhocks, Mr. Wordsworth, is no longer with us. She has not even lived in England for years, yet that is how celebrated her writing is.

Giovanni, by contrast, speaks the language of soldiers. His is the tongue of the streets of Rome, of the men who shed their blood to defend her. It's a poetry that I know and love and find beautiful, but a different sort of poetry from that which the genteel Brownings speak.

It's something we have both begun to feel and notice, I realize, not just here in Florence. Giovanni's learning, his schooling in the Roman streets, it sets him apart from most of the other people in my life with whom I am close. Waldo, Eliza, the Hawthornes, even Thoreau—I don't see Giovanni having much to speak of with them. I can't imagine him sharing a common tongue with my philosopher friends from Massachusetts, even if he were to learn English. Perhaps Greeley, with his gritty drive to see the true and unvarnished life of the denizens of New York City, could find some common ground with my husband. But even so, Giovanni's learning has only ever come from the school of his modest and urban life. He, the Roman, would be the last man I know to quote Virgil. That's fine with me, but it does give me pause when I think about braiding him into my broader life, if and when our period of exile does lead to the next phase. *How can it even be done?* I wonder.

I put all of these thoughts to the side, quelling these concerns for now, as I am eager to meet Mrs. Browning, and Giovanni doesn't seem to mind our leaving him to a quiet afternoon at home. Besides, Nino deserves a few hours with a new friend. As do I.

WE GIVE OUR names to the butler at the door and a moment later, Nino and I are shown into the Brownings' gracious drawing room, a space of green walls and bright red furniture. A chandelier casts a glow over the dark wooden bookshelves and framed paintings. There's a cozy fire beneath the mantel, and a lady who appears slightly older than me sits on a couch of plush crimson, propped up by a mountain of pillows. She does not rise as we enter. "Ah, my dear Margaret Fuller Ossoli," the woman says in a refined English accent, beckoning Nino and me toward her. "Please, do come in. Take a seat here with me."

"Thank you," I say, clutching Nino's hand as we step into the room. The dark-haired lady fixes me with a pointed stare, the hint of a smile tugging on her lips. She is attractive in a striking way, her eyes intense, a waterfall of dark ringlets framing her narrow face. "I am Elizabeth," she says, though I hardly need to hear it. "But you? You have so many titles: editress of *The Dial*, foreign correspondent for the *New-York Tribune*. And now I hear you are Countess of Ossoli." Her bright eyes slide to Nino at my side, and her smile becomes full as she adds: "And, of course, Mamma."

"That is correct," I say, giving my hostess a quick curtsey in greeting. "Margaret will do just fine. Mrs. Browning, it is a pure delight to meet you at last."

"And you, my dear. But please, call me Elizabeth. Sit, sit. Welcome to our Casa Guidi."

Nino clings to me as I take the offered seat across from our hostess. Just then, a little boy comes wobbling into the salon, a nursemaid following close as a shadow. "Ah!" Elizabeth raises her hands to the little lad. "Here is my Pen. Hello, my darling one. And your son is called?"

"This is Angelo," I say, pressing a reassuring hand to my son's shoulder. "We call him Nino."

"Nino, isn't he a darling?" Elizabeth remarks, her voice like a coo.

The two boys lock gazes, and I see Nino offer a coy smile before he presses his face into my skirts. Elizabeth asks the nursemaid in quick and easy Italian to retrieve a basket of toys from the nearby shelf, which the lady begins to spread across the carpeted floor. I see how Nino softens, growing intrigued, and within a few minutes the pair are playing together on the carpet with a lineup of stuffed lions, laughing and growling at each other.

Elizabeth eventually rends her gaze from her son, saying to me in a low, confiding tone: "Four heartbreaks before him, and then that angel stayed with us."

"Oh my," I say, my hand flying to my heart. "I am so sorry."

"Have you ever . . . lost a babe?"

"No." I shake my head. "In fact, it was quite the opposite. That child arrived to me stout—but he came as quite a surprise." I've never spoken this fact aloud before, that Nino was conceived out of wedlock. Not even Mother knows the true order of things. But something about Elizabeth's unapologetic manner, about the fact that she ran off with Robert, defying her father, showing little care for his disinheritance of her, rejecting the society match for which she was intended, makes me feel emboldened to speak the truth now in this parlor.

And I can see that I haven't misjudged her when Elizabeth flashes me a warm and earnest grin, saying: "Bravo for you, my girl." She's not offended; she doesn't even disapprove. If anything, she seems to approve of my candor. "But where is your dashing Italian nobleman now?"

"Oh, he must send his regrets, unfortunately. He was sorry to miss you. He was feeling . . . well, he wasn't feeling himself today." I shift in my seat. It's true, what I've said, that Giovanni wasn't feeling all that well. And yet now I'm equivocating on his behalf.

"Well, you shall have to give your count my regards," Elizabeth says. "And it's just as well, for my Robert is away, too. Making New Year's visits in the country. So we are a pair of doting mothers with our little baby birds."

"I'm perfectly content with the company," I say, throwing a look toward Nino and then back toward my hostess.

"As am I," she agrees. "I've been mad to meet you, my dear. I will confess, it sent ripples through Florentine gossip circles when the pair . . . or rather, the *trio* of you arrived from Rome."

Now I lean back in my seat. "Oh?"

"It was sensational, my darling." Elizabeth folds her hands together in her lap, resting them atop the froth of her plum-colored skirt. "I don't know whether a woman has come into town with such a great story, well, since *I* arrived. You do know I love a great story. And particularly a great love story. And that's what yours is."

This sends a warm feeling coursing through me, and I can't help but let out a small laugh. As the boys babble and play at our feet, Elizabeth pours out a traditional afternoon tea on the table between us, complete with strong black tea and cream, and biscuits from a tin that we could have found in London. Soon both my stomach and my heart feel full. Everything about the gathering is pleasant: Elizabeth's lively conversation, her affable and open manner, the witty banter in my native tongue. The fact that my child eventually trots off, so happy and comfortable, with the first playmate of his age since Rieti. It appears we are both equally delighted to be here.

My hostess seems just as content with our company, and she flashes an inquisitive grin as she tips forward in her seat. "But, my darling, you must tell me the truth: How are you finding Florence?"

"The truth?" I take a sip of tea and consider my words for a moment, answering: "I'm finding Florence to be cold."

Elizabeth laughs at this, the sound like a silver bell. "Do you mean the weather?"

"Mostly the weather," I answer. "I've lived through a great number of cold winters, having lived in Boston, Cambridge, New York, but I suppose I'd grown accustomed to Rome."

"Ah, yes. Of course you had." She studies me a moment, and I resist the urge to fidget under her searching gaze. Then, eventually, she asks: "Do you miss it very much?"

"I do," I say, my tone full of feeling. Rome felt like my city in a way that Florence, though beautiful, does not. But I hasten to add: "Though, when I say that I miss it, well, not as it is now. I miss Rome as it *was*. As we believed it could be."

Elizabeth, her eyes narrowed, nods. And in her expression I see that she understands me. I go on: "But Giovanni and I are both in agreement: we can't go back there now. We will only return once Rome is free."

Elizabeth turns her teacup in its saucer, considering what I've said, before she asks: "You really do believe that day shall come?"

"Oh, I don't simply believe it. I know it."

"Really? You must tell me how you can be so hopeful."

I lower my teacup. "It'll be a few years. But the Romans have had a taste of freedom, and they won't let that go. They'll throw off their occupiers." Both Giovanni and I believe this—we've spoken about it at length. It is one of the few things that keeps our hearts from being utterly shattered: our indelible belief that Rome is not lost. At least, not forever. "What's more," I say, "we still believe that Italy will be one country someday."

Elizabeth pinches her teacup in her fingers, frowning. "My dear, I am sorry to say it, but now you sound like a barmy prophetess."

"Perhaps." I shrug, smiling. "It would not be the first time someone has thought me mad."

Elizabeth throws me a smirk over the top of her teacup. "Well, my dear Margaret, until that time, until you may return to the Rome that both you and your count consider your true earthly home, do we get to keep you here in Florence?"

"I don't know, to be perfectly honest," I say, my words halting as I stare down into my empty cup. "Florence has never been the place where we thought to settle. It's been a haven, to be sure. But . . ."

"Then where? America?"

"Perhaps," I reply. The truth is that I had thought it an impossibility for the longest time, America. Once I had married Giovanni and delivered a son in Rome. But with all that has happened, with the fact that *Rome* has become the impossibility in the present, and my family back home now knows about my husband and son, well, I'm thinking of America more and more lately. Speaking about it with Nino, and even with Giovanni. Thinking of my family there, and my friends. Florence is not a home to either of us. But America— could it be a refuge for a time?

We hear the giggles of our children in the next room. Elizabeth's eyes slide toward the doorway and she smiles. Taking another sip of tea, she looks back to me and says: "I am so happy they've become friends. In fact, I'm not sure who is enjoying their playmate more—me or my son."

I laugh as she goes on: "My Pen has been desperate for a companion. We will want to borrow Nino all the time now."

"As often as you like."

"I can't run about with him, as you see." Elizabeth fixes me with a direct gaze and then explains: the back pains have plagued her since she was a young woman, leading to the loss of her leg muscles. The same reason why she did not rise when we entered her salon. Now she moves about entirely in a rolling chair, or in the arms of a servant or her devoted husband. I take all of this in, absorbing it with attentive silence. Perhaps her awareness of her own weaknesses and her young and forced reckoning with her own limitations have given her the gifts to write with such warmth and pathos. Perhaps it's even emboldened her to embrace the power of her mind, since the power of her body has abandoned her.

"It can be hard for Pen, being cooped up indoors when Mamma cannot do much away from this couch," she says, letting out a quiet sigh. "It's a common misunderstanding that London has a bitter winter. But really it's not all that punishing. It's gray and rainy, to be sure, but it's not often bitter cold, the way it can be here."

"Right," I say.

"You were in London on your way here, were you not?"

"I was," I answer.

"Yes, I read your columns along your journey. Marvelous work."

This fills me with a warm satisfaction, even pride, to think that Elizabeth Barrett Browning has enjoyed my work. And it emboldens me to say: "In fact, the great disappointment of my time in London was that I missed you. I believe you had just come here with . . ."

"With my Robert, yes." Elizabeth flashes a mischievous smile. "And then you were on to Paris?"

"Yes."

"You met George Sand there, didn't you?"

"I did," I answer, my tone bright.

Elizabeth tips her head back. "I could turn green with envy. You must tell me what she was like."

Now it's my turn to flash a mischievous smile. "Oh, she was every bit as brilliant as you've heard she is. And then more." I tell her about Sand, about her pants, the cape, the cigar. The deep richness of her voice, the shocking blaze of her eyes, her curtains of dark hair. Her unapologetic embrace of her famous lover. Elizabeth listens to all of it, rapt.

"There are so few of us, you see," Elizabeth says, once I've finished. "Sand is one of us. Mary Wollstonecraft. The *fallen* women who are willing to speak out. But if we do it, my dear, then we shall invite others to join us in our boldness. And soon there shall be more. And then the next day, even more."

Elizabeth's words land somewhere deep inside me, beneath my bones, hitting where my heart is beating, and fast. Elizabeth Barrett Browning is speaking to me in a language I've always known and have always sought to find in others. Oh, but it feels good to meet a kindred soul, and to meet in conversation that feels like the vital and worthy truth. My voice is low and throaty as I lean forward and answer her: "I agree, Elizabeth. We mustn't allow our voices, or our pens, to fall silent."

She, too, tilts forward. To my surprise, she takes my hand, and her palm is warm. She gives me a squeeze as she says: "And we won't."

We drink more tea. Elizabeth refills my cup and we drink even more as the conversation continues to unspool between us. And then, somehow, the city outside her windows has gone dark. "Look at that, my dear Margaret. We've devoured the time and yet my appetite remains as ravenous as ever for you and your conversation. I regret to say that, it being New Year's Day, I've dismissed most of the household staff; we plan to have just a light supper of cold turkey and some bread rolls and cheese. Would you and Nino like to stay on to take supper with us?"

"We'd be delighted," I answer.

After a delicious and relaxed meal, Elizabeth turns to the topic of my current work, and I share with her my true feelings, speaking with a frankness that I have not yet had the opportunity to voice. "I believe that this book on Rome will be the most important thing I've done to date," I say.

Elizabeth holds me in her warm gaze, eventually offering a single nod. She looks to Nino, who sits on the floor beside her Pen, and then she looks back to me as she says: "Then, my dear, you've given the world two gifts from your time in Rome. The precious child and the important book, both of which shall change the world."

I sit there with Elizabeth as the first day of the New Year comes to a close. It has been a good day, a day that began in the cold and the dark but has ended in the comfort of a bright drawing room and a convivial conversation. And with it, the enlivening warmth of a new and most welcome friendship.

Chapter Fifty-Four

Spring 1850

T HE WORDS DO COME, THE PAGES FILL, AND BY THE
time spring returns to Florence, I have a book. A full and
written book. One precious copy that rests on top of my desk. On
many nights, after Nino is tucked in and asleep, Giovanni and I sit
by the fire and I do my best to read aloud to my husband, selecting
passages that I translate on the spot, until my head begins to ache
or he becomes too overwrought with the emotions that these
memories elicit.

Pages arrive to me, as well. Elizabeth writes with regular invitations to tea or luncheon at her home near the Palazzo Pitti, invitations that Nino and I happily accept. Mother writes regularly,
ravenous for news of the grandson she longs to meet. Missives to
which I gladly reply, overflowing with maternal adoration as I describe Nino's golden curls, his new babbles in Italian and English,
his delight at running through Florence's piazzas, tossing pebbles
into the Neptune Fountain outside the Palazzo Vecchio.

Waldo writes, also. He is eager to read my book, assuring me that
the American public is ready for it. Greeley sends me updates on
Mary and Arthur, as well as clippings of my columns and readers'
reactions. I miss them. I miss all of them—more, now, perhaps because the chaos of Rome has subsided and I have the time to think
of them. I do wish to see them again.

But then, in one delivery of the evening post, a message arrives
to me of particular interest, and one that catches me quite by surprise. The page is folded and tucked into Mother's letter; she's for-

warded it along as she suspects that the note's writer does not know how to reach me here in Florence. I unfurl the page and see a fine, elegant hand, one that strikes me as vaguely familiar. It is from Elizabeth Cady Stanton. A jolt of memory; yes, I know her. A young bride, living in Boston, and a regular attendee of my earliest Conversation series. A bright woman, I recall, and an earnest advocate for the rights of women.

As I read her note, as I absorb the power of her words, the blood begins to swell inside me, causing my veins to throb. Elizabeth Cady Stanton has joined forces with other like-minded women, two of them named Lucretia Mott and Susan B. Anthony, and they've been holding rallies and gatherings for women, most recently in Seneca Falls, New York. This year they plan to hold an inaugural meeting of what they are calling the National Woman's Rights Convention, the first-ever gathering in America of this kind—and they wish for me to serve as their president. *"You are the founding Mother of our movement, Miss Fuller, and thus it is our ardent wish to confide in you the leadership of this assembly."*

I sit there, in the silence of my writing room, my heart racing. I look down, read the note a second time. Then I look up, astounded. I rise to stand and stride quickly out of the room to find Giovanni. He's seated in his usual spot, the faded armchair by the fire, his soldier's jacket unbuttoned down the front. I approach him in silence and I see the surprise in his eyes as I fold my body into his, curling into his lap as I have not done in some time. We hold each other, and I tuck my head into the slope of his shoulder, feeling the steady thrum of his heartbeat. Or perhaps it's mine. After several minutes I lift the paper in my hands, showing him the letter.

He can't read it, it is in English, but I explain what Elizabeth Cady Stanton has asked of me. The name Elizabeth Cady Stanton means nothing to him, nor do the names Susan B. Anthony or Lucretia Mott. I doubt many gentlemen in *America* even know their names, their work—but my Roman soldier certainly does not. Nevertheless I explain to him all that she has said, writing to me, it seems, from a world away, and yet piercing my heart with the contents of her letter. And then I tell my husband the truth: I miss America. It's the first time I've said it aloud. The tears come, catching me by surprise, as I speak to Giovanni, admitting to him how I miss my family, my friends.

Here with him I've been prepared to work—and even die—for our dreams of Italy and a free Rome, but there is also much work that needs to be done in America. While we wait for the Romans to rise again, to drive out the occupiers, which we both believe will happen, can we not go to America for a time, where we will be safe? Where we can work for greater rights for the people there, as well. Where we will have the comfort of loved ones and community. Where Nino will have the chance to meet and know those who can love him best of all.

I lay my arguments before him and then I fall silent. A log pops in the hearth, but otherwise there's a throbbing quiet that fills the room. My husband says nothing for a long time, eventually looking down at his hands. Perhaps seeing, with a new clarity, how useless they have become here.

There is more, but I can't say it; at least, not right now. My work, my book, is brilliant. I can see that. But it is not for the Italians. It will prosper and flourish, but in America. It is written in English, and I need English publishers and readers to help it become what it is meant to be. But I keep that part to myself for now, deciding to bide my time. I've said enough for tonight. And I believe that my husband, though he has said nothing, has heard it all.

EASTER COMES AND, with it, a blessed break from the gray and chilly rains. The morning dawns with miraculous sunshine and a silky blue sky that fills the entire city with good cheer, and that lively mood reaches the three of us. We set out together on Easter Sunday for mass at the Duomo. It is a special day for me and Giovanni, as it is the anniversary of our first meeting and then, the year later, our lifelong vows to each other. And now here is Nino, a year and a half old, healthy and thriving. As we hold hands, I feel Giovanni giving me gentle squeezes, I see how he tosses me tender looks as we walk with the crowds into the packed and incense-rich basilica, and I return the warm gestures.

The service does much to lift our souls. I love to see how Nino thrills at the powerful music, at the way my husband belts out his deep voice in song with the rest of the close-packed worshippers. Our cheery and active little boy, usually more content to be hopping and running, sits mostly still for the entire service, enraptured by the colorful scene around us. When the mass ends and we are beginning to slowly file out, surrounded by the throngs, Nino does begin to squirm and point. "Papa, Papa!" He wriggles in Giovanni's arms.

"He wants to climb, there," Giovanni says over the din, and I follow the direction of his gaze through the crowds. "The stairs of the bell tower."

Nino is at an age when now, having mastered running, he wants to climb everything. "Papa!" He begins to kick his legs while still in Giovanni's arms, eager to be let loose.

Then, with a glimmer in his eyes that I have not seen in weeks, perhaps months, Giovanni says to me: *"Andiamo."*

Let's go. Together.

How can I say no?

In all our time here in Florence, I've not yet climbed this tower, the stunning triumph of early Renaissance architecture, which pierces the Tuscan sky almost three hundred feet above the piazza. My son is wild to do it, and my husband appears eager to do *something*. "Yes," I say, looking up at the lively medley of white, green, and red patterns on the marble walls. "Let's go up."

We enter the narrow, winding stairway in single file, me first, then Giovanni holding Nino a few steps behind me. "It must be hundreds of steps," Giovanni says as I look up, taking the first few steps at a steady pace.

"Andiamo!" Nino repeats his father's words. We do as he says. After a few minutes of climbing, when I can hear that we are both heaving with our breaths, we come out onto the tower's first open level. "Don't stop here," Giovanni insists, continuing his long strides across the landing. "This will spoil the view." I am so happy to hear my husband's voice this animated that I agree to his suggestion, not pausing to take a break and catch my breath. Instead I lead the way toward the next flight of stairs that will take us even higher.

We continue our climb. After a few minutes my breaths sound

more like ragged panting. Nino is clapping, excited by all this climbing. I turn around, pausing as I throw a look to my husband. *"Tutto bene?"* I ask.

Giovanni smiles, letting out a full exhale, then he nods. "We're getting closer," he says, as if encouraging me to keep going. I continue to climb.

Many steps later we come out to the second open level, this time looking down on a sweeping view. We pause to take it in, panting in appreciative silence. The city of Florence flows beneath us, a teeming sea, its colorful Easter crowd now appearing like a small and distant shoal of fish. Red and orange rooftops rise up on both sides of the Arno, the scene pierced by the spires of so many churches and basilicas. A blue sky meets the surrounding hills of Tuscany, where the elegant villas and gardens are terraced into the slopes.

But still, we are not at the top. Without words, since our breath is now too labored, we make our way straight toward the final flight of stairs that will bring us to our marble summit. "I bet it's been at least three hundred steps," I say through my uneven breaths.

We pick up our pace, our footsteps echoing in the narrow, winding tower. "That's twenty-five steps since the last landing," Giovanni rasps. "We cannot have too many more to go."

"We are nearly—" I am saying, but then I hear a noise that immediately silences me—faint at first, then steadily growing. A low groaning, as though the walls around us are rubbing against one another. I pause and look to my husband. The bell tower sounds like a creaky ship being tossed on an ocean wave. We've stopped our climb at this point. "What is that?" I ask, my chest heaving.

Then, unexpectedly, above the sound of the groaning walls and the Easter crowds below, there's a clamor like the pounding of a cannon. The walls around us quake, and the thunder of the cathedral's ancient, powerful bells explodes all around us. I gasp in surprise, bracing myself on the wall as Nino squeals in rapturous delight.

Giovanni pulls his timepiece from his pocket. "Twelve noon," he observes, shouting over the booming of the bells. We are standing in Florence's most majestic tower, home to its seven storied bells, at high noon on Easter Sunday, and the peals surround us as they ring out for all of Tuscany. Giovanni and I look at each other and we begin to laugh, his eyes as wide as mine must surely be. The sounds of our surprise and our cheers mingle with the sacred music and we are overcome. I'm on a higher step and I lean down toward my husband, toward my son in his arms, and the three of us embrace. Giovanni wraps an arm around my waist and pulls me even closer, as Nino burrows his golden head into the space between us. We are braided together, a rope, a cord that will never come untied.

The bells ring out twelve times. And then, after the twelfth and final bell, as the walls of the tower thrum all around us in the aftermath, as Nino laughs in his exuberant delight, Giovanni leans closer and whispers into my ear: "We can go, Margherita."

I look into the warmth of his dark eyes, confused by his meaning. He goes on: "We will go to America. I will go with you. Anywhere you are, it will be home for me."

Chapter Fifty-Five

"I TAKE IT AS A GOOD OMEN, MY DEAR," ELIZABETH says, peering at me from her pillowed perch on her red couch. "A most favorable omen, indeed, that the steamship to bear you across the Atlantic shall be called the *Elizabeth*. Even if I do not wish to bid you farewell." My friend gives me a heartfelt smile as we sit together in her gracious salon, our two boys playing on the carpet at our feet. I try my best to offer her a smile in reply, but she sees the wobble of my features.

Elizabeth narrows her all-seeing eyes and leans toward me. "What is it?"

"You are correct, we will be crossing on the *Elizabeth*. . . ."

"Yes?"

"Only, it's not a steamship."

Elizabeth throws a glance toward her son, who has knocked down a tower that Nino has built with the blocks. Then she looks back to me, saying: "I don't understand."

"We have booked passage on . . . well—"

"Out with it, my dear, whatever are you trying to say?"

"It's a cargo ship, rather than a steamer."

"A *cargo* ship?" Elizabeth nearly chokes on the word.

I nod, looking down at the boys, then back toward my friend. "The captain has some space remaining for private passengers on his crossing from Livorno to New York."

Elizabeth lets out a puff of air. "If you don't mind being stuffed in the cargo hold next to drums of olive oil and crates of onions," she grumbles. She means it as a joke, but I manage only a shaky grin. It is true—our accommodations will be far less comfortable than if we were to make the crossing on a ship intended for passengers, rather than merchandise. "But . . . how long will the voyage take?" Elizabeth asks.

"Several months," I answer, trying to keep my tone level. "Nino is quite excited to see such a large ship."

"Months?" Elizabeth's dark eyebrows tilt upward. "But . . . a steamer would have you there in weeks."

"Yes, I know. My steamer coming here took twelve days," I say. *But the Springs were paying*—this part I do not say aloud.

Elizabeth leans back against her cushions, exasperated, and then fixes me with a pointed gaze. Eventually, heaving a sigh, she shakes her head full of dark ringlets and says, "No, no, no, my dear. This simply won't do. Why didn't you book passage on one of the Cunard vessels? Or the White Star Line? They are new, but I've heard fine things."

I glance down at my hands, noting the smears of ink along my fingers. The cost of three transatlantic crossings on a Cunard steamship, or anything of the sort, even if we were to book third class— well, it would have been far beyond our budget. Hundreds of dollars beyond our budget.

Elizabeth, guessing the cause of my quiet, interjects: "My dear Margaret, Robert and I would have gladly loaned you the necessary funds. You need only to have asked."

"Thank you," I say, my voice low as I meet her eyes. "I do know that. You are most generous." I could have written to Mother to ask for the funds, as well. Or even Waldo, or Horace, had I been truly desperate. But the truth is, I did not want to ask a friend for the funds. Not when we could afford a perfectly adequate ship to make the journey without going into debt. I'm returning to America after years away, and I do not wish to start out on my back foot— borrowing, apologizing, explaining the need for necessary economies. I'm proud of the life I have built—the family we have built. I need not apologize, even if some small sacrifices may be necessary in the immediate future.

Besides, I read all the time of the shipwrecks that happen with these luxurious but too-fast steamers, like the *Fair Mathilde*, which only just recently sank in the waters near England. All souls on board perished, their expensive tickets doing them absolutely no good. No, a slower, less luxurious, steadier merchant vessel will do just fine. It will give us time as a family to prepare for all that is to come once we do eventually disembark onto American soil.

And, once I am back in America, where my book will be published—to great interest, I believe, as do Horace and Waldo—as well as any number of my articles and essays, then our financial woes shall be behind us. Some small economies may be necessary now, but they will get us to the place where our lot will surely improve. A longer journey on the sea will not be any undue hardship. We will come through it very well, just as we've come through far worse.

NOW THERE REMAINS just the matter of packing up our life in Florence and moving it all across the Atlantic. It's quite a different prospect, boxing up a household when it is not only my own but my baby's and my husband's, as well. Once our tickets are booked, our departure date set for the middle of May, I throw myself into packing, and the remaining weeks fill with a flurry of plans and errands.

For Nino there are piles of baby linens to launder and fold, as we will not have much opportunity to wash any of his clothes or diapers while at sea—I'm warned that fresh water will be scarce throughout the journey. Also we make plans to purchase and bring a goat of our own on board, so that we will have milk throughout the long crossing. Giovanni secures several crates of lemons and oranges, to fend off the scurvy that takes so many ill-prepared sailors at sea. We amass a months-long supply of hard breads and crackers, tins of salted meats and fish, hard cheeses, apples, olives, fruit jellies, and a crate with a pair of hens for eggs and, eventually, meat. We pack a chest filled with the medicines that our local doctor tells us we should have on hand for any variety of problems that may arise while at sea: phials for earaches, powders for dyspepsia, ointments and wound dressings for scrapes, and, of course, pastilles for our most likely ailment, seasickness.

For myself the packing includes my clothes and books, my undergarments, and the personal letters I've kept throughout these years in Italy. Last to go, and kept on top of my personal valise to ensure easy access, is my portable escritoire desk. My heart lurches as I tuck it in beside a soft shawl, my fingers handling it with the tenderness of a mother handling a newborn. Locked within that escritoire is my most treasured piece of cargo: my one copy of my completed manuscript on the Roman revolution.

In our final days in Florence I am determined to soak in every last drop of Italian beauty, knowing that it will be a few years, at least, before our life conditions and the conditions in Rome will be such that we can safely return. I gobble up fresh figs and mozzarella from the vendors on the streets. I stroll with Nino along the Arno, gazing up at the Tuscan hillsides and the painfully beautiful blue of the sky. I feast my eyes on my last glimpses of Raphael, Michelangelo, and Titian—marble and oil and gold. Oh, how I will miss all of the sights, sounds, and tastes of this rich and artful life, this place that presents a feast to all of the senses each day.

At last all of our luggage is packed and ready, prepared to be loaded into the coach for our ride to Livorno, then transferred onto the small *barca* that will bear us several miles out to sea and finally onto the *Elizabeth*.

On our final afternoon in Florence, I make one last visit to Casa Guidi, the home of my new but cherished friend. Elizabeth Barrett Browning, a late addition to my life in Italy, is now perhaps one of the best things to come from it, after Nino and Giovanni.

"But it is not the end for us, my dear," she says, sensing my sadness now that the journey has finally arrived. "You shall come back to us in triumph."

She flashes me a smile and I return it, though my eyes are blurred with tears.

And then, tilting her head and setting her dark waves aflutter, she adds: "Only, when you find me to be an old pile on this couch, you must lie and tell me that I have not aged a day."

I cannot help but laugh at this. "I shall be the one who ages," I say. "That's right. Your birthday will fall during your crossing, won't it?" "Yes." I nod. "I'll turn forty while at sea."

"There you go," she says. "Your husband is giving you America as a birthday gift. How lovely." She leans back against her sofa, folding her hands in her lap, and then she fixes me with a sideways glance. "But my goodness, not yet forty, and look at all that you've managed. It fatigues me just to think of all that you'll get done in the next forty. And that precious child." She looks down at our boys, then back to me. "You tell me you travel light, my dear, but you are returning home with the greatest of treasures. And your dashing count. Why, I can imagine a great number of things, and yet I cannot imagine how America will react to the return of Margaret Fuller, Marchesa Ossoli, mother, wife, and author of the defining book of her time. You must write and give me all the delicious details. Promise?"

"I promise I'll write," I reply, managing, I believe, a bright tone to mirror her enthusiasm. The fact is that I *have* been mostly excited for the return—to see Mother, to introduce her to Nino and Giovanni—and yet, I cannot help but feel the cloud that passes over me now, adding a weight to the thoughts that already swirl in my mind. Nino is young, not yet two years old; I doubt he'll even remember this time in Italy. He has a lively mind and a winsome disposition, so I do not worry about him. But how will Giovanni adjust to life in America? How will he find my family, my friends? How will he feel, being in a place unlike all that he has ever known?

Elizabeth is studying me, and she interjects now: "My darling, if it is the scandal of marrying a Roman Catholic that you fear, I tell you this: no one reads the books about the boring women who follow the rules."

At this I can only offer a grateful laugh. I wish it were only the fear of scandal that filled me with dread. But I don't want to dwell on my dreary thoughts. Not today, in my last hours with my dear friend. "Oh, Elizabeth, I wish I could bottle you up and bring you along with me," I say. "I'll miss your brilliance. Those many long days at sea would pass much more favorably with you beside me."

She shakes her head. "One sea crossing was quite enough. You won't find me sailing back in the other direction. I'll wait here until you return to me."

I hear the bells begin to peal outside. Evening is falling over Florence, and darkness will not be far behind. It is time for us to take our leave, sad as it may be. It is time for me to get Nino home. We all need a good night's rest. There are long days ahead that will require all our strength.

As I lean toward my friend, taking her hands in mine before we both fold into a hug, I feel a tremor pass through me. It is not just the sadness of our coming separation, my departure from this land that has felt like my home. It is a flash of memory, crawling up from within the folds of my mind. I blink, the room tilting around me. And then I am in another sitting room, taking my leave of another friend, another kindred spirit who has connected to my soul. Only, I am at the start of a very different journey. I am telling Waldo: "'*Possunt quia posse videntur.*'"

One of the many quotes that Father insisted I memorize and carry with me through life. *They can conquer who believe they can.* Virgil's *Aeneid*. The founding of Rome. And what I realize now, as these words fly to my mind and then out of my lips, is that it was the oarsmen who said it, as they pushed their ships ever farther, into lands unknown, undaunted. A journey to find, and to found, and to become.

Chapter Fifty-Six

Livorno
Spring 1850

"**B**ARCA! BARCA!"

"Ship, yes. You see the ship, my darling," I say as my son writhes in my husband's arms, delighted by the vessel before us and eager to clamber aboard.

It takes hours, and we bob beside the Livorno shoreline in our small loading craft, watching as the crew hoists an endless procession of goods to be transported to America on this massive vessel: marble, olive oil, crates of wine, almonds, silk, leather, carpets, clothing. I marvel that there shall be any room left for us.

When at last we are waved forward, I throw a glance toward Giovanni and see the grim set of his jaw. Ossolis are not oceangoing people. They have been rooted, grounded, in the streets of Rome for centuries. He has already traveled farther from his home today than ever before in his life. And like me, he is not overly fond of the water. Now I am trying not to think of the prophecy he shared with me just the night before as we lay in bed, restless ahead of the long crossing. "It's an old belief in our family," he confessed, whispering in the dark so as not to wake Nino. "Any Ossoli who tries to leave Italy on the water will meet an end at sea."

I blink, forcing that troubling thought out of my mind, along with the many nightmares I've had over the course of my own life having to do with water or shipwrecks. Instead I focus on Nino's joy and delight. He is enchanted with the boat, mesmerized by its webs of rope and timber. He is fascinated with the crewmen who fly about, calling out to one another in their bursts of rapid Italian.

Nino is also enamored of the small goat that we are bringing on board, and he reaches for her now like he would a beloved dog. Perhaps we should get him a pet puppy when we settle in America.

Finally, it is our turn, and we are helped aboard, Giovanni holding Nino tight in his arms as we wobble onto the deck. There is a uniformed man who stands ready to greet us. "Count Ossoli, Countess Ossoli?"

He's a young man in a sea captain's hat; he can't be older than I am, and he is greeting us with a broad, sun-chapped smile. I am momentarily taken aback by his English, and more so by his American accent, as he says: "Captain Seth Hasty, at your service."

"Hello, Captain." I raise my hand to my sunbonnet, hoping to steady its flapping brim as I return the man's stare. "You're American?"

"I am." He flashes a bearded grin. "A New Englander, like yourself. From Maine. 'Course, I knew of you when you were Margaret Fuller."

"I'm still Margaret Fuller," I say, giving the captain a smile.

"Well, then, Margaret Fuller"—he nods, touching the brim of his cap—"it is my honor to bring you home."

ONCE ALL IN our small number of passengers have safely boarded, the crewmen get to work. The anchor is hoisted up out of the aqua Italian waters. The wind pours into our sails. The *Elizabeth* groans and heaves as she sets out on our journey, bearing us west, on a course that will take us out into the Mediterranean.

I look up at the sky and give thanks for the broad sweep of gentle blue. The water spreads smooth before us. I pray that these temperate conditions will continue when we reach the Atlantic and for the remainder of our journey.

That evening we meet the captain's wife, Catherine, a lovely young woman who invites us to take breakfast with her in the small but comfortable dining room the following morning. She does not seem to mind the disruption that Nino's presence means as we sit at the table.

We settle into the rhythms of the ship, the three of us, and Nino seems to take happily to life at sea. Our cabin is small but pleasant enough, and the mild water allows us to move about without any paralyzing seasickness. To my delight, Giovanni spends several hours in the mornings practicing English. Soon he and Nino will be able to babble together as they learn. Nino loves romping around the ship, up and down the stairs, walking the goat like he would a dog and delighting in watching the crewmen shimmy along the rigging.

DAYS LATER, ON the evening before my birthday, I catch the first glimpse of the stunning Rock of Gibraltar, that former playground of the god Hercules that now serves as the threshold to the wide-open waters of the Atlantic. I am standing alone at the deck railing, Giovanni and Nino having run off to chase a seagull. It is dusk; the next time I glimpse the sunlight, a new decade of my life will have dawned.

I pull in a deep, salty breath and close my eyes, allowing the fading and gentle gold of evening to wash my skin. I tip my head up to receive its last drops of warmth like a blessing. With eyes shut, my mind fills with an image, and I recall sitting on my beloved rock by the Concord River, the sounds of the birds and the birches dancing along the warm air. As the picture shifts, I am perched high on the stony green banks of New York, watching the ships glide up and down the East River. And then I see the ancient rocks of Rome, the fountains ravaged and emptied, the crumbling wall slashed blood-red on the last night of freedom.

I open my eyes, blinking, coming back to the present and the Strait of Gibraltar, taking in the black jut of the monolith that climbs up out of the sea before me. This mountain of immovable shale and limestone, this resting place for tired birds, this gateway between oceans and countries and continents. The sun has slipped farther and now the fortress rock is a shadowed shape as, beyond it, the vast waters of the Atlantic roll and reach and, on the far side, break onto the shores of my waiting homeland.

"Mamma!" I turn at the sound of my name. Nino comes trotting back toward me, his father one step behind him.

"Yes, my darling?" I lean forward, picking up my boy and giving him a twirl, which sets off a peal of delighted giggles. I can't help but laugh, as well.

"Mamma! I saw a seagull!" Nino's voice is high and giddy.

"Did you, my dearest one?"

"He flew away."

"Where to?" I ask, staring into the deep blue of his cheerful eyes.

"To the sky, Mamma. Where birds live forever."

Giovanni is beside us. "I think I'll bring little *signore* belowdecks with me now." He places a kiss on my cheek and then takes Nino in his arms. "We will dress for supper. Come, Nino, *amore mio*, we must go make ourselves handsome. It's almost your mamma's birthday, we want to look our best, no?"

"That sounds wonderful," I say. "I'll join you in a moment." Another kiss, and then my husband is off, my baby in his arms.

My heart swells as I watch the pair of them walk away together, their two dark heads tipped toward each other, their figures outlined in the wispy light of the warm evening.

Once they are gone, and the deck is quiet, I turn and look back out over the water. The wind has picked up and now it is whipping my hair. I reach up to pull back a curl, tucking it into my comb, my fingers lingering on the cold silver. I trace the delicate outline of the butterfly and I cannot help but smile. What a life this butterfly has made. A life of stories. Stories of travel, of transformation, of sowing and growing. And even though the ocean unfurls before me, even though the shore remains distant still, I know that, in a most meaningful way, I have already arrived. I tuck the butterfly pin deeper into my hair, and the thought flies to my mind: I have grown, I've transformed. I have become.

Epilogue

L OUISA MAY ALCOTT STARES AT THE PAPER WITH
trembling fingers.

Ordinarily a letter from Thoreau would fill her with hearty delight, but not this note. Not these words. Dreadful, shattering words. Margaret Fuller, along with her baby and husband, is gone. Dead off the coast of New York's Fire Island after the ship carrying her home to America crashed and sank. In spite of his devoted and diligent search, Thoreau has been able to find nothing of her body, nor a single page of the precious book she was bearing home with such excitement. Instead, Thoreau writes that he found the beach *"smooth and bare,"* with only a scattering of human bones, stripped by the sea and its creatures. Beside them, her husband's jacket.

Louisa lowers the page, unable to read more. Feeling as though she might be sick if she does. Margaret is gone. The words strike Louisa as impossible. As she knows they will do to Mr. Emerson, as well. And Hawthorne and Greeley and so many others. She blinks, her eyes stinging. And then her gaze lands on the other papers strewn across her desk, a newspaper she fetched that morning but has not yet read.

There is an image above the news article, and Louisa studies it. She sees them there, a line of formidable soldiers clad in white, and she scans the accompanying text, reading of how the National Woman's Rights Convention shall soon meet for the first time. The speakers and delegates there will include Elizabeth Cady Stanton,

Susan B. Anthony, Sojourner Truth, Lucretia Mott, and many others.

Margaret must *be there*, Louisa thinks, again unable to reason out her friend's absence.

Margaret, to whom these women look as their leader, the mother of their movement. Margaret, whose fiery heart and words ignited the very flames that now light their way toward a brighter day for women—for all.

Louisa pushes back from the desk, unable to sit in this room a moment longer. She charges down the stairs and out into the yard, stunned by the glorious green of summer in Concord. Oh, how Margaret loved these days. But she'll never again be here. She'll never again take a walk through Waldo's gardens or out past Fairyland Pond to Walden. Just as she'll never see the women who gather at this convention to honor her call and carry on her work.

Louisa blinks against the bright sunshine, momentarily overcome. Gone at forty. Far too soon, when still there is so much work to be done. Why, Margaret was only just getting them all started.

And that's when Louisa realizes it: Margaret has gotten them started. Hers was the flame that first lit the way. Now it falls to her, Louisa May Alcott, and the countless others who grew stronger in the radiant glow of her brilliance, to keep the march moving forward.

Margaret *will* be there, Louisa realizes, when the women gather. She will be there when they begin the convention in silence to honor and mourn their founding mother. She will be there as they grow in number, as they debate and they work and they march. When they dare to proclaim that women deserve the rights, same as any man, to vote, to work, to learn, and to lead. Margaret will be there in the mind of every girl who grows bold and asks questions of herself and her world. *To become*, as Margaret would have said, and as Louisa hears the voice in her mind, she can't help but smile. Margaret, whose body is lost but whose words will never die. The butterfly who has shown her, and countless others, that it is not only her right, but her sacred obligation, to fly.

Author's Note

If indeed it was Margaret Fuller whose "radiant genius and fiery heart was perhaps the real centre" of this incredible period of creativity and human drama—as was claimed by Ralph Waldo Emerson—then why do so few people know the extent of her legacy? Or even her name? That was the question that prompted my initial search to learn more of the fascinating details of Margaret Fuller's life, and then spurred me on to write this work of historical fiction inspired by her life and legacy.

As the opening epigraph of this book makes plain, to write about Margaret Fuller felt like a bold undertaking. It felt formidable, even presumptuous, because her mind, her life force, and her story were all so outsized. This was a woman and a writer, after all, who inspired one of her contemporaries, John Van der Zee Sears, to boast that he could "read Dante in the original Italian, Hegel in the original German, and perhaps the hardest task of all, Margaret Fuller in the original English."

It started for me on a rainy Memorial Day weekend three years ago, shortly after the birth of my third daughter. We had family visiting from out of town and inclement weather forced us to scrap all our plans and remain indoors. Sitting in the kitchen, my mother-in-law handed me a book titled *American Bloomsbury*, a work of nonfiction that takes up the lives of the Concord genius cluster of Louisa May Alcott, Ralph Waldo Emerson, Margaret Fuller, Nathaniel Hawthorne, and Henry David Thoreau. I knew every single one of the names, except Margaret's. I'd read the works written by each of them, except Margaret. I knew a fair amount about their personal lives, as well—except Margaret's. And yet, from out of this star-studded constellation, it was Margaret Fuller who jumped off the page as I read. Her story was far and away the most fascinating; I was entranced by the inspiring, shocking, romantic, and ultimately tragic facts of her life. I, like Emerson, felt she was the leading lady at the center of this great American story. Yet somehow this was the first time I was learning about her. I was obsessed, and I had to know more.

I went to Concord. I walked the lanes and the fields that Margaret and her friends adored. I sat on top of her beloved sun-warmed boulder, the place where she loved to read and write and watch the river. I followed the well-worn path from her guest bedroom into Waldo's study. I visited the places where these people talked, thought, fought, and created: the Concord River, Bush, Fairyland Pond, the North Bridge, Walden Pond, Heywood Meadows, Monument Square. I saw, all over town, homages and testimonials to the Transcendentalists. Inns have suites labeled in their honor. Streets and storefronts bear their names. Sleepy Hollow Cemetery holds their graves as these friends rest in perpetuity in one another's society. All, except for Margaret. The gang is all there, except for her.

I knew I had met my next book. This novel is an invitation to readers to enter into an imagined world inspired by the *radiant genius and fiery heart* of Margaret, our guide and leading lady.

As an English major and a lover of books I, like countless others, have been treated to a hearty diet of the American Transcendentalists and their peers. We all had the assignments in high school to read *The Scarlet Letter, Walden,* and *Moby-Dick.* But I daresay that few of us are assigned lessons studying Margaret Fuller in English or history classes—though we should be.

Nathaniel Hawthorne published his most celebrated work, *The Scarlet Letter,* the same year that Margaret Fuller died in a shipwreck just yards from the shores of America. His heroine in that classic novel, Hester Prynne, is a brave and defiant woman who takes a lover and then faces the ensuing scandal to bear his child. She is a strong-willed brunette who finds inspiration and freedom in the woods with the company of the flowers and the birds, much like Margaret did so often during their days together in Concord. Most, including Sophia Hawthorne, saw Margaret when they read of the now-iconic character of Hester Prynne.

Henry David Thoreau did write alongside Margaret Fuller for *The Dial* magazine, and he did float alongside her down the rivers of Concord before removing himself to the woods at Walden Pond to write his iconic work. Louisa May Alcott did admire the worldly and brilliant woman who came so often to Concord throughout the Alcott girls' youth. In 1868, when Louisa May Alcott published her classic coming-of-age novel, *Little Women*, she changed the name of the eldest sister from Anna to Margaret.

And the relationships in the Emerson home were as fraught and complicated as this work of fiction would have us believe. Margaret came often to Bush, a place that she called "the Paradise of thought," much to Waldo's delight and Lidian's chagrin. Hawthorne observed, "[Waldo] apotheosized [Margaret] as the greatest woman, I believe, of ancient or modern times, and the one figure in the world worth considering." Words such as these, and the moments that inspired them, did certainly lend themselves to the drama that a writer of historical fiction craves.

Margaret undoubtedly had times of great happiness among her fellow thinkers and writers in Concord, and yet, the impression I got was that she did not quite fit in. She did make that clever quip about how there was not enough "Discord" in that picturesque little village of Concord. I believe that the choices she made and the life she felt called to lead were enough to render her, in the end, an outsider among the clique.

New York was a much bigger pond in which to swim, with discord and chaos aplenty, and Margaret did make history as a female newspaper editor working with Horace Greeley, covering everything from the poetry of Elizabeth Barrett Browning to the writing of Frederick Douglass to the music of Ludwig van Beethoven. While living with the Greeleys, Margaret mixed with the New York literati, including Walt Whitman and Edgar Allan Poe. And yes, Poe and Margaret had infamous rows, and Poe did in fact write, "Humanity is divided into men, women, and Margaret Fuller."

The details of Margaret's many travels and solo adventures are true to the history, and there were even more journeys than those I included. It was no small matter for a woman to travel on her own at that time to Niagara Falls or Chicago—or, certainly, Rome. Margaret did it all, with stops in England to befriend William Wordsworth and France to befriend George Sand and Frédéric Chopin, of course.

Margaret truly did feel that once she arrived in Rome, she was in the place where her true nature could thrive and flourish, and flourish she did. Margaret worked as the first American foreign newspaper correspondent, and she embraced the experience of living abroad with the fullness of her enthusiasm and passion. She did take Giovanni Ossoli as her lover, conceiving a child before marrying in secret.

And yet, her story continued to evolve and take further unanticipated and dramatic swerves. Margaret did work in a hospital during the Roman revolution while Giovanni served in the army and their baby remained (tragically) hidden in the countryside. Margaret's was one of the first homes that the newly returned leader Giuseppe Mazzini visited when he arrived in Rome at the formation of the republic. I did not embellish any of the details of this time or these experiences; the raw material of the history was beyond anything I could have conjured.

Tragically, and chillingly, Margaret did in fact have recurring nightmares of drowning and a fear of the water her entire life, just as her husband, Giovanni, did know of a family prophecy that he would lose his life at sea were he to leave Rome.

The shipwreck also claimed Margaret's manuscript on her experiences during the Roman revolution, the book that she considered the greatest and most important work of her life.

Other works and threads of her legacy do live on, even if far too few people are aware of her seminal impact. Margaret Fuller's popular Conversations in Boston were attended by all sorts of women in her day, and one of her attendees was the young Elizabeth Cady Stanton, whose name we all know of as central in the fight for women's suffrage. Fuller's *Woman in the Nineteenth Century* was and is considered by many to be the original document of the American women's rights movement.

In this book, as in real life, Margaret was sailing home just as American women were getting ready to attend the inaugural meeting of the National Woman's Rights Convention. The founders of that movement were vocal about how they saw Margaret Fuller as a leader. We can only imagine the impact she might have had, had she been able to attend the meeting that fall in Worcester, Massachusetts, and all the resulting rallies, marches, and historic moments to come out of it. Alas, fate intervened and instead the convention opened with a moment of silence in Margaret's honor. It feels wildly unfair that Margaret was not permitted to do more or witness the movement she helped to inspire.

After Margaret Fuller's tragic death and the loss of her final work, Emerson, Greeley, and other friends mobilized to produce her memoir. Upon publication, *Memoirs of Margaret Fuller Ossoli* became the bestselling book in America. It was surpassed only when *Uncle Tom's Cabin* was published.

Margaret's life story was both epic and intimate. In so many ways she lived with an energy and spirit that were larger than life, and yet she was always unflinchingly honest about her human vulnerabilities and foibles. This combination lends itself to the writing of historical fiction with all the ingredients I could wish for. In those instances where I did deliberately take liberties with the timeline or the specifics of the historic details, that was in an effort to serve the narrative and hopefully hone the experience for the reader.

Those who are particularly well acquainted with the history of Concord likely noticed that I have Thoreau living with the Emersons at Bush a few years prior to when he took up residence in the small bedroom over their staircase. Thoreau was studying at Harvard in 1836, and while he spent a significant amount of time in his hometown of Concord that year, he would have resided with his family just up the lane. That said, Ellen Emerson asserts in *The Life of Lidian Jackson Emerson* that her father, Ralph Waldo Emerson, began his friendship with Thoreau that year. (She also states that was the year in which Thoreau befriended the Emersons' chickens.) Because that was also the summer in which Margaret first arrived at Bush and Concord, I made this adjustment in order to introduce Thoreau to Margaret and to readers earlier in the narrative. I felt, and I hope the reader agrees, that there can be no such thing as too much Thoreau.

Similarly, those fortunate readers who are well acquainted with Orchard House and the Emerson house will know that the two homes are approximately 0.4 miles apart, which, for me, took a little over five very enjoyable minutes to walk. That said, there were many times through the years when the Alcotts stayed in homes much closer to Bush. The Alcotts, as the reader likely inferred, moved a lot. Even within Concord. They did not take up residence in Orchard House until the late 1850s. And yet, Orchard House is the iconic Alcott home, forever memorialized in the beloved book *Little Women* and its multiple film adaptations. Rather than burden the reader with the moving targets of the many Alcott homes, I decided to plant our stake at Orchard House and give the Alcotts the stability of residing in that final family home a few years earlier than was in fact historically the case.

In Italy, I also made a few adjustments for the purposes of plotting and storytelling. Giovanni in fact had three older brothers, not one. Since they were elusive figures, those Ossoli men, notable in the history and in this story more for the support they withheld— rather than their actual presence in or relationship to Giovanni's life—I decided not to encumber the reader with an entire roster, but instead decided that one unsympathetic and withholding older brother could sufficiently fill the role.

And those who are familiar with the nomenclature of the Italian nobility will likely inquire as to why Giovanni was referred to with the noble title of *marchese*, or "marquis," when he was not the eldest son. This is a question that has puzzled a number of readers through the years. Giovanni would have more accurately been referred to as *dei Marchesi d'Ossoli*, meaning *of* the Ossoli noble family. For whatever reason, Margaret and those in her life always referred to her husband (once they knew he existed) as Marchese Giovanni Ossoli. And Romans referred to Margaret Fuller as Marchesa Ossoli. I deferred to their example on that.

As the years have passed, Margaret Fuller's life story has slipped further from the public's awareness and imagination, while the legacies of her close friends continue to thrive and flourish today. You'd be hard-pressed to find a high school English program that doesn't include the works of Hawthorne, Emerson, Alcott, Poe, Thoreau, Melville, and the rest of her friends and contemporaries. This is my offering to show that it's not only Margaret Fuller's work and her legacy that are most worthy and compelling, but so, too, is the story *behind* her stories: namely, the inspiring and incredible tale of her brave, bold, and colorful life.

Acknowledgments

Now for the note that could easily stretch longer than this book. I would like to begin by thanking all of my readers. Your support, enthusiasm, curiosity, and warmth keep me going, fueled to find more inspiration and to deliver more books that I hope will be worthy of you. Thank you.

I am so grateful, as both a writer and a reader, to the countless librarians and booksellers who spend every day supporting books and connecting our work with the readers who will give those books their wings. My heartfelt thanks to all booksellers and librarians everywhere. I can't wait to continue working with all of you to connect with your communities, and I thank you for your expertise and enthusiasm.

This past decade in publishing has me convinced that writers and their people are some of the most supportive, talented, hard-working, and collaborative human beings in the world. There is this entire network of writers with whom I've had the privilege of connecting—both in person and virtually—and truly, it feels like we are a big tribe. We read one another's early work, we blurb one another's covers, we host conversations and events together, we share content, we chuckle and commiserate on social media, email, and text, we meet up for meals or drinks. You all make this solitary job feel like part of a full and united community. Thank you. You humble and inspire me.

And speaking of our warm and supportive community, I am so thankful to the book influencers, bloggers, readers, and reviewers who are out there reading, sharing, reviewing, and doing all they can to support books and writers. My heartfelt thanks to Jenna Bush, Lee Woodruff, Hoda Kotb, Kathie Lee Gifford, Christine Gardner, Carol Fitzgerald, Andrea Peskind Katz, Zibby Owens, Suzanne Weinstein Leopold, Lauren Blank Margolin, Robin Kall Homonoff, Jennifer Tropea O'Regan, Pamela Klinger-Horn, Bobbi Dumas, Sharlene Martin Moore, Tonni Callan, Jamie Rosenblit, Lindsey Wood, and so many others, and all the organizers of festivals and events and online forums where we connect with readers. This is the part where I cringe because I just know I am forgetting too many important names and for that I am deeply sorry. But please know, I am so grateful!

This book, and my entire life as a writer, would not be possible without Lacy Lynch, my agent, partner, and dear friend. Book ten, Lacy! This one is for you, with admiration and appreciation, you brave and bold force. And my thanks also to Haley Reynolds, Dabney Rice, Jan Miller, Shannon Marven, and the entire family at Dupree Miller. I'm forever amazed by and thankful to Lauren Auslander and her incredible team at LUNA Entertainment.

Thanks to my editor, Kara Cesare, for championing this book with such care and working as my partner with genuine encouragement and invaluable wisdom. I could not imagine writing with anyone else. Thank you for believing in me and working with me. My deepest thanks to the entire team at Ballantine, including Jesse Shuman, Kim Hovey, Loren Noveck and her brilliant copyediting team, Taylor Noel, Debbie Aroff, Michelle Jasmine, Chelsea Woodward, Kara Welsh, Jennifer Hershey, Susan Corcoran, Jen Garza, Virginia Norey, Paolo Pepe and the art department, Gina Centrello, and Sanyu Dillon. I am the luckiest author to work with you all, and I am thankful every day.

None of this would happen without my family and friends, who fill me up and sustain me. I started out with a big family, and then I married into an even bigger family. I love you and I am grateful for you all: my siblings, Owen, Teddy, and Emily; in-laws, siblings by marriage, nieces and nephews, cousins, aunts and uncles. Louisa and Nelson, thank you for Dave (and Lulu: for this book idea!). Mom and Dad, you believed in me as staunchly as Margaret Fuller's parents believed in her, but you allowed me to read Shakespeare without shame, and for that I am grateful.

I have girlfriends who began this life journey with me when we could barely talk and I've added to this golden sisterhood at every phase of life—grade school, high school, college, early professional days, and now this wild and beautiful ride of motherhood. You are my people. You give so much color, richness, and beauty to this life.

And last, but furthest from least, my love and thanks to my husband, Dave, and our three incredible daughters. I am so thankful that you are mine and I am yours.

The research for this book was especially enjoyable, because who would not relish total immersion into the beauty and history that is Concord, Massachusetts?

The Ralph Waldo Emerson House, or Bush, is a unique and special place. I am particularly thankful to Marie Gordinier and Kristi Martin for their time, their expertise, their enthusiasm and passion for all things Emerson and Concord. I will always count sitting in Margaret's beloved bedroom reading chair and looking out over the green views that she cherished as one of my life's treasured moments. For those who are interested in learning more or visiting Bush—and seeing it largely as Margaret and Waldo did—please see ralphwaldoemersonhouse.org. I highly recommend a visit.

Orchard House is the gem you would expect it to be from reading Alcott's adored writing on her family home. I am particularly thankful to Diane for the time she spent showing me the house and grounds, and for answering my many questions. It's just a short walk from Bush, and a lovely one, so I'd suggest a visit here, as well: louisamayalcott.org.

From there, it's a quick and beautiful stroll out to Fairyland and Walden Pond or up to the Old Manse, where you can plunge into the history of the Hawthornes and so much more. I suggest taking a seat on Margaret's beloved boulders beside the river, then taking an amble across the Old North Bridge through Minute Man National Historical Park. History is the furthest thing from boring, and I'm so thankful to Concord for celebrating and sharing its rich and important role in it.

Marya, my book subjects seem to follow you. From New York

to Washington, D.C., and now to Massachusetts. Thank you for meeting me in the midst of my research trip, and for always sharing this love of history and adventure. Where are we going next?

For those who would like to continue reading about Margaret Fuller and her time, there are many works that make that possible. Beginning with her own words, I would suggest *Woman in the Nineteenth Century* and *Memoirs of Margaret Fuller Ossoli*. I am deeply grateful and indebted to the countless brilliant and talented scholars and biographers who have distilled the thousands of pages of letters, writings, journals, and primary sources of Margaret and her correspondents. Reading Margaret Fuller in the original English, no less! I am humbled by these skilled researchers and writers who have managed to present her complex and full life through comprehensible and compulsively readable narratives. I would like to make special mention of Megan Marshall's stunning biography *Margaret Fuller: A New American Life* and John Matteson's brilliant work *The Lives of Margaret Fuller: A Biography*. Thank you. Your works illuminate Margaret Fuller and every aspect of her life as a woman, a thinker, a writer, a friend, an activist, a lover, an advocate, and so much more. I highly recommend both.

Further suggested reading:

Memoirs of Margaret Fuller Ossoli, by Margaret Fuller, edited by R. W. Emerson, W. H. Channing, and J. F. Clarke

Woman in the Nineteenth Century, by Margaret Fuller

The Essential Margaret Fuller: Autobiographical Writings, Summer on the Lakes, Reviews and Essays, by Margaret Fuller, edited by Jeffrey Steele

The Lives of Margaret Fuller: A Biography, by John Matteson

Margaret Fuller: A New American Life, by Megan Marshall

American Bloomsbury: Louisa May Alcott, Ralph Waldo Emerson, Margaret Fuller, Nathaniel Hawthorne, and Henry David Thoreau; Their Lives, Their Loves, Their Work, by Susan Cheever

Emerson Among the Eccentrics: A Group Portrait, by Carlos Baker

The Life of Lidian Jackson Emerson, by Ellen Tucker Emerson
Two-Way Mirror: The Life of Elizabeth Barrett Browning, by
   Fiona Sampson
Little Women, by Louisa May Alcott
The Scarlet Letter, by Nathaniel Hawthorne
Walden, by Henry David Thoreau
Essays by Ralph Waldo Emerson, including "Nature," "Self-
   Reliance," "Experience," "The American Scholar," "The
   Over-Soul," and others

About the Author

ALLISON PATAKI is the *New York Times* bestselling author of *The Traitor's Wife, The Accidental Empress, Sisi, Where the Light Falls* (with Owen Pataki), *The Queen's Fortune*, and *The Magnificent Lives of Marjorie Post*, as well as the memoir *Beauty in the Broken Places* and two children's books (with Marya Myers), *Nelly Takes New York* and *Poppy Takes Paris*. Her novels have been translated into more than twenty languages. A former news writer and producer, Pataki has written for *The New York Times*, ABC News, HuffPost, *USA Today*, Fox News, and other outlets. She has appeared on *Today, Good Morning America, Fox & Friends, Good Day New York, Good Day Chicago*, and *Morning Joe*. Pataki graduated cum laude from Yale University, is a member of the Historical Novel Society and a certified yoga instructor, and lives in New York with her husband and family.

allisonpataki.com
Facebook.com/AllisonPatakiPage
Twitter: @AllisonPataki
Instagram: @allisonpataki

About the Type

This book was set in Berling. Designed in 1951 by Karl-Erik Forsberg (1914–95) for the type foundry Berlingska Stilgjuteri AB in Lund, Sweden, it was released the same year in foundry type by H. Berthold AG. A classic old-face design, its generous proportions and inclined serifs make it highly legible.